Bestial Noise

Bestial Noise

The *Tin House*
Fiction Reader

A
BLOOMSBURY
TIN HOUSE
BOOK

Published by Bloomsbury, New York and London
Distributed to the trade by Holtzbrinck Publishers

Library of Congress Cataloging-in-Publication Data has been applied for.

ISBN 1-58234-334-9

1 3 5 7 9 10 8 6 4 2

First U.S. Edition 2003

Typeset by Hewer Text Limited, Edinburgh
Printed in the United States of America by
RR Donnelley & Sons, Harrisonburg

CONTENTS

If you want a fresh, revelatory cross section of current American short fiction – a big if, I know, unless you're a writer sizing up the competition, a reader trying to find out what you've missed, or a sociologist looking for clues as to what the hell is wrong with everybody nowadays – you couldn't do better than this anthology. I don't say this only because *Tin House* is paying me the big bucks to write the foreword and because several of my friends have pieces in it. And I'm not claiming you'd do worse with a recent *Best American Short Stories* or O. Henry collection – the bucks aren't that big – but at least this book isn't so damn august. No John Updike, no Joyce Carol Oates, no Alice Munro. No Alices of any variety, in fact. Nor any Nadines, Tonis, Margarets, Sauls, Philips, or Richards. Oh, you've still got your big-deal writers here – Dorothy Allison, Lydia Davis, Stuart Dybek, Mary Gaitskill, Aleksandar Hemon, Amy Hempel, James Kelman, David Leavitt, Jonathan Lethem – as well as the euphemistic "new voices" you're understandably wary of. But the closest you'll come to a literary pooh-bah is David Foster Wallace – that is, not even in the ballpark. Suit you? Just this once? Suits me.

Some of these names probably make you afraid – or, on the other hand, make you hopeful – that what you've got here is a bunch of that way-out stuff. Just calm down. *Bestial Noise* has plenty of traditional well-made realist stories – just not by the usual suspects. One, a honey called "The Vision," is by Lethem, probably the last guy you'd expect; it involves hip parlor games and subtle aggression between a deceptively normal man on the make and an old schoolmate who used to dress up as a character from Marvel Comics. In Ron Carlson's coincidentally similar "Evil Eye Allen," the narrator serves as assistant to a high school friend who entertains at parties with a combination of magic act, performance art, and free-form psychotherapy; by the end, Carlson has managed a triple epiphany – a feat at least as tricky as any of Evil Eye's. And Kevin Canty's "Red Dress" could pass for a story John Cheever never got around to writing: a little boy tends bar for his hard-drinking parents' parties, has a mishap you should've seen coming, gets caught in a shameful act you also should've seen coming, and ends his story – suddenly in adulthood – with a last line Cheever himself would've been proud to cop.

Since you've been around the block a little, naturally you'll suspect that the better pieces here come from the lesser-known writers. You know the truisms: that editors set the bar higher for them than for writers with established reputations, and that big-name writers sell the finest flowerings of their genius to *The New Yorker* and stick cutting-edge – formerly known as "small" – magazines like *Tin House* with the seeds and stems. Probably yes to the first truism. Tom Barbash, Tara Ison, Michael Lowenthal, and Nancy Reisman – all with first books out, but none with intimidatingly recognizable names – must have met somebody's rigorous standards, and they clearly set their own. In Barbash's "The Break," a mother and her nineteen-year-old son have either a congenial and tolerant relationship or a struggle to the death going on – or both. Ison's "Ball," about a young woman, her lover, and her dog, inexorably reveals one character as a monster of neediness: for a while there you think it's the dog. Long before Lowenthal's "Over Boy" morphs into an absolutely convincing account of tripping on Ecstasy, it's won your trust with such indelible images as a "shovel-faced" bouncer outside a club. Reisman's "Illumination," set in 1930s Buffalo, puts you inescapably in the head of a legal secretary crushed by a burdensome family – and burdened with a crush on another woman.

But forget that second truism. Even if the high-paying, high-profile magazines had space to publish all the high-quality stories by high-end writers, they'd still miss stuff right and left out of sheer human fallibility. And experienced writers know that mainstream magazines have their limits. Allison's harrowing "Compassion" might be too long and densely detailed. (*We understand that this is supposed to be a lingering death, but many of us here felt . . .*) Hempel's elegantly heartbroken "Beach Town" might be too short and spare. (*Many of us here felt that your narrator needs a back story; doesn't she have anything better to do than spy on the neighbors?*) Davis's – well, what can I say but elegantly heartbroken? – "Letter to a Funeral Parlor" might be too short and too plotless. (*Many of us here felt that this was basically a riff on the word "cremains."*) Kelman's "Yeh, These Stages," ditto. (*What's the motivation for "the kind of despair that made suicide a positive move"; many of us here felt it was merely existential.*) Stuart Dybek's "Fiction," ditto. (*While we understand that the narrator "wanted to tell you a story without telling the story," many of us here felt . . .*) And Wallace's "On His Deathbed, Holding Your Hand, the Acclaimed New Young Off-Broadway Playwright's Father Begs a Boon" might be too dark and eccentric. (*Many of us here felt that the father comes off as improbably loveless – the reader has no one to root for. And are you sure you want both "new" and "young"?*) Pieces like these need places like *Tin House*.

But for thoughtful contemporary writers – and there don't seem to be any exceptions here – experimentalism is no longer a cause or an issue; literary history in the sense of forward progress ended long ago, and the old avant-garde is now the tradition. Leavitt's "Heaped Earth" substitutes Nabokov's John Ray Jr. for Dirk Bogarde in the 1960 film *Song Without End* (although, slyboots that he is, Leavitt names neither Nabokov, Bogarde, nor the film). Kelman's debt to Beckett is as clear as that of Wallace's "On His Deathbed" to Kafka's "The Judgment," or of Jim Shepard's "Alicia and Emmett with the 17th Lancers at Balaclava" (juxtaposing the charge of the Light Brigade and a contemporary child's cancer) to the pastiches of Donald Barthelme. Today experimentation has less to do with form than with writers testing the limits of their own ability. A brilliantly chosen word is an experiment. "A little trickle of bright red blood debuted out of Dan's left nostril" (Helen Schulman, "The Interview"). So is a devastating line of dialogue. "Just let me ask you something," one of Allison's characters asks a woman who's going on about God's plan for us all. "Have you had cancer yet?" And so is a flight of drily manic humor. The main character in Gaitskill's "A Bestial Noise" thinks that if her family "could be placed in a more congenial environment – say, in another solar system where they would not be bound by the personality requirements and bodily structure of human beings – they would do extraordinarily well."

Reading through these stories allowed me to savor work by some of my favorite writers, to discover writers I didn't know or ought to have known long ago, and to reconsider a couple of writers I'd thought were way overrated. (Maybe it's just the limited exposure, but they read okay to me here.) But I found all of these pieces together even more moving than if I'd encountered them one by one. Which is odd, at least for me. "No poet or novelist wishes he were the only one who ever lived," W. H. Auden once wrote (he must've meant short-story writers too), "but most of them wish they were the only one alive, and quite a number fondly believe their wish has been granted." I'd go Auden one better: every writer, in the process of writing, needs to believe this. Each of these stories creates a separate and distinct world with its own landscape, language, and laws of behavior, and most of them do it convincingly enough to make you forget all the others while you're reading. But if you step back, you can see there's a community here. Not in the sense that all these writers know each other, or necessarily regard each other as comrades – let alone equals – or even have much use for each other's work. But so much clean, clear, direct prose in so many different voices makes me think this contemptible and terrifying fin de siècle – which will probably be the fin de all of us – is a weirdly exhilarating time for writers and readers, at least for as long as they're writing and reading.

DAVID GATES

A BESTIAL NOISE
Mary Gaitskill

Elizabeth woke too early again on Saturday morning. She sat up, opened the curtains, and looked out. It was a bright day in early spring. The branches of the maple tree in the front yard were shocking against the white house across the street. Beyond the white house were fir trees and soft blue sky. Each thing – tree, house, fir trees, sky – was defined and distinct according to the elegant and beautiful character of this planet. But to Elizabeth they seemed undifferentiated: a single vast organism breathing slowly and deeply outside her window, as dense as her own body, full of tissue, blood, bones, all the tiny things you can't see that keep everything going. She felt like a space traveler staring out of her capsule, like a moronic invader blind to her own world. She closed the curtain.

Elizabeth was pregnant. She was only eight weeks pregnant but still she felt it powerfully. She felt like an hourglass being crazily tipped back and forth, except instead of sand the glass was filled with homunculi, all screaming and clawing and holding each other for balance – some bravely trying to assist the others – as the glass swung top to bottom. She was forty-two years old and she had not expected to get pregnant. For most of her life she hadn't wanted it, not one bit. There were certain terrible moments when she wasn't even sure she wanted it now, and this morning was turning into one of those moments.

It was as if there were a tiny, faceted sensor in her brain that stored terrible information where she wouldn't have to think about it – except that her unstable system had triggered an alarm and the sensor had gone crazy, sending an unbroken shriek of warning in the form of grotesque images, surging into each other with the implacable truth of dreams:

A starving polar bear collapsed on its side, so emaciated it looked more like a dog than a bear. The sun had gotten too hot too fast and melted the ice it hunted on. It lifted its head and let it fall again. The core of its world had been broken.

Five-year-old girls grew breasts and pubic hair. Was it because of pesticides that mimicked estrogen? Was it because the girls had too many fat cells? Their parents gave them drugs that produced symptoms of menopause and then had to take them to therapy in order to cope with their emotions.

Millions of Africans died of AIDS, leaving millions of orphaned children. A magazine printed a photograph of a dying African woman. She lay in an empty room on a cot covered by a piece of cloth. Her skeletal body was exhausted by its slow descent through limitless suffering, and her eyes stared up from the pit. But her spirit came up through her eyes in full force. Her spirit was soft and it was powerful, and it could hold her suffering, and it would stay with her until she fell into darkness.

Thousands of Americans died of AIDS too. They also died of diet drugs, liposuction, and anorexia. Their pictures were in magazines too. They were smiling from wedding photos, school yearbooks, family albums. Their eyes were bright with happiness and want. One woman looked nearly out of her mind with happiness and wanting of more of it, and terror of being without it. "I'd rather die than be fat!" cried a nineteen-year-old anorexic. And then she'd died.

Elizabeth's heart pounded. She groped over her night table for the packet of crackers she kept there to calm her stomach. The salty biscuit was dry in her mouth, and she had drunk the water she had put on the table the night before. Muttering irritably, she rolled from bed and went to the bathroom to drink from the tap. She bent over the sink and slurped the cold, faintly metallic water running sideways into her mouth, the faucet visually tinged with tiny toothpaste flecks.

She remembered the first time Matt had said it: "I want to make you pregnant." They were fucking, and the words opened a scalding pit in her imagination. He wanted to see her breasts swell with milk, he wanted to feel her giant belly from behind. She pictured herself swelling, straining until her body showed its fleshy seam, slowly bursting, screaming as she broke open. Her mind abject before her cunt, her words dissolved, her personality irrelevant. They had made it a fantasy of abjection, sometimes his, sometimes hers. They made sounds of pretend abjection, grunts and bestial moans, making fun and playing. Except that something earnest and yearning started creeping into the sounds, then something fierce, like a roar – and then it had happened for real.

She stood and wiped her mouth. She imagined ice plant growing over the ground with impossible speed, its fleshy leaves glistening with vesicles, growing hungrily and busily, devouring the earth and feeding it too. It was a signal from another part of her brain, saying "But wait! Look at this!" She pictured Matt pointing at the ice plant and giving a roar of triumph and solidarity. "It grow!" he would roar. "Life good!" She would roar back, they would crouch down with their legs wide apart, raise up their fists and jump around roaring. They did this when they were happy and excited; they did it a lot. If they were in public, and couldn't roar, they instead made faces of bestial satiety and uttered grunts of affirmation.

She grunted to herself as she turned off the water and left the room. She thought of going to Matt's room to get under the covers with him and decided she wanted a snack first. She put on her thick socks and went downstairs. The curtains were still drawn so the house was dim and a little cold. She put on the teakettle and looked into the refrigerator. She had been thinking bread and cheese, but when she saw the tinfoiled remains of the Chinese food they'd had the night before – crispy Peking duck! – she began to salivate. She took out the container and peeled back the tinfoil; the crisp, fatty meat was irresistible. She got herself a glass of cranberry juice for sweetness, poured salt on the meat, and sat at the kitchen table eating crispy duck with her fingers in a trance of pleasure. She felt like she had when she was eight years old and had for some reason come home from school a few hours early and found that her mother wasn't home. Because she was alone, she got a chicken drumstick from the fridge, salted it, and ate it while watching cartoons on TV. It was a wonderful sensation of independence and solitude and salt.

Then came her family, crashing in. Her father a boiling tumbleweed, her mother a wet amoeba of love, her sister a geyser of pain squeezed off with a tourniquet of madness and will. When people asked her to describe her family she said, "They're like people who've been sent on a camping trip with a tent and no stakes." What she meant was, there wasn't anything wrong with them; she always thought that if they could be placed in a more congenial environment – say, in another solar system where they would not be bound by the personality requirements and bodily structure of human beings, they would do extraordinarily well. Someplace where you didn't need a tent.

She especially thought this of her sister, Angela: a beauty at nine, with a tender mouth and huge gray eyes full of gravity and joy, she had the face of a wooden totem by the age of fifteen. The story Elizabeth always told: When Angela was in high school, a psychologist came to visit her science class in order to demonstrate psychology to them. He gave each student a deck of cards and told them to arrange them in a pattern, so that he could explain what the patterns meant at the end of the exercise. He went around the class, analyzing everyone according to their card pattern. When he came to Angela, he stood and frowned. "What did you do?" he asked her. She could not tell him. He reshuffled her cards and told her to do it again. She did, repeating the pattern. He shook his head. "I have never seen anything like that before," he said, and then went on to the next student. The teacher made a face. "It figures," she said.

The physical flavor of crispy duck ran together with the emotional flavor of her sister and her handful of unwanted cards: pain with sweetness. Memories came to her like several different tastes all at once, hard to sort. She remembered lying on the thin maize carpet of her childhood home, feeling the furnace make the floor hum slightly as the warmth came up through it. It was like feeling her mother's body through her sweater. *One Thousand and One Strings* was playing on the stereo. Listening to *One Thousand and One Strings* felt like flying through a peaceful sky filled with light, limitless yet absolutely safe. It made you picture everything moving outward in an endless, revelatory triumph. She put her face down eye-level with the floor; the small house grew vast, and the thin maize carpet became a happy traveler, live as a rippling field of grasses in a Technicolor movie, rambling through the bedrooms, the living room, Daddy's private room. The music was all smooth, like pudding in the mouth, and the carpet was rough and nubbly, with bare patches and lumps under the legs of Grandmother's table. She got up on the couch and lay against Mama. Mama was rough and nubbly too, with tiny watery noises in her stomach, and secret voices all trying to talk to Elizabeth while Mama listened to music and read her magazine. Her mother didn't know about the voices, even though they were hers. They said things without words, and because we live in a world of words, nobody listened and because nobody listened Mama forgot about them herself. But Elizabeth was new in the world of words; she had just come out of her mother's body, and she couldn't help but listen. The voices knew this, and they reached for her. Some of the voices reached with sadness and fear. Others were gentle and intrepid as the sky in *One Thousand and One Strings*. Some were all rage, like a flailing ax, rage at everything, including Elizabeth. Others were delighted and loving, like children themselves, wanting to play. Some were a hole of need, a hole made of sucking, tactile voices that clutched at Elizabeth and tried to pull her in. Elizabeth was afraid of the voices; they were a tangled knot she did not want to get lost in. So she went past them, whistling and looking straight ahead like a traveler in a haunted place. She sent her attention further down, searching for the solid thing underneath them all; her mother's furnace, running deep inside her, sending warmth and power and blind, muscular love.

Elizabeth sat in her cold kitchen, eight weeks pregnant with a faint acrid nausea in her mouth. She heard another voice, a voice inside her now, the sound of her sister screaming. Angela had screamed at night and was told to shut up, to stop being a baby. They did not realize that she had spinal meningitis. When they finally did realize it, they took Angela to the hospital, where she screamed for Mama not to leave while Mama waved goodbye.

Now Angela was thirty-eight, and her voice sounded like a scream had gotten stuck in it. It was jagged and too bright except when it sounded half dead. She'd been a beggar on the street since she'd gotten fired from a chain pharmacy for stealing drugs. She came in and out of their lives like a figure in a dream, calling from pay phones to ask for money. Except for the previous year, when she had been hospitalized after a stroke bashed in one side of her face and made her walk with a limp. Then they knew where she was, and went to visit her. Their mother tried to get Angela to come live with her but Angela said no; she preferred her freedom.

Angela had been overjoyed to hear that Elizabeth was pregnant. "I think it's really going to ground you," she said. Then she paused and Elizabeth heard her through the pay phone, working for breath after the long sentence.

She didn't feel the furnace, thought Elizabeth. *That was the problem. She got lost.*

She put away the food and headed up the stairs to Matt's room.

Probably their friends wondered about their having separate bedrooms; possibly some of the married ones envied the arrangement. It had been a condition of their moving in together, and Elizabeth was grateful to Matt for understanding, even sharing her special need to not have his corporeal reality pressed upon her at all times. Of course, this special need would be literally pissed on by the approaching infant, who would soon – again, literally – be pressed upon her at all times, starting from the inside. Her first feeling about this was one of soft, blind opening, like a viscous plant efflorescing in a nature show. Then the hourglass tipped. She felt lost in the middle of her mother's voices, except they were her voices now, a winding knot that she could not sort, yelling one thing, then another.

She opened Matt's door; he was still asleep, she could tell even though he was faced away from her toward the wall. She crouched on the floor with her hands planted in front of her and made a monster face. They liked to do that: sneak up, crouch, make a face, and wait for the other person to see. She waited. He stirred but he didn't turn. She uttered a soft guttural sigh. You could deliver a baby squatting on the floor. You could fuck that way too, and once they had, him behind her. He'd said, "Do you want a baby? Do you want a baby?" and there was the scalding pit. She'd let out a bellow, like a cow with a hot ass. She was joking, but she was liking it too. She pictured a woman kneeling with her butt in the air, her face dissolved in want, bellowing "just give me a baby!" All the middle-aged, Pilates-trained, surgically enhanced women progressing in their therapy and loaded with fertility drugs, finally letting it all out. The queen throwing her fit. She bellowed like a cow with a crown on its head, charging through the forest.

She emitted a sultry little noise at Matt's sleeping form. He lifted his head and turned, an affable dog with rumpled skin and sleepy eyes, answering her with his own noise, a doggish question mark on the end of it. She came off the floor and into the bed, under the covers with their chests touching. Even half asleep, his body was busy with the sniffing, scratching, licking, proudly trotting energy of a loyal pack animal.

"Matt," she asked, "do you remember Elsie the cow?"

"Sort of. What was she?"

"The cow on the cartons of milk. She had big soft eyes and she wore a crown." Mama took the milk in from the chute in the kitchen where the milkman delivered it for breakfast. A slur of Mama in her flannel robe, moving in the kitchen.

"She didn't have a crown," said Matt. "I remember. She wore a garland of flowers." He paused. "Her husband was Beauregard the bull."

He ran his hand down her body, slipping it into her pajama bottoms to feel the rough hair on her crotch.

"I'm in a horrible mood," she said.

He hesitated, then withdrew his hand.

"I feel like we're living in an enemy world," she said. "Or I am anyway."

"Enemy world how?"

"I'm thinking about Angela. How she was destroyed by the world."

"She isn't destroyed. We just talked to her."

"She's destroyed."

"She's homeless. She's not destroyed."

"Oh come on!"

"Anyway, you aren't Angela."

"But I'm like her."

"No, you're not. You have friends and you're able to –"

"I don't really have friends. I'm able to perform socially better than Angela. I understand the codes better. I know the ways you're supposed to arrange the cards." Matt of course had heard the story.

"What about Liane?"

"Liane? Are you kidding?"

"Well, she was your friend for a while."

"But she turned on me." She was vomiting self-pity, and she couldn't stop it; the hourglass had turned into a carnival ride where they spin you upside down and then make you hang there. Besides, it was true! "People are always turning on me. I've never had a real friend except Doreen, and she's in Texas. And anyway, she's crazy."

"People turn on each other," said Matt. "I've turned on people, so have you."

"I know," she said. "That's what I mean. The world is so ugly. I feel like I'm another species, like my whole family is another species and now I'm creating another one. Why? They killed my father and they're killing my sister, and those fuckers at the office would kill me if they could. In a primitive society, they'd stone me. Why would a baby want to be here?"

The ride flipped around again and everyone screamed. Matt was sitting up looking like a concerned middle-aged man who'd never made a bestial noise in his life.

"Beth," he said. "Your dad died of cancer and Angela, well, if she wants to kill herself, that's her choice. And what are you talking about, the people in the office? You were really liking them last week."

How to explain? She did like them, even Liane, who last month had joined forces with the bitch who'd tried to get her fired. Just last week she had sat in a meeting looking at them all in wonderment; it seemed as if their discontented, ironic personalities were flimsy costumes they could barely keep in place, and that she could see beneath the absurd makeup and false noses just enough to intuit the innocence and strangeness flashing, deerlike, beneath. Even the sweet personalities seemed a garish imitation of the real, the hidden sweetness she could sense the way she had sensed her mother's purring furnace.

But now they just seemed like pigs. They seemed worse than pigs. They seemed purposefully twisted, as if they had deliberately taken the raw matter of their selfhood and distorted it beyond recognition, covering it with complex masking, barbed wire, and booby traps, anything to hide and pervert the essence beneath.

"Your co-workers are not going to stone you. You're too tough and besides, you're pregnant – once they know that, they'll cut you a lot of slack."

"Yeah, you're probably right. It'll all get better when they can ID me as one more stupid cow." She stood up. "Just a minute."

Quickly, she went back down the hall to the bathroom. A light sweat broke on her forehead as she knelt before the toilet. She lifted the lid, leaned forward, and puked. When she and Angela were little and they got sick, Mama would sit with them and stroke their backs while they puked into a yellow bucket. There were no crazy voices then, just her strong, warm hand. Elizabeth's mind followed the example of her mother's hand, and was gentle with her puking body.

When she was finished she felt calm, dense, and heavy. She rinsed her mouth and sat on the edge of the tub. She pictured a dense, heavy demon, a creature of flesh and stone, sitting with its chin in its hand. She imagined herself inside it, the whole room inside it. Matt was there too, in another room. Somewhere in it was the office and everybody that worked there, somewhere else was her mother, making tea and watching television. They might be in the liver section, where they were saturated with bitterness and bile, or they might be near the heart, saturated with the tremendous, singing energy of blood. Wherever they lived, they went about their lives, amid the inner organs of the demon. Outside, something else was happening, but that's not where they were.

Earth, she thought. *Physical life.*

She pictured her child, the size of a fingernail, deep in her own demon body. She pictured him questing through it, as if through a living mountain, guided by a strand of gossamer, finding his way out.

She went back to the bedroom and sat on the bed.

"I'm sorry," she said. "I know I'm being weird."

"Well," he said, "I was sort of wondering. Do you want to kill them?"

"Who?"

"Like the people at work. Anybody, everybody."

"No," she said. "I don't want to kill them. But I'd like to replace them."

"With what?"

"I don't know." She considered a moment. "Maybe cartoons?"

He threw back his head and laughed, and she loved him laughing, as if her self-pity were a cartoon with a wonderful character that you liked no matter what. Now she was only half in the mucky richness inside of the demon and half in a place of light and shimmering particles. She shifted back and forth between the two places, enjoying both of them. She pictured their child, age two or three, sitting in a sunny room, rubbing both hands in finger paints, palms down, smearing the heavy paper with wonderful purple and red mud. He would like the mucky richness too. Or maybe not. He might be finicky and ethereal, all light and surface. He might think she was gross! She smiled and got under the blankets with Matt. They put their arms around each other, and each tiny, sensitive hair of her personality extended to feel each tiny, sensitive hair of his.

"What kind of cartoons?" he asked.

"I don't know. Something nice for him to play with."

"Maybe Pokémon?"

"No! I'm so sick of those!"

"I'll bet he'll like them though."

Matt put his hand on her belly. She put her hand on his; they made soft lowing noises of herd animal recognition. She tried to recall the ice plant, but instead she got pictures of the people who'd died of diet drugs or liposuction, their eyes wanting more and starving to get it. They were made to want like the plants were made to grow. Their want was as persistent as roots through concrete, twisting and turning, finding every way to want and every way to satisfy and then wanting again. It suddenly seemed to her that if you untwisted the want, you would see a different version of the growing. If one was terrible, so was the other. Her father used to say, "I hate nature. Nature is trying to kill us, and if we didn't fight it twenty-four hours a day, it would kill us. I wish they could just pave the whole damn thing over so all you'd have to do would be hose it down every once in a while." She smiled; her father had been funny.

"You know," said Matt, "I wouldn't blame you if you did want to kill people. I think it's pretty normal. I was thinking of killing Ted Agrew just last night."

"Who's he?"

Matt produced plays in a small theater, and the people he worked with came and went.

"The director of that company, Blue Bug. You met him, he wears ridiculous glasses and he tells horrible sex stories, like dogs ejaculating on women's faces and stuff."

"Oh, yeah."

"I imagined coming up behind him and stabbing him in the back of the neck with an ice pick."

"You couldn't do that, Matt, you're too short."

"I could too!" He sat up and made the face of a retarded psychopath, one hand clutching an imaginary ice pick. "Like this!"

They laughed and pressed against each other. But this time the closeness agitated instead of comforted her, and she pulled away.

"The thing about Angela." She frowned and lay on her back. "My parents always said she was a crybaby, and she was. But it was like, it was like she wasn't wired like everybody else and so they couldn't help her grow up. Because she couldn't receive their signals."

"Ummm!"

"That's what I mean about enemy world. Not that people are actively trying to kill her. Just that they can't recognize what she has and so it's rotting. Like Africa. It's so beautiful and its spirit is so big. And it doesn't do any good. It's dying anyway. Because the world doesn't know that spirit anymore."

They were quiet a moment. The heat came on and the vent behind Matt's bed began to ping and tick. Elizabeth considered all the things that worked without thinking: machines, plants, bacteria, bugs, the hearts of mammals. She pictured a vending machine: a waxed paper cup rattling into place and thin, sugary hot chocolate streaming into it.

"I feel it too sometimes," said Matt, "the enemy world thing. In a different way. I feel like a small tugboat chugging through hostile waters. I cast my searchlight up on the hill – and there's Ted Agrew's smirking face, illuminated and staring down."

"But people aren't your enemy," said Elizabeth. "People like you. You don't have these alien feelers coming out of your forehead. You have this earthy thing that makes them feel safe. They don't realize you want to stab them in the neck with an ice pick."

"Then the baby will have it too. He'll have that and the feelers. He'll have everything. And as soon as he's old enough, we'll send him to African dance class so he'll find out about African spirit."

"But it won't help if *he* knows about it, that's not the point. The world is killing Africa. It doesn't care about the dances."

Matt sighed. "You're just being self-indulgent now. The world is not killing Africa."

"But it is! That's what I'm saying. The climate that has been created by other cultures is antithetical to the spirit of Africa. Africa is being spiritually suffocated. That's why they're getting AIDS and having those wars."

"Okay," said Matt. "Okay. We'll arm the house like the Swiss Family Robinson and stay in."

"Then they'd just get us for being crazy."

Matt was silent for so long that she thought he might be fed up. She considered apologizing, but she was suddenly too tired. A cloud covered the sun; the room became soft and dim. Matt put his hand on her stomach. He sang: "Roses love sunshine / Violets love dew / Angels in heaven / Know I love you." He kept singing, except instead of words he sang soft little syllables: "Ma ma ma MA ma . . ."

Tenderness opened inside her with erotic force. It was impossible to close herself to it. She thought of her mother and father with longing, as if she were saying goodbye, and yet at the same time, as if they would be with her for as long as she lived. Strangely, she thought of her co-worker and former friend, the treacherous Liane. She thought of her asleep, her ovaries cycling through, making blood and eggs while her head dreamed, innocent of treachery. She thought of her own body building flesh and bone, tiny nails and teeth and an unknowable, electrical brain. She pictured Angela, holding her arms up like she was calling something down from the sky. The hair on Elizabeth's arms stood up. The eye on the collapsed side of her sister's face looked out as if from an exalted secret place. She was calling all her hidden power from the world beyond the stroke to bless her sister's baby.

The cloud moved off the sun and a pool of light spilled across the floor, full of trembling shadows: nervous little branches, a preening bird, a flying bird, water dripping off the roof. The rippling shadows of heat and air. She imagined Christopher – because suddenly she knew his name – working his way through the density of her body to the light, following the cord that guided him to her. Because she wanted him. She wanted him.

JACOB'S BATH
David Schickler

The legend of Jacob's bath began on May 1, 1948, the day Jacob Wolf married Rachel Cohen.

The wedding took place in the West 89th Street synagogue and the reception was at the Plaza Hotel. Jacob and Rachel's mothers – both named Amy – coordinated these events. Both families had histories of propriety in Manhattan. Centuries back, the Wolfs had been Romanian tailors. They now owned Wolf's Big and Tall on West 72nd, where they trimmed the prominent and took in the monstrous. It was rumored that Sherman Wolf, Jacob's father, had been personal tailor to both the mayor and the Scapalletti crime bosses. The exact clientele of Wolf's Big and Tall was never known publicly. What was known publicly was that the Wolfs were in league with giant men, men whose paws you were afraid to shake. That's what made it such a disgrace when, in the summer of 1943, twenty-four-year-old Jacob Wolf, Sherman's only son, took work as a jingle writer.

"A what?" Sherman Wolf stared at his boy. "What're you handing me, here?"

"I'll write jingles," said Jacob. "Songs for products."

"Songs for products?" Sherman Wolf was six foot seven. His son was five eleven.

"What songs?" demanded Sherman. "What products? What're you handing me?"

"It's for the radio, Dad." Jacob sighed. "It's for a conglomerate."

"What now? What're you handing me? A condiment?"

Jacob sighed again. The conglomerate was a team of businesses whose common association mystified Jacob. All he knew was that a man had offered him a paying job writing jingles. If the man called and said, we need a poodle-collar song, that's what Jacob wrote. If a thirty-second-long ode to mouthwash was required, Jacob would create a thirty-second-long ode to mouthwash.

"A conglomerate is a team of businesses, Dad."

Sherman looked down on his son. They stood facing each other in the drawing room of Sherman and Amy's penthouse on West 74th Street. The penthouse contained two original paintings by August Macke. It also contained a black grand piano that Sherman had bought when Jacob was a boy. At an early age, Jacob had shown musical talent and a chronic deficiency in athletics, and Sherman hoped to promote the former. True, his son was short and a disgrace at stickball. But, with arduous training, perhaps Jacob could become a musical genius of stormy temperament, a kind of Jewish Mozart who would bang out his tragedies at Carnegie Hall or the Met. Sherman wasn't averse to culture. But he presupposed that his only male offspring would crave power, notoriety of some respectable cast. A war was on, and anything that smacked of the trivial was disgraceful to Sherman Wolf.

"Amy," barked Sherman, "get in here. The boy wants to join a condiment."

So Sherman and Jacob never agreed about Jacob's profession. In 1944, when Jacob netted a fat paycheck for his Grearson's Soap Flakes jingle, Sherman held his tongue. He did the same during his son's 1946 Bear Belly Cupcakes phase. But, in the fall of 1947, Sherman's patience died when he heard the following ditty on the radio:

> *It's time to be kind*
> *to your child's behind.*
> *Switch to Kyper's . . .*
> *the dapper diapers!*

"Diapers can't be dapper," fumed Sherman. "Men's clothes are dapper. Suits and vests, dammit."

"It sounded good," said Jacob.

"Besides," said Sherman, "I know Mitch Kyper. He dresses like shit."

"Dapper diapers," explained Jacob. "Alliteration, Dad."

Sherman threw up his hands. His exasperation and embarrassment over Jacob seemed like divine decrees, permanent curses on his life. All he wanted was for his son to be a man. A man worked hard, played cards, drank whiskey, thought about women's tits. A man paid for things, and then, if he wasn't sick or dead, he laughed. But a man did not write songs about toothpaste and hair cream.

"He just needs a wife," Amy Wolf told her husband.

In January 1948, Jacob Wolf found his wife. To Sherman and Amy's undying relief, the girl was Rachel Cohen, daughter of Alex and Amy Cohen of West 79th Street. Alex Cohen was the sports editor of the *New York Times*. His family hadn't been in news for as many generations as Wolfs had been cutting cloth, but Alex's published opinions about the Yankees and the Giants were sober and correct. Alex Cohen, Sherman Wolf felt, was not a man of levity. Alex understood the honor a man bore when he crushed an opponent, whether that opponent was Adolf Hitler or the Boston Red Sox. Sherman hoped that some of Alex's nobility had come down to his daughter Rachel – as much nobility, anyway, as a woman could carry – and he hoped in turn that Rachel's nobility might rub off on Jacob.

As for Rachel, she loved Jacob. She was twenty-two when they met, and she worked as a fact checker in the *Times*'s features department. Rachel was responsible for discovering and accurately reporting to her superiors the exact height of Benito Mussolini, or the wing speed of the hummingbird, or the precise ingredients in the vichyssoise at Duranigan's of Madison Avenue. In fact, Rachel was at Duranigan's, arguing with the chef – who had agreed over the phone to publish some recipes, but was now being tight-lipped and haughty – when she noticed Jacob Wolf eating lunch alone at a corner table. She'd seen Jacob while growing up, at temple on 89th, but she'd never *noticed* him. She'd never noticed the particularly strong cut of his jaw, or the frailty of his fingers. She'd never been privy to the sadness, the unselfconscious melancholy with which Jacob ate a Reuben sandwich when he figured no one was looking.

"My God," whispered Rachel. "Jacob Wolf?"

"I say nothing." The chef shook his head in triumph. "The vichyssoise, it is private."

Rachel floated out of the kitchen, toward her lone and future lover, who glanced up to meet her gaze.

"Private," the chef hollered after Rachel. "You hear?"

Four months later, Jacob and Rachel married. It was a regal wedding. Cousins poured in from Long Island and Washington, D.C. Pure white long-stem roses were strewn on the synagogue floor. Susan March, Rachel's close friend and fellow fact checker, was the maid of honor. Susan wore a dress that revealed her excellent calves, and many guests felt privately that Susan was more beautiful than Rachel.

At the Plaza reception, under Amy and Amy's discerning command, steak tartare was served, and Parisian champagne, and then lemon sorbet and then dinner. All the best people in Manhattan attended, including June Madagascar, the Broadway soprano, and the comedian Robby Jax, and ominously tall men in waistcoats. Dancing was permitted, children smiled, and a cavalcade of gifts was bestowed on the bride and groom. All of the gifts were impeccable. There were silver knives and opal jewelry. There were bottles of wine and examples of art. There was nothing lewd, grotesque, comical, or personal: no lingerie, no cash, no recordings of jazz, no books. Every gift pointed toward a useful, lavish life.

Presiding over the night was six-foot-seven Sherman Wolf. True, Alex Cohen had footed the bill, but that was nothing magnanimous. It was Sherman who imbued the night with class: he sank his teeth into steak tartare, he danced with wives, he shook hands with his cousin Ida to end a long-standing feud. Above all, Sherman was happy. No goofy jingle writers had appeared – Sherman had feared there might be a union of them – to sing stupid songs or snort laughter. For the evening's end, a limousine had been hired to pull up to the front doors of the Plaza and spirit Jacob and his bride off to an Adirondack mountain resort. Finally, in the reception's pièce de résistance, the governor himself appeared for fifteen minutes. He kissed the bride, pounded the groom's shoulder, then took Sherman aside for some intimate words.

Amid all this wonder was Jacob Wolf, twenty-eight, newly married and utterly dismayed. Jacob sat at the head table beside Rachel and watched the night go unhappily by. The Plaza was glorious, of course. The food was glorious, and the lighting, and the violin music, and even Jacob's snot-nosed cousin Lucy from New Haven had somehow lost her baby fat and vulgar tongue and become glorious, too. But Jacob was not built for glory. He'd known this all his life. He smiled at his and Rachel's guests because they wished him well, but, in his heart, he was terrified of these people. Contrary to myth, there was nothing pretentious or phony about them. They were everything they believed themselves to be. They were rich, shiny, intelligent, and, Jacob guessed, they were moral champions of every perseverance. It was exactly their goodness that chilled Jacob's heart. For he knew himself to be a flawed, simple man. He wrote breezy, foolish song lyrics for a living and was content to do so. He took long walks in Central Park, not so as to appreciate nature or become fit, but rather for no reason whatever. He'd chosen Rachel as a wife because she'd been an easy catch. She'd walked up to him at Duranigan's, and, through body language and the English language, made it known to Jacob that she was available. They dated for a month, and Rachel said things that made Jacob laugh. She had a capable body, as did Jacob – though they didn't sleep together before their honeymoon – and Rachel neither loved nor disdained the jingles Jacob wrote. Out of what might have been joy but was certainly relief, Jacob asked Rachel to be his wife. She immediately said yes, and that was that.

Or perhaps not, thought Jacob, looking out at his reception. Perhaps the power that shone so exquisitely in these guests lay dormant inside Rachel, too. Jacob lived in the Preemption apartment building on West 82nd, and he planned for Rachel to move in with him after the honeymoon. But how long would she be content there? Maybe a month into the marriage she would demand magic: a move to the Upper East Side, tickets to *Carmen*, papaya for breakfast. What if she suddenly decided that California was an important place? Or craved oysters? Or wanted to discuss Churchill?

Rachel squeezed Jacob's hand. "You look worried."

"I'm not," said Jacob.

"You're lying. Stop worrying."

Jacob looked at his new wife. He looked at her sparkling gown, her cleavage, her rather ugly eyebrows.

Rachel shrugged. "I'm just a girl," she said. "You're just a guy."

Thank God, thought Jacob.

The legend of Jacob's bath began later that night, in the mountains.

Jacob and Rachel's honeymoon lodge was called Blackberry House. It was a compromise between a Vanderbilt retreat and a modern bed-and-breakfast. The house itself was vast and wooden and just an hour south of Canada. The ground-floor common room was paneled and studious. It featured bearskin rugs, racks of antlers, and a chessboard with pieces cut from tusk. The bedrooms, however, were warm and dear, with quilts on the beds, lighted candles, and, in the bathrooms, freestanding tubs with brass lion's feet. In Jacob and Amy's room – The Blackberry Room – there was an antique loom, and a giant dormer window that looked out over Raquette Lake. Outside this window, on the roof, in the moonlight, was a skunk.

"There's a skunk out there," said Rachel. She still wore her wedding dress. She pointed at the roof, looked out at the night. It was spring in the Adirondacks, but the windowpanes were cold.

"It's two in the morning," said Rachel. "There's a skunk outside our window."

Perhaps Jacob should have been thinking about consummation. Instead, he was wondering how a skunk could possibly scale a three-story building.

"*Mephitis mephitis*," said Rachel. "That's Latin for the common skunk."

For the *Times*, Rachel had once checked animal facts.

"How'd he get up there?" said Jacob.

The man and his bride watched the skunk. The skunk was black and white and did not currently smell bad.

Rachel removed her shoes, rubbed her feet. "I don't know how romantic this is. A *Mephitis mephitis* outside our window on our honeymoon night."

Jacob didn't reply.

"I'm going to take a bath," said Rachel.

She went into the bathroom, closed the door. Jacob stayed looking at the skunk. It wasn't moving. It was planted five feet from the window, in plain view of Jacob and Rachel's nuptial bed.

Jacob heard the chirp of pipes, the running of water. His wife, he knew, was up to something feminine. As he thought this, Jacob decided to get rid of the skunk.

"Honey?" called Rachel. "What're you doing?"

Steam leaked from the crack under the bathroom door.

"Nothing," said Jacob.

He removed his good leather shoe, put it on his left hand like a shield. With his right hand, Jacob opened the window, slowly, just a few inches. He stuck his left hand outside.

"Go away, skunk," whispered Jacob, waving his shoe. "Hit the road."

The skunk looked at Jacob. It seemed terribly bored.

"Fuck off," hissed Jacob. "Scram."

He glared at the skunk. He waved his shoe carefully.

"Shoo, now," he said.

Jacob kept waving his shoe. He didn't want the skunk to fall to its death, necessarily. He just wanted it to move to a different part of the roof, to eavesdrop somewhere else. As it turned out, the skunk did neither of these things. What it did was, it pulled a one-eighty and sprayed Jacob's shoe.

"Oh, shit."

Jacob pulled his hand out of the shoe, yanked himself back inside. He closed the window as quickly as he could, leaving his shoe outside. But it was too late.

"Uh-oh," said Rachel from the bathroom.

"I'm sorry," called Jacob.

He stood up, plugged his nose. The stench was unbearable.

"You'd better come in here," said Jacob's wife.

I've ruined it, thought Jacob. I've ruined our honeymoon.

"Come on," said Rachel.

She was standing, wrapped in thick, white towels. One towel wrapped around her hair, turban style. The other was fixed over her breasts and came down to her thighs. There was a scab on her knee.

"We'd better plug the door," said Rachel. She took an extra towel from a shelf, lay it across the crack under the door.

"I tried to get rid of the damn thing," said Jacob. "It sprayed my shoe."

Rachel had been in the tub. She was wet beneath her towels.

"I'm sorry," said Jacob.

"It's all right," said Rachel.

The air was fogged. Jacob looked at his woman, at the way she'd wrapped herself in towels. It was a manner in which women often wrapped themselves in towels, one for the hair, one for the body. It wasn't original, but it was something men never did. Jacob liked it.

"Um." Jacob blushed. After all, under the towels was his wife.

"He only sprayed my shoe," said Jacob. "He didn't get me."

Rachel giggled. She wrinkled her nose. "He got you," she said.

Jacob laughed. Rachel laughed, too. They fell silent, watching each other.

"Maybe you should get in the tub," suggested Rachel.

Jacob panicked. He'd heard about women who made love in bathtubs.

"I don't know about that," he said.

"You smell," said Rachel. "Undress, and get in the tub."

Rachel smiled. Jacob took her smile to mean she wouldn't get kinky. So he relaxed. He undressed slowly, letting her see him. He got in the tub.

Rachel picked up Jacob's clothes, threw them outside the door. She closed the door, knelt by the tub.

"You're . . . um." Jacob was eye level with Rachel's bosom. "Are you going to . . ."

"I'm not getting in there with you," said Rachel.

"Oh, fine," said Jacob quickly.

"I've already had my bath."

"Exactly."

"I don't take long baths."

"Yes. No problem."

Rachel lay her cheek on the side of the tub. She looked at Jacob's body in the hot, clear water. She saw all of him.

"Rachel," said Jacob. He was embarrassed now, sitting in the tub, water to his neck. He felt like a boy.

Some of Rachel's hair fell from her towel, mingled with the water. She reached out, stroked Jacob's neck.

"I love your neck," she said. "Your neck and your jaw."

Jacob let her touch his face. She was his wife.

"I love you," he said.

Rachel sighed happily.

"I do," said Jacob.

Rachel stopped rubbing Jacob's jaw.

Now what? thought Jacob.

Rachel picked up a white cotton washcloth. She lathered it on a bar of soap. The soap smelled like wintergreen.

"What're you doing?" asked Jacob. He kept his eyes on the washcloth.

Rachel rubbed the washcloth till it foamed. She arranged the cloth over her hand, dipped her hand under the water. She massaged her husband's chest.

"Be quiet," said Rachel. "I'm going to give you a bath."

Jacob obeyed his wife. He remained quiet, and she did what she said she would. She gave her man a bath.

In the bath's early stages, Jacob laughed. He had ticklish underarms, and he was self-conscious about his body. But, as Rachel proceeded to wash him head to toe, Jacob stopped laughing. His wife was committed to her action. She scrubbed her new husband carefully. She was firm with his hands – which had been tainted by skunk – and hard on his feet. She worked thoroughly on his torso, but she was tender with his groin. Finally, overwhelmed with the care being shown him, Jacob closed his eyes. A mellow joy stole over him. For weeks, he'd been planning for tonight – for his conquest of Rachel's body – but now his plans faded. He still wanted to make love to her in the bed, but right now something simpler was happening. Rachel's fingers were tending his skin, grooming him wetly, kindly.

"You like this?" whispered Rachel.

Jacob kept his eyes shut. His body had gone over to goose bumps, and his mouth came open in surprise. Jacob felt sure, suddenly, that Rachel had never bathed another man.

"Hmmm." Rachel's throat was pleased.

"You like this," she whispered.

The bulk of Jacob and Rachel's honeymoon was their business. But one warm fact remained: after a meal and a walk in the forest, Rachel gave Jacob a bath every night. Within three days, husband and wife were hooked on the ritual. They came to enjoy it not as a luxury, a sign of some new, candied life, but as a necessity. It was as if Jacob had been climbing a mountain all his years and had come now to a decent peak, where there was a woman and a well of water. The woman was there to strengthen the man, to quench his thirst, and the man loved the woman and he was grateful. It wasn't about equity: Jacob never bathed Rachel. He was ready to perform a lifetime of chores for her, but this isn't about that. This is about the bath: the legend.

Jacob and Rachel returned to Manhattan. Rachel returned to checking facts, Jacob to writing jingles. They moved into Jacob's place in the Preemption apartment building.

The Preemption was special for three reasons. It featured the oldest working Otis elevator in Manhattan, a hand-operated antique with mahogany doors at each floor. The Preemption also featured a peculiar doorman, a Negro man named Sender. Sender wore a blue suit like a train conductor, and he never seemed to age or leave his post. Some Preemption residents guessed that Sender was not quite fifty, some that he was over one hundred, but nobody could beat him at arm wrestling. He had an oval scar on his forehead between and just above his eyes. Whispers went around every October that Sender had been born with a third eye, and that the doctors had removed it from his forehead when they cut his umbilical cord.

rd, fatefully unique characteristic of the Preemption was the Elias Rook, the building's original designer and owner, had freestanding bathtubs in every apartment. Elias Rook finished the building in 1890, but he was an endowed, strict Presbyterian, and he had eternity in mind when he fashioned the Preemption. As a result, the apartment floors and walls were cut from the sturdiest oak. The glass on each vaulted window was inches thick. The tubs, however, were the masterpieces. They were cast iron with white enamel coatings, brass pipes, and brass fittings. If a fact checker like Rachel ever bothered to research the Preemption, she might discover the incredible truth that not a single resident had ever, in over a century, suffered foul water, broken pipes or even crumbled enamel in their tubs. Of course, over the years, most tubs had been converted into showers, Jacob's included. It was against Preemption rules to remove the original tubs – which were cemented into place anyway – so most residents hired plumbers to raise a pipe like a mast and fit the mast with a shower head. These people – the majority – then fenced their tubs in with plastic curtains, showered quickly, and returned to the world. But a few Preemptioneers never erected showers. They stewed themselves slowly in their tubs, their old-fashioned cauldrons, and they thought of Sender, and they pondered the Preemption's elevator, which also never broke, and they were not afraid.

The day Jacob and Rachel Wolf returned from the Adirondacks, Jacob dismantled his shower. From then on, every night of their marriage, Rachel bathed Jacob. She bathed him on November 20th, 1953, the day their first son, Elias, was born. It wasn't something Rachel told her family or the doctors at St. Luke's hospital. She just did it: She checked into St. Luke's in the morning, gave birth to Elias, and was home by nightfall to bathe her husband.

Rachel made it home to bathe Jacob, too, on April 8th, 1956, the day her mother died of a brain aneurysm. She bathed Jacob on every Sabbath, and on Jewish holidays. She bathed him during full moons and the World Series, bathed him when she was angry and when he was cruel. Jacob, for his part, made it home for his bath every night. On July 30th, 1958, the night he received an award at Rockefeller Center for his

Jeremiah's Mustard jingle, Jacob refused a fifth beer at Duranigan's and caught a cab home for his bath. On August 23rd, 1969, in a hotel room at the Plaza, fifty-year-old Jacob Wolf ended his affair with Broadway pianist Melodie "Three-Four Time" Sykes. He rushed home, convulsing with sobs, and climbed into the tub for his wife.

For decades, nobody knew the secret, the private font, of Jacob and Rachel's marriage. Their parents didn't know. Neither did their neighbors, or their children, Elias and Sarah. These latter figured, all through their adolescence, that their parents were simply horny. They watched Jacob and Rachel disappear every night into the master bedroom, which connected to the bathroom. When Elias and Sarah heard tub water running, they assumed that sex was being achieved, and that they themselves had been conceived in warm water. This led to some teenage confusion for Elias, who deduced that young women were at their most pliable and libidinous if you scuttled them into a shower and soaked them down. Sarah, of course, was like-minded, right up until college. If a boy or man ran hot water anywhere within two rooms of her, she collapsed into giggles or scampered off in fright.

The legend of Jacob's bath went public in January, 1991. Jacob was seventy-two, Rachel was sixty-five, and the Gulf War was on. Jacob's mother had died five years before, and his father, the mighty Sherman Wolf, was ninety years old. Sherman had shrunk almost a foot. He lived now at Benjamin Home, a convalescence house on the Upper East Side. The facilities at Benjamin Home were extravagant. The beds were firm, with good wooden frames, the halls were carpeted, the nurses kind. Sherman Wolf growled at the old women who played canasta in the lounge. He followed the war proceedings religiously on his television and in the papers. In his heart, though, Sherman was anxious. The world had remained Big and Tall, but he had not. His lungs ached when he took deep breaths. He suffered from arthritis, poor hearing, and cold spells that made his limbs shiver. On top of it all, there was a madman in Iraq, and Sherman was convinced that this madman would soon attack Benjamin Home and, more specifically, Sherman himself.

"Dad," said Jacob. "No one's going to attack you."

"What?" Sherman glared at his boy, not comprehending. "What're you handing me?"

Jacob visited Benjamin Home every Sunday, and often during the week.

"Nobody's going to hurt you, Dad. I won't let them."

Sherman stared at Jacob in disbelief.

"You?" he muttered. "You can't stop the madman."

"Don't worry about the madman." Jacob arranged a quilt on his father's shoulders. It was a quilt Jacob's mother, Amy, had made.

"You." Sherman looked away and sighed. "You jingle writer."

Jacob's bath became famous because of Susan March, Rachel's maid of honor and colleague from way back. They'd started out together as fact checkers at the *Times*. When Rachel left work to raise Elias and Sarah, Susan March stayed in news. She worked at the *Times* for five decades, writing her way through Watergate, break dancing, the Troubles in Belfast. By the late 1970s, Susan had her own biweekly column, March Madness. The column ran the gamut from political satire to denouncements of fashion. Typically, Susan would send up some grotesque: a world figure of freakish disposition, or some no-name with a startling agenda. It was in March Madness that America first heard interviewed Dana Smith, the lover of accused serial killer Bobby Bobbington.

"I'll only talk to Susan," sobbed Dana, and she meant it.

Susan March also took swashbuckling offense to Denmark's 1986 Mongoloid Crisis – to the point, some said, that she swung key Senate votes on the issue. All in all, Susan's career attested that she had an eye for what mattered to the world, or at least to America. Susan had, apparently, a prudent heart, a savvy pen, and a willingness to touch the morally electric.

The catch came on New Year's Day morning, 1991. Susan March was in a cab, traveling down Fifth Avenue. It was 4 A.M. Susan was returning home from a party, and she was drunk. It was one of those nights when alcohol had made her perceptive and depressed, and Susan gazed forlornly at the city as the cab sped along. It was snowing outside. There were very few other cars. The cabbie had figured Susan for a tourist and was narrating the sights of Fifth Avenue.

"There's Trump Tower," said the cabbie. "There's St. Patrick's Cathedral. There's two people fucking."

Susan started, blinked, looked hard. There indeed, on the steps of St. Patrick's, were two teenagers in the snow. The cabbie had slowed down to get a good look, so Susan got one, too. She wished she could've said the teenagers were making love, ringing in the New Year with healthy abandon, but the cabbie was right. The teenagers were fucking. The girl's face winced. The boy had bunched the girl's dress and coat up around her neck, but his own pants were only at his thighs. The nakedness, the snow and the pain all belonged to the girl, and Susan was about to roll down her window and cry rape when the girl smiled. It was a hideous smile, Susan thought: permissive, rude, greedy, not to mention sacrilegious.

The cabbie shrugged.

"On we go," he said.

Susan couldn't sleep when she got home. She kept thinking about the teenagers. In her younger, brasher years, she would've dashed off an angry column about public mores, about sex, privacy, decency. The trouble was, Susan herself felt suddenly, completely indecent. Everything about the previous night had been unhealthy: not just the teenagers, but the party Susan attended. It had been a gathering of heavyweights: news anchors, models, actors, some respected journalists, and even a supposed hit man named Mr. Bruce. What disgusted Susan wasn't the gin and cigars, or the presence of a killer, or even the rutting of a girl. What disgusted Susan was that she'd made a life out of embracing these things, giving them credence by writing about them. She was well into her sixties, and she'd never married, or been to Disneyland, or learned to sing. Instead, she'd drawn a bead on the large, savage habits of the globe: murder, extortion, hatred, crimes against women and the earth. She'd stared long at these awful truths. The problem was, as Nietzsche said, when you look long into an abyss, the abyss also looks into you. That New Year's morning, Susan March made a terrible realization: she craved baseness. Some fiber of her soul longed to kill, as Mr. Bruce did, or to cleanse countries with napalm, or to be taken viciously by a man on the steps of a church. Not only did Susan want these atrocities, she wanted them so badly that she'd never erected the means to fight them off. She had no husband, no children, no balm to ease her days. And her arrogance, her pride in her lifelong, clear-eyed independence died hard that New Year's morning: or so Susan thought, anyway.

Susan threw up. She wept and shook. She tried to remember the lyrics to an Irish lullaby and couldn't. She stared at her bathroom mirror for an hour, repulsed by the creases in her face, the marks of what she'd once considered wisdom. By 9 A.M., Susan was on her couch, sniffling, clinging to Biter and Beater, her two cats, when the phone rang. Susan was in no shape to speak, but when she listened to the voice on the machine, she sighed with relief. It was Rachel Wolf calling, reminding Susan of their annual New Year's brunch appointment at Duranigan's. It was a ritual they'd kept up for twenty years.

"See you at eleven," said Rachel's cheerful voice. The machine clicked off.

Susan dried her eyes. She lay on the couch, recovering, thinking.

Brunch, she thought. Brunch, what a wonderful word.

It's so simple, Susan thought. She believed she was having an epiphany.

Brunch, Susan thought. Brunch and tradition and talking with a friend. Could a sixty-five-year-old, hungover woman write about such things, perhaps, instead of railing against misery?

Susan hugged Biter and Beater. She took a shower.

"What'd you do last night?" asked Rachel. She was eating eggs and potatoes with garlic and parsley.

Susan ate cinnamon toast. "Party. Uptown."

Rachel smiled.

She has a good face, thought Susan. Warm and wholesome, like toast.

"The jet set?" asked Rachel.

Susan nodded. "What'd you do, Raych?"

Rachel's hair was entirely gray, but long enough that she could still pull it back. Like a young girl's hair, thought Susan.

"The usual," said Rachel.

Susan leaned forward. "And what is the usual?"

Rachel smiled. "Oh, you know."

Susan shook her head. "No." Her voice quavered. "No, Raych, I really don't."

Rachel looked at her friend. Her face became serious. She was a mother of two and a grandmother of five. She could see when someone she loved was in trouble, in need.

"Well, Jacob fixed us two porterhouse steaks, like he always does on New Year's Eve. We had a little wine. Then Elias called, and later Sarah."

Susan waited. "And then?"

Rachel hesitated. It had been forty-three years, and they – she and Jacob – had never told anyone about what they did every night. But no one had ever needed to hear it, and now here was Rachel's friend. Here was Susan March, with a black death in her eyes that Rachel had only seen once before: when Elias had been admitted to a psychiatric ward for three months, suicidal over the loss of a woman. That death, that hole in the desire to live, made Rachel shiver for her friend as she had for her son. It was all she needed for a forty-three-year secret to end.

"And then," said Rachel simply, "I gave my husband his bath."

Out came the legend. With the pace of a child, Susan asked questions. Rachel answered them. She told the story of her honeymoon. She told about the skunk and the bathing. As she spoke, she forgot her eggs and potatoes. She related the days and nights of her marriage plainly and truly, without sentiment. She told how Jacob's bath wasn't about sex, but about devotion, and love. She even admitted, because she thought her friend needed her to, that Jacob had once had an affair, an affair she'd known about the entire time it went on.

"She was a girl in an orchestra," Rachel said. "Jacob met her for her lunch breaks, and they'd go to hotels."

"The bastard," whispered Susan.

Rachel stiffened. "He was home every night for his bath."

"But he lied to you! He was cheating!"

Rachel stared at her friend, who didn't understand men.

"I was devoted to him," she said evenly. "I was his wife, and I loved him. The affair stopped."

Susan licked her lips, astounded, thirsty.

"And you still bathe him every night?"

"Every night."

Susan's eyes brimmed. "That's so beautiful."

Rachel rolled her eyes. "Don't cry, Susan."

"But it's so beautiful." Susan March sighed.

Rachel frowned. For the first time, she sensed the danger of what she'd said and to whom she'd said it.

"It's just my life," she said.

"But it's so . . . so . . . *saintly*."

Rachel sat up straight. "For God's sake, Susan. I shouldn't have said anything."

Susan reached for her friend's hand. She reached for it earnestly, with the deep, soulful conviction of a person declaring war.

"But I'm so glad you did, Raych." She squeezed Rachel's palm. "I'm so glad you did."

Susan March devoted one day of her column to the legend of Jacob's bath. In what she thought was an act of homage, she used Jacob and Rachel Wolf's real names and told their intimate tale to the world. It was a column, Susan decided, that hallmarked her new hope in mankind. No more would she rage against the irrational, the evil, awful, and absurd. There was another option, she said in March Madness, for the true rebel, and that option was radical decency. Like Jacob and Rachel Wolf, people had but to choose a simple, decent action and devote themselves to it daily, entirely, without fail. It was the key to happiness, wrote Susan.

"Oh my God," whispered Jacob. He was reading the paper, reading about himself, his nightly bath.

"I'm sorry," begged Rachel.

"She gave the name of our building." Jacob's voice shook with fury. Rachel hung her head.

The Wolfs got letters. If Susan March had devoted a day of her column to a couple's bathing ritual, then that couple and that ritual deserved scrutiny and laud. One curious, desperate married couple even cornered Jacob in the Preemption's lobby.

"You could form a spousal cleansing club," said the husband.

"No, I couldn't," said Jacob.

"You could inspire the elderly," said the wife.

"Go to hell," said Jacob.

There were critics, too. A few acquaintances shook their heads sadly at Jacob and Rachel, convinced that the Wolfs had been hushing up decades of perversity. There was speculation that Elias and Sarah had been psychologically warped by their parents' habit, and were even now practicing similar rites with their loved ones. The worst of this came from Sherman Wolf.

"What're you handing me?" Sherman was wrapped in his quilt, glaring at Jacob.

"Dad," began Jacob.

"No." Sherman made a bony fist. "There's a madman in Iraq, and my son is taking baths with his wife. I read this in the paper."

"I don't take baths with Rachel," explained Jacob. He was blushing, though, livid inside. Some nurses had smiled at him today. They knew.

"She gives me baths," said Jacob quietly.

"Shut your mouth," said Sherman.

"All right, Dad."

Sherman hunkered down in his quilt. He coughed feebly.

"You were never a man," he croaked.

Jacob set his jaw. He thought of a jingle he'd once written for a greeting-card company. He thought of the myth of Pandora, and the way Rachel never got soap in his eyes.

"I'm sorry, Dad," said Jacob.

The assault lingered in Jacob's mind, turned to a paranoia. Each night, he still climbed naked into his tub, and Rachel still washed him. She sang him bits of songs he loved and petted back his hair. But something had died. Jacob felt it. Whether they'd mailed him letters or not, certain inhabitants of the island now considered him and Rachel to be profound. Strange couples that they'd never met were surely aping them, Jacob thought. Men were submerging themselves in hot water, and women who loved these men were washing them. If such bathing had been brainless, coincidental – just a man and a woman and soap and water – Jacob could have stood it. But he knew what the world wanted. It wanted glory. It wanted the act of a wife bathing her husband to be capable of banishing adultery, impotence, boredom.

"I can't take it." Jacob stood abruptly, climbed out of the tub.

"What?" Rachel wrapped a robe around her husband, tried to calm him.

Jacob paced. He wasn't articulate.

"People," he said. "I can't take people."

Rachel hugged her husband from behind, stopped his movement. The back of his neck was crazy with gray hairs. She nuzzled these.

"I love you," she said.

Jacob wasn't caving so easily.

"Susan March is an intrusive bitch," he said.

I've ruined it, thought Rachel.

"Yes," she said.

They stood there, Rachel holding Jacob. Jacob's knees were gangly, dripping.

"I love you," said Rachel.

Jacob sighed. He wanted there to be a fight. But there wouldn't be.

"I do," said Rachel.

His wife's hands were belted together on Jacob's stomach. He covered them with his own.

"I love you, too," he said.

The phone rang. Jacob left the bathroom, answered the phone.

"Hello?" he said.

"Good evening," said the phone. "This is Benjamin Home. Is this Jacob Wolf?"

Jacob closed his eyes. He got ready.

"Yes," he said.

Jacob and Rachel went together. Jacob's father had had a stroke. The left side of his face and body were paralyzed, and he couldn't speak. He could hear, though.

"I'd like to see him alone first," Jacob told Rachel.

They were at Benjamin Home, standing outside Sherman's room.

"All right," said Rachel.

Jacob went in.

Sherman looked terrible. There were tubes in his arms. Half of his face had fallen: the skin slacked, the eye lolled in its socket, the left side of his mouth sagged. His living eye, his right eye, looked radically, pleadingly afraid. It was fixed on a nurse, a young woman sitting at Sherman's bedside. She whispered kind words to Sherman, and with a washcloth, she wiped off his chin the drool that poured from his addled lips.

It was very simple. Jacob walked to the bedside, took the cloth from the nurse.

"I'll do that," said Jacob. "I'm his son."

The nurse nodded, left.

"Dad," said Jacob.

Sherman's eye panicked, roamed.

"Sherman Wolf." Jacob moved his face closer. "Dad."

Sherman's eye found Jacob. The old man's lips tried to work. The drool came forth, spilling down Sherman's neck.

"No, Dad," said Jacob. "No talking."

Jacob settled his father's head on the pillow. He swabbed drool off his father's chin, neck, shoulder.

Sherman's eye tried to rally its forces. It tried to resist. But in the end it relaxed, and the son moved the cloth over his father, tending him in a manner that would become a habit.

LETTER TO A FUNERAL PARLOR
Lydia Davis

Dear Sir,

I am writing to you to object to the word "cremains," which was used by your representative when he met with my mother and me two days after my father's death.

We had no objection to your representative, personally, who was respectful and friendly and dealt with us in a sensitive way. He did not try to sell us an expensive urn, for instance.

What startled and disturbed us was the word "cremains." You in the business must have invented this word and you are used to it. We the public do not hear it very often. We don't lose a close friend or a family member very many times in our life, and years pass in between, if we are lucky. Even less often do we have to discuss what is to be done with a family member or close friend after their death.

We noticed that before the death of my father you and your representative used the words "loved one" to refer to him. That was comfortable for us, even if the ways in which we loved him were complicated.

Then we were sitting there in our chairs in the living room trying not to weep in front of your representative, who was opposite us on the sofa, and we were very tired first from sitting up with my father, and then from worrying about whether he was comfortable as he was dying, and then from worrying about where he might be now that he was dead, and your representative referred to him as "the cremains."

At first we did not even know what he meant. Then, when we realized, we were frankly upset. "Cremains" sounds like something invented as a milk substitute in coffee, like Cremora, or Coffee-Mate. Or it sounds like some kind of chipped beef dish.

As one who works with words for a living, I must say that any invented word, like "Porta Potti" or "pooper-scooper," has a cheerful or even jovial ring to it that I don't think you really intended when you invented the word "cremains." In fact, my father himself, who was a professor of English and is now being called "the cremains," would have pointed out to you the alliteration in "Porta Potti" and the rhyme in "pooper-scooper." Then he would have told you that "cremains" falls into the same category as "brunch" and is known as a portmanteau word.

There is nothing wrong with inventing words, especially in a business. But a grieving family is not prepared for this one. We are not even used to our loved one being gone. You could very well continue to employ the term "ashes." We are used to it from the Bible, and are even comforted by it. We would not misunderstand. We would know that these ashes are not like the ashes in a fireplace.

Yours sincerely.

THE VISION
Jonathan Lethem

I first met the kid known as the Vision at second base, during a kickball game in the P.S. 29 gymnasium, fifth grade. That's what passed for physical education in 1974: a giant rubbery ball, faded red and pebbled like a bathmat, more bowled than pitched in the direction of home plate. A better kick got the ball aloft, and a fly was nearly uncatchable – after the outfielder stepped aside, as he or she invariably did, nearly anything in the air was a home run. Everyone fell down, there'd be a kid on his ass at each base as you went past. Alternately, a mistimed kick scudded back idiotically to the pitcher, and you were thrown out at first.

The Vision booted a double. His real name was Adam Cressner, but he believed himself or anyway claimed to be the Vision: the brooding, superpowered android from Marvel Comics' *Avengers*. The comic book Vision had the power to vary the density of his body, becoming a ghost if he wished to float through walls or doors, becoming diamond hard if he wished to stop bullets like Superman. Adam Cressner couldn't do any of this. This day he wasn't even wearing his cape or costume, but under black curls his broad face was smeared unevenly with red food dye, as it always was. I was fascinated. The Vision had come to be taken for granted at Public School 29, but I'd never seen him up close.

"Nice kick," I ventured, to Adam Cressner's back. The Vision had assumed a stance of readiness, one foot on the painted base, hands dangling between his knees Lou Brock style. "Ultron-5 constructed me well," replied the Vision in the mournful monotone of a synthetic humanoid. Before I could speak again the ball was in the air, and Adam Cressner had scooted home to score, not pausing as he rounded third.

Now the Vision was a grown man in a sweatshirt moving an open Martini & Rossi cartonload of compact discs into the basement entrance of the next-door brownstone. I spotted Captain Beefheart, Sonny Sharrock, Eugene Chadbourne. I'd been returning from the corner bodega with a quart of milk when I recognized him instantly, even without his red face and green hood, or the yellow cape he'd worn in winter months. "Adam Cressner?" I asked. I made it a question to be polite: it was Adam Cressner.

"Do I know you?" Cressner's hair was still curly and loose, his eyes still wild blue.

"Not really. We went to school together."

"Purchase?"

"P.S. Twenty-nine, fifth grade." I pointed thumbwise in the direction of Cobble Hill. I didn't want to say: *You were the Vision, man!* But I supposed in a way I'd just said it. "Joel Porush."

"Possibly I remember you." He said this with a weird premeditated hardness, as if not *remembering* but *possibly remembering* was a firm policy.

"Migrated back to the old neighborhood?"

Cressner placed the box at the slate lip of the basement stairwell and stepped around his gate to take my hand. "By the time we had a down payment we could barely afford this part of the city," he said. "But Roberta doesn't care that I grew up around here. She became entranced with the neighborhood reports in the City Section."

"Wife?"

"Paramour."

"Ah." This left me with nothing to say except "I should have you guys over for drinks."

The Vision lifted one Nimoy-esque eyebrow.

"When you get in and catch your breath, of course." *You and the paramour.*

I met Roberta at the border of our two backyards, the next Sunday. The rear gardens through the middle of the block were divided by rows of potted plants but no fence, allowing easy passage of cats and conversation. These communal yards were a legacy from the seventies that most new owners hadn't chosen to reverse. I had a basement renter's usual garden privileges, and was watering the plants which formed the border when Roberta Jar appeared at her back door. She introduced herself, and explained that she and Cressner had bought the house.

"Yes, I met Adam a few days ago," I said. "I know him, actually. From around here."

"Oh?"

I'd supposed he'd told her of our encounter in front, mentioned being recognized by a schoolmate. Now I had to wonder whether to explain Cressner's childhood fame. "We were at grade school together, on Henry Street. Long before this was a fashionable address. Surely he's walked you past his alma mater."

"Adam doesn't reminisce," said Roberta Jar coolly and, I thought, strangely. The assertion which could have been fond or defiant had managed to be neither. I thought of how Adam had *possibly remembered*, the week before.

"Funny, I do nothing else," I said. I hoped it was a charming line. Roberta Jar didn't smile, but her eyes flashed a little encouragement.

"Does it pay well?" she asked.

"Only when something gets optioned for the movies."

"How often is that?"

"It's like the lottery," I said. "Ninety-nine percent of the time, nothing. But that one time and you're golden."

I'd been blunted from the fact of my instinctive attraction to Roberta Jar, in those first moments, by her towering height. Roberta was six-two or -three, I calculated, and with none of that hunched manner with which women apologize for great height or sizeable breasts. So I'd been awed before being struck. By this time, though, I was struck too. *Paramour-pyramid-pylon*, I fooled with in my head.

I mentioned again having the two of them over for a drink. My evenings were very free since parting from Gia Maucelli, and I was stuck on what I'd blurted to Adam Cressner and had visualized ever since – a grownup encounter, involving wine and sophisticated talk. No longer a couple, I still socialized like one in my imagination. Cressner and his tall woman would visit my apartment for drinks.

They'd see the couple I'd been by Gia's phantom-limb absence, and ratify the couple I'd likely be again by the fact of themselves. In other words, perhaps Roberta Jar had a friend she could set me up with.

"Maybe," she said, utterly disinterested. "Or you could come along tonight. We're having a few people in."

"A housewarming party?"

"Actually, we're playing a game. You'd like it."

"Truth-or-dare, spin-the-bottle sort of thing?"

"More interesting than that. It's called Mafia. You should come – I think we still need a fifteenth."

For bridge or a dinner party you might need a fourth or sixth – Roberta Jar and Adam Cressner needed a fifteenth. That was how close to essential I'd been encouraged to feel myself to be.

"How do you play Mafia?"

"It's hard to explain, but not to play."

I turned up with wine, still imposing my paradigm, but it was a beer thing I'd turned up at. Adam Cressner ushered me into the parlor, which was restored – new white marble fireplace and mantel, freshly remodeled plaster-rosette ceiling, blond polished floor – but unfurnished, and full instead of gray metal folding chairs like those you'd find in a church basement. The chairs were packed with Adam and Roberta's friends, all drinking from bottles and laughing noisily, too caught up to bother with introductions – when I counted I found myself precisely fifteenth. Roberta Jar was part of the circle, tall in her chair. I wondered if she stood taller than Adam – this was the first time I'd seen them together.

Adam had just been explaining the game, and he started again for me. I was one of four or five in the group who'd never played. Others threw in comments and suggestions as Adam explained the rules. "I'll be the narrator," Adam told us. "That means I'm not playing the game, but leading you through it."

"We want you to play, Adam," someone shouted. "Someone else can narrate. We've played, we know how."

"No, you need a strong narrator," said Adam. "You're an unruly bunch." I imagined I heard in his tone a hint of the Vision's selfless patronage of humanity.

According to the rules of Mafia, the group of fourteen comprised a "village" – except that three of us were "mafia" instead: false villagers working to bring the village down. These identities were assigned by dealt cards, black for village, red for mafia. The game then unfolded in cycles of "night" and "day." Night was when we closed our eyes and lowered our heads – "The village is asleep," Adam explained – with the exception of the three mafiosi. They instead kept their eyes open, and by an exchange of glances silently conspired to select a villager to kill. The victim would be informed of his or her death by the narrator, when night was over, and then make an orderly exit from the game.

Day, by contrast, was chaos, a period of free talk and paranoia among the sincere and baffled villagers – who, of course, included three dissembling mafiosi. Each day closed with the village agreeing by democratic vote on a suspect to banish. This McCarthyesque ritual lynching brought about night, and another attack from the Mafia. And so on. The Mafia won if they winnowed the village down to two or three, a number they could dominate in any voting, before the village purged all mafiosi from its ranks. It seemed to me like relentless jargonish nonsense, but I worked on a beer (telling Roberta the wine was "for the cellar"), checked out the women, and allowed myself to be swept into the group's flow. We began our first day in the village, peppered by Adam-the-narrator's portentous reminders, such as "Dead, keep your silence." I'd drawn a black card: villager.

Our village was young and boisterous, full of hot, beer-bright faces whose attachments I couldn't judge. It was also splendidly bloodthirsty. "It pretty much doesn't matter who we vote out on the first day," some veteran player announced. "We don't have any information yet." I wondered how we were meant to gather information at any point in the agitated cross talk, but never mind. A regular named Barth was quickly exiled, on grounds of past performance – he'd proven such a generally deceptive player he couldn't be trusted now. Roberta, who with her stature and chesty volume was strongly dominant in the village, led this charge. Barth succumbed to our lynch mob under groaning protest. "Night" fell, we "slept," and when day came again Adam announced that a woman named Kelly had been taken out by the mafia.

Kelly's murder drew shouts and giggles of surprise. Why had they picked her? Perhaps *this* was the information which would lead us to an informed lynching, instead of Barth's whimsical sacrifice. The village again plunged into an uproar of accusations and deflection. I turned to the woman beside me, a sylphlike girl with dyed-black shortish hair, who hadn't spoken. "Are you in the Mafia?" I asked her, not quite whispering.

She blinked at me. "I'm a villager."

"Me too." I told her my name, and she told me hers – Doe. Our exchange was easily covered by the shouts of the village leadership, mainly Roberta Jar and a couple of strident men, as they led our next purge.

"First time?" Doe asked.

"Yes."

"That doesn't mean you aren't lying to me."

"No, it doesn't," I said. "But I'm not. Whom do you suspect?"

"I'm hopeless at this." Unashamed, she met my eye. I felt a pang. Doe was everything Roberta Jar was not: diminutive, vulnerable, and, I began to hope, single.

"We'll work together," I suggested. "Be watchful."

Mafia was a kind of fun, I decided. It elicited from us heaps of behavior: embarrassment and self-reproach, chummy consensus building which curdled at a moment's notice to feints of real paranoia and isolation, even measures of self-righteous, persecuted fury. The intensity was enthralling, but it was also strangely hollow, because it lacked any real content. For all the theatrics, we revealed nothing of ourselves, told no tales. It was that for which I yearned.

It was the morning of the third day that I fell under suspicion. Irrevocably, as it turned out. "I think we're ignoring the new people," said Roberta Jar. "I've seen it again and again, some newcomer draws the Mafia card and sits there, playing innocent and silent, just mowing the village down while we argue. I think we ought to look at Joel, for instance. He isn't saying *anything*."

"I heard him talking to Doe," someone volunteered. "They have some little thing going on the side."

"Both Mafia, then," said one of the leader-men, whose every pronouncement was full of unearned certainty. "Take them both out."

"I'm a villager," I said. This was the standard protest, despite its deep meaninglessness: who wouldn't say that? Someone laughed at me sharply for being unpersuasive. Before I'd assembled a better defense, hands shot up all around the circle. Even Doe voted for my banishment.

Adam Cressner then shepherded the village into night. "The dead usually wander off where they can talk without disturbing the village," he stage-whispered across their bowed heads. I took the hint. As I moved into the hall, Adam returned to narration: "Mafia, open your eyes, and silently agree on someone to kill." I wondered who the dastards were.

The zombies who'd vacated the parlor were gathered out on the brownstone's stoop, smoking cigarettes and gabbling. They spotted me peering through the front door's doubled glass panes. I made a gesture meant to be interpretable as *be right there, just going for a pee.* Someone waved back. I went downstairs.

The half-basement's front room was furnished as a suburban den, with a stereo and large-screen TV, and walls lined with CDs, laser discs, and books, many of them expensive museum catalogs, compendiums of film stills, photo essays from boutique imprints. I spotted a brightly colored paperback on a shelf of oversize volumes on art and antiquities: *Origins*, by Stan Lee, a reprint-compendium of comic books introducing various Marvel characters, Spider-Man, Iron Man, the Fantastic Four. A sequel, *Son of Origins*, was shelved beside it. I browsed both, but the Vision wasn't included. He wasn't the sort of character who'd had such a prominent debut – more of a cult figure, I recalled. Like Rhoda or Fraser, he'd been an unplanned star, spun from an ensemble.

The pop art panels looked thin and fraudulent on white paper, instead of the soft, yellowed rag of the old comics from which they'd been reprinted. Nevertheless, I felt a howling nostalgia rise in me at the sight of the Silver Surfer and Daredevil, characters who'd meant a tremendous amount to me for a brief moment in junior high, then been utterly forgotten. I'd discovered Marvel Comics a year or two after leaving P.S. 29 and Adam Cressner behind. The oddness of Adam's choice in identifying with the Vision had had a troubling chicken-or-egg quality to me, then – did the character seem so depressed and diffident to me *because* of Adam's red face paint? The answer wasn't in *Origins*, or *Son of Origins*.

I replaced the books on the shelf and went digging in the walk-in closet instead.

"Hello?" Someone had entered the room behind me. It was Doe, swinging a beer bottle elegantly by the neck.

"Oh, hi," I said.

"What are you doing?"

"Looking for something."

"Something?"

"A costume, or a cape," I said. "It's a long story." I emerged from the closet, which seemed to hold only wool coats and ski gear anyway. "Did you get voted out of the village?"

"Right after you."

"Sorry. I guess I dragged us both down with that suspicious side talk. A rookie mistake."

"It's okay. They were right to. I was in the mafia."

"Ah. Now I feel truly foolish."

"Don't. It was brave of you to speak up at all. The first time I played I just cowered." Her tiny mouth was perfect apart from one incisor that seemed to have been inserted sideways for variation, like a domino.

"How do you know Adam and Roberta?"

"Adam was my dissertation advisor. At Columbia." Doe squinted at me oddly, expectantly, perhaps sensing I didn't know the first thing about Adam. She was right and wrong, of course.

"I'm just the friendly neighbor," I said. I considered how the word *friendly* could mean *not-an-actual-friend* – like friendish, or friendlike. "Is this a whole, ah, Columbia group, upstairs?" I wondered what the man who'd been the Vision would teach: android identity politics?

"Just that guy Barth who got killed. The rest I don't know. Adam and Roberta seem to collect people from all over the place."

"They're not big on introductions, are they? They prefer keeping everyone in the dark, and dependent on them."

"Maybe they figure we're grownups and can take care of ourselves."

I'd touched the limits of Doe's disloyalty, and been admonished. I rather liked it. "Yes, of course," I agreed. "The way we are, now, for instance. You and I, I mean. Taking care of ourselves."

Doe only blinked, as when, in the circle upstairs, I'd probed her mafia status.

There commenced a clunking and scraping of chairs above our heads. The village had shrunk, or dissolved. I stepped forward and took Doe's hand, thinking I only had a minute. I had less, as it happened. For a giantess Roberta Jar moved silently, and now she was in the doorway. Doe's hand slipped from mine as a newt darts from view on a forest path.

"Game over?" I asked.

"Yes," said Roberta, cat-ate-canaryishly. "The Mafia won."

"The Mafia always wins," said Doe, a little petulantly, I thought, given her own affiliation.

"Not really," said Roberta. "But they have had their way recently, it's true."

"They did fine without *my* help," mused Doe. This accounted for her bitterness: she'd wanted to prove essential.

We returned upstairs on a quest for more beer. The smokers had returned from the stoop, and villagers and Mafia alike mingled in excited dissection of the game's plot: *I-told-you-so* was the general thrust. There was hopeful talk of another game, but Val and Irene, a couple with baby-sitter problems, had to go. A few more defections followed, and suddenly we didn't have numbers enough for a village. "Don't everybody go," said Adam, as one after another made their excuses. "The night is young."

Seven of us remained. Happily, this included Doe. There were also two younger men vying for the attention of an Asian woman named Flour. Perhaps predictably, it was singles who'd stayed – us with nothing to rush home to. We sat in the sea of empty bottles and abandoned chairs, a ghost village. But Adam Cressner and Roberta Jar seemed glad to have us. He went downstairs and soon Chet Baker emanated from speakers in the parlor's corners. Roberta lowered the lights.

"I know a game," I said.

"Yes?" said Roberta.

"It's called 'I Never.' It's a drinking game, though. We all have to have an alcoholic beverage in our hands."

Adam plopped two fresh sixes of pale ale at our feet. I explained the rules: each of us in turn made a statement – a true statement – beginning with the words *I never*. Those in the circle who'd done the things the speaker hadn't were required to confess their experience, by sipping their beer. Thus the worldly among us were made to grow embarrassed, and intoxicated, and thus secrets were flushed into the open.

"For example, I'll start," I said. "I've never had sex on an airplane."

Adam and Roberta smiled at one another and tipped their bottles. Flour also wet her lips, and one of her suitors as well. Doe and the second of Flour's men were in my more innocent camp.

"Excellent," I said. "The rest is just a matter of thinking of good questions." I felt now an unexpectedly sharp appetite for this game – I wanted Adam and Roberta, and Doe too, to see how false the drama of Mafia was compared to our real lives. Of course, after my example we first had to endure a tentative round of inquiries into sex on trains, in restaurant coatrooms, in film projection booths, etc. When my turn came again I ratcheted things up a notch.

"I've never had sex with anyone in this room," I said.

Adam and Roberta clinked bottles, toasting smug coupledom.

Then Doe raised her drink and gulped, eyes closed. "*Oooh,*" said one of the single men. I did the easy math, then inspected Roberta for her reaction. If anything, she looked ready to toast Doe's confession as well. Certainly it came as no surprise.

"I've . . . never . . ." Flour thought hard, eager to fill the loud silence. We were eager to have her fill it. "I've . . . never . . . had sex with a married person."

"Good one," congratulated one of her suitors.

I was forced to drink to this, as were our sybaritic hosts – and, yes, Doe. Her long-lashed eyes remained cast down to the floor, or squeezed as if in pain.

It was Adam's turn. "I've never killed anything bigger than a cockroach," he said.

Neither had I. Nor Roberta Jar, nor the woman named Flour or her two wannabe boyfriends. No, it was Doe again who had been trapped by the odd question, who raised her bottle once more to her thin-pressed lips. I wasn't sure she actually drank, but I wasn't about to call her on it.

It's the nature of I Never, as in other of life's arenas, that though explanations aren't called for in the rules one often feels compelled to explain. I can't claim our circle didn't look to Doe for some gloss on her lonely confession.

"I was five," she began, and there was something ominous in the specificity: not *four or five*, or *five or six*. "My uncle had given me a new kitten, and I was playing alone in the yard with it, with some string. I hadn't even given the kitten a name yet." Doe looked at Adam Cressner, as if the whole game had devolved to the authority of his eerie question. "There was a tree in the yard, it's still there" – she spoke as though hypnotized, and seeing the tree float before her – "my parents still have the house. I used to climb the tree, and I had the idea I would take the kitten up the tree with me. I tied the string around the kitten's neck" – here Flour gasped – "and tried to pulley it up with me, across a branch."

Her tale's Clint-Eastwoodian climax having been telegraphed by Adam's question, Doe was permitted a graceful elision. "A neighbor saw the whole thing from a window across the yard. He thought I'd done it on purpose, and he told my parents."

"Did they believe you?" asked Roberta Jar, clinically impassive.

"I don't know," said Doe, raising her eyebrows. "It didn't matter, really. Ever since then I think something broke inside me . . . when my parents made me understand that the kitten wasn't alive anymore . . . there's always been a part of me missing."

"That's *horrible*," said one of Flour's men.

"I mean, I still have a capacity for happiness," said Doe matter-of-factly, almost impatiently. It was as though she wanted to protect us from her story now, felt bad for telling it.

We meditated in silence on what we'd learned. Someone guzzled their beer, not as a gesture within the game, just to do it: a quiet pop of bottle-mouth unsealing from lips was audible in a break between songs, Chet Baker finishing "I Fall in Love Too Easily," then, absurdly, beginning "Everything Happens to Me." I'd have been tempted to put my arm around Doe's shoulders, or even lead her from the room, if she as much as met my eye. She didn't. Tears streaked Flour's ivory cheeks instead.

Adam Cressner began speaking. At first it seemed a hollow gambit, an attempt to distract us from Doe's testimony by non sequitur. "When I was last in Germany, I visited the Glyptoteck in Munich," he said. "It's full of statuary the Europeans ripped out of the old temples. They've got a Roman copy of a Greek marble by Boethos – the original's in the Vatican – showing a boy with a goose. The bird's practically as big as the boy, and they're wrestling. The kid's got the goose by the neck. A museum guard came up behind me, he saw I was transfixed by this sculpture, and he uttered this line I'll never forget, it shot through me like a bolt: '*Spielend, doch, mit toedlichem Griff.*' He thinks it's a game, but he's choking the goose. But in the guard's High German it was more allusive and grand – 'playing, but with a deadly grip.' "

"Like something from Rilke," said Roberta Jar.

Oh yes, I thought viciously, *Rilke* and *High German* after four or five beers. You're both such fine people. However slow my uptake, a picture formed: I now supposed Doe's dissertation had been in art history, for example. And that Adam Cressner and Roberta Jar had together known, from intimate experience, how easily Doe might be induced to turn herself inside out for us.

I wanted revenge on Doe's behalf. "*I never,*" I said loudly.

All stared. I began again. "*I never pretended I was a character from a comic book.* Never, say, dressed up in a superhero costume, not even on Halloween." I glared at Adam Cressner: let him eat cape.

It was Roberta Jar who drew our attention, though, by lifting her bottle high, as if to toast again before she sipped. We looked to her as we had to Doe.

"I met a man once," Roberta said. "I liked this man, well, very, very much. This was eight years ago now." She lolled her big head, a little shy to tell it, though her voice was still strong and resonant in her chest. "When we began to see one another, this man and I, there was something between us that was difficult, a secret – a secret priority in his life. It had to do with this, exactly: dressing up as a character from a comic book. And this priority was difficult for both of us."

She'd turned my hostile joke into another confession, to give Doe company. We listened wide eyed – I caught Flour glancing at me, likely wondering how I'd known to ask the question, as I'd wondered before at Adam Cressner. As for Adam, he sat quietly adoring his paramour while she spilled on.

"I realized I had to learn as much about this as I could, or it would beat us, and I was determined not to be beaten. I discovered that the comic book character in question had gotten married to another character, called the Scarlet Witch. I thought this was very unusual, two married superheroes, and I took it as a good sign. So, I went shopping for fabric, and hand-sewed a Scarlet Witch costume. Tights, and pink boots, a sort of pink headpiece to hold back my hair. I did a good job, really impressed myself. It was the most sustained arts-and-crafts project of my life, actually."

Roberta paused, and in the silence we were allowed to sense the result of her efforts, a climax as inevitable and in its way horrible as the kitten's execution. I wondered if Adam still wore the red food coloring for face paint, or whether he'd found some better method, easier to remove when he wanted to pass for a mere Columbia professor. I thought of the Scarlet Witch as I knew her from Marvel Comics, an exotic beauty whose powers, loosely defined as "sorcery," mostly consisted of throwing up pink force fields, but whose real achievement was a stoical, unwavering devotion to her Spock-like emotional mute of a husband.

I looked again to Adam Cressner. I still faintly wished for the satisfaction of an unmasking, but his eyes gave me nothing. Adam Cressner was as little interested in my impressions of his Visionhood as he'd been at second base, all those years ago. He hadn't even sipped his beer to confess the truth.

"I have to go," said Doe suddenly. She flinched her head from me, from all of us, hastily gathered a load of beer bottles into the kitchen, and rinsed them in the sink. I wondered if she'd also been enticed into a costume – Ant-Girl, or Thumbelina.

"Well, anyway, that's my story," said Roberta, the sardonic twang restored to her voice. One of the men gave an artificial laugh, barely adequate to break the tension. It was only now that Adam Cressner followed the game's protocol and also drank. I'd had my answer, though not as I'd wanted it, from Adam's mouth. I don't even know whether Flour or the two men had any understanding of what had happened – for all Roberta had told us, the man in question could have been someone other than Adam. Strangely, it was as if he and I were allies, having each forced confession from the other's woman. Except that neither woman was mine, and both might be his.

"A beautiful story it is," said Adam Cressner. "With that we'll see our dear guests to the door, yes?"

No one resisted. The spell was broken. *We* were in some way broken, shattered by the game, unable to recover any sense of delight in one another's company, if we'd ever had that – I no longer knew. We cleared bottles, shuffled chairs, mumbled excuses, made promises to be in touch, to forward one another's e-mail addresses, which rang hollow. Within ten minutes we were out on the pavement, each headed home alone. At least I think we were alone. Certainly Doe strolled away, apart from the others, a tiny figure vanishing on the pavement, before I'd turned my back and descended into my basement entrance, before I'd even had a chance to wish her good night or kiss her equivocally on the cheek. It's possible one of Flour's suitors followed her home, but I doubt it. It had all been a little much for us poor singles, the tyranny of the Vision and the Scarlet Witch.

ILLUMINATION
Nancy Reisman

Buffalo, 1933

Lucia Mazzano is a loaf of bread. Black hair pinned into a tight rosette, black lashes, olive neck, olive fingers, tapered, small, her dress a long flute, yellow of forsythia, yellow of butter. The young lawyers fawn and loiter at her desk, the older ones wink, Moshe Schumacher grins: fat Moshe, fat boss, herring breath and stench of cigars. "Good morning," Lucia says, and returns to her filing, while Moshe Schumacher lights up and watches her legs. She's young, at the job a month, Catholic in a firm that hires Jewish.

From her own desk, Jo watches the men parade, pretends she's alone in another building, concentrates on typing *in such instance, the injured party shall be granted no less and no more than one-third the proceeds*, carbon paper the indigo sky after dusk.

And when Schumacher finally leaves, Lucia crosses the office from her desk to Jo's and holds out her hands. Bread, Jo thinks.

"Take a look." Lucia holds a pile of buttons, shiny black geometric hills. Her palms are pink. "For the jacket I'm making. Aren't they smart?"

Smart? Yet Jo reaches over, takes one, and there's a tightening low in her belly when she runs her finger over the ridges and polished planes.

"Sophisticated," Jo says.

Lucia's teeth: white against her carmine lipstick.

Bread. A hard thing to refuse, if you are Jo, if you picture your life as filament tracking back and forth between your father's house and

the lawyer's typewriter, between men obsessed with order: brown
suits, black ledgers, tobacco clouds. Weekday hours partitioned by
documents: wills, contracts, letters, motions, pleadings, orders of
the court filed alphabetically by client, daily and chronologically, so
the story unfolds backward as you read from the top. Evening:
dinner at the appointed hour, fish and potatoes, eggs and noodles,
chicken for Friday night. A pot of tea at eight and the dishes
washed, the dining table cleared and rubbed with linseed oil. Then
pipe smoke seeps up from the parlor, the evenings her father stays
in.

Even her body seems reduced to wire: sealed, unerring, mono-
chrome. So unlike her sisters, the married ones, spawning in the
neighborhoods off Hertel. Or unmarried Celia, who can't keep her
own thoughts straight, who starts for the department store and ends
up at the soup kitchen or the burlesque. *A half-step from vagrancy.*
Celia would spawn if she could, *try to keep her from rutting in alleys.*
Not the kind of thing you say aloud.

Jo's brother Irving, a bachelor, comes and goes as he pleases and
leaves his dirty clothes at the top of the stairs.

Pour the tea at eight, precisely; five minutes past and her father
will begin to sniff and glance about, ten minutes and in an irritated
tone he'll call her name. Pour tea and then he works in silence on
his store ledgers. Celia listens to the radio. Jo reads the newspaper
and bathes and retires early, so she can wake before dawn, when
the others are asleep: then it's as if the house is hers. Nothing
encroaches and she can fill the emptiness as she chooses. Lately
she's allowed herself to pretend her family has vanished and the
sleep belongs to someone else. A woman, young, with black lashes,
her yellow dress hanging over a chair. Lucia Mazzano in the
predawn light, asleep in the next room while the tea steeps and
Jo considers breakfast. Jo curls into the sofa and drifts and does not
rise. The furnace blows and ticks. Wet breeze against the house: the
lake ice is almost melted. Late April, and the dampness has its own
weight.

The light arrives. Her father stirs. He'll be downstairs soon, waiting for breakfast, and Irving will follow, and then Celia, loud and clinging.

And the house is again an alien thing.

In the fifth week of Lucia Mazzano, Jo is called away from the office. It's Tuesday, early afternoon, she hasn't yet taken lunch. Celia again. This time, a coffee shop. It's Minnie Greenglass who calls, Minnie Greenglass from Hadassah, Minnie who even in high school didn't say much to Jo, she was mousy then, her last name Rabinowitz, but now she's married and plump and in the habit of hiring maids. When Jo steps through the doorway of Schroeder's Coffee & Lunch, Minnie's in a lush burgundy suit and new heels and pearls, talking with her hands. Celia really is a lovely woman, Minnie tells the owner, but she has troubles, has some terrible days, and this is one. "We all know about troubles," Minnie says.

Celia is docile, sitting at a counter stool next to Minnie Greenglass and the skeptical owner, neck bent, lipstick reddening the corners of her mouth. The counter in front of her is strewn with broken pie. At a nearby table a man thumbs a paper and glares at Jo. He's blue-eyed, German-handsome, slightly dissolute. Blotches of purple mar the right panel of his shirt.

Schroeder the owner sizes up Jo. His forehead is wide and meaty, his mouth a thin slit. "The lovely woman disturbed my customers," he tells Jo. "And wouldn't pay."

"Please accept our apologies," Jo says. She tries to be small, innocuous, but Schroeder frowns.

"Minnie, thank you," she says. Lays a hand on Celia's shoulder. "How much is the bill?"

"Mrs. Greenglass has taken care of it," Schroeder says.

"Minnie, what do I owe you?"

"It's nothing," Minnie says.

"No, really."

"I'm happy to help," Minnie says. "Celia and I go back a long way."

"That's kind of you," Jo says. Schroeder and Minnie Greenglass lean close together, a unified smugness, and Jo urges Celia by the elbow. "Very kind," Jo says.

"Very kind," Celia repeats, and after a pause. "Sorry. Thank you. Sorry."

The streetcar, the walk over to Delaware and Lancaster, the white frame house rising into pastel green – bursting elm buds, frilly maples. Celia doesn't explain. Won't. And Jo is left to puzzle out the incident using Minnie Greenglass's summary and the raw evidence: pie stains, the averted eyes of the female customers, the raised eyebrows of the men. Celia slumps and in the hazy light seems frailer than usual. Her hands are small and bony and she doesn't know what to do with them, finally tucks them into her coat pockets. At the house, she heads directly to her bedroom, coat on, and lies down on the bed. Jo offers to help her with her shoes, which she allows. "What were you doing?" Jo says.

"Nothing," Celia says. "Goodbye."

When Jo hesitates, Celia starts to hum. And it is safe to leave her now: she'll stay in her room for the rest of the afternoon. It's what she does after being humiliated.

Jo's been away from the office two hours: she'll have to work late. As she returns, she tells Lucia, "My sister is unwell."

"Oh no." Lucia's neck and face flush pink.

"Sorry to leave you alone here."

Lucia shakes her head. "I'll pray to Saint Michael."

And then they are both typing, there is only the sound of typing and breathing, the occasional shuffling of paper, a suggestion of leaves.

It's not the first time Lucia has mentioned saints: the Blessed Virgin Mary, Saint Francis, Saint Luke, Saint Vincent de Paul, Saint Joseph, Saint Agnes, Saint Catherine, Saint Nicholas, Saint Michael, Saint Stephen, Saint Mark, Saint Anthony, Saint Jude. She's studied their lives and deaths, talks of them as if they lived next door. When Lucia describes their torments, Jo sees a chorus of macabre dolls, most of them missing parts.

But no, Lucia tells her, after death they are restored. After death they are beautiful and holy.

"Saint Cecilia," Lucia says, "unsuccessfully beheaded." That Sunday, Jo wakes early, thinking of Lucia's wrists, the point just below her palm where the veins branch, slim bones, delicate skin, imprint of cologne. Jo's walking up Delaware when the bells begin, stitching Sunday together. Saint Everything, ringing in tandem. If you let yourself into the heart of the city and walk, the calls come from the neighborhoods.

Once, last year, the windows of her father's jewelry store were soaped with *Christ killers* in Polish. Catholics, and not the first with their threats and profanity and soap. But imagine Lucia in her yellow dress, her hands extended, those sweet wrists, while the bells multiply, the chimes hovering over Lucia and her mother and their army of saints, Lucia praying to Saint Michael for Celia's health, Lucia with her eyes closed, mouthing the Rosary, mouthing *Hail Mary Mother of Grace*. Picture her in the grass, *Mother of Grace*, she says, black hair loose against the green. Her saints descend and rise, miraculous, their eyes restored, their breasts intact, necks swanlike, uncorrupted. They are blessing the onions. They are feeding the birds.

Jo follows the bells. Thick clouds slide over Saint Louis's elaborate spire, the door of the church opens into – what? A dark vestibule, beyond which Jo cannot see, only invent. Outside: pale husbands in tight suits, wives – brunette, earnest, fake flowers pinned to their hats – herding children who are scrubbed miniatures of the parents, all of them approaching the entry with careful steps. The door closes and the sounds of the pipe organ leak out into the street. Once Mass has begun, Jo ascends the stone stairs, touches the thick door, and sniffs the air, which smells like evaporating rain and wax and libraries. *Illumination*, Lucia says. *Miracles can happen anywhere*. As the organ bleats and Latin harmonies rise from the choir, Jo closes her eyes and leans into the door.

That night, when Jo is alone again, she conjures the thick wood and old rain and thinks yes, Lucia illuminated, floating in the yellow dress, holding out her hands, offering buttons and transcendence.

Wind pulls at the dress, there's a dampness between Jo's legs. In the vision, Jo is wearing a brown fedora. She's near enough to touch Lucia's hem.

In daylight, Jo types pleadings and imagines the texture of Lucia's skin, while Lucia organizes files and takes letters for a jittery, myopic attorney named Feigenbaum. As usual, Feigenbaum leans too close to Lucia; Jo's impulse is to swat him away. She turns instead to the windows, imagines the neckline of Lucia's dress plunging, Jo herself sailing up to the highest branches of the elms. An unaccustomed lightness overtakes her.

Such pleasure feels new, addictive. *The elms*, Jo tells herself, *remember the elms*, and her fantasies multiply, deepen by the day: Lucia beneath the trees in Delaware Park, her dress gauzy and sheer; Lucia in repose, waking in a low-lit bedroom, her breasts exposed, repeating Jo's name in a voice laced with desire. The fantasies multiply despite Lucia's long hemlines and safe necklines and careful office behavior, intensify with the thrill of secrecy, a giddy ache that overcomes Jo at the typewriter. They multiply despite all signs that Lucia – with her talk of gabardine and linen, infant nephews, holiday cooking – is really no different from Minnie Greenglass before marriage, no different from Jo's married sisters, who come around with their babies in prams, who enter the house and sigh, tell Jo to see a dentist, a hairdresser, a tailor, who make Celia wash her face and bribe her with cakes and leave, back to their husbands, their marital beds, their mahjongg games and flower arrangements and charitable works. Jo pretends otherwise, imagines the dark thatch between Lucia's legs. Pretends the saints, in all their eccentricity, hold sway. Pretends that the ordinary is a disguise Lucia will shed in time.

For now, Jo adopts disguises of her own. Clothes are only clothes, but the ones she wears – heavy cotton dresses dulled from wash – will get her nowhere with Lucia. In early June she counts out her savings and shops downtown Main Street, acquires a pale blue suit, a cream-and-plum-striped dress, three blouses in pastel and white, a beige skirt, new leather pumps. Visits a beauty parlor on Hertel, where a plump, efficient woman named May cuts and curls her hair and insists on regular appointments.

"Beautiful," Lucia says, and fingers the sleeve of Jo's silk blouse. Wonders aloud if it's French. Offers Jo a lipstick. And Jo takes the tube, peers into Lucia's compact and dabs the color on her mouth. Lucia hovers, waiting for the result.

"Pink Bouquet," Lucia says, "that's you."

For the moment, Jo accepts this: she is as much Pink Bouquet as anything else. A small price for Lucia's approval.

On Friday night, when Celia lights the candles, Jo silently prays to the candlesticks and the tin ceiling *Blessed art Thou, O Lord our God, bless and keep Lucia and bring her to me*. But then her father barks the other blessings, his tone of accusation seeping into the food. Irving opens a second bottle of sugary wine, having drained the first: he's sloppy and loud, though harmless. The ceiling does not change, the table does not change, and Jo thinks, fleetingly, of shul – services? should she go? – and then, depressingly, of Minnie Greenglass.

How long will it take? How long before Lucia can see Jo as Jo cannot even see herself? Consecutive Sundays, Jo dresses simply, pins on a small blue hat, sits across from Saint Gregory's, Saint Michael's, Saint Joseph's, and watches the parishioners arrive. On a weekday afternoon she walks into Saint Mary of Sorrows. There is a scattering of women, each alone, in separate church pews. A table of candles beside the Virgin Mary, a city of small flames, leaning and nodding in the slight draft. One of the women crosses herself and kneels to the Virgin, leaves a coin in the box and lights a candle. When she's gone, Jo leaves a coin and lights one of her own, as if she speaks the language of the Virgin. As if Mary might recognize her longing and dispense grace.

At home, her father seems to recognize nothing. He does not mention the blue suit, the lipstick, the stylish sweep of Jo's bangs. Not her new pumps or his missing fedora or the tobacco she has recently pinched from his study. He does not look at her the way he looks at her married sisters – appraising, pleased – despite the white silk. It's too late for that; how long has she deliberately made herself plain? He regards her as if she were a kitchen table. Reminds her to fix the loose porch rail.

Irving follows their father's lead, gives her suit a glance, shrugs. Only Celia remarks: she stands in doorways, holding the cat, sizing up Jo's clothes, assessing her face. *Pretty one*, Celia says. *You are the prettiest one.*

"Jo, take a letter," Moshe Schumacher says, flicking his eyes over the plum-and-cream dress. "Well. You got yourself a beau?" and she smiles at him the way Lucia smiles at him, calm, benign, follows him to his office, sits in the side chair taking shorthand while he paces and gestures with thick hands. Today she feels as if she's inhabiting someone else's skin, a body over her own. Only her fingers are recognizable. Worth it, she tells herself, and begins the second letter, her notes fast and fluid, and words imprinting themselves and drifting: *Dear, it is a pleasure, when we next meet, I remind you, please call, I look forward, most sincerely.*

At her desk, typing, she glances over to Lucia, who is explaining Atty. Levy's handwriting to Atty. Levy. Lucia rolls her eyes at Jo, smiles. In that moment, what else does Jo need? Most sincerely a pleasure. *Most sincerely, please join me. Most sincerely, yes.* In the afternoon Moshe Schumacher leaves for court. The other attorneys are burrowed in their offices, and Lucia stands beside Jo's desk, her dress a field of white dots over peach.

"What Mr. Schumacher asked," Lucia says, "about a beau?" Drops her voice to a near whisper. Her face is flushed, she's absently stroking a loose strand of hair. Smiles. And for an instant, Jo hovers at the edge of anticipated joy, up in the elms, Lucia floating, they are far from the office and the house on Lancaster, they are falling into the grass, Jo immersed in the green of the lawn, the black of Lucia's hair. There's a two-second delay before Jo registers the name *Anthony*, which Lucia embroiders with sighs. A city clerk, Lucia says, eyes the color of walnuts. On Wednesdays after work Lucia does not go to Mass, but instead meets this clerk, who buys her cups of coffee, and rides the streetcar with her back to her neighborhood.

Jo's throat dries and she's overcome by a choking sensation, like fishbones needling her esophagus. "That's lovely," she says. There's a slight distortion in the sounds from the street, a whining echo, and the light in the room splits into patches, which seem to swim away from each other.

"It's still a secret." There's a low thrill in Lucia's voice. "He hasn't met my father yet."

"You look happy." Jo searches for a handkerchief, then pretends she is backlogged with her work for the day. She squints at her own shorthand, coughs, leaves the room to fill a glass with water. Her slip clings to her thighs as she walks, the dress moving as her body moves, though it seems to be someone else's. In the ladies' room she splashes water on her face. It will not last, she tells herself. She ignores the water glass and drinks from her hands. Surely Lucia will not fall for the polite door-opening, for the cups of coffee and escorts home, transparent rituals that mean nothing. This Anthony will exit Lucia's life as quickly as he's entered it. Perhaps he will prove himself unworthy. Perhaps he will die. Jo regains control of her throat, slicks on the Pink Bouquet, crosses the hall to the office. "Your dress," she tells Lucia. "Lovely."

For a few hours, a numb calm descends, a state Jo associates with frostbite and emergencies. She stays late at the office, and after Lucia leaves, after the last client and even the attorneys leave, she crosses the room to the desk along the wall and opens Lucia's cabinet of active files. Her hands move over the folders, fingers pick at documents and pull them out, a simple shifting of rectangles. She takes a real estate agreement from the Saltzman file and slides it into the Schwartz file.

On the streetcar home, Jo's exhausted. She stumbles into the house and up to bed. Dusk: the afternoon's seeped away through the trees, which are black against a backdrop of indigo. The streetlight casts a yellow the color of bruises almost healed. New rain, honeysuckle blooming on the side of the house. It makes you yearn the way radio symphony does, the way Lucia's wrists do. And then Celia's in the bedroom doorway calling, "Jo? What about dinner?"

In the morning, while the house is hers, Jo tries on her father's spare fedora, soft brown darkened by rain, slightly misshapen. For a while, her face assembles itself. For a while the desire to break out of her body abates.

In summer, Celia spends whole days in the garden: this seems to keep her out of trouble. But if it rains for too long, Celia's agitated, distraught; she paces, chews her hair. "What is it?" Jo asks her. "What now?" When Jo gets home from work, Celia demands to play gin rummy and checkers, games she quickly abandons. Bad signs, Jo knows, but who can keep track? It's enough to make dinner, brew the eight o'clock tea. Jo smokes her father's tobacco on the back porch, while the rain falls and Celia rants: today the postman ignored her. But evening company is not enough for Celia, not if the rain persists, which it does. In the morning, she follows Jo to work. Not the first time: occasionally, Jo buys her coffee and sends her home. But now the streetcar lurches, the passengers lurch, the scents of lake water, soap, wet leather shoes mix with old smoke while Celia breathes into Jo's ear, "You hate me, don't you?"

"Not this," Jo says. "Why aren't you home?"

"I hate you too," Celia says.

"Don't be stupid," Jo says, "You hate the rain."

"Stupid," Celia says. "That's what you think."

"What is it you want? You want a danish?"

"Hate," Celia says. "The truth is out." She points to a young man hunched over a newspaper. "He doesn't hate me."

It's the sort of maneuver that can escalate in seconds: harassment of strangers, angry conductors, annoyed police. The man wisely stays hunched. "Let's get off," Jo says.

"No. I'm riding. I paid."

What choice does Jo have? She takes the streetcar past her office stop, down to the base of Main Street and uptown again, rain pummeling the packed car, until Celia calms down and Jo can get her home. But it's a lost day. Jo convinces Celia to change into dry clothes – "I don't hate you. Try this dress." – brews tea, and, at Celia's request, rolls out pie dough, washes strawberries, measures sugar. When the pies are in the oven, Jo chews a finger of horseradish. Her body seems to flatten and gray until its lines are indistinguishable from the walls. It's only the horseradish, the daily tobacco, reminding her she is separate.

Celia sits on the porch and hums. Water draining from the roof ticks over garden tools and mud. Once the rain stops, she moves down to the flower beds. Yellow print cotton dress, thick apron, bare feet. She's pulling weeds from between wet calla lilies, damp patches spreading over her dress. The peonies are blooming, the grass is again thick, seductive. Watching Celia move through the yard, Jo can almost forget her wildness. She's almost a picture of holy.

Wine helps. After dinner, even when there is no rain, Jo pours herself the sugary kosher wine; a glass or two and the day's disturbances retreat. Trouble appears as if on the far shore of the river, tiny, increasingly remote: city clerks waving to Lucia, Celia's petty thefts. From the near shore you can sift through Lucia's stories, decide what to save, what to erase: the Archangel Gabriel, leading the Herald Angels; Saint Agnes, the Virgin, accused of witchcraft; Anthony the clerk bringing snapdragons to Lucia's mother. When Lucia speaks, her face seems incandescent. Keep that. Keep Agnes's death sentence, the white and yellow snaps, the singing angels. Forget Saint Cecilia's damaged neck. Let the rest blur and fall away.

It's July, a Sunday at Old Saint Joseph's: Jo's across the street, beside a sycamore. Parishioners arrive, dark suits in the heat, long dresses and small hats, automobiles parking with slow deliberation. Jo no longer watches their faces, only their bodies moving through the heavy air, the fluttering arms of the women, the solemn gaits of the men. But her reverie is interrupted by the O of Lucia, today in deep blue, hair pinned beneath a matching hat with a tiny veil, a flock of family around her. Lucia does not look at the street or the sycamore, but ahead to the entrance of the church, increasing her pace. Follow her gaze and there he is, a handsome suit holding a hat, hair a cap of black, dark eyes and long lashes floating above a flash of teeth. A body bending toward her,

and she toward him; he is bowing to the family at the door, he is taking
her arm in their presence. The church entry swallows them and they do
not reappear. The door closes. Jo waits for it to reopen, but of course it
does not; the service begins and she paces. Her legs move independently, carrying her in circles around the church, up one block and
down the next: up over down across, up over down across. The breeze
increases and she is a thin vertical line moving over the horizontal of
the sidewalk, the city is a scattering of rays, and the sky fills with its
customary banks of clouds, occasional patches of blue among the
bloated layers. She breaks into even finer lines – arms, fingers, legs – all
in flat continuous motion down one side street, up another, now away
from the church and onto broader avenues, until she's in front of a
department store on Main Street. Only there does she notice her
location and the blank interval that brought her from Old Saint
Joseph's. Think. Think. She can imagine the route as if to give
directions, but not today's version, not the particulars of open windows and parked cars and broken curbstones. The sky seems half
familiar. Did she walk the whole way or was there, at some point, a
streetcar? She cannot remember a streetcar. This isn't like her, she's
never lost time this way; it's Celia who appears at unplanned destina-
tions, forgetting how she got there, panic in her face when you ask
what happened.

Supper and collapse, sweat and collapse, bitter insomnia, stifled
weeping, open weeping, sharpness in the belly: two days. Two days
of moving from the bed only to relieve herself and make her way back,
of pretending *Father, I am ill with flu. Best to stay away.* Celia hovers
outside the door, disappears, returns with water Jo will not drink,
toast she ignores, sugary strawberry pie, cold tea, souring glasses of
milk.

By Tuesday night Jo is empty, body slack, worn out. No weeping,
no tremors, no waves of nausea, just an awareness of indigo air and
the outlines of curtains. Eventually she sleeps. Wednesday morning,
when she sits at the edge of the bed, the room appears to have shifted,
but how? The bureau, framed pictures, and rocking chair remain

themselves. The glass cover of a bookshelf is open – as she left it? Clock tick, faucet drip, barking dog, footsteps on the street, insect fizz. Ordinary, expected sounds. Where was she? Already a blank. She closes her eyes and sees blotches of light shaped like pits and fruit. Where? A vague, untouchable *there*, and didn't *there* include a woman? A line of color, white or perhaps blue? Pale blue or something deeper?

There is one person who loves her, and it is Celia.

When Jo arrives back at work, the office appears unchanged; she approaches her desk the way she has for years, before Lucia Mazzano, barely glancing to the desk along the far wall, acknowledging nothing but the need for more light, the necessary adjustments to the blinds. "How are you, Jo?" Lucia says. She's on her feet, listing in the direction of Jo's desk: Jo glances up long enough to register a blurred, slim figure, green topped with black. She can't focus any longer than that, even if she wills herself to, not in that direction. She nods and bows her head over her desk of files. "Better, then," Lucia says, her voice filtered through air as dense as glass.

Jo remains silent. Isn't that all she has – insulating silence, the silence of retreat? She rolls paper into the typewriter and imagines the monotone percussives filling out into a chant. For an hour, two hours, she types beautifully, unthinkingly. Nods hello to Moshe Schumacher. Nods to Attorneys Feigenbaum and Levy. Takes her lunch in silence, the noise of downtown passing around her, the afternoon light glossy and peculiar. She waits until the end of the day, unaware that she is waiting. The office emptied, she returns to Lucia's files, which she has not touched since the first day of Anthony. This time, Jo rearranges the papers in the Markson file, ruining the chronology. Closes the cabinet. Closes the office. Cooks fish and noodles for dinner, pours her father's tea, sleeps the night without interruption.

By the end of the week, Jo's wearing the cream-and-plum dress to work, bringing Lucia breakfast rolls and coffee, regularly riffling Lucia's files. Lucia smiles her carmine-and-white smile. There's talk of Anthony, Lucia's family warming to him, the invitations to dinner, of the lingering goodbyes and ecstatic hellos, kisses in the theater. Outside the office, a light rain has begun to fall, occasional plinks against the glass. Kisses in the theater, imagine, and his hands, where were his hands? "Delicious coffee," Lucia says, and the theater evaporates. "Thank you."

"Of course," Jo says. Nods. Sets her fingers on the keyboard.

She sticks to the easy misfiles, chooses the busiest and most distracted days. The attorneys appear at Lucia's desk, at first inquiring mildly, then demanding: *The cover letter for the Cohen agreement? Have you seen it? Brodsky case, Motion to Amend – don't you have it? Find it. Now.*

"It's in the file," Lucia repeats, checking her desk, the basket of documents to be filed, the floor, the wastebasket, the desktop again. "I'll have it for you in a few minutes," she says, and the attorneys wait, impatient. She's flushed, miserable-looking. "I'm sure I filed them," Lucia tells Jo. "I know I did."

The deadline on Brodsky arrives. Jo nods in the direction of the attorneys' offices. "One of them probably has it. I'll help you look." Together they search the files, trying different dates, searching out other Brodsky matters, checking under the client's first name, Jacob. Try the files on either side: Blumenthal. Broadman. Bryson.

It's in Broadman. The attorneys nod and retreat.

"Such stupid mistakes," Lucia says.

"Don't give it a second thought," Jo says. "These things happen."

Twice, Jo stays late retyping Lucia's work, this time with errors.

Two weeks of misfiles and Lucia does not smile at the attorneys, does not speak of Anthony, does not mention the saints. There is no talk of lipstick: there is almost no talk. As if she's absorbed Jo's silence. She stops objecting when the attorneys point out errors, turns beseechingly to Jo. *Let me help*, Jo says. *I can proofread. I'll take the Lipsky pleadings. Why don't I file that last group of letters?* Once, Jo asks Moshe Schumacher to wait while she helps Lucia correct an error.

He stares at Lucia, his mouth a flat pout. "Miss Mazzano will have to do that herself," he says.

"I understand," Jo says, and then, more quietly, "Give her time." To which he makes no answer.

Jo can't remember her dreams, but that is familiar, the old way. She does not consider the grass, observing instead the space between trees, the neighboring yards. Continues to smoke tobacco in the evenings behind the house, while Celia watches without comment, the orange cat rumbling, its eyes pressed shut. There is no pleasure in smoking, no pleasure in anything. But also no tremors, no bitter cramps or ragged breathing.

It's a Monday morning in early August when Lucia is called to Moshe Schumacher's office. She leaves her desk for no more than five minutes, returning tight-lipped. Pale blue dress, hair pulled back tightly, head bent, her gestures jagged and fast. From her desk drawer she grabs up a compact, a handkerchief, a palm-sized print of the Virgin.

"What happened?" Jo says.

Lucia's lashes are wet spikes against her face. She forgets herself and bites at her knuckle.

"What is it?" And Jo crosses to Lucia's desk, shocked: in that instant she does not remember the sabotage. She touches Lucia's shoulder. "What can I do?" Jo is sincere, she could even save Lucia, earn her gratitude. It's a chance, isn't it? To prove, finally, that though Lucia has been foolish she can still be forgiven, that with Jo she can be redeemed.

"He's got another girl lined up," Lucia says. She steps away and organizes her desktop into rectangles and squares – files, stationery, message slips – and beyond it the parquet floor extends to the sharp lines of the windows. Lucia herself is blue curves. She hands Jo a lipstick. "It's a new one," she says. "Why don't you keep it?" she says. And then she's at the door.

Jo mumbles Oh, and thank you and Oh, but already Lucia is fleeing, an echo of footsteps in the hall.

At her desk, Jo completes a letter in the matter of Brodsky v. Ludwig.

Celia weeds and waters and the zinnias bloom. Delphinium, snapdragons, honeysuckle, common daisies, roses in yellow and red and white. Some of these Celia cuts and brings into the house; others she won't dare touch. Peas blossom and mature, green tomatoes fatten. It's best to think only of the colors, to be empty except for yellow against green against red. The back porch is the only place Jo can breathe, at least for a while; she can't cook dinner unless the porch door is open, and she won't sit at the dining room table, despite her father's complaints.

At summer's end, Moshe Schumacher's cousin Gert, a terse, stout woman in her forties, takes up Lucia Mazzano's desk. Daily, Jo falls into the percussive hum of the typewriter, works precisely and without thought. She walks instead of taking the streetcar and her body seems as light as a lifted fever. Still, the cooling nights are marred by poor sleep, which seems connected to no one but Celia: Jo imagines Celia humming through wounds in her throat; imagines the roses in the yard blooming over Celia's body until she falls beneath their weight, until she is buried in roses. Their malignant proliferation speeds on, obliterating the house. Even when Jo is awake, the humming persists, mixed with patternless ticking and faint sporadic bells.

RANA FEGRINA
Dylan Landis

Lorelei Yassky keeps a switchblade in her sock.
Lorelei Yassky has B.O.

Lorelei Yassky did it in her parents' bed and a week later they had crabs so bad they were in their *armpits*.

The Gospel of Lorelei Yassky is graven into desks with house keys and the blood of Bics; it is written in the glances of girls – low arcs of knowing that span the hallways and ping off the metal lockers.

Lorelei Yassky walks with her books soldered to her chest.

Lorelei Yassky bites her nails until a quarter-moon of roseate nailbed rises at the top of each finger. When she laughs, her eyes narrow; the laugh is bitter and quick in her throat.

Lorelei Yassky once stuck a hot dog up inside herself and couldn't get it out and her parents had to drive her to the hospital.

Lorelei Yassky eats lunch with two older girls: Ivy who has a forehead broad as a man's, and a girl whose brother Keith went to jail for almost killing a guy. Ivy and the other girl are blond the way Lorelei is blond, with ribbons of brown raveling along their side parts. They are juniors. They could get Keith to fuck you up. No one calls them a slut.

In the beginning is the word and there is no making it go away. Leah's finger polishes the dark scars in her honeyed desk: the jagged *S*, the glottal *LUT*. The word is appended to the initials *L.Y.* In Leah's mind the name *Lorelei* is a ribbon unfurling. She traces the secretive O and the lascivious curl of that *EI* at the end, like the tip of someone's tongue.

When she gets tired of reading her desk she tries reading Mr. Jabor's

T-shirt backward, searching for hidden meaning. Forward it says I'D RATHER BE WRITING MY NOVEL in inky typewriter type.

Mr. Jabor's hair stands straight up which is why he cuts it to a fuzz. His arms jut from his sleeves like splints and he has earnest knees, perpetually bent. Mr. Jabor is the only teacher Leah knows who comes to work in sneakers. She gets a good look at them because she sits in the second row, and Mr. Jabor reads poetry standing on his desk.

The kids are supposed to call him Rick.

"Walt is not just another dead poet, ladies and gentlemen," Rick says. A cigarette bobs and jabs in the corner of his mouth. The freshman English class stares at him much of the time, waiting for him to light up. Sometimes he does.

"Listen to this," says Rick. "This is so good it'll make you want to pee in your pants."

Leah considers the option. In three and a half periods she will have to carve something far more elemental than a word into the thoracic-abdominal cavity of *Rana fegrina*, a creature as tender and green as a gingko leaf. Everyone will look at her because she got a bad lab partner, a partner who has been held back and has B.O., and this will somehow appear to be Leah's fault and she will have to mouth-breathe for the entire fifty-five minutes.

"*The atmosphere is not a perfume,*" says Rick, his knees shooting off little sparks with each bounce. "*It has no taste of the distillation, it is odorless, it is for my mouth forever, I am in love with it.*"

Rick's sneakers squeak on his desk and Leah looks away. She hates Rick's sneakers for being so excitable and sympathetic and she hates the name Walt.

Rick has been reading poetry to them all semester, Coleridge who was an opium addict and John Donne whose son died, and the one who peed in his pants over a Grecian urn, Keats. No matter what Rick says, Leah cannot name one thing that poetry heals. For example, poetry does not heal adenocarcinoma of the lung. Leah's father smells like formaldehyde and he's still alive, and that is a mystery not even Walt can explain.

She writes on the inside cover of her notebook: *Rana Levinson. Leah Fegrina. Rana Leah Fegrina.*

"*I will go to the bank by the wood and become undisguised and naked,*" says Rick. "*I am mad for it to be in contact with me.*"

Leah hears tittering. Peripheral movement of hands, a shard of briefly floating white: a note is being passed. Leah does not have the kind of school friendships that involve communication by note, or even, for the most part, by speech. This is due partly to her being a girl five-nine with acutely red hair, which causes people to look at her, which causes her to think that large bells are clanging above her head.

Rick grips his book with both hands, like a preacher. "This man is talking about rejoicing in the physical universe," he says. "Are you listening? Because some of you really need to hear this." *My respiration and inspiration, the beating of my heart, the passing of blood and air through my lungs.*

It is thirty seconds to 10:35. Even Rick can see that. The instant his shoulders deflate, backpacks slam onto desks; fingers fly over clasps.

"Wait!" yells Rick. "Gimme one thing you learned from Walt. One thing."

"Get naked in the woods," says Andy Sak.

Leah doesn't turn around because Andy Sakellarios is too lovely to look at directly, just as when Leah's father opens his eyes anymore in his metal bed and looks directly at his daughter, she has to study a crease in the sheet. The crease floats over his chest like the ghost of his scar. Leah knows that Andy Sak's mouth is slightly open, like a cup. She knows that the curvature of his skull is elegant in the way that mathematicians use the word.

"Yeah?" says Rick. "You're close. Relish the natural world, and remember that you are a part of it."

Kingdom Animalia. Subkingdom Metazoa. Section Deuterostomia. Phylum Chordata. Subphylum Vertebrata. These are the places where Leah seeks beauty: in the classification of living things, in books arranged by height, in closets with hangers precisely one and one-

half inches apart and clothing zoned by color. She seeks purity in the
blamelessness of a clean-swept desk. She seeks forgiveness in each new
sheet of loose-leaf paper. Class Amphibia. Order Anura. Biological
name Rana Fegrina of the long green hands.

They've had three days to memorize the exact position of the frog in
the biological universe. Leah was born with the words in her bones;
she took ten minutes.

"Remember the finger-prick?" says Mr. Lack. "If you had trouble
with the finger-prick, raise your hand."

The arms of girls shoot into the air. Leah's rises halfway. A few boys
who had trouble with the finger-prick start shoving, or maybe it's the
word that gets them going. Not *finger*. The other one. Lorelei Yassky
doesn't raise her hand. She's ransacked the dissection kit without
waiting for instructions and is stroking the scalpel down the inside of
her arm, dragging it lightly, almost weightlessly, so no weal of red
unrolls behind it.

Leah takes a small step back.

"Those of you with hands aloft," says Mr. Lack, clasping his own
behind his back and strolling among the lab tables, "may have a little
trouble with today's dissection. For this subpopulation I have one
piece of advice." He gathers the moment. "Get over it," he says.

Leah watches the point of the scalpel whisper across Lorelei
Yassky's wrist.

"Get over it, people," says Mr. Lack. "Be glad the frogs are dead. In
my day we pithed our frogs." He holds an invisible needle high in the
air and stirs.

Lorelei dips her head. "That's the eighth plague," she says behind a
curtain of hair. "Pithing frogs."

Rana Fegrina is larger than Leah expected; he is nearly the size of
her hand, with limbs extended in full leap. Did he die this way, or did
they flatten him under a book? Most of his green has drained away.
Chlorophyll, Leah thinks stupidly, as Mr. Lack turns and strolls down
her aisle.

"And any girl who utters the words 'Eew, it's so gross,' regardless of
intonation, loses ten points," says Mr. Lack. He wheels around,

guided by sonar. "Boys lose twenty-five," he snaps. "And *Miss* Yassky, please desist from the dissection of your own hand."

Lorelei lowers the scalpel until it is the merest inch above the lab table. Then she drops it. It sounds like a tiny piece of glass breaking.

"Miss Yassky joins us for the second year," says Mr. Lack.

The top of Leah's head bursts into flame. She takes another step back. Lorelei spreads her fingers, revealing a small red smear in the vicinity of her lifeline. Then she hides it in her fist.

"Open your kits," says Mr. Lack, "pin the frog, and decide which among you shall make the first cut."

Leah is now standing four feet from her partner. It won't do. She steps closer to Lorelei. All she smells is formaldehyde. Rana Fegrina, on his back on the dissection tray, looks up at her through the blind eye of his belly.

"I'll pin if you cut," whispers Leah, looking at the frog instead of at Lorelei.

"I cut last year," says Lorelei.

Lorelei's voice has exactly the same drape as her hair. Leah can't tell if she's being ironic. Also, she has never stood this close to a slut. She thought a slut would have yellow teeth. She wants to check Lorelei's teeth and sniff her neck and rifle her backpack for notes and pierce the curtain of hair with her finger, as if breaking the sleek vane of a feather. She wants to say: Is it true?

"I'll do absolutely everything if you just cut," says Leah, frantic. As a sign of good faith she plucks up the first pin and positions it over Rana Fegrina's gray-green palm. She has to duck her head so she won't see it break the skin. Instead she concentrates on Lorelei Yassky's bell-bottoms. They are perfect, these bell-bottoms. They clump over Lorelei's sneakers in front, and in back they're frayed from being stood on. The jeans taper and flare as if they had been breathed onto Lorelei Yassky by God.

Leah counts to twenty for each of the four pins, two for the hands and two for the feet. Rana Fegrina does not struggle.

"Look at him," says Lorelei. "He died for your sins. You know what's weird about frogs?"

"Are you going to cut?" says Leah. Her voice is a handkerchief fluttering on a twig. She clears her throat. She wonders if there is such a thing as pushing Lorelei too far.

"What's weird about frogs," says Lorelei, "is they only recognize food when it moves. You set a dead fly in front of a frog, he'll fucking starve."

Leah imagines Rana Fegrina crouched before his dinner – a fly sizzling on a tiny white plate, size of a fingernail. Rana Fegrina secretes an ancient green wisdom through his pores. Rana Fegrina knows that time is a circle. Rana Fegrina knows that all things will pass. Rana Fegrina knows that sometimes a girl has to wait in the hall because her father is going to the bathroom in his bed. Rana Fegrina knows where the love goes when the body dies. The frog's thoughts coil along his hidden tongue, deadly as a bullwhip.

Leah decides to attempt a string of sentences.

"My mother's like that," she says. "She only recognizes food when it has no calories. If you put a steak in front of my mother she'd starve too."

Lorelei picks up the scissors in her right hand and, with the tweezers in her left, nips up the skin above Rana Fegrina's groin. She doesn't read the directions; she's done this before. "My mother's a heifer," says Lorelei. She wrinkles her nose, jabs a scissor-blade into the pickled skin and snips, unzipping the body cavity. "You put a steak in front of my mother she'll ask for thirds."

The heart of Rana Fegrina is a five-chambered thing. Three chambers have walls like the webbing between Rana's toes: the sinus venosus, the right auricle, and the left auricle. But two chambers are muscled like a father's biceps: the ventricle and the truncus arteriosus.

The heart of Rana Fegrina contains doors that open in one direction only.

The heart of Rana Fegrina cannot be broken. It can only be stopped.

What Leah suddenly notices, as she unsettles the liver with her probe and exposes the tiny purse of a gallbladder, is how Lorelei leans in so close that crabs could even now be leaping from her hair to Leah's. She imagines the crabs as a matrix of tiny translucent spiders so that if she were to actually look, Lorelei Yassky's pubes and scalp might appear to be a moving, shimmering mass.

She holds her breath.

"God, how do they get all these organs in one friggin' frog," says Lorelei.

Leah wonders if disgust is not that different from awe. She prods the gallbladder, marks it on her lab sheet. She says, "I think it's kind of beautiful."

"You need a doctor," says Lorelei.

"I just mean – " The probe starts trembling. She tucks the gall bladder back into its bed between the lobes. "I just mean the frog has everything it needs to be a frog," says Leah.

"You need an ambulance," says Lorelei.

"No, listen," says Leah, desperate to make sense. What is it her mother says? A perfect room has everything it needs and nothing else; it has a fireplace and a sofa and good lighting – but this is nothing Lorelei would want to hear.

Lorelei smirks. It is a sound she makes in her nose. "Have it your way," she says.

Leah looks at the wreckage that is Rana Fegrina, the flaps of bellyskin spread and pinned, the tumble of innards unspooled. She thinks of her jewelry box, dumped out on her bed.

"Ugly-beautiful," says Leah.

"Huh," says Lorelei.

Leah nudges a small nugget with the probe, holds it there in case Lorelei wants to see. But Lorelei is looking into the cup of her palm. "Kidney?" says Leah.

"Look, don't wait for me," says Lorelei. The edge of her knife is in her voice. Leah understands suddenly that the knife is a thing deep inside Lorelei; it is not a thing you would find in her sock.

Leah withdraws the probe. She slides her lab sheet into a central position on the table, where she has to reach over somewhat to write. On the sheet is a mimeographed drawing of Rana, splayed and radiating lines from the organs. At the end of each line is another line for the organ's name. Leah has filled in most of hers.

Pancreas, she writes.

When Lorelei copies she could be filling in a grocery list. She drops the *r* from pancreas. The red smear in her palm stays hidden as she writes, a stain in the chamber of a shell.

"I could help you," Leah says.

"You missed stuff," says Lorelei, pushing the lab sheet toward Leah with the eraser end of her pencil.

Ureter. Cloaca.

"I could," says Leah. "For the final." Because now she sees something inside herself as clearly as she sees the knife in Lorelei: one single ability, the classification of living things, that could maybe save a person's life. Lorelei calls to her from under the waves, and she, Leah, walks into the water. Lorelei sits alone and wide-legged on a low wall after lunch, and Leah is the one who stops, extends a pack of Winstons. Other kids glance at them but they are safe in a fold of shadow, and Leah believes it is the shadow of Keith. Lorelei saying, *You'll get a reputation if you hang with me.* Lorelei saying: *I never had a friend like you.*

"Give it up," says Lorelei, her writing hand still in a nautilus around the pencil. "I got a D on the midterm."

Lorelei whispering: *The whole hot dog thing, Ivy started that, it was all a big lie.*

"I could tutor you," says Leah. "For nothing. I could get you a B."

She watches Lorelei yank the pins from Rana Fegrina and walk across the room with the tray. She watches Rana Fegrina slide into the trash as if he had never lived. She wonders what the body releases when it dies; she wonders if there is something she has forgotten to say.

"Wake up," says Lorelei. "It's next fucking Wednesday."

It takes Leah a minute to realize they are still talking about the final. She tries to look Lorelei in the eye. She almost gets there, but the machinery stops when she is looking at Lorelei's mouth.

Lorelei saying, *Trust me.* Her breath sweet.

"I could do it," Leah says. "After school. I just have to go home first."

This is not exactly true. The apartment is empty. Her mother will wait in a green vinyl hospital chair with a book on French furniture until they take away her husband's tray. Leah goes home every day and cleans her room because it is a thing she has to do. She works from a list of rotating jobs – burnish desk with lemon oil, dust behind books, line books up like teeth along edge of shelf, clean inside bureau drawers, recouple socks. By Saturday morning her room quivers like a heart in its new skin so that she is afraid to touch anything.

Lorelei looks at the ceiling as if seeking patience in the perforated tile. The movement slides the blunt gold edge of her hair down to the bone-wings on her back. Then she starts writing a number on a corner of Leah's lab sheet. Leah yanks it away. A green film glides down over Lorelei's expression like the secret eyelid of a cat.

"He'll make me do it over," Leah says.

They are not allowed to have notebooks at the lab tables. Leah pushes up her sleeve. Lorelei Yassky is halfway through the ballpoint tattoo of her home address when Leah detects it – the small, sharp twang of seaweed and salt.

Low tide.

She filters it through her memory.

It is the smell of seaweed thirsting on the sand; it is the smell of the horseshoe crab's shell after the crab has been returned to the physical universe.

It is the smell of Rana Fegrina, disemboweled for her sins.

It is the smell of Phisohex after the patient has been bathed – sponged and rolled and patted dry behind the curtain by a nurse in sympathetic shoes, a nurse who talks as if tending a frightened child.

It is gray ammonia sloshed from an orderly's yellow bucket, it is the Sea Breeze her mother strokes onto her father's slackening neck.

It is the smell of the body releasing. It is a tinge of lemony sweat.

It is the smell of B.O., though Leah cannot be certain whether it is Lorelei's or her own, and Whitman is wrong: the atmosphere is a perfume. It tastes of the distillation. She is in love with it, it is the beating of her heart.

ALICIA AND EMMETT WITH THE 17th LANCERS AT BALACLAVA
Jim Shepard

A licia and Emmett find themselves with the 17th Lancers at Balaclava. Emmett's a captain of one of the inner squadrons. He loves Alicia, has loved her since he met her in college. They have big decisions to make, things to work out, and they have no time for this. It's a gorgeous October day, crisp, blue, chilly, with the sun warming their backs. The entire brigade has fanned out loosely around them in parade order, the only noise the light step of the horses' hooves on the soft grass and the faint jingle of bits and accoutrements.

Alicia's mount takes a few mincing steps and then holds quietly steady. Its tail switches back and forth. She's waiting for the order he holds in his hands. She's on a pearl charger, her back erect in the saddle, her scarlet and royal blue tunic laced round and dazzlingly breasted with intricate gold braid, her furred pelisse lined with crimson silk, her brown hair swirling out from below her bearskin hussar's cap, her thighs in tight, cherry pants, gripping and controlling her mount.

Emmett has in his hand the fourth order of the day, for October 25th, 1854: "*Lord Raglan wishes the cavalry to advance rapidly to the front – follow the enemy and try and prevent the enemy from carrying away the guns. Troop Horse Artillery may accompany. French cavalry is on your left. Immediate.*"

As an order, from where Emmett sits, it's alternately inchoate and nonsensical. What enemy? Follow where? There's no one in sight except the vast main force of Russians all the way down the end of the valley. But what difference does his bafflement make? What else in history does the Light Brigade do but charge?

And the order is almost beside the point. He can feel how much everyone around him is itching to act. They've been up since before dawn and they've been on and off their mounts like this for three and a half hours. They breakfasted on biscuits and hard-boiled eggs and water from their flasks. Earlier that morning, from more or less this very spot, they watched the Heavy Brigade perform one of the great cavalry feats of all time, charging uphill – diagonally! through the ruins of a vineyard! – to break the downhill charge of a body of Russian cavalry four thousand strong. The Heavy Brigade – the Scots Greys, the Innskillings, and the 5th Dragoons, with the 4th Dragoons and the Royals in the second wave – had been able to muster less than five hundred troopers, after the morning's losses to dysentery and cholera.

After the Heavy Brigade's charge, the entire mass of Russian cavalry had broken and fled back over the Causeway Heights and down the North Valley to the east, passing, though some way off, right in front of the Light Brigade. Tactical situations like that – fleeting opportunities to turn breakthroughs into routs – were the reason units like the Light Brigade existed. The Brigade had remained, in its own eyes, shamefully inactive. It had been under orders not to move from its position, and its commanding officers had refused the initiative. Some of the men had wept. "My God, my God, what a chance we are losing!" the officer to Emmett's right had exclaimed, repeatedly slapping his leg with the flat of his sword.

Alicia's mount dawdles back and forth one horse's length in front of the center of the line. Her trumpeter waits half a horse length behind her and to her right. She looks over her shoulder at Emmett. Her expression radiates the kind of poise that improves the manners of children and calms the hopelessly upset.

The captain of the next squadron over catches his eye and gestures with his chin toward Alicia. Emmett glances at his horse's withers, his white leather gloves at rest over his pommel, and then catches the captain's drift: It's Emmett's order to deliver. He surveys the front row of lancers. He admires the precision of the line of square-topped lancer caps. The gilded chin-chains glitter like jewelry. Each cap is loosely leashed to a shoulder loop with a gold cord. The jackets are dark blue with a plain white Prussian collar and white piping. The pants are gray with double white stripes down the seam. The lances are nine feet long with swallow-tailed pennons, white over red, and are at rest in leather lance buckets attached to the stirrups. Each of the lancers seems to be looking at him.

He claps his calves on his charger's flanks and it trots forward at an angle. Alicia's mount turns and backsteps to meet him. He's impressed with her horsemanship.

He extends the written order, arm straight from the shoulder. Her face is set off like a cameo by the chin-strapped severity of her hussar's cap. Her eyes regard him with composure. The crimson cloth-bag atop her bearskin cap ruffles in the wind. She lifts the note from his grip.

She reads it, her lips moving. They're painted a cool and delicate red. Her hair's thick and straight, sweeping to the base of her neck from under the cap and fanning out in the slight breeze. Her skin smells faintly of vanilla.

She turns to the east. The cloudless sky extends all the way down the valley. The valley is a grassy, undulating plain, five miles by two, a half-mile north of the small town and harbor of Balaclava. The country is steppe, mostly bare and treeless. A mile or so back there was a small stream, with a bridge and a post house. The land ahead is as green and unmarked as a parade ground. The grass is firm and springy and smells slightly of thyme. The slope is gentle and downward. The place is absolutely made for a cavalry charge.

Ridges, busy with Russian infantry digging in and passing ammunition, extend like walls on both sides of the valley. Scrub growth lines a natural ditch along one side. It all leads like a sinister perspective drawing to the sprawl that fills the far end of the valley, every so often giving off glints of light: the main force of Russian infantry and cavalry, fronted by the Russian guns.

Alicia and Emmett have been married for four years. They have one boy, Oscar, who's three. Four days ago when Alicia was wrestling him into his onesie, she noticed lumps below his lymph nodes. She'd noticed them a few weeks earlier, and these were already bigger and more irregularly shaped. Their pediatrician hadn't returned their calls until after the long weekend, and then had heard her description and interrupted her to tell her to bring him in right away.

Emmett put in two years working with fabric at RISD before getting his Ph.D. in history. He told people he made Art Clothes. He got a lot of attention from his studio teachers for what they called his postcolonial pastiches, but really all he was doing was collaging his favorite bits from Victorian costume. He left academia for jobs as a historical advisor and/or assistant costume designer for movies involving the nineteenth-century British army. Every so often a director wanted the look of crimson jackets when the brigade wore blue, but for the most part he's handsomely paid to fly over to England and root around regimental mess and museum collections, and what could be better than that?

Alicia is pleasantly surprised by the movie money but otherwise finds that world of enthusiasts and curators and collectors and various other kinds of shut-ins to be both emasculated and childishly self-involved. Emmett finds her position hard to refute. On both sides of the Atlantic, archives teem with bachelors with bad teeth and embarrassed, furtive smiles who live with their moms. Every so often they leave their stuffy archives to hang around hobby shops, or, in bigger cities, military modeling shops, correcting each other on the year in which the Scots Greys changed the lining color of their sabretaches.

Emmett's got a monster break staring him in the face: the opportunity to be sole technical advisor for a seventy-million-dollar remake of *The Charge of the Light Brigade*, a payday in the high five figures. And it's not just the money. The Crimean campaign is what got him interested in the nineteenth century British Army to begin with. This movie *cannot* be made without him; he'll hang himself from a shower head if it is. But the people in Los Angeles are not going to delay his presentation; he's either on board this week or he's not. He's supposed to demonstrate what he knows, demonstrate that he'll be a pleasure to work with, and demonstrate, delicately, that he might have the occasional good *idea*, as well, all in his late-morning meeting and following lunch.

He really should be out there now, schmoozing. He *has* to be out there by Tuesday. Tomorrow, Monday, they hope to hear from the doctors about Oscar.

He and Alicia can consult by phone, Emmett has suggested. He can be back in New Jersey by Thursday morning. It's only a matter of dealing with the complications long-distance for a few days before being right back in person, ready to give his all to the crisis.

It was that way of putting it that may have exacerbated the problem.

One of the complications involves what Alicia calls his neck-deep wallowing in narcissism. A series of calm but humiliating talks on the subject at the kitchen table after Oscar's bedtime has sketched in the outlines of the problem. He almost always thinks about others only as they drift into view, while at the same time he pisses and moans about the way others lose track of him. About his own self-absorption he pretends to be as innocent as a horse. The inkling that others aren't spending their entire time thinking about his feelings rankles him.

His situation is to be distinguished from vanity, the two of them agree. He has no problems with vanity – someone who looks the way he does couldn't afford to – but Alicia has been dismayed in recent months by how smoothly and relentlessly he's been able to relate everything that happens to others back to himself.

Oscar's a three-year-old, *their* three-year-old, who may be in a dire situation. Alicia is beside herself with worry. She really needs Emmett to demonstrate certain kinds of support right now which Emmett seems incapable of demonstrating. When she tells him this, he flashes on Lord Cardigan's admonition to one of his subordinates in command of the second line, right before the charge: "I expect your best support – mind, your best support." His subordinate, irritated at the implication, is reported to have loudly replied, "You shall have it, my lord."

The Light Brigade thing isn't the only project around, Alicia reminds him. There's also that other thing. By "that other thing," she means the planned remake of *Khartoum*, with Adam Sandler as Gordon.

There's some other kind of tang in the air, as well, a fresh, laundered smell. This is all a terrible mistake, but a glorious one. Of course the attack is intended for the eminently stormable Causeway Heights, where the Russians have carried at the point of the bayonet some redoubts and captured the British twelve-pound guns. But the Light Brigade can see only the massed army at the end of the valley, and the order is fatally vague. It's as if a dachshund, turned loose to sic a kitten that it didn't know was nearby, decided instead to go after what it *could* see: a bear flanked by wolves. Emmett trots along behind his wife and her trumpeter as she arranges the brigade for its advance. The first line will consist of the 13th Light Dragoons on the right and Emmett's 17th Lancers on the left. The 11th Hussars, brilliant as parakeets, are to be pulled back four hundred yards to form the support line. The reserve, four hundred yards behind the 11th, is to be handled by the 8th Hussars and the 4th Light Dragoons.

She waits quietly in her saddle, her back to the enemy, while the troop officers dress and redress the lines to her instructions.

"There's not a lot I can do once we get the doctor's word, anyway," Emmett remarks, beside her. "We may not even have immediate decisions to make."

"It's not just about Oscar," Alicia tells him. She's drawn her saber and has it at slope swords, at rest against her shoulder, the regulation position when at the halt. "It's not even just about Oscar and me. It's about being able to focus on something other than what you want."

The trumpeter looks away, not wishing to eavesdrop. The front of his cap features a gilt plate with the queen's arms over the regimental badge of a skull and crossbones, with OR GLORY inscribed beneath. His bugle is slung forward and his trumpet slung behind him.

"Do you know how much this means to me?" Emmett asks. He feels as though he hasn't made that clear. "It's not like I do this all the time."

"It *is* like you do this all the time," Alicia answers. She's weeping. She wipes her cheek and then examines the fingertips of her leather gloves.

The troop officers signal each regiment's readiness. Alicia brings her mount around, Emmett following. This entire week neither of them have been backing down, snapping miserably at each other while

Oscar peered up at them from below. In the middle of the night he's been waking up with night terrors, the night-light no help. The idiots commanding the Light Brigade were afterward compared to two pairs of scissors that went snip snip snip without doing each other any harm while chopping to pieces the poor devils between them. Alicia raises her sword. The trumpeter sounds the advance, repeating the four notes twice.

The lines step forward, accelerating smoothly into a trot. Ahead they flush the occasional hare. For a hundred yards there's only the quick thump of hooves on turf and the shake of equipment. From the ridges on their flanks there's complete silence, ominous and ceremonial. The Russians peering down at them are serenely puzzled as to what they could possibly be doing.

At first they cover the same ground they would have had the attack been on the Causeway Heights. The Russian battalions on the heights form infantry squares, bristling hedgehogs of rifles enfilading outward, to prepare for the charge.

But the brigade continues down the valley, trotting by in profile and in range.

It proceeds a few hundred yards unscathed, the Russians still at a loss. The trooper to Emmett's left has his eyes tightly closed but otherwise is sitting erect.

Then from the north, the fire starts, and then from the south. The silence evaporates and the roar is total. Riders go down on all sides, spinning into each other, mounts slipping to their bellies.

"Oscar sad," Oscar now says as he wanders the house in the mornings after his waffle and apple slices. When he hears his parents fighting he makes what Alicia calls his kabuki face. His little lumps are visible when the light's right. At a stoplight this week he asked for an explanation of the red light. They told him it meant Stop.

"What about yellow?" he asked.

"Go Slow," Alicia said. She teared up all the time now. While they waited for the news, it was like every single thing he said was impossibly poignant.

"What about green?"

"Go," Alicia said.

"What about purple?" His head was back against the headrest of his safety seat. He looked tired. He looked out his window, distracted.

"There is no purple light," Alicia said.

"Yeah there is," Oscar said.

"Then what's purple mean?" Emmett asked.

"Purple means Go Like Crazy," Oscar said.

Alicia's always been the better parent. And she was sacrificing right and left before Oscar even showed up. She got her degree in landscape architecture and walked away from an on-the-map firm in Providence when Emmett decided he was an academic. Then she left even the hole-in-the-wall firm in Vermont when he bailed on teaching at Middlebury. Now she gets whatever work she can, haggling patiently with suburbanites who want to do something half Japanese with the area near the birdbath. She set up her drafting table and materials and piled the books she saved in the space adjoining the laundry room in the finished basement. With Oscar, most days she doesn't get down there.

The bullets sound on the hard caps and saddlery like gravel flung at wood. The end of the valley is an unbroken white bank of gunsmoke and haze with the occasional flash of orange. Under such fire, the instinct for advancing cavalry is to quicken the pace, and then to charge, to get into close quarters where the horses' momentum and power can be brought to bear as soon as possible. The trooper to Emmett's left is lashed backward, his chin chain spinning in the air where his head had just been. The air is a maelstrom. Each instant they survive seems inconceivable. In the roar one trooper, then two, then three shoot ahead. "Steady, steady, the 17th Lancers," Alicia calls without looking back, her voice hoarse.

The cannons gouge huge holes in the lines, men and horses in groups of two or three seeming to flash backward and disappear. Sticky mists bloom and pass, and a fleck of bone appears on Emmett's glove. Their lines close up as they continue. The concussions jolt them in their saddles, like someone giving them a rough shove. With the gaps filling in so reliably, the Light Brigade as a target is always equally dense, so every shot and shell has a field day. Halfway to the guns the first line is only half as long as when it began. Emmett spurs his horse so that it's level with Alicia's. They're riding knee to knee.

"I never felt like I was *sure* I should be doing any one thing," Emmett tells her. "This is the first thing I was ever sure I should be doing."

A shell concusses thirty yards to their right and something windmills past in his peripheral vision. Alicia ducks her head and shakes it once to clear her eyesight. "So much for getting married," she says bitterly. "So much for having Oscar."

"You know what I mean," he says. Something incandescent from all the way down the valley helixes past his ear. There's a ringing and then the ringing goes away. The Russian fire from the front is now all-consuming. Officers can be heard as the men can no longer tolerate the pace: *Close ranks! Close in! Back the left! Close ranks!*

Come on! someone yells from the rear, and the back lines are all in a gallop, their gallop becoming headlong, forcing the forward lines to charge or be overwhelmed, and the last shouts audible are *Close in! Close in!* before the noise sweeps everything before it. Alicia and Emmett are at the apex, deafened, bloodthirsty, maddened by what they've been through, aiming for the gaps between the cannon mouths, so close they can see the gunners' expressions.

Grit in his teeth and soot in his eyes. Ten horses' lengths, six, two, and one gunner seems to have picked him out. He locks on Emmett's eyes. The entire battery fires.

"It's the doctor," Alicia says, holding out her Nokia. "You answer it."

He's been flattened, unhorsed, and he's on his back and elbows. The top of his head feels grated. His horse seems to have gone away. Alicia's on one hand and her knees. Her hussar's cap is gone and her hair is splaying upward as if from static electricity. There's a spray pattern of darker blood on her cherry pants.

He takes the phone and puts a finger in his other ear to try and hear. The doctor's voice says something like *retro gooner*.

The second line is thundering over them. An officer getting to his feet a few yards down the line is poleaxed by a flash of chestnut. A trooper from the 11th vaults Alicia, wearing the wrong headgear: some incoherent mishmash of a French dragoon's helmet and a shako, with a plume no less. The sky and smoke have gone monochromatic and the cacophony has morphed to include stirring theme music. The next guy flying past Alicia is Errol Flynn, his horse galloping impossibly fast, under-cranked. Flynn's bareheaded and holding a lance. Color pours back into the world like seawater swamping a boat. John Gielgud's standing over him doing his prissy, citrus-eating squint. Gielgud's commander in chief's expeditionary cap is historically accurate and features a pleasing fan of crimson and white feathers. This is the Tony Richardson version.

Whatever you're about to hear, you'll recover from, he realizes about himself, still holding the phone.

After their fourth date, Alicia took him to see her great-aunt, dying of cancer. It was a three-hour drive. On the way, she explained how Rosalie was one of those relatives who saved you from your parents by demonstrating that not all adults were psychotic. And of course, the last few years Alicia'd been busy with school and neglected her. And now it was too late.

Rosalie was so bad off they'd let her come home. She was on a sofa that had been dragged onto the sunporch. She was on what he assumed was inadequate pain medication. She studied his face as if that was one of the last things she could do for Alicia.

"Do you think she's as wonderful as I do?" she asked, with Alicia sitting there. He told her he did. And then when Alicia was laid low with strep he drove up to Rosalie's without her and without telling her and sat there in the sun room just keeping the woman company, his mind emptied of its own agenda.

There's some presence but the situation is treatable, seems to be the gist of what the doctor's saying. Alicia's on all fours, her attention on his expression, her pelisse in wrack and ruin across her back. There's a smudge on the end of her nose.

They're more or less at the very wheels of the guns, around which there's now pitched fighting. Russian cavalry has counterattacked and there's a lot of Cut Three and Guard Four. It's hard not to see it as derring-do. Alicia's got her back to it, waiting for his information. Behind her two horses are on their sides, washed with blood and spooning. Over them goes Oscar on a gray Thoroughbred, his safety seat wedged between the saddle's pommel and cantle. The impact of the landing tips the seat, and out he tumbles. He lands in Errol Flynn's lap. Nigel Bruce – another Warner Bros. standby – lies beside Flynn, also mortally wounded. Broken lances crook up out of the ground in different directions and the brigade's colors are planted just behind them, fluttering fiercely.

"What did he say?" Alicia calls into his face.

"He said he's never seen a couple as much in love as we are," Emmett calls back.

"What did he say about *Oscar*?" Alicia says with exasperation. Behind her Oscar's gotten to his feet, Flynn holding one hand and Bruce the other. He sees his father and sticks out his lower lip: the big boy who survives all bonks.

Alicia turns to follow Emmett's look and sees him. Above his proud little head sabers cut and parry. Someone turns with a lance and then claps a gauntleted hand to his breast and arches his back, as if miming *O! I am struck!*

Who had the right to give my boy this? Emmett's thinking. *Who says any presence – one fucking particle of presence – is acceptable?* He's flummoxed by the force of his feeling. A caisson's powder tray detonates and the cannon barrel and carriage and wheels behind Oscar erupt outward, the blast wave sweeping the bodies like the wind over grass. Flynn and Bruce are rolled under and in an instant Oscar kites from their hands to his mother and father. Alicia has one hand up and Emmett has both. They're thinking not of their own bodies, but of his: luminous with the explosions powering it, intricate with its own history of neglect and care, and inexhaustible in what it's taught and what it teaches.

YEH, THESE STAGES
James Kelman

I T DAWNED on me I hadnay been listening to music a long time. Quite a lot of days. That was a sign of how things had been, my psychological state.

Not necessarily depressed. But maybe just out of things, on a sort of downside keel, no wind, just drifting about with the sails slack, not knowing fuck all about what I was doing, not capable of thinking such thoughts. My partner had been gone for a while now and even going to bed was nothing to look forward to. I hadnt made the fucking thing since she left. The sheets and pillows disgusted me, the oily bit where my head lay. I wasnt washing properly, not one solitary shower in at least ten days. Falling apart! I saw myself in the typical male role, helpless without a woman, the poor wee boy syndrome. Yet this wasnay me. It was annoying to think I had let it go this far. Time to get a grip. I began in a straightforward way. I stuck on some music and let it blast out. I opened the curtains then the windows. Then I was fuckt. I sat down on the edge of the bed and felt like killing myself. It got worse, I was into the kind of despair that makes suicide a positive move. I heard somebody chapping the door. Fuck them, whoever it was.

Which wasn't my real thought. At that moment my state of mind meant this sort of thought was beyond me. I just didnt budge, mentally or physically. I was staring at the floor, wondering about something to do with certain dods of oose and fluff, I think, if they might have been unusual insects, some uncharted species, it isnay as if science knows everything or has ever discovered everything. Even living organisms, some dont fucking even count; they arenay even worthy of being verified as extant, they arenay even worthy of reaching the state of the fucking dodo, an entry into an encyclopedia.

The chapping on the door, when it occurred to me that this indeed is what had happened; it took a bit of time to hit me. I wasnt capable of being there in the head at the same time the chapping was happening, I was behind the time the way it should be if you happen to be in an ordinary psychological condition, not well-being – who cares about well-being – but just an average sort of routine condition. There was a song I liked, I had been listening to, not recently, fairly recently, a couple of weeks, ten days, who knows – but it got to something, it was to do with it, the state I was in, the depth, that song was reaching down there, and it wasnt even the song it was the backing instrument, whatever the fuck it was, a box-accordion maybe, it was a depth, it was reaching some kind of depth, that way sunlight pierces right down through water, looking up and seeing it so far above, seaweed flowing by yer skalp. Needless to say by the time I opened the thing, the door, whoever it was had vanished, if somebody had been there, if at all. So this human absence there on the doorstep. I found I was scratching my bolls. I definitely needed to shower. Desperate. This human absence on the doorstep.

I tried to keep the train of thought going but didnay succeed. It was just overwhelming, the state I was in. Imagine being in such a state! Christ almighty. But at least I knew it was a stage. Or I thought I did. I hoped it was. I had that hope. I turned back and I didnt want to open my door, not any further, I was not wanting to go into the room, I wasnt wanting to. I was really scared.

But it wasnay a way to be, I knew that. Fucking hell man come on, come on, it's only yer woman's away for a few days, ye're not getting it the gether properly, that's all. I pushed open the door and saw it staring back at me, all these fucking bits and pieces; mainly they were hers, they belonged to her, but they were all out of place and topsy-turvy. Come on I said be practical be practical. And there was the television. It was a magnetic force, drawing my wrist, pulling me towards it, right into it, the other world, where my world was not, I got sucked in, I could get sucked in, even now, even so, even yet: just close yer eyes, keep yer way, tacking through the debris, the fucking wash, five stops and reach and ye shall find. So that made me smile, the syntax, then the sea, the fucking sea. I was seeing the stuff now, I stepped forward and picked up an empty can of lager. It was so easy. I just reached down and lifted the fucker and squashed it, dumped it into a polybag that was lying there, I must have put it there for the purpose at some earlier time, an energetic instant. But I knew I had to watch myself and be attentive to these practical acts and not get sidetracked. There was the ashtray surrounded by ash and where was the hoover? but before that get the debris get the debris. And I replaced the bits and pieces, and then when I got into the kitchenette and saw the state of that! I just put in the stopper thing in the sink and piled in the dishes and the cutlery. Ran the tap, sprinkled the washing-up liquid. Saw the squeegee thing and started cleaning the floor, I wanted to sluice it. And all the empty ginger bottles, I stuffed them into another polybag. Absolutely no bother, I was well away. I was laughing to myself. Christ almighty man I knew it for sure, she was coming back, I knew she was coming back, maybe even that selfsame fucking afternoon, I knew it, I knew it for sure. Maybe she would even bring me a present. Christ, yeh, crazy, crazy.

THE BREAK
Tom Barbash

I t was her son's second night home for Christmas break, and the mother had taken him to a pizza place on Columbus Avenue called Buongiorno, their favorite. The boy was enjoying all the attention. The conversation revolved around him and his friends. He was talking about someone at school who had lost her mind, a pale, pretty girl who'd been institutionalized and who sent a scrawled-over copy of *The Great Gatsby* to a friend of the boy's. In the margins she had pointed out all the similarities between the characters' situations and what she believed to be hers and that of the boy's friend. She had earmarked pages and scrawled messages. *You are Gatsby*, she wrote on the back of the book. *I am Daisy.*

The boy's mother pictured the girl in a hospital ward, aligning her fortunes with tragic heroines, ripping through the classics with a pen. At least, the boy's mother thought, the insanity was literary. They were taking school seriously, she thought, and she liked that her son seemed to have some compassion for the woman (more than she did; she was simply glad it wasn't he who'd been the target).

She liked the person he was becoming, liked the way he treated others. He'd had a girlfriend in the spring and then another over the summer and the mother had liked how he opened doors for them, how he listened to what they said, and how he talked of them when they weren't around. Now both of those were over and done with. She didn't know much about how they'd ended, only that he'd kept in touch with one and not the other. From time to time the boy glanced toward the front door of the restaurant at the hostess station. The hostess smiled over at them. The boy's mother was getting used to this. Her son had begun to fill out in the last year, his sophomore year at college, and had become the sort of young man women smiled at, and not only girls his age. Recently one of the mother's friends saw a picture of him in a T-shirt and jeans and had said, "*look out.*"

The pizza was good and the boy ate a lot of it. The mother looked over and caught the eye of the hostess. A good ten years older than the boy, and not what you'd call pretty. Though thin and busty, she had a somewhat pinched nose and a dull cast to her eyes. The mother imagined that she often went home with men she met at the restaurant. The girls the son had dated were smart and pretty and charming. This woman was not. Her son didn't seem to notice her but was talking about the coming summer and how he wanted to travel around Eastern Europe, Romania maybe, or Hungary. He'd work half the summer and then take off. He wasn't going to ask for any money, he said. How's the book going? he asked the mother.

She had been writing a book about Hollywood in the 1950s. She told him about the last three chapters, one on the advent of television and the other two on the end of the studio system. He asked good questions, made suggestions. He was funny. He was her friend.

He left for a moment for the bathroom. The mother watched the hostess watching her son as he crossed the room, as though he were a chef's special she was hoping to try. The hostess walked back toward the kitchen. The mother couldn't see either of them now. It's nothing, she told herself.

But then she was peering around the partition to see what was happening. The hostess was lingering eight or ten feet from the men's room. How incredibly pathetic, the mother thought.

The boy stepped out. She said something. He said something. Then he was back at the table.

"Should we get dessert?"

"What did that woman say to you?"

"Nothing."

"I saw her say *something.*"

"Oh, you know, how's it going? How's your meal?"

She was acting like a jealous wife, she thought.

"I think she likes you," the mother said, though not encouragingly.

The boy smiled, then changed the subject.

They stopped at an ice cream place on the way home, a store the boy had worked at three summers before. Back home they watched the second half of *Anatomy of a Murder* on TV, then the mother said she was going to sleep. The boy stayed in the family room to watch more TV.

The mother read for a while. She thought of calling her husband, but then didn't because she would probably bring up the hostess, then feel ridiculous for doing so. She'd make it a bigger deal than it needed to be. It had been a nice night, she thought. They'd have a few weeks of these and then he'd be gone again, and she'd be alone in the house. She liked his company, and lately she'd been starting to understand that *this* was the reward for all the work you did, these years of friendship. You watched them become the sort of people you wanted to know.

In the middle of the night she heard voices and she wondered if he'd turned the volume up too loud. She walked back to the family room. The doors were partially open. She peered in and there was the hostess, her shirt off and one of her considerable breasts in her son's mouth. Her son's shirt was off, and his eyes were closed. The hostess was straddling the boy's lap, her chin resting atop his head as he nursed and nuzzled.

She stepped back out and closed the door.

"Shit," she heard the boy.

The mother was surprised by what she felt then – not embarrassed, even for him. She felt enraged and invaded, as though someone had broken into her home and stolen something valuable.

"Can you come out here a moment?" the mother said.

He walked out, his hair messed, but his pants still on.

"I'd like her to leave."

His eyes were on the ground. He looked ashamed, and she knew she wasn't being entirely fair here.

"And keep your voices down."

She tried to pinpoint what it was exactly that bothered her about the hostess because she wouldn't have minded if it were her son's girlfriend over. She was neither a prude nor a moralist.

There was something about her son picking up a stranger and bringing her back, and using a dinner out with her to do it, that made her feel used and betrayed.

Then she thought: he's nineteen. He can do what he likes.

She heard the two of them leave through the front door. Her son was walking the woman home, she supposed, which was the right thing to do.

Around twenty minutes later he'd returned. He didn't knock on her door to complain or apologize. He went to his room and closed the door.

They said nothing about the incident at breakfast the next morning. They read different sections of the paper, and talked about what classes he was taking in spring.

The next day the mother was walking to the subway and she passed the pizza place. The hostess looked up from her seating list and saw her through the window. They made eye contact. The hostess smiled, affably and unappealingly (one of her teeth might have been gray). The mother kept walking.

The mother made dinner that night, rosemary chicken and steamed vegetables. The boy was going out with some friends afterward. The mother knew the friends, Oscar, whose father was a producer for *Nightline*, and Kevin, a math major at Dartmouth who always smelled of coffee. The boy was not home by two o'clock, nor by three. At around four he returned. She thought better of confronting him. There were things she wouldn't know, and that would have to be okay. Still, she dreamed that night that he'd brought home two women, strippers, and they had tied him to the leather armchair in the family room.

She said nothing the next day. Her work was going slowly. She tried to keep her mind on Howard Hawks and Elia Kazan, but her thoughts kept returning to the hostess. She had altered the atmosphere surrounding the boy's time home. And now the mother was having trouble meeting her self-imposed deadlines. She went by the restaurant the following afternoon after the lunch tables had cleared. The hostess was refilling hot pepper and grated cheese dispensers.

"Do you know who I am?" the mother asked, when she stopped by.

"You're Phillip's mother."

She didn't like her using his name, though of course it would have been strange for her not to know it by now. "Yes," she said.

"I'm Holly." She said it as though the mother had heard all about someone named Holly.

"He's nineteen, you know."

"I know."

"It's none of my business."

"No, I guess it isn't. Can I get you a table?"

She talked with her husband that day. She didn't tell him what she'd seen, simply that Phillip was dating a hostess from Buongiorno's.

"So?"

"So I don't like it."

"Don't be such a snob."

"You haven't seen her."

"What's wrong with her?"

"You'd know if you saw her," she said. Then added, "She's easy."

"How do you know?"

"I saw the two of them."

"You saw them."

"You know."

"Having sex."

"Practically."

"Do you want me to talk with him?"

"No. I just wanted to know what you think."

"I think it's fairly normal, don't you?"

It was nearly two years since the mother and father had decided to undergo a trial separation. The mother had believed it was her decision, because he had fought it. But once they'd gone through with it, he had more easily adapted to the new set of circumstances. Now the husband lived in Seattle, a few blocks from the fish and vegetable stalls of Pike Place Market. The mother had spent time there in graduate school, and then again two years ago when they'd decided to travel around the Pacific Northwest. She hadn't known then he'd been thinking of moving there, once the boy left for college. He was the one who was supposed to be exiled, but while he had landed within a lively social circle, the mother had found it hard to find any sort of community. She had been the less social of the two and now she was in his town with his friends. There were three or four people who stuck closely by her, but most of their friends had stopped calling or inviting her to parties. Not that she would have gone, necessarily. She hadn't been feeling particularly social. She was abstractly aware of the toll the separation had taken on her. She'd been needing a glass of red wine or two in the evening to get to sleep, and some nights she couldn't resist calling him, knowing it was the West Coast and he'd still be awake. She wouldn't talk about their problems, she'd simply talk of her day and matters outside of them and then listen to his advice, or she'd ask about his life out there and he'd tell her, as though they were new friends beginning to learn about one another. Her work meanwhile had flourished; she'd finished one book, started another, and had begun contributing magazine pieces. There were many times when she thought to herself – I love my life, but they were all times when she was alone and wrapped inside her writing, or reading, or out on a long sumptuous walk in Central Park. She had grown to respect and learn from solitude, something she'd had little of in the past. Another good thing was that she'd become closer to her son. In the past she'd felt like a supporting actress to her husband's incessant starring role. Now when the boy came home it was easy, like having a great roommate. He cooked sometimes, or at least set the table and did the dishes. They talked about everything, except the boy's father. She knew they were still close, but the boy seemed to understand the competition between his parents. He'd made the mother feel as though he was on her side without ever really taking sides. She pictured her husband's life out there amid Starbucks and Microsoft. He was working now for a software company in new product development. He had stock shares. He had a kayak and a mountain bike. He was fifty, and he still looked thirty-five. She was forty-five and looked it. She imagined her husband with a younger woman. And when she pressed the boy after his visit west for Thanksgiving, he affirmed there was someone younger who the father was occasionally seeing. Someone thirty.

Friday night they went out to a movie together, a black comedy her son had been talking about for days, and afterward they walked the fifteen blocks home. The boy had laughed throughout, but now she was dissecting the story, explaining how it could have been better. She was pointing out inconsistencies in the plot, and funny parts she'd found more depressing than funny, until she saw that she was in essence ruining his experience of it.

"I guess it did kind of suck," he said.

"Don't you ever just go to a movie to enjoy it?" her husband asked, when he called that night. This had been a favorite argument of theirs.

"Sure," she said. "But I don't enjoy crap. I wish I did. I'm tired of disliking things."

As she went to sleep that night she heard her son slipping out. Without thinking of what she was doing, she threw on her long coat and boots and followed him, her nightgown on underneath. The night was cold and mostly empty. A homeless man slept at the door of a dry cleaner's. A few bankers or lawyers scuttled home for a few hours' sleep; others, ties loosened, were out having late drinks around window tables of the neighborhood eateries. Most of the stores were decorated for Christmas with lights and Santas; the Gap had a reindeer in a down vest. A thin man with small wire-rimmed glasses waited while his dog watered a bare tree. The boy walked by the restaurant and picked up the hostess. When she walked out the door, they rounded a corner and kissed hungrily, illicitly, like adulterers in a bad movie when they've sneaked from the dinner party into the kitchen. Having seen him in love before, and sweetly, it was odd and depressing to see him this way: as a man with an impersonal libido.

He talked animatedly to her as they walked. About what? the mother wondered, and then she realized he was describing a scene from the movie they'd been to. He stopped in the middle of the block to finish, the streetlight above him casting his gestures in long, graceful shadows. The action sounded so much more compelling in his words than it had been on the screen, he had in fact added details and lines of dialogue that improved it. He was similar to his father in that way. Anything that happened sounded better coming from her son. It occurred to the mother that he was better suited for enjoying the world than she was. The boy laughed and the hostess just watched him. She kissed him seductively, her hands running from his chest to his shoulders. And then she did something that made the mother queasy. She ran her hand between his legs. It happened so fast the mother wasn't sure she hadn't rubbed his thigh or grasped for something in his front pocket.

"*Helloo*," the hostess said.

He's a college sophomore, the mother wanted to say. He still plays knock-hockey with his friends who come over, still collects rare stamps.

They went and had a drink at a nearby tavern. The mother watched through a window as the boy ordered drinks at the bar and brought them back to the table. It had gotten colder out, the wind had hardened, and the mother thought briefly of returning home. She was driven by curiosity, or perhaps by the impulse that causes some people to watch cars crash into each other, or fires overtake homes. At the same time she felt protective of the son she'd raised. She supposed fathers went through this all the time with their daughters – the sudden and alarming realization that their offspring had become eye candy for the masses, not simply for the right boys, who would be scrutinized and carefully selected. The hostess leaned ahead, resting her assets on the table before her. She was making girlish facial expressions, attempting to present herself as his age, which she definitely wasn't. She wasn't old. She was between their ages. The same age, the mother thought, as the woman who dated the boy's father. She imagined the two of them in Seattle after the boy graduated, double-dating roommates, sisters perhaps, who would argue when they were together in the women's room who would get Dad and who'd sleep with Junior.

At the moment she'd decided to head home, she heard her name called. She turned and started walking, but the voice followed. "Elaine. Elaine, is that you?"

She stopped then; it was Joyce Taft, from the fifth floor of her apartment building.

"Hi, Joyce."

"I thought so. Are you all right? I saw you standing out here. It's awfully cold out."

"Yes, I'm fine."

Joyce was examining her, as if hunting for clues to explain this behavior. The mother wondered if the neck of her nightgown was showing above her coat. She thought she should say something else so she said, "I just came out to clear my head." Joyce nodded and the mother understood she would soon become a story Joyce would tell to a half-dozen people in the building: *She's been like that ever since Warren moved out.*

"I'm heading home, if you'd like company," Joyce said.

The mother looked at the window; they were walking toward the front cash register.

"Thanks, sure," the mother said.

He was back home at around five. The mother and the boy didn't see each other until the early evening.

That night as they stood in the kitchen, she managed to get him to say he'd been seeing the hostess.

"I don't want you to see her again," she said.

"Why not?"

"Because I don't."

"I like her."

"You like her."

"I do," he said, as though defending a great principle.

"Is she your girlfriend?"

"No."

"What is she?"

"She's a friend. Am I getting the fifth degree here? Do I need a lawyer present?"

"You can do what you want."

"I've had a good week."

She didn't know what he meant by the comment.

"Go ahead and screw her if you want," she said, unfortunately, pointlessly.

Her boy did a strange thing then. He started crying.

He didn't go out that night or the next. He watched TV on his own, or read in her study. He wasn't friendly or particularly unfriendly.

After three nights of this the mother asked, "What happened to the hostess?"

"Nothing," he said.

"Nothing?"

"I blew her off."

And that was that. He went out with friends that weekend and for a few nights did nothing. She'd walk by the hostess and draw looks and then she stopped walking by.

One day on her way home she felt the hostess following her.

"What did you tell him?" the hostess said.

The mother turned and faced her. The hostess had on a thick navy turtleneck sweater over tight black jeans. She had a small stack of Buongiorno's menus in one hand, as though to remind the mother of where she'd just sprung from.

"I told him I didn't want him seeing you."

"Why?"

"Because I don't want him to. He's nineteen, what are you?"

"Twenty-eight."

"He's just a kid."

"No he's not." She raised her eyebrows. "*Believe* me, he's not."

The mother's hand jumped out and slapped the woman. The woman slapped the mother back, and then they were yelling at each other and swinging their arms. A waiter and the stout old manager ran out to break it up.

"Pathetic bitch," the hostess said beneath her breath.

She had always imagined a life for her son that would exceed her own: more travel, better clothes and food, a little land maybe, near a body of water; an unimpeachably bright, elegant, and decent partner, whom the mother could imagine as a daughter, the one she'd never had, for whom she could now buy sweaters and stylish scarves and sign the gift cards, *Love, Elaine.* But what if what she wanted wasn't what he wanted? What if this hostess was what he wanted? Her awful little apartment, her abject little life. And what if they had children and they looked not like him at all, but like her? She pictured two children, four and six with the hostess's face, those small dull eyes and those sunken nostrils.

It occurred to her the hostess would tell her son about the incident. She'd describe the mother as crazy, and the boy might agree.

She called the boy's father and there was no answer. It was eleven-thirty New York time. She tried again at one and reached him. After a little banter about her writing, he asked, "What's up?"

"I hit her," surprised at her own disclosure. "And she hit me back."

"Who?"

"The hostess."

The line went silent, and the mother considered telling him she was joking.

"You hit her?"

"Yes. It was a mistake, okay? But she hit me as well. The people from the restaurant broke it up."

"I don't know what to say. Let it go. It's his life. Jesus, Elaine, you hit her?"

"I didn't call to be *upbraided*."

She dreamed the hostess was pregnant and that she'd given her son a disease.

She didn't see the hostess in the restaurant window after that. One day she saw in the doorway the manager who'd broken up the fight. She asked him what had happened to the hostess.

"We let her go," he said.

"Over the incident?" the mother asked.

"Yes of course. We don't condone that kind of thing. I hope you and your husband will come back and eat with us again," the man said.

Two days later she met with her editor. They went to lunch to talk about the new pages, which were about the failed-birthday-party scene in *East of Eden* (the moment that launched the late 1950s and '60s youth culture, she postulated) and the influence of the Beats and the French new wave, and when the mother returned to the office, she found herself speaking at great length on all these subjects with the receptionist, a sophomore at Bowdoin College in Maine, an English major, with green eyes and lovely teeth, who wanted someday to be an editor. She had read the mother's last two books.

"What I loved about them both was how personal they were. Whatever you're writing about it's as if you're speaking to one person, to a good friend. That's what you make the reader feel like. You made me feel like it. I felt smart reading your books; smarter than I usually feel, anyhow." She laughed.

There were still ten days left in her son's vacation.

"Do you have a boyfriend?" the mother asked.

They would go to the movies and then get Indian food. He was doing her a favor, the mother said, because the girl might end up editing one of her books someday. The night started slowly, but before long the boy was telling his stories, and the girl listening, then telling a few of her own. The mother prodded them both with questions. They had much in common, she thought. But there were enough differences for them to learn from one another. When the girl excused herself to go to the rest room, the mother said, "Is this awkward? I mean my coming along like this."

The boy smiled, "No. It's kind of fun really. It's like being on the Charlie Rose show."

"I'll head home after this and you can do whatever you want."

On their walk back to the apartment the girl asked more questions of the mother, how and where she worked, which authors she liked to read. Many of them the girl too had read. What was gratifying was how well the boy held his own in the conversation. He was never entirely an intellectual, but he was smart, and inquisitive, and there was reason to believe he'd grow into an interesting, expansive adult, given the right company.

Already they were laughing easily at each other's jokes. And besides, there was nothing wrong with the fact that the girl was a knockout – at least by the mother's standards.

Christmas Eve the mother filled the boy's old red-and-white stocking with candy he wouldn't eat, a book, and two CDs she knew he wanted. The next morning they listened to Christmas carols and opened their gifts. She encouraged the boy to open his father's gifts in front of her. There was a beautiful blue ski parka, to accompany the skis she had bought him (they'd worked this out weeks ago on the phone) and as a surprise to the mother and the boy, a laptop computer.

She had been outspent again, but she didn't mind.

She had given him something better.

They saw each other the next three evenings, and they were planning on going to a New Year's Eve party at a Soho restaurant that the girl's high school friends had rented out. The mother got them theater tickets for a show December 29, and this time she resisted going with them. She would go to a late movie by herself so that they could get settled in the apartment after the show. Part of this, she knew, was an attempt to make up for getting in his way with the hostess, but he'd someday understand, or maybe he already did.

It had turned out so well, she thought. He seemed happier. The girl could visit him at school. And the mother thought there were advantages to having a girlfriend at another college. First of all, long-distance relationships were often the most romantic. Secondly, they left you more time for your friends and your schoolwork. Relationships in college were difficult to maintain. There were so many distractions, and those distractions were healthy. The boy was on an intramural basketball team and played bass guitar in a band. It didn't matter that by his own admission the team wasn't very good and neither was the band. She didn't want him to have to give up anything.

The night they went to the theater, the mother went to a late showing of a trite Tom Hanks movie that was set in her neighborhood and made it look like a decent place in which to fall in love. When she returned she was pleased to hear the sound of the stereo, of the two of them staying up late. She peered in before she went to sleep at midnight, and they were together on the couch looking at an atlas. The boy was showing her where he planned to travel over the summer. The mother pictured them in a curtained train compartment, rolling through the Romanian countryside, poring over a guidebook.

"Good night you two," she said.

And her son blew her a kiss.

When she woke again it was two-thirty or maybe three and the music was playing still, or again. She went to get herself a glass of water. They were talking and though she still felt hazy and half asleep, she realized it wasn't the girl's voice she was hearing. The girl was gone, and somehow he'd managed to get the hostess to come over for a nightcap. Tag team. *Here come the reinforcements.* It gave her a terrible sinking feeling. She retreated into her room and tried to remind herself that it was his life and that he was over eighteen and could do what he wanted. But the more time passed and the more she thought of the two of them in there, the angrier she got. Not merely on her own behalf, but on behalf of the girl. It was so ugly and pointless what the boy was doing, so soulless. She tried to go to sleep again and forget it all but she couldn't help placing herself in the girl's shoes. She might be thinking of the boy right now, and of the countries they'd visit together. And tomorrow when they went out again the boy would tell her nothing of what he'd done with the hostess, nor would he seem different.

She wouldn't abide this. Not in her house, and not with a woman she'd come to blows with, no matter whose fault it had been. She walked to the study and threw the doors open.

"I want you to get the fuck out of here," she said.

But there was no one in the room except the boy. He was alone watching TV. There was a bowl of ice cream before him and a can of 7 UP.

He seemed not angry then but frightened, the way one might feel while watching a spouse put her hand through a glass door panel, which her husband had watched her do. It happened in the period when she'd thought he'd been screwing around. He hadn't, though he admitted he'd come close once. The boy never knew anything of this.

Now he was walking toward the mother. She was crying soundlessly, and she felt as though she might never stop.

"My God, Mom, what's going on? What's this about?"

On the TV the woman, Barbara Stanwyck, was running her fingers through Henry Fonda's hair. The mother had seen the movie a half dozen times, but she'd managed not to recognize the dialogue.

"I thought . . ."

"I know . . . I know," he said. He said it as one might say it to a child who'd thought she heard a ghost.

She didn't have to explain anything, she realized; he knew her better than she did right then and maybe he had for a while. Her son. It was as though her irrational behavior had promoted him to the role of the wise and clement adult. And while she felt significant pride in this, she feared now that he'd plan to spend his coming vacations in Seattle, or Europe, or Colorado. He was unlikely to spend another Christmas in New York with her.

"Come on," he said, as though reading her thoughts. "Let's watch the rest of this."

"All right," she said, and she let him fill her in on what she'd missed.

Before the end of the movie, he fell asleep. She turned the TV off and threw a blanket over him.

It was four now, one o'clock in Seattle. There was an off chance he could still be up, but of course there was no guarantee he would be alone. She imagined calling him, and him consoling her with his new girlfriend in bed next to him, and afterwards, he'd say, "She's still having a rough time of it." And it would even score points with the woman who would see how gracious and tolerant he was. She thought then about the hostess, because it was she who had started all this. What was it the mother had hated so much? She was no criminal, and she hadn't treated the boy badly as far as the mother knew.

She had simply seemed too desperate, too lonely, too hungry. Her needs were too naked. The mother could imagine someone like that consuming her boy, swallowing him up, before he had the chance to see the world and become the person she knew he could be. He snored softly now, with the beginnings of a cold, she knew, because when he was a child it would begin that way: a mild sawing sound, a sniffle the next morning, and a temperature the following night. She would douse it with soups and juices, and she would secretly enjoy the days he was too sick to go to school and had to stay home with her. It was in the time they'd first moved to the village, in that odd little apartment on Tenth Street with the stained-glass window and the false fireplace they bottom-lit to resemble embers, and the acres of built-in bookshelves, and the café down the street where they'd listen to bad poetry, and the tiny crowded market where she'd buy bread and fish. Her husband would be reading in bed, waiting for her. She would watch her sleeping son for ten minutes or twenty, and marvel at all his possibilities, a life that young, so full of wonder and unstained hope.

INSIDE OUT
Chris Offutt

Today's deceased required little preparation on my part. A young man is simpler than an old lady who needs extensive makeup and hairstyling. Her breasts have to be taped so they'll stick up when she's lying on her back. Deceased lungs are empty, and the bosom falls into the armpits. The bereaved don't like the looks of that. Thank god for duct tape. It's the little things that get repeat business. As Great Uncle said, you've got to cater the dead to the living.

My official title is Director of Grief Proceedings, which has a more savory connotation than Mortician or Undertaker. What I really am is a businessman, the only one who gets everyone's business, regardless of station in life. Many people believe that I understand death, but I don't; I understand the bereaved. The fancier death is made to appear, the more the mourning seems to matter. We crave an afterlife because otherwise our dead grandfather is the same as a possum hit by a car and swelling in the ditch. My job is to dress up death and transform Grandpa from outdoor roadkill to an indoor centerpiece surrounded by flowers.

I shooed the bereaved away on schedule and sat in my office completing the bill. Someone knocked on the door. The bereaved often think my occupation can offer insight into sorrow, which is like assuming the worker at the Salvation Army knows why someone donated a toaster. I am not a therapist. I am a professional of the mortuary arts with fifteen years' experience in Lexington, Kentucky. My livelihood is based on the perpetual public expression of sympathy when, quite frankly, I don't care. I keep this to myself. I keep a great deal to myself.

A woman entered my office. Her open shirt revealed the intricacies of her collarbones like a topographical map of an exotic country. I arranged a sincere expression on my face and used my most dolorous voice.

"I'm afraid that the viewing hours have ended, but I can allow a final goodbye to your loved one."

"No thank you," she said. "I've said all the goodbyes I've got. Don't you ever get tired of saying them? I bet that's all you do – goodbye, goodbye, goodbye."

"Won't you please have a seat?"

She entered my office as if stepping into a throne room that was rightfully hers. I thought of lost royalty, an illegitimate child waiting to discover her birthright. Her neck was lovely and strong.

"My name is Lucy Moore," she said.

"Please tell me how I can serve you, Ms. Moore."

"Thank you," she said. "But I have to say, when someone says that to me, I get suspicious. Men especially. A man's idea of serving me is mostly a long ways from mine."

"I'm afraid I don't quite understand."

"I'm afraid you do."

Of course I knew what she was talking about. Death produces an irrational need for tidiness and a surprising amount of spontaneous sex. I've found people in the coatroom, the foyer, the restroom, even the chapel. Great Uncle warned me of this. In adamant terms he said I should deflect a woman's attempt to seek temporary solace in my arms. It would be short-lived and bad for business.

"Ms. Moore, it is my duty to serve the family. I retrieve the deceased from the hospital, prepare them for viewing, and arrange for cemetery proceedings. If you are here to discuss such provisions, I suggest we make an appointment."

"I was a friend of the man in the other room – Billy Chandler."

Great Uncle taught me that calling the deceased by name would hinder my ability to perform the necessary tasks. It was similar to naming livestock intended for slaughter. She passed me a manila envelope containing the last will and testament of William Chandler. It was signed by the deceased and counter-signed by his attorney. He bestowed his liquid assets to alternative energy research, his books to a community library, and his household belongings to a homeless shelter. His collection of animal skulls was bequeathed to the Portland Museum of Natural History. Lucy Moore was the sole individual recipient of goods. In explicit terms, it was made very clear that she was to receive the personal and actual skull of the deceased.

I inhaled and pressed each of my fingertips against its mate on the opposite hand. I exhaled while slowly relaxing the pressure. Great Uncle taught me to do this when facing a bereaved upset over the cost of arrangements.

"Are you with a TV show?" I said. "Is this some kind of promotion?"

"No, it's real."

"Are you protesting the amount of real estate given over to cemeteries? Because I'm with you on that. I can be of service."

"No," she said.

"Animal rights. You throw animal blood on people wearing furs."

"Of course not. That's disgusting."

"So is taking a human skull."

"Are you saying you can't do it?"

"Oh, it's my department, all right. In the trade we call it a skull extraction or a cranial harvest."

She didn't smile and I called my attorney, who requested an immediate fax of all documents. People are eager to provide me with assistance. They believe that if they are prompt and competent with death, death will do the same for them. What they secretly want is a financial break on an eventual coffin, a deal I always offer, since I can eat 10 percent without batting an eye. We had half an hour to wait for the legal response to her request, which was not only a first for me, but quite possibly for the entire industry. Lucy Moore exuded a remarkable repose. People who aren't afraid of life have no fear of death, and I was surprised to find myself admiring her resolve.

"Was Mr. Chandler a special friend?" I said.

"My whole life there's always a man telling me what to say and what to wear and how to act. But not Billy."

"A close friend."

"Are you married?" she said.

"Divorced. No kids. And you?"

"Never married."

"Most people," I said, "meet their spouse at work, but I work alone, and I never get involved with a client. That makes it difficult because in the long run everyone becomes a client."

"You made a joke."

"Yes."

"I hate when people laugh at their own jokes," she said. "It's worse when nobody thinks it's funny. Then the person usually laughs harder. Know what I mean?"

I nodded.

"But a smile is okay," she said. "You're allowed to smile."

"Great Uncle taught me never to smile because a smiling undertaker is a fearsome sight."

"That is the saddest thing I've ever heard."

"Great Uncle passed on, and I am proud to continue."

"So you inherited a funeral home," she said. "How about a tour?"

"It is against policy to conduct tours."

"I might be some sicko, right? Or maybe I'm just curious. And don't go giving me that curiosity killed the cat stuff, I've heard it all my life and it makes no sense. Besides, I'd be in the right place. Can you imagine being an undertaker for cats? All those lives. No business."

She laughed then, a low tone.

"See," she said. "You smiled. Glory be, what would Great Uncle say? Come on, let's have a look. I won't touch a thing."

She rose from her chair with surprising grace, considering the swiftness of motion. Her jeans were old, frayed at the cuffs. She was one of those spectacular women who actually looked better when she dressed down. She was as beguiling as a card trick. I wanted to touch her, which was startling because I had recently lost my curiosity for bare skin in general. People are reluctant to shake hands with me. Lurking in the back of everyone's mind lies the omnipresent possibility that an undertaker is somehow inexplicably drawn to unnatural relations with the dead. This is tantamount to thinking that a plumber might eventually begin eating from the toilet.

I led Lucy Moore into a private chamber, where a portrait of Great Uncle hung on the wall.

"This was my former office," I said. "After Great Uncle passed, I made this room a history of the business. The artist is local and enjoys a strong reputation. He recently painted the wife of the lieutenant governor."

"Nice frame," she said.

"Yes, quite tasteful. I chose that. It is burnished dark cherry, also available in a casket. The color is musteline."

"You don't have to sell me. I'm not in the market."

"Yes, of course. I apologize."

"I never heard of the color musteline."

"Me neither. Great Uncle called it Monkey Brown."

She laughed again, a sound I wanted to hear forever.

"Tell me about him," she said. "Uncle Monkey Brown."

Hair wisped into her eyes. Mine was trimmed weekly by a barber whose brother had died intestate and destitute in Cincinnati and for whom I had arranged an elaborate funeral without charge. It was a justifiable expense, I felt. The barber's family was very large and all would eventually die.

"Great Uncle learned embalming during World War II when he was stationed in Alaska. He came home at the same time that funeral homes were opening, which was also the golden era of home building in Lexington. In those days, most people died in their own bed instead of a hospital and the family prepared the body and held final viewings at home. Each house had a special room called the funeral parlor. With the emergence of professional undertakers, every home gained an extra room that Great Uncle began to call 'the living room.' The term swept the country like influenza, which frankly never hurt our business."

"Ah," she said, "another joke."

"One of Great Uncle's, I'm afraid."

The fluorescent tubes swathed us with a garish flickering that made my eyes hurt. I wanted to be in the same room with her forever.

"When I was a boy Great Uncle used to give me a ride in the city ambulance. He let me turn on the siren and the red light, and we'd fly down Savoy Road. It's my fondest memory from childhood."

"That is the second saddest thing I've heard."

"What is your fondest memory of home?"

"Leaving."

A part of me envied not only her honesty, but the fact that she had left. I have lived all my life in my hometown and never regretted it. Sometimes though, usually at night, a sense of dissatisfaction crept through me like a shadow. I thought of running away and starting again in a place where people didn't avoid me on the street. I wished I could be a supper guest, a block parent, a board member of an arts organization. I craved a different wardrobe and a flashy car. I wanted to be liked by people who knew nothing about me.

"Do you ever wish you could go somewhere new?" I said.

"I change jobs a lot," she said. "Waitress, copy shop, temp sec. I tend to burn my bridges."

"That sounds sad to me."

"I don't have an occupation or an inheritance. I'm always new, a constant visitor."

"I am never a visitor. No one invites me anywhere. When I run into people at stores, they hurry away. The worst part is that no child ever comes to my house on Halloween. I leave the porch light on. I carve happy pumpkins. Nothing works. Every year the children skip my house."

"Kids do things they're afraid of all the time. It's the parents who won't let them come to your door."

The planes of her face worked together as if made smooth by a craftsman's touch. Her jaw ran taut to her chin, yet there was a softness present that I wanted to trace with the back of my finger. She turned away abruptly and moved along the wall of various framed photographs and awards. She didn't notice my official commission as a Kentucky Colonel.

"What's this picture?" she said.

"That's Man o' War. It's from the *New York Times*, 1947. Great

Uncle embalmed him. He invented a special sling to hoist him into an oak casket. It was six feet by ten feet and weighed half a ton. That horse took twenty-three bottles of embalming fluid. Afterward Great Uncle 'retired' the tools. They now reside on permanent exhibit in the Texas Musuem of the Mortuary Arts. I would prefer to have them remain in Kentucky, but the Texans quite generously provided a substantial fee that was tax-deductible. I take a cavalier approach to taxes since morticians are rarely audited. When it comes to death, even the IRS would rather not know."

"How'd Man o' War die?"

"Heart attack."

"Is this what I think it is?"

She was pointing a delicate finger toward Man o' War's loins. He lay on his side in the immense casket, his penis proudly exposed rather than tucked demurely from sight. The photograph had been cropped to hint at what lay beyond the edge of the frame, as if the horse had been circumcised.

"Yes, it is," I said. "Man o' War sired three hundred eighty-six foals."

"Believe me, that sort of thing means a lot more to a man than to a woman."

The room suddenly seemed like a pathetic attempt to chronicle a record that no one particularly cared about – including me. I am no fan of horse racing. Anyone can become a Kentucky Colonel, and no one really cares about mortuary awards. I was looking at a picture of a dead man and a dead horse and feeling proud. It occurred to me that my photo was next to join them.

We walked to the foyer, and I felt thunderstruck by her very presence. To prevent staring at the contours of her posture, I admired my parking lot through the windows. I keep it freshly blacktopped and clearly marked with bright yellow lines. The machinations of death are clean, well lit, and orderly. More automobile burglaries occur at funeral homes than anywhere else because people commonly leave their cars unlocked. I am proud of my lot, which is the most secure in town.

"It's peaceful here," she said. "I'll give you that. I like the quiet."

"It's my world."

"And the dead. Don't forget your bread and butter."

I guided her through the visitation rooms, well appointed in dark paneling with potted plants and alcove lights. Pastel sofas were placed against the walls. Many years ago I converted a room previously used for private moments into a smoking area. The smell of cigarettes served as an excellent antidote to the pervasive reek of perfume. Before attending services, most women feel compelled to douse themselves as if applying bug spray. Lucy wore no scent that I could detect.

We entered the coffin showroom. They were arranged hierarchically by cost, with the most expensive occupying the best light. Over the years I have noticed that a poor family wants a fancy funeral, and the wealthy want to get out cheap. The absolute top of the line – mahogany rails, brass finishings on all the joints, silk interior – is invariably chosen by adult children who had seldom visited the deceased. As Great Uncle used to say – guilt translates to gilt.

"So," Lucy said, "how much do these boxes run?"

"Between two and ten thousand."

"That's a lot of money."

"All the general public sees is the price tag."

"It's like eye doctors who sell glasses. How can you trust what they say? They run a test, tell you how bad your eyes are, and sell you a pair of glasses on the spot. The exam is cheap, but the glasses cost a fortune."

"You have no idea of my expenses."

"I bet you're tight as the end of a woodpile."

"Naturally we have slumps when no one dies, but we can never complain."

"Then you get a rush. Like lunch hour."

"Cremation is on the rise," I said. "It's faster and cheaper. It is also a scam, since no bereaved actually receives the ashes of the deceased. You get a smorgasbord of that week's incineration. Consider for a moment – when you vacuum your house, do you change the bag after each room? Of course not. And no funeral home cleans the ash hopper between procedures. My competitors think it's a betrayal for me to expose this practice, but I believe the public has the right to know. Especially since I can charge a higher rate to guarantee the ashes are those of the deceased."

Gleaming empty boxes surrounded us, the lids open like mouths. The only sound was Lucy's breathing and the white noise of my own blood rushing through my veins. I wondered vaguely how fast blood moves and if the velocity differs with each person. The flow of blood slows as it gets farther from the heart.

"Do you do autopsies?" Lucy asked.

"No, that procedure is performed at a morgue by a medical examiner."

"Then what do you do?"

"Drain the body of fluid. Extract air from the organs. Introduce an embalming agent."

"That's it?"

"That's a lot. It's not fast, and once you start you have to finish. Sometimes there are difficulties, depending on cause of death."

"What do you mean?"

"If the family wants an open casket and death was due to head trauma, my task can be quite challenging."

"How about a quick peek?"

I shrugged and led her to the lab, where an alarm system accepted my digital code. We passed through a small corridor, and I unlocked the heavy lab door.

"What's that smell?" she said.

"Embalming fluid. Some people consider it the scent of death, but I find it soothing. I associate death with the bouquets that fill the visitation rooms. Flowers die here, not people."

I turned on the powerful overhead lights to a stainless steel table, storage cabinets, and shelves. My instruments were carefully stored. Everything was orderly. I felt pleased and relaxed, as anyone does upon entering the place of work. Aside from medical personnel and the occasional anatomy student, no one visited my lab.

"Embalming," I said, "is not as necessary as people believe. Our food is so full of preservatives that the deceased take twenty years longer to decompose. That doesn't mean we'll live longer."

"Another joke," she said. "What's the point of embalming anyhow?"

"If you get the deceased in the ground quickly enough, it's not necessary. The only reason we embalm is for viewing. At death, the skin draws away from the fingernails, giving the illusion that they continue to grow. The face stretches so tight it can pull wrinkles away, making the person seem still alive. The organs swell until they burst and blood is forced out of the mouth. This is what gave rise to the vampire myth – a deceased feeding on blood and remaining young with fingernails that grow."

"So you embalm a body because people are scared of vampires."

She released a stream of laughter that echoed from the tile floor to the high ceilings. I remembered Great Uncle's delight in my attention twenty years ago. His weak jokes were attempts to amuse me in the same manner that I was now trying with Lucy. She turned to the door. I wanted to prolong her presence but wasn't sure how.

"Kentucky doesn't have a female funeral director," I said. "You are patient, smart, and steady. You could be a pioneer in the field."

"No way, Jose. I like the living."

"An effective system of mourning is one that blurs the line between the living and the dead. When the baby boomers die, we'll need you."

"When the boomers die, we'll need ground space."

We returned to my office and faced each other across my walnut desk, bequeathed by Great Uncle when he entered his early retirement. The phone rang. My lawyer had communicated with the deceased's attorney, who was dismayed that the beneficiary was actually seeking her inheritance. My options were limited – give her the skull, buy her off, fight in court.

I thanked him and replaced the telephone on the receiver. This funeral home was built on the basis of a horse and I was not going to lose it over a skull.

"My attorney believes you to be a valid heir."

"No surprise there."

"Have you thought this through?"

"I believe that's your job."

"Should I ship you the skull after removal and cleaning? Or maybe you want me to just cut off his head and give it to you in a duffel bag right now?"

"Shipping is fine."

"First of all, it's illegal to mutilate human remains. To honor the will, we have to inform the family and delay the funeral. Then we'll go to court. That means newspapers. The media will undoubtedly portray you as a contemporary ghoul."

"It doesn't matter to me."

"It does to me. I can't have citizens think I'm over here giving away body parts. We need to work out a compromise."

"All my life men have told me that. I'm sick to death of it, Mister Undertaker Man. Why is it that men always want women to bend but don't want to give an inch?"

"I can't answer for other men."

"That's what they all say."

"You can do whatever you want with your body. You can pierce it or tattoo it or give it to science. Donating body parts to private parties is ahead of the curve. I respect the foresight of your friend. It might be the wave of the future. But it's just not feasible to hand over his skull."

"Feasible doesn't have a hand in it. Neither does compromise. Or your business."

"That's selfish."

"I'm not here for myself. I'm here for him."

"Maybe you need to meet a different man."

"I finally did," she said. "He went and died on me. There were times when just knowing he was out there kept me going. We never even kissed, but he was my backup man. Now I don't have anyone – in back, in front, or on the side."

"I can provide you with a fully articulated skeleton discarded by a medical library or an art school. The skulls are intact except for the cranial cavity, which is always open for removal of the brain. It latches together like a screen door. You can have an Asian peasant or an

American who died in prison. Perfectly legal. Delivered to your door free of charge."

"I want Billy's."

"Why?"

I enjoyed the prolonged silence that ensued. The room faded as if she were able to dispel time and space by speaking. Her voice was tinged by a mountain lilt that became more pronounced the longer she spoke.

"I'm not the collector type. Billy got me started on bones. He liked to walk in the woods without a plan or a map. He found skulls hand over fist. It was like they found him. He thought he kept part of the animal alive by saving the bones. Life was what he liked, not death.

"Bones are hard to find because they get scattered. Billy showed me where to look – along rivers, and on cliffs. Animals die at the high and low spots of the world. Other animals gnaw their bones for calcium and they go for the skull first because it's thin. Finding one is rare. Billy said a skull was the last footprint you left. He had gobs of them. He set them on shelves. We always talked how a human skull would be the prize for a collection, but they're hard to find. If you do, you're supposed to call the police. One place to look is Civil War battle sites. We didn't want that because it felt like prospecting or something. They got a place in New York called Manfred's Mandibles where you can order all the bones you want, but we never thought that way.

"Billy knew a lot of people from traveling and they sent him things in the mail – bones, shells, feathers. A neighbor sent him a camel skull years after he moved away. I think people gave him so much because he never wanted anything. Nothing. He never asked anyone for a thing. He wanted nothing. He wanted to find bones without meaning to. The whole thing was to come across a skull by accident.

"I started living that way in general. Thinking inside out, I called it. If I wanted to escape from my life, that really meant there was something inside of me that wanted out. If something was eating at me, I was hungry for something else. If I felt sorrow, it meant joy was trying to find me. Thinking inside out changed my life. For the first time I was a little bit happy. I quit wanting. All my life I'd wanted more but I turned that inside out. The less I wanted, the more I got.

"Then Billy moved to Portland for a job. My thinking went back the way it was before. At Christmas I mailed him a skull. For his birthday I sent a letter saying he could have my skull if something happened to me. He sent me the will. It was supposed to be fun. Then he died."

She stopped talking as if all the air had leaked from her head. Her face held a forlorn quality, buttressed by a scaffold of strength, like an old building that was half-renovated. After a lifetime of professional compassion, I was shocked to feel genuine sympathy for her. For years I'd handled the dead, massaging their muscles to help the embalming fluid enter the veins. Like anyone I wanted to be more than a statistic at the courthouse, more than a name engraved on a rock in a grassy field, more than a thirty-line obituary in the Sunday paper. I wanted to live on, but would never leave an heir. Four million years of genetic memory ended with my death – I was history turned inside out.

"Lucy, you should consider your trip here as a hike in the woods. Amid the concrete flora and fauna of the city, you stumble across something by accident – a human skull. It's not the skull of a friend, or a prisoner, or a forgotten soldier. It's my skull you found. Mine. An average skull of an average man."

I turned my head side to side for her scrutiny. She gazed at me as if I were a deceased twitching on the embalming table. Her eyes were heavy-lidded and lovely of lash. She never blinked. "Through my industry contacts I can guarantee a swift and simple process of acquisition. No fuss. No courts. No media."

"You don't know me," she said.

"It's not about you. I'm trying to think inside out. Undertakers are never remembered after their death. I have directed over three thousand funerals and have nothing to show for the work. Nothing. All of my achievement is slowly rotting under the earth. Great Uncle was remembered for a horse, but I have done nothing. When I die, my business rivals will prepare my body. No one will attend my funeral. Who mourns the mortician? Not a soul."

She reached across the desk and placed her hand on mine. Her skin was soft and very warm. The feeling I'd previously had drained away as if pumped from my body, replaced by something new and fresh with a completely different purpose. She slowly moved her hand beneath mine, turning her palm until the inside of our hands touched each other.

"You are a good man," she said. "I don't meet many."

"With your help," I said, "I can live forever."

"If you think inside out," she said, "death means permanent life."

"Will you take my skull?"

"Yes."

I stepped around the desk and traced her jaw with the back of my fingers. Her eyes never left mine. She tipped her head to my caress, her breath warm on my hand.

"You understand," she said.

"What?"

"I want to turn my loneliness inside out."

"Forever?"

"For now."

I pressed my forehead against hers. The sudden warmth of her skin flowed through my body. I felt as if I knew her a thousand years ago and a thousand years from now.

Slowly I rolled my head against hers. Our breath mingled. The lashes of our eyes brushed each other as if straining to entwine. I moved my cheekbone along hers, first one side, then the other. My lips touched hers. Our mouths turned inside out.

KAVITA THROUGH GLASS
Emily Ishem Raboteau

Now that he had won a lifetime supply of colored glass, Hassan Hagihossein felt he could endure the vagaries of Ramadan and Kavita Paltooram's moods. He was no longer tempted by Pete's Pancake House. He was no longer kneeling at his wife's feet offering her mango chutney and almond gelato and other mouth-watering things he could not touch until the sun went down. He was content simply to sit in the rattan chair, turning the pieces of glass over and over in his hands, loosely pondering his dissertation or the arc of Kavita's distended belly or nothing at all.

It was the ninth month of the Islamic lunar calendar as well as the ninth month of Kavita's pregnancy. It was also nine days since Kavita had stopped talking to him. None of the significance of this was lost on Hassan, who was a mathematician as well as a loosely practicing Muslim.

The pieces of colored glass were smooth and flattish and oblong, shaped like teardrops roughly the size of robin's eggs. They fit in his palms perfectly. Each piece was punctured with a delicate hole at one end. It had crossed Hassan's mind that these were designed to be craft items, that he ought to make a chandelier out of them, or bead curtains or something of that nature. But he was positive Kavita would find a colored glass chandelier or bead curtains tacky and he wasn't sure he would find them beautiful himself anymore if he had to look at them all clustered together in one aggregate form.

Kavita was an architect and didn't like "things," which is to say that she didn't like clutter. She preferred open space, negative space, and the color white. She had decorated their apartment sparely. The little furniture there was was white. So were the appliances, the dishes, the bedspread, the towels, and the sheets. Hassan was made to keep his library in a closet fitted with shelves so as not to break up the whiteness of the walls with the colored spines of his books.

Kavita added to the sparseness of the place by lolling about in the nude. She cooked and cleaned this way as well, brown and lithe and utterly naked. This made him blush. Hassan regarded her body as a perfect arrangement of spheres, a planetary form, a heavenly thing, a thing that might turn his eyeballs to salt if he looked too long, and so he tried not to.

During the first few months of their marriage, he had found the apartment antiseptic and cold. He found himself afraid of breaking things, although there really was nothing to break. He felt like he was stuck on the set of a movie about the future. Because of these feelings, he was childishly insistent that Kavita let him keep his rattan chair from college. He knew that the chair was an eyesore. He knew that it pained Kavita to have it in the living room, but for a long time it was the only thing he found comfortable about their home.

Later, he began to find the apartment peaceful. He understood Kavita's design sense more when he found himself opting to work at home rather than in his tiny office over at the math department. It was like living in a tabula rasa. White is a color without depth, he thought, or a thing without depth, since it is not a color at all, but a thing that makes depth possible. Ideas like this came to him, and new ways of solving problems.

One afternoon, as he sat quadrilating aspect ratios at the kitchen table, he was struck by the slow movement of a rectangle of soft not-yellow afternoon sunlight sliding across the white wall opposite him. It was moving infinitesimally. It was shifting its shape. He perceived its path, and it was telling him something about the basic probability of time that he could not put into numbers or words. Then a cloud crossed the sun and the shape was suddenly not there. The wall appeared to be a different shade of white than it was before. He was surprised to find his eyes stung with tears.

In that moment he felt he understood Kavita Paltooram more than he ever had and more than he ever would. And later that week when he skulked home from a disappointing multivariable calculus section in which he realized he was not transferring his passion for gradient functions to a group of stunningly disinterested undergraduates, he wasn't even upset to find that the rattan chair had been painted white as a bleached bone. He was simply glad to be home.

Once in a while he would find arabesque strands of his wife's black hair shed on the white furniture or the white bathroom tiles and he would read them like calligraphy. Today she wants me to pay the electric bill, he would figure, or today she wants me to bring home a cantaloupe. Almost always he was right.

That was before Kavita became pregnant. That was before she locked herself in the bathroom to urinate on a magic stick and refused to come out for two hours while Hassan paced the white rooms like a tiger on eggshells, wanting to pound down the door but not daring even to knock. Not daring even to tap. That was before she finally came out of the bathroom wielding the little magic stick with two pink lines, looking like a decidedly different person. Like a person with pointed edges instead of round ones. That was before she became impossible to read, left to right or right to left.

"I'm going for a walk," she had said, "and I don't want to be followed." As if he was a stalker and not her husband of three years. That night he divided the time it took for her to come home into nanoseconds, suffered an outrageous hollow craving for pancakes, and neglected to praise Allah for his blessings. When three hours passed without a sign of her, Hassan reached for the phone and dialed his father long-distance in Rasht to ask if this was normal behavior for women who've just discovered they are pregnant.

"It most certainly is not, my son, and don't say I didn't warn you. What did you expect? You married a Hindu from New Jersey."

"Don't start with that. I should think you'd be happy. You're going to be a grandfather."

"Of what?"

"Of a baby."

"That's not what I meant."

"I know what you meant."

"You know everything, Ph.D. So why consult with your father at all?"

"I don't want to argue."

"Why not consult me before the marriage? Why not marry Khaled's daughter instead as we arranged?"

"Khaled's daughter was twelve."

"Khaled's daughter was more beautiful than the moon!"

"I didn't call to argue."

"And she knew how to respect men. Now she's married to Zaid's idiot son. The one who drives his motorcycle like a maniac. It's a shame."

"I told you I don't want to argue. I'm just not sure what to do."

"You do what they all do in that godless country. You go buy a box of cigars and smoke them all."

It was true that Gulmuhammed Hagihossein had warned his son. He had opposed Kavita Paltooram from the moment he first laid eyes on her, which was the first time Hassan had seen her as well. Afterward it astonished Hassan that in his four years at Columbia he had never once noticed her, and it struck him as fateful rather than random that they should meet on graduation day before almost separating paths forever. It was fate that brought the Paltoorams to sit for their celebration supper at the round lacquered table in Lucky Cheng's Four Star Halal No Pork Chinese Restaurant next to the very one where Hassan sat glumly between his father and his square black graduation cap.

"Avert your eyes from her flesh," Gulmuhammed insisted in Farsi, even as he stared with his son at the indescribable midriff of Kavita, bedecked in her blood-red sari.

Hassan's mother had worn a hijab up until the day she swelled like a cresting wave after being stung on the tongue by a wasp in the kitchen while preparing a khaviar. After that she was wrapped in a shroud by a brood of shrieking neighbor women and covered with two thick yards of Iranian earth. Watching Kavita at Lucky Cheng's, it occurred to Hassan that he could not remember his mother's hair. Kavita's hair reached to her waist. It was oiled in a blue-black braid that snaked over her shoulder like a question mark. The Hagihosseins stared at her impossible curves. "That woman is wicked. Completely shameless. It is clear that she will break a man's heart one day for sport with her wiles," Hassan's father intoned.

She wore the sari exclusively to please her parents. That much was clear. Hassan understood this because he was wearing a starched galabiya for the exact same reason. He also recognized the customary apologetic look that first-generation offspring wear in public with their mothers. As Mrs. Paltooram sat weeping like a camel over her vegetable lo mein (not from sadness, but from joy because her daughter was going to be successful), as Gulmuhammed sat pontificating over his kung pao chicken about performing ablutions (and chastising his son for becoming too American), Hassan's eyes locked with Kavita's. They rolled their eyes and smiled.

That was the beginning. On the streets of New York, where they started their courtship, she was approached by Mexicans and responded in halting Spanish while he, more often than not, was mistaken for a light-skinned black man on account of his woolly hair. This amused them. They pondered how confusing their children would be, if they ever had any.

When she became pregnant, he was himself confused. When she became pregnant and started the night walks, he became strangely bewildered by language. It wasn't that he had lost his grip on English so much as that he couldn't connect signifiers and signified anymore. He would falter in the middle of a sentence even though he knew the string of words coming out of his mouth was correct.

Is this thing really called an elbow? he thought. And if so, is my knuckle the elbow of my finger? Is my wrist an elbow? Is Kavita's waist an ankle? They are both slender and they both bend and they are both the color of cinnamon. Is a joint on the body an angle or the possibility of an angle? Is Kavita's little finger a cinnamon stick? No, a cinnamon stick does not bend like an elbow.

He worked furiously on his dissertation, *On Finsler Geometric Manifolds and Their Applications to Teichmueller Spaces*, to rid himself of his vicious thought cycles. This failed to work. He just found himself thinking about his wife in elementary mathematical terms. For example, he imagined Kavita and himself as the axis on a graph plotting the growth of their child. He also tried using Kavita and the baby as the set of coordinates and tried to design an algorithm to classify the shape of their future as a family. He thought of them as a triangle, of course, but one whose boundaries he could not begin to measure.

Kavita's night walks became regular. He assumed she had taken a lover. He doubted his paternity. He doubted his doubt. Every time she left she would admonish him not to follow her. Of course the night came when he decided to do just that.

She was walking very fast. Hassan kept three-quarters of a block behind her, trying to move in the shadows and keep cover behind parked cars. He felt ridiculous. His shirt was sweat-stuck to his back like a postage stamp. Kavita crossed a street. The wind lifted her hair so that several thick strands of it pointed backward in his direction like accusing fingers, but she did not turn her head. He realized she was making a beeline for the campus. At one point she leaned against a tree and brought one foot up against the trunk to adjust her sandal strap. The gesture hurt him physically. He realized Kavita was monumentally graceful. She began walking again. He let himself lag farther behind. From a distance he watched his wife stop in front of the University's Art and Architecture Building, a gray monstrosity of a structure. She pushed through the revolving door and was gone. Hassan began to breathe again.

She is taking a class, he thought, straightening his tie. That's all. She is continuing her education. Still, he was nagged by the fact that this should be kept secret from him, and he was left with the troubling image of Kavita being swallowed up by the building, like a tiny sea horse in the striated mouth of a humpbacked whale. Then he thought of their child growing in her. A pearl in the belly of a sea horse in the belly of a whale. A pearl. A precious thing. The night was heavy and wet. "Allah Akbar," he said to no one in particular. He kept saying it as he followed Kavita's trajectory backward to their white home. "Allah Akbar, Allah Akbar." God is great.

In the third month of her pregnancy, Hassan drove Kavita to the Corning glass factory. He picked the factory because he'd noticed her reading a library book on stained-glass windows and thought it might be of interest. She was growing more distant from him every day and he hoped an excursion might draw them together.

Upstate, the leaves were blazing, almost radioactive tones of red and yellow somersaulting to the road. Kavita was silent in the car. Veiled without a veil. She had the window rolled down on the passenger side and her hair was whipping around like a system of angry black vectors, hiding her face and revealing it in turn. An equation came to Hassan as he took in the simultaneous motion of the leaves falling down and her hair lifting up. He understood these things to be linked. The equation was this:

$$Distance \div Longing = Desire$$

Hassan quickly dismissed the equation as nonsensical. Longing and desire were too close in meaning to be considered separate variables. There wasn't a word in the English language to describe the cause and effect of Kavita Paltooram's remoteness on his heart. He was very hungry.

"Would you like a tuna fish sandwich?" he asked her. He'd packed them an elaborate lunch. "An éclair?"

"Where are you taking me, Hassan?" she answered. Her voice was tired.

"It's a surprise. I can keep a secret just as well as you."

Kavita gathered her heavy hair, tied it in a knot at the nape of her neck and closed her eyes.

"Would you like some cashew nuts?"

"No."

"Would you like a pickle?"

"No. I'm going to take a nap." Her eyelashes cast long elliptical shadows down her cheekbones. While she slept, Hassan wound up eating everything, both her portion and his own.

Inside the factory, they watched a man blow a tiny glass sparrow from a long spinning pipe. Hassan watched Kavita watching the beak and the wings harden out of liquid glass. On her face was the trace of a smile.

She carefully chose a set of wineglasses from the gift shop. Before they left, Hassan entered a contest. He wrote three words on a slip of paper: Delicate, Durable, Divine. It was supposed to be a new slogan for the cover of the CorningWare catalog. He had been trying to describe his wife. On the car ride home he thought about how none of the words was right.

The second time Hassan followed Kavita to the Art and Architecture Building, he waited until she came out. He chose a bench near Stanhope Hall because it afforded him a view of the revolving door while obscuring him slightly behind the Rockefeller statue. While he waited he ate through the large bag of jelly beans Kavita had turned down because they hurt her teeth, and he thought about what he could say to her to make her love him. He had a lot of things he wanted to tell her. Whenever he tried his tongue got tied.

"Kavita," he wanted to say, "in my country, a bowl of goldfish on the table means an auspicious new year. A sturgeon fish can live a hundred years. My grandfather was a fisherman. He couldn't spell his own name. My grandmother was a poet. She wove her verse into Persian rugs and traded them to an Englishman. One rug for two lambs. Her loom was lost in the war. My grandmother's name was Khadijah. Her mother's name was Khadijah. Khadijah was the first wife of the Prophet. Khadijah was also my mother's name. My mother wore a hijab from her head to her toes. I do not remember the color of her hair. Every woman in my family has named her daughter Khadijah for the past two thousand years."

Before she became pregnant, Hassan didn't think like this. Before she became pregnant, he thought of himself primarily as a mathematician and, as such, a citizen of the world. The roster of names in his department read like a litany of united nations: Imran Abbaspour, Antonio Cavaricci, Saul Diamond, Ricardo González de los Santos, Hank Hansell, N'gugi Obioha, Nicolas Paraskavopolous, Olga Rasvanovic, Hoc Sung, Almamy Suri-Tunis, Li Wang, Toshio Yamamoto.

Three-quarters of the members of the Applied Probability Research Group could barely speak enough English to ask what time it was, yet they were understood just so long as their equations were sound. Yet, here he sat, gorged on gourmet jelly beans, not knowing how to talk to his wife.

After exactly two hours, Kavita emerged in a thin wave of students. She was noticeably pregnant. She was talking to a very tall man. Hassan watched in horror as this man stooped over his wife and picked something from her shoulder. Was it a hair? Were this man's fingers touching Kavita's hair? He watched her say goodbye. He waited until she turned a corner to tail the man. He followed the man across the quad and underground to the all-night library where he noticed under fluorescent lights that the man was blond and blue-eyed and had a mustache that resembled a baby caterpillar crawling on his upper lip.

This was the night Hassan unraveled. He dreamed Kavita gave birth to a moth with blue eyes and wings that extended to the roof. He called his father in Rasht. He let the phone ring twenty-seven times. Gulmuhammed was not at home. On another night he dreamed he asked Kavita why she had married him.

"Out of kindness," she replied, "so that you could get your green card."

He had to ask Toshio to cover his multivariable calculus section two weeks in a row because he feared he wouldn't be able to hold a piece of chalk without dropping it. In one week he ate five Hungryman breakfasts at Pete's Pancake House. When he weighed himself on the white bathroom scale, he discovered to his dismay that he'd gained nearly twenty pounds.

The third time Hassan followed Kavita to the Art and Architecture Building was Lailat-ut Qadr. It was raining, and he'd been fasting. For Ramadan, for clarity. He waited a half hour and went inside. He'd never set foot in the building before, but as if guided by instinct, as if making a hajj of doom, he found the classroom without really trying.

It smelled of turpentine. A dozen students sat like a solar system in a semicircle with paintbrushes clutched in their hands or held between their teeth. In front of each student was a canvas. On each canvas was a naked Kavita. Kavita herself was sprawled out at the semicircle's center on a filthy couch, her belly rounder than the sun and twice as painful for him to look at.

Hassan reached for the closest thing he could grab. Later he would remember the gesture with embarrassment. His hand found a thing. It was a coffee can full of soaking brushes. He flung it as hard as he could without aiming at anything and not knowing why. A woman gasped. The can grazed the corner of one of the canvases, knocking it to the floor and splashing turpentine on at least three people. One of them was the blond-haired blue-eyed man. Hassan fixated on him.

"What is your name?" he demanded. His voice didn't sound like his voice.

"Excuse me? What's going on here?" asked the man, rising to his feet.

"What is your name?" repeated Hassan.

"I'm Burt. Burt Larson." He came toward Hassan with his arms held out in a placating way that reminded Hassan of a jellyfish. "We don't want any trouble here, man."

Hassan spun on his heels and fled through the rain. His socks were wet. It was Lailat-ut Qadr, the night of power, and his socks were soaking wet. When he got home he had to breathe into a paper bag because he was hiccuping violently. He rewrote the scene so that he broke a canvas over the blond man's head, threw a blanket over Kavita, and led her out of the Art and Architecture Building by the hand.

That was the day Kavita Paltooram stopped talking to him altogether. Which at first was fine because he didn't want to talk to her either. She had shared her body with a circle of strangers. She was just as far away as before. The difference now was that she seemed far away and *dirty*. He busied himself in Finsler Manifolds and stayed away from the apartment. He made astonishing progress with his dissertation. He attributed this clarity to his fast and also to Kavita's imperfection.

Then he dreamed again about the moth. This time it was gargantuan, with feelers as long as trees and wings as shaggy as a llama's fur. In the dream, Kavita was mounted on the moth and carried away into the blue sky. She was naked, of course, but small as a dot on the back of the moth. In the dream, as the moth carried his wife toward the sun, he was filled with longing. Hassan woke up gut-wrenchingly hungry.

On the ninth day of her silent treatment, the glass arrived. "*Congratulations, Mr. Hagihossein,*" read the card. "*Your slogan was chosen for our catalog! We send you these timeless treasures with gratitude. Sincerely, Peter Simpkin, Executive President, Corning, Inc.*"

There were dozens of pieces. Hassan sat in the rattan chair turning them over in his hands. He held up a blue piece over one eye and watched Kavita through it. She had just taken a shower and was wearing her white bathrobe. Through the glass, her body was distorted. Her edges were running. She looked like she was underwater, a drowning angel. It occurred to Hassan that he didn't know how to make her happy. He didn't know how to speak her language. Kavita did not think in the terms of water. Kavita, who had grown up in Teaneck and taken perhaps one desultory trip to the Jersey shore every other summer, could not understand what it had meant to grow up on the rim of the Caspian Sea. This is why the glass pieces, which put his mind at rest, did not mean the same thing to her. She didn't know what it was to hunt a beach for sea glass.

Hassan fished in his toolbox for some wire. He moved to the kitchen table and began sketching a design.

"Kavita," he called.

She came.

"Do you see? I am making a mobile to hang above the baby's crib."

She was silent.

He looked up at her and saw that her eyes were bloodshot. He steadied his voice. "If it's a girl, I want to name her Khadijah."

Kavita fingered an orange piece of glass.

"It was my mother's name," he explained, placing his hand gingerly on her hip.

"I know," she said. "It's beautiful."

"Yes. And it sounds like yours."

She moved his hand to her navel and held it in place with her own. A riptide tore his stomach like a hunger pang. Her body gave him gooseflesh. She opened her mouth to speak then shut it, as if reconsidering.

"Yes? You were going to say something?" he begged.

Kavita spoke slowly. "Do you realize you never look at me?" Her voice was soft like sand under bare feet. "I can't remember the last time you touched me."

Hassan stood. He swallowed. He didn't know the name for the way his wife's hair smelled. He gathered it in his fists and combed his fingers through to its snarling ends. Then, with the wet tips of Kavita's hair, he painted concentric circles on his face. Over his eyebrows, temples, cheekbones. By which he meant to say, "You are all I look at. You are all I see."

FICTION
Stuart Dybek

Through a rift in the mist, a moon the shade of water-stained silk. A night to begin, to begin again. Someone whistling a tune impossible to find on a piano, an elusive melody that resides, perhaps, in the spaces between the keys where there once seemed to be only silence. He wants to tell her a story without telling a story. One in which the silence between words is necessary in order to make audible the faint whistle of her breath as he enters her.

Or rather than a sound, or even the absence of sound, the story might at first be no more than a scent: a measure of the time spent folded in a cedar drawer that's detectable on a silk camisole. For illumination, other than the moonlight (now momentarily clouded), it's lit by the flicker of an almond candle against a bureau mirror that imprisons light as a jewel does a flame.

The amber pendant she wears tonight, for instance, a gem that he's begun to suspect has not yet fossilized into form. It's still flowing undiscernibly like a bead of clover honey between the cleft of her breasts. Each night it changes shape – one night an ellipse, on another a tear, or a globe, lunette or gibbous, as if it moves through phases like an amber moon. Each morning it has captured something new – moss, lichen, pine needles. On one morning he notices a wasp, no doubt extinct, from the time before the invention of language, preserved in such perfect detail that it looks dangerous, still able to sting. On another morning the faint hum of a trapped bee, and on another, there's a glint of prehistoric sun along a captured mayfly's wings. When she grazes down his body and her honey-colored hair and the dangling pendant brush across his skin, he can feel the warmth of sunlight trapped in amber. Or is that simply body heat?

The story could have begun with the faint hum of a bee. Is something so arbitrary as a beginning even required? He wants to tell her a story without a beginning; no, rather a story that is a succession of beginnings, a story that goes through phases like a moon, the telling of which requires the proper spacing of a night sky between each phase.

Imagine the words strung out across the darkness, and the silent spaces between them as the emptiness that binds a snowfall together, or turns a hundred starlings rising from a wire into a single flock, or countless stars into a constellation. A story of stars, or starlings. A story of falling snow. Of words swept up and bound like whirling leaves. Or, after the leaves have settled, a story of mist.

What chance did words have beside the distraction of her body? He wanted to go where language couldn't take him, wanted to listen to her breath break speechless from its cage of parentheses, to wordlessly travel her skin like that flush that would spread between her nape and breasts. What was that stretch of body called? He wanted a narrative that led to all the places where her body was still undiscovered, unclaimed, unnamed.

Fiction, which he'd heard defined as "the lie that tells a deeper truth," was at once too paradoxical and yet not mysterious enough. What was necessary was a simpler kind of lie, one that didn't turn back upon itself and violate the very meaning of lying. A lie without denouement, epiphany, or escape into revelation, a lie that remained elusive. The only lie he needed was the one that would permit them to keep on going as they had.

It wasn't the shock of recognition, but the shock of what had become unrecognizable that he now listened for. It wasn't a suspension of disbelief, but a suspension of common sense that loving her required.

Might unconnected details be enough, arranged and rearranged in any order? A scent of cedar released by body heat from a water-stained camisole. The grain of the hair she'd shaved from her underarms, detectable against his lips. The fading mark of a pendant impressed on her skin by the weight of his body. (If not a resinous trail left by a bead

of amber along her breasts, then it's her sweat that's honey.) Another
night upon which this might end – might end again – for good this time
– someone out on the misty street, whistling a melody impossible to re-
create . . .

I wanted to tell you a story without telling the story.

CHOSEN PEOPLE
Lisa Zeidner

B.J. liked to pick up women at the Holocaust Memorial Museum. He liked to choose one, track her reactions to the cattle cars and heaped cadavers, and approach after the tour of the carnage, when she emerged, dazed and blinking, into the tastefully solemn Hall of Remembrance.

Imperfectly shaven in a leather jacket the supple brown of a chocolate Lab, B.J. could have been a resistance fighter. A five o'clock shadow of danger combined with courtliness: he could have been a count moonlighting as a pilot, because trying times demand trying measures. Shy behind wire rims, his eyes suggested that love was a brilliant weed that could sprout from the cement of the world's brutality.

This was not untrue. Even in the camps, people must have found crevices of time and space in which to have sex. To stay alive, you must hang on to desire.

B.J. liked Jewish women. Not that he had any burning desire to marry one again. Pale but not, generally, pasty, their long faces, framed by dark hair, were appealingly out-of-time, someone else's ancestral daguerreotypes. Some were jumpy as whippets, but he could enjoy that in controlled doses; could bolt one down like absinthe or Turkish coffee.

B.J. himself was a Southern boy – a Bobby Joe, in point of fact, though he'd never own up to that here, or to the equally trite initials. For Holocaust museum purposes, he was Rob. The accent was not a problem. An advantage, even. For the women he followed the trim asses of were not the ones who came to this shrine with a holy sense of belonging. On the contrary, he wanted the ones who could not accept a man like their fathers, but whose rage and ambivalence were so deep, so unruly, that they would never be so obvious as to date, say, a black bongo player with dreadlocks who plays for change in the subway. Rob is an *architect*, they could huff.

He was not even circumcised. Of course that would not generally be evident until later. Likewise, the women could not know, when informed of his profession, that he was a failed architect (was there, really, any other kind?). A low-level CADD operator, detailer of hideous, derivative, squat strip malls and office parks, whose workday offered little more outlet for creativity than your average data-entry clerk for a credit-reporting bureau. Despite the reality, "architect" as a profession still managed to sound dashing. Further it gave him and the women something to discuss, since everyone knew that the architecture of the Holocaust museum was supposed to be interesting.

B.J. did not tell the women how much he disliked the architecture, and not merely out of professional jealousy, this being the kind of project he himself would never enjoy, despite having dutifully learned to hash-sling phrases like "conceptual parti" in grad school. He loved bridges and arches, steel and brick, thought them luscious and noble; he resented the materials themselves being symbolically linked with the Third Reich. He even had a mental bumper sticker to sum up his objection to the unfair bad-reputation-by-association:

Stainless steel didn't kill Jews. Nazis did.

His ex-wife's brother – whom he still saw, since Mike was still his physician, and his friend – was the only person he had told about his use of the venue. Mike got "a kick" out of B.J. and considered it brilliantly subversive to hit on women in front of a portentously enlarged photo of Kristallnacht rather than, say, a curvy Matisse nude. B.J. did not find this praise condescending, since Mike was far more complicated than he seemed. He too had married outside his class and faith, suffering the scorn of his family. The men shared a conviction that miscegenation not only produced better and better-looking human beings, but was the very cornerstone of progress and civilization. Look at the English – their fine, refined race begot by wave after wave of invasion.

"You guys can't possibly believe that," B.J.'s ex-wife, Elaine, had scoffed, at the Thanksgiving dinner close to a decade ago when the topic had come up. "It's such kindergarten bullshit. You're actually proposing history as a nice-nice Rainbow Coalition, perfectly balanced and harmonious, like some Pepsi ad?"

"Not harmonious," Mike had shot back, "but definitely *vive la difference*. And there's scientific evidence for it, too. All those studies where they ask women to sniff the armpits of worn men's shirts, see who they want to screw. They like the B.O. most different from their own. The nose knows – the gene pool wants to vary up its act. Unless you're Amish."

"God, you're a dolt," Elaine had huffed. Mike was the little brother. He had not yet finished medical school. His brand-new girlfriend and wife-to-be, a placid, fine-boned WASP, had looked alarmed during this exchange; as soon as was polite, she'd left to busy herself in the kitchen. B.J. himself had played the impressionable newcomer at one point, the trembling hick right out of *The Rocky Horror Picture Show*, witnessing the brutality of the family's wit. Elaine had eventually remarried a nice, ambitious Jewish stock-market guy who served on the board of directors of many significant Manhattan cultural institutions, condescending to people like B.J. on a daily basis. When her first child was born, she'd begun to keep kosher, which had shocked B.J. deeply. The only explanation he could devise was that she needed an excuse to design a kitchen with many, many different cabinets and preparation areas, but Mike said that it was very common for people to discover their devout inner children when they became parents.

B.J. stood by what they'd said. One thing you must hand to sex: it is democratic. Aside from whips and chains, studs and black leather, or movies where Nazi soldiers snatch their snatch from the line of the doomed, sex, like death, is a great equalizer. An ass, grabbed, knows no race or place. Paradoxically, however, sex renders you more vulnerable to falling in love, and love returns you to the dangerous myth of individuality. The conviction that a life – say, your own – can matter in the great meat grinder of history. This is what B.J. contemplated as he watched footage of emaciated bodies being cleared away by bulldozer. Someone once wanted to kiss, solely, each one of those mouths. Each tongue, each tooth *connected*. To commit a sexual act in the face of death was therefore not sacrilege, but sanctimony.

"What we have tried to do," the architect was quoted as saying in *Progressive Architecture*, "is to construct symbolic forms that in some cases were very banal, ought to be banal, and in other cases are more abstract and open ended." No shit, Sherlock. *Banal* summed up neatly, for B.J., the museum's elevator. Once you surrender your timed pass to a uniformed guard, you take an identification card that "tells the story of a real person who lived during the Holocaust" and board a somber elevator – steel, of course – to deliver you to the exhibitions. People face forward and fold their hands before them, reverent as churchgoers, but their eyes are avid, awaiting the horrors above. When you are an American, confident that the worst thing likely to ever happen to you is to be trapped in an elevator for several hours with sweaty strangers, you take amusement-park rides, bungee-jump, watch disaster movies about airplanes or high-rises.

A pickpocket could work very efficiently in the Holocaust museum elevator. That would be amusingly craven. The elevator often made B.J. think of one of his nephew's Nintendo 64 games. "Yah-poo!" Super Mario exclaims as he jumps from platform to platform above quicksand, abysses.

Sometimes B.J. found her right there in the elevator. It wasn't appearance that drew him so much as movement. Something swift would twitch in her: a pang of pre-lunch hunger or need to look down at her new shoes. Exactly twice, women had already been taking his measure. (He had not lied to Mike about his small success rate at this enterprise, nor was it his fault that to Mike, still married, any ratio of call to response was impressive.) Those women were, not surprisingly, among the willing. Mandy, recovering from a breakup, sweetly timid, then immediately, skipping afterglow, accusatory. Like reliving his entire marriage in time-lapse. Ildiko, tourist from Budapest, zesty as Popeye. Generally B.J. did not gravitate toward tourists. Ideal as they'd be logistically (with, even, their own hotel rooms), B.J. could not be accused of wanting to carve the names of his conquests on a commemorative wall. He fully expected to marry again, and this certainly was more likely with someone he could meet for dinner by Metro than with Anna from Amsterdam. Still, he was ready to go where love led him.

Wasn't one of the Holocaust's lessons that you must be willing to leave your Picassos on the wall and bail? People deluded themselves that in the Jews' place they would have bravely boarded the ship at the first sign of trouble, but that is merely the safety of hindsight. There was no Vietnam Museum on the Washington Mall – too much ambiguity. Better to bemoan cartoon Nazis in their armbands.

Once you got off the elevator, the hallways were designed to chunnel you through the exhibitions, but here, as on the highway, people rudely passed. Most of the women who appealed to B.J. dawdled behind their companions if they had them, spending longer than usual on something less obvious than the Auschwitz room, where people can elbow each other to rubberneck at the crematoriums. They were in front of the huge photo of the fifteen thousand pounds of human hair (think of all the wigs, B.J. once heard someone note, that hair could have made for the women of Brooklyn's Orthodox community), or even poring over the guest register near the gift shop ("This really sucks, man," one teenager had written. "Love, Beavis and Butt-head").

The very young women, with their vacant expressions and low-riding jeans over cloddish shoes, did not much appeal to him. You couldn't blame them for not knowing the history of their grandparents' war, but B.J. felt himself way too jaded for the kind of dewy-eyed exploration a woman that young would demand. He was no Casanova; he brought to bed all of his dashed hopes; sex, he knew even as he felt himself flush from pleasure at a trim hip, pursed lip, or balletic walk, would disappoint him as had everything else, and this disappointment was not something Prozac could cure, though Mike had suggested it once, casually.

Only an idiot, B.J. believed, would *not* be depressed. Arms and clitorises were being chopped off all over the globe, in what was generously called the Third World but was really the Ninth or Tenth, by preteens with Uzis who made the Gestapo look like Cub Scouts – what exactly was that lesson the Holocaust was supposed to have taught us? – while in the home of the brave and the free, Commerce had triumphed so totally that even museums were voyeuristic entertainment centers. In all fairness, the architecture of the Third Reich was perfectly tasteful – an updating of the very neoclassicism that had inspired the Washington Mall. Whereas the "tasteful" Holocaust museum gave away, as party favors, passports of genuine Jews! *Please turn page at end of 4th floor*, the instructions offered, to help people get into the spirit! The whole country one gigantic shopping mall, B.J. himself a humble manservant.

That Saturday he had failed to engage a sultry, knock-kneed woman in the Hall of Remembrance. Her blue-black, frankly artificial hair was cropped close, like a camp inmate's or Mia Farrow's in *Rosemary's Baby*. She'd spent a long time in the Resistance section, one of B.J.'s favorite haunts, squinting at the pullquote about Irene Gut Opdyke, who saved eighteen people by playing mistress to a major in Tarnopol. At the end of the exhibitions B.J. zeroed in. But she would not even look at him, even though she was lost and impatient, in search of something. Her boyfriend, it turned out. B.J. venomously witnessed their reunion kiss.

The museum had installed a container for recycling the identification cards, since it had become embarrassing to have the sad histories of dead Jews littering the grass outside as people left. B.J. watched now, mesmerized, as a black child of about ten removed the bubble gum from his mouth, smashed it between the pages of his passport, and gleefully dropped the passport in the recycling container. You were not even allowed to note, anymore, that a person was black.

"Charming," someone said, at his side, in an accent so close to his own that it had to be – Georgia? Tennessee? But tempered by college and – Manhattan? She was all in black. A trim, blondish, heavily freckled woman. "Just the spot where I'd take a kid. But hey, as we all know, slavery was much, much worse. 'Course *I'm* not allowed to say that, being a *plantation owner* and all. Guess what? Slavery isn't new. Ask the Greeks. The potato famine wasn't all that much fun either, and let me ask you: Do *you* know your ancestors' names? Can *you* trace your lineage right back to the king? Who has their own names, in this country? Smith? Taylor? I'm surprised, by the way, that you like her," and here she jerked her head toward the jet-black-haired woman. "Seems a little . . ." She stared at B.J., challenging.

"Come here often?" she asked.

He wondered how long she had been watching him. Had he actually been stalked? He had not noticed her at all, anywhere, which, given his vigilance, seemed impossible. The way she had just laid her political cards on the table to a stranger – it seemed bold enough to qualify as deranged, although her posture (arms folded, head tucked chinward) seemed guarded enough. What made her suspect he was a reasonable recipient for un-politically-correct invective? Did he look, despite the Oliver Peoples specs and cool shoes, like a *good ole boy*?

"So what do you think?" he asked, making a sweep with his hands to indicate the room.

Her eyes registered surprise, which she choked off. She had not recognized him as a co-Confederate until he spoke. On what basis, then, had he been selected? Bachelorhood alone?

"Thought I just said," she answered. "I just want to make it known, however: *Mass murder is a bad thing.* I'm totally against it. Slavery, too. *Extremely* poor idea."

"Of the architecture, I mean."

She sighed. She drew his attention downward to the point of one of her ankle boots, which she now aligned, in a mildly parodic ballet position, with the grout joint on one of the triangular granite floor tiles. "Triangles," she said. "Mind you, I don't have anything *against* triangles. A nifty change from right angles. But is it supposed to *mean* something? Okay, a Jewish star – I understand it's pointy – but to have the edges look threatening, like ice picks: I don't get it. I mean . . . why?"

That was the moment when B.J. knew he could fall in love.

"Have you seen the famous sharp-edged building corner of Pei's addition to the National Gallery?" he asked.

She nodded. The nod might have meant she had, or had not. He went on.

"A thirty-degree angle in Tennessee marble. Technical feat, no bout adout it. Everybody needs to come up and say, Bet that was hard to do, then stroke it, so the entire expensively produced and elegant joint is all worn down, turned black."

"Care to show me?" she asked.

B.J. realized that he was breathing hard, from the effort of having to evaluate her all at once rather than surreptitiously, in stages. She made a sweep like the one he'd done, about the room, to show her willingness to be inspected by Quality Control. But the erstwhile object of B.J.'s affection, with her tiny silver backpack and her galoot boyfriend, was ready to leave, taking a path that demanded their inserting themselves right between B.J. and this new woman. B.J. recognized, now, the error of his ways. Blue-hair suddenly seemed ridiculous, Olive Oyl-ish, clearly inferior to this woman with her pageboy, in her priestly black, who was "neat as a pin," as his mother would say, except for the random splatter art of the freckles.

B.J. was not particularly attracted to her. But that wasn't the point. Or rather, that was exactly the point. What do you know about people by how they look? We're all supposed to be enlightened enough to declare, *Nothing*. Phrenology, not science at all. Red hair no more makes someone "fiery" than freckles make them "spunky." And yet. And yet. We all make our instantaneous judgments. He had been selected, here, on the basis of something. He wanted to trust her enough to see where things led.

He knew that his next gesture was important, and he didn't have long to invent it. He was thrilled to have to act with no facts. He looked at her gravely. He shifted position so that he could offer his arm. "I'll show you," he said. Wordlessly, with a wince of shyness, she took the arm with both of hers in a quaint way that seemed to require long white gloves.

B.J. had a flash of this encounter's ultimate position in the line of encounters he had enjoyed here. For this to be the Final Solution to his thus-far failed personal life, a life as blind and botched as history itself, shouldn't he and this woman find a handicapped bathroom somewhere, go at it? Any old dark semiprivate alcove. A tour of the Holocaust museum made small spaces seem claustrophobic: the bunk beds at Auschwitz like the head-to-foot sardine layout of the galleys of slave ships; Anne Frank's minuscule apartment, shared with strangers, so she couldn't even find a private place to write small in her diary. But in love, small spaces are bowers. Secret gardens. Her hands around his arm were so thrilling that the fantasy he'd been mentally playing out, mentally bragging about later to Mike – which involved, for some reason, her having her period, them not caring – dissolved into a powerful feeling of *safety*.

They would come back here together always, he knew. A private ritual. Mike would be best man. He would take some flak in his family. For all B.J. knew, she would not like it much either. "Hey," he could imagine himself saying, "I *like* Mike."

Her name, he was about to learn, was Rebecca, and she was one of a handful of Jews to grow up in North Carolina, where her father was: *an architect*. An architect who had been actively involved with the civil rights movement in the fifties and was now fixated on his hatred of the Nation of Islam, which had actually accused his ancestors of perpetrating the slave trade. The sundry straggling colonial Jews with capital to invest, rather than the Portuguese! When it came time for B.J. to tell Rebecca that he was an architect, her response would be, "I'm so sorry for you." When he tried out the line, *Funny, you don't look Jewish*, she'd laugh. Her mother was a Georgia belle, awakened by love into political conscience. Her maternal grandfather and B.J.'s grandfather (either of his would have done, but only one was alive) could sit together at the wedding, emboldened by champagne to admit to each other that they're not entirely sure the Holocaust ever happened. This museum was unlikely to change their minds: they were not so old and naïve as to not know that photographs could be rigged. Even old black-and-white footage.

"Wait," Rebecca said. They had not moved, B.J. realized, from the recycling container. It had taken only a second for him to spin out this whole premonition of their joint destiny – their lives flashing before his eyes.

"Shall we?" Rebecca asked.

They found their identification cards, in unison checked the last pages. Both his and her tour guides to the museum had survived their separate death camps, emigrated to the United States in 1947. B.J. pointed out that their twosome might have met on the ship. She retilted her chin in a way that seemed to suggest a lot, most of it contradictory: that this meeting was indeed fated, as meant-to-be as if it had happened on Ellis Island; that she might not stick around for more than lunch. They dropped the identification cards in the container for reincarnation and once more Rebecca took his arm.

B.J. had this thought as her hand landed. *She's the kind of woman who will cry when she comes.* Never at the standard sentimental things, though. Never at dead heroes in movies. For that second he enjoyed the absolute conviction of the premonition, as strong as his belief that they would marry: that her strong shudders would so deeply move her, she would weep. He was wrong, actually, but by the time he discovered he was wrong, it would no longer matter.

On the way out, Rebecca did something that made B.J. so fond of her it caused him a sharp pain in his gut. As they walked past a brushed stainless steel railing, she had to release one of her arms to touch it. As a boy B.J. had stroked everything he passed on the walk home from school, drawn to each new texture, so that his hands and nails were always filthy, cut, and splintered. Maybe all boys did this. The ones who didn't stop became architects. His ex-wife had berated him about just this habit: *Stop touching things!* But the architect's daughter put down just the pads of her fingers on the steel, as if blessing it, or savoring the material's coolness.

"Pretty," she said.

THAW
Max Ludington

There were about ten people in the place, all men. Jerry went to the bartender.

"Someone call a cab?" he asked.

"Yeah," the bartender pointed over at the pool table. "Billy! Your cab's here."

A big Indian with hair as long as Jerry's looked up from the shot he was about to take. "Already?" he said. "Hang on till I finish this game."

Jerry walked around the bar. His lungs were still cold from the negative temperature outside. "Where you headed to?" He wouldn't mind waiting if the guy was going into Minneapolis, but he wouldn't wait long for a fare going around the corner.

"Here and there. Don't worry about it." The man was about thirty, Jerry's age, wearing a Harley-Davidson T-shirt, a leather biker vest, jeans, and cowboy boots. His black hair fell freely around his face and shoulders.

"Well, I wouldn't mind knowing what direction we're headed," said Jerry. The Indian's drifting eyes took in Jerry's black jeans and sweater, leather jacket, biker boots, blond ponytail, and goatee. He gave Jerry an approving grin. "Name's Billy." He offered his hand. His handshake was respectfully firm. He leaned back down to take his shot and missed.

"Is it the money you're worried about?" Billy burrowed a hand into his jeans and pulled out a roll of cash. He peeled off a hundred-dollar bill. "I'm going to keep you tied up for a while," he said, handing it to Jerry. "I need a driver. That right there's got to buy me at least a couple hours. You in?"

Jerry looked down at the bill. "You got me, brother. Hell yes."

Billy laughed. "All right then. Rack 'em up. I'm sick of playing against myself."

"Tell you what," said Jerry, "you rack 'em, and I'll call my girlfriend and tell her I'm not coming home now so she doesn't make dinner for me."

"You do that," said Billy.

When Betsy answered, Jerry said, "Baby, I know we had a date for tonight, but I just picked up a fare down here in Chaska, a chauffeur job. He laid a hundred bucks on me for starters."

"How long will you be?" she asked.

"I don't know. As long as he keeps laying C-notes on me I'll stay with him. Do you still want me to come over if it's late?"

"I want you here now."

"I know. I'll try not to be too late. Okay?"

"Okay."

Billy wanted to put twenty on a game of eight-ball, but Jerry declined. Billy broke the rack and nothing dropped. Jerry sank three balls on his first turn, Billy sank one – an easy tap-in – before missing again, then Jerry ran the rest of the table.

"You should have made that bet," said Billy.

"Yeah, I guess."

"Fuck it. Let's go. I want to go down to the rez, swing by my house and then into the casino for a bit."

At the car Billy said, "I don't like riding in back. Bad memories." Jerry moved the maps and newspapers he kept on the passenger side, and Billy slid in next to him. They headed east and the road hugged the frozen coils of the river for a few miles out of Chaska. They crossed the arched, gently down-sloping Ferry Bridge southbound; the iced river below was blown clean of snow, flat and white-veined like cut quartz. They followed County 83 onto the Sioux reservation. On both sides of the road, fields were lit by the setting sun and hay was mounded evenly through them. The snow had partially melted a few days earlier in a warm snap, and with their bare tops and snow-skirted sides, the haystacks looked like primitive huts. They threw a pattern of long overlapping shadows and the tops of the stacks to the west shone moist and bright with refraction. Jerry didn't know anything about farming, but it struck him as strange that hay was sitting stacked in the fields in midwinter. The symmetry of the mounds reminded him of parts of his hometown – Daly City, California – seen from the highway, with small, single-level white and cream houses laid out in endless rows. Jerry was saving for his first visit home since he had gone into rehab in Minneapolis two years earlier.

Billy directed Jerry to his house, which was set back in some pine woods on an unpaved dead-end road in a cluster of dwellings ranging from trailers to brand-new family homes. Billy's place was a small white ranch house flanked by a satellite dish – which was half as big as the house – and a new red Chevy four-by-four pickup jacked up on knobby tires and a custom suspension, yellow racing stripe down the side. Jerry pulled alongside the truck.

"She's a beaut, ain't she?" said Billy. "And I can't even drive her except around the property. I got my Harley in the garage too, and when spring comes I'm going out of state for a ride where the cops don't know me. You ride, don't you?"

"Yeah, I used to, but I don't have a bike right now." Jerry admired the truck's tires, the tops of which came to his window. "What happened? You lose your license?"

Billy laughed. "Yeah, they said if they catch me behind the wheel again, drunk or sober, they'll put me away for a long time."

"Lucky you got me," said Jerry.

Billy went inside and Jerry waited in the car, engine running in the subzero cold. The sky would soon give up the last of its light. Jerry sat and watched his exhaust blow slowly down over the windshield and spiral off into the pine trees. He lit a cigarette and cracked his window. He thought about his trip home in a couple of months. His parents weren't there anymore his father had driven off a highway overpass a year before Jerry cleaned up. The accident had been spectacular enough to make the local news. Jerry had seen it on a stolen TV with tinfoil rabbit ears in an Oakland squat. The news copter got a perfect shot with the demolished guardrail in the foreground and the flattened smoking Cadillac below it, flipped sunny-side-down. Jerry remembered saying, "Check that shit out," to a roomful of junkies who weren't listening. He didn't find out until the next day whose car it was.

His mother had married a guy who owned a discount department store and moved to Palm Springs. But Jerry's sister and her family were still in Daly City, and he wouldn't mind seeing his one real friend, Miguel, so long as Miguel had his shit somewhat together. Jerry would go in April when the winter business slacked off. By then he would have plenty of money saved for a plane ticket, a rental car, and presents for his sister's kids. He was thinking he might take Betsy if it worked out between them.

Mystic Lake Casino was a short drive from Billy's house. For miles around at night, the spotlights were visible, set in a ring on the roof so the beams formed a giant teepee in the sky. "Biggest Indian casino in the Midwest," said Billy as they pulled into the huge parking lot. "The only one bigger is that one in Connecticut." His voice dropped low and became mock serious. "You want to know how much we make off this thing?"

"Sure," said Jerry.

"Well, total, I don't know. But let's just say I get a very big check every month. Very big," he said, his voice reverential.

"Every month, huh? That must be nice."

"Fucking right, long as you live on the rez. I ain't rich, though."

"How do you figure?"

"Because rich people got a certain attitude. I ain't that. I'm just a regular guy with a shitload of money. It don't mean shit to me. It don't make me think I'm better than you. But I'm glad I have it anyway, know what I mean?" Billy slapped Jerry's shoulder and laughed. The sweet tang of booze wafted Jerry's way.

"I guess I do," Jerry said, laughing with him.

Inside, they walked through the maze of slot machines and blackjack tables. Billy nodded to all the drink girls and a few of them smiled as if they knew him. He raised his hand to a tall Indian pit boss with a waist-length black ponytail, dressed in the blue blazer and gray slacks of management-level employees. "Hey, Julius," Billy said. Julius gave him a grim stare and a small nod. "That's my cousin," Billy said to Jerry. He broke a hundred at the change booth and handed Jerry twenty to play with.

Billy went to a nearby bank of dollar slots and Jerry started playing five-dollar hands of blackjack. The last time he had been in the casino, a month and a half earlier, he had brought Betsy with him. She put twenty dollars into the slots while he won over a hundred at blackjack. She got all worked up, said it made her feel queasy, and vowed never to gamble again.

They had met two weeks before that, when her car was in the shop and she called a cab to take her home from the school where she taught kindergarten. She had moved fast that first night, and now that made him wonder. Jerry had never had any trouble attracting women, but he wasn't used to women of her type. He wondered what this petite blond teacher, who had gone to graduate school, saw in him. He wanted to think it was something he hadn't known he possessed, or hadn't been willing to acknowledge in himself. She seemed crazy about him, but sometimes he thought he was a fling for her, a walk on the wild side before she settled down with Mr. Right. Since he had gotten clean, Jerry's wild side didn't go much past his clothes and hair.

On the way to her place in his cab, her blond curls bouncing in the rearview, Betsy chatted him up about what it was like to be a cabdriver. Near the end of the trip she leaned forward and put her thin forearm over the back of his seat. "Well," she said, "another lonely Friday night. I'm just going to curl up with my cat and watch some movies, I guess."

"That sounds nice," said Jerry.

"What about you?" she asked. "Got big plans for tonight?"

"No, not really. I'll probably just hang at home, too."

"You want to maybe get a couple of movies and watch them together?" Jerry played it cool, like he had been expecting it. In the video store she made plain, innocent suggestions for movies, and he agreed with them.

Partway through the first movie he made a pass at her and they spent half an hour fooling around on the couch. When she started taking off her shirt, Jerry had an unfamiliar impulse to stop her. He pulled his hand from under the shirt. He kissed her again and said, "I want to take you out."

"Right now?"

"No," he sat back and pulled her shirt down, "tomorrow night."

She looked confused. "You mean you don't want to do anything now?"

"Let me take my statement a little further." Her narrow body was across his lap and his hand was around the back of her neck. "I want to come over here and pick you up at seven tomorrow night and take you out to a nice restaurant." He kissed her. "From there we'll go to a movie." He kissed her again, harder. "Then we'll come back here and I'll rip your clothes off."

She stayed silent, staring at him.

"Hey," he said, "if that's not what you want it's all right. If you just want the one night, we can rip our clothes off right now."

She stared at him a second longer and then turned loose a crooked smile he knew he could get hooked on. "No, you just surprised me," she said. "Tomorrow night sounds lovely."

That was the last time he saw that smile. He hadn't managed to surprise her in quite the same way since. Her everyday smile was generic – it pulled the corners of her mouth straight back and thinned her already straight lips – and he imagined it was the smile she gave her students when they completed a pretty collage, or cleaned their play areas nicely. It didn't do much for him. She did have some things he loved, though: freckles spattered all over, dense in the vee of her neck, thinning onto her breasts, and petering out in her shaved white armpits; and she had quirky little hips, even if she didn't really know how to use them. She would learn, he kept telling himself. She was smart without using it against him. And she probably would never lie to him, an idea he was still trying to get used to.

Jerry was fifteen dollars ahead when Billy tapped him on the shoulder.

"Check it out." Billy was holding two large plastic cups filled with silver dollars. "Now we go downtown. Have some real fun."

On the way off the reservation, Billy told Jerry to go to Sultan's, an upscale strip club where his ex-girlfriend worked. He hadn't seen her in a while, he told Jerry. It had ended badly. He wasn't even sure she still worked there.

Jerry eased the car into a turn at fifty and the power steering hummed. It needed some fluid. It was night now, and Jerry thought of the frozen haystacks on both sides of the dark road. He wondered; if he let go of the wheel halfway through the long turn and let the car take its own course into the field, would it thump safely into one of the big mounds of hay, or thread them and slam into the forest on the other side?

"If she's there, I think she'll be glad to see me," said Billy. He paused. "It's probably better if she's not there anyway. We'll have more fun. You're coming in with me, right?"

Jerry thought of Betsy. "I don't know if I want to pay the cover."

"No, no, no, no. Fuck that, man. Everything's on me, food, drinks, cover, everything."

"In that case."

Sultan's was dark and high-ceilinged. Lights flashed around the stage, where a tall brunette was dancing to Aerosmith's "Crazy," slowly liberating herself from a gray business suit. Billy paid their cover charge, then slipped the hulking Scandinavian doorman an extra twenty and said, "Get us a corner table, will you, Sven?"

"Sure, Billy," said the man. His name tag said *Ron*.

Jerry had been in the club once before, with a skinny junkie named Annie. He had met her in rehab and fucked her for about a month after they got out. It had been her idea to come to the strip club. She said she liked looking at the dancers, and looking at her man staring at them. They went to her place afterward and had sex with the lights off, and in the middle of it she asked him if he was imagining that she was one of the dancers. Jerry thought it was what she wanted, so he told the truth, he said yes. That turned out to be the wrong answer, and she pushed him off and said she wanted to talk "about us." He got up, got dressed, and went home. He didn't call her after that. He saw her at an NA meeting a few weeks later and she didn't seem to hold it against him.

A hostess in a mini-tuxedo shirt and black garters led them to their table. Billy tipped her twenty dollars and ordered a bottle of champagne.

"I'll just have a Coke," said Jerry.

"Come on," said Billy. "Have a little nip with me."

"No thanks. Strict policy, never when I'm driving." Jerry didn't see any point in talking about sobriety.

When the waitress brought the drinks, Billy tipped her ten dollars and said, "Is Diana here tonight?"

"I don't think I know her."

"Tall blonde. Her stage name is Cheyenne."

"Oh, Cheyenne. No, she's not here tonight. I haven't seen her around in a while."

They watched the stage dancers, and Billy drank the champagne before starting in on mixed drinks. Dancers crowded around their table wanting to give them private dances, and every so often Billy paid for one. "Private" dances, done on a pedestal placed in front of the customer, cost ten dollars. Billy paid twenty or fifty for each one. Jerry shook his head politely when they asked him. He kept his eyes mainly on the stage, not wanting to stare at Billy's private dances. At one point all the dancers in the club paraded in a chorus line onstage, meant to entice reluctant customers to take their pick.

"Which one do you think is the hottest?" Billy asked.

Jerry was munching on a plate of fried cheese sticks with tomato sauce. He studied the dancers on the stage and picked out a thin, lithe woman with small breasts and perfect legs. She was shaped like Betsy. "That little redhead there is pretty nice looking."

"Her?" said Billy. "Come on. What about all those big titties up there?"

"I got nothing against them. But there's something about that girl I like." Jerry let his eyes stray down the line of dancers and they landed on the only other small-breasted woman there. She had grown her hair and dyed it blond, and put on just enough weight to make her ass worth shaking, but there was no mistaking Annie.

"Okay. I guess I see it," said Billy, and raised his hand to call the waitress over. Billy said to her, "Tell that little redhead there to come over here and bring a friend when she's done onstage."

"On second thought, make it the blonde fourth from the end in the white outfit," Jerry said.

The waitress followed Jerry's eyes. "Okay, that's Nina," she said.

"You heard the man." Billy handed her a ten while searching the stage for Jerry's choice. "Jesus, you like them small titties, don't you?" Billy slipped Jerry a fifty. "Here, this is for her to dance for you."

"You don't need to do that," said Jerry.

"Hey, just take it. But make sure you get at least two songs and some conversation for it. Don't let her short you."

"Hi there." Their table was on a slightly raised area against the wall, and Annie was speaking from the lower level, right next to him, smiling and holding onto the round brass railing. Her see-through teddy was trimmed with fake white fur.

"How are you, Annie?" Jerry smiled.

"I'm good. It's good to see you, Jerry," she said, beaming at him.

She came around the railing and up two steps. Before she sat down she leaned over and kissed his cheek. He put his hand on her shoulder, and she pushed it away gently and said, "No hands in here. It's really strict. The security guys get pissed. And in here I'm Nina." Her face had gained color and a little healthy flesh. Her lips were thin and shapely, forming a shallow M, like a compound bow. She let her solid slender thigh lie along his and touched his forearm when she spoke. She looked over at Billy, who was engrossed in his own dancer. "Hey there, Billy. Long time."

Billy turned toward her and brightened with half-recognition. "Hey. What's up?"

"Not too much. Seen Diana lately?"

"No. She still work here?"

"Off and on," said Annie. Billy's dancer put two fingers on his cheek and turned his head back to her. Annie faced Jerry. "How do you know Billy?" she asked.

Without turning his head, Billy answered for him, "Oh, we go way back, me and Jerry. Ain't that right, buddy?"

"That's right," Jerry said.

"I know Billy's old girlfriend," said Annie. "She's great. She's really crazy about him."

"How long have you been working here?" Jerry asked.

"Oh, a while now. At least a year. You remember we came here together?"

"Yeah, I remember."

"Want me to give you a dance?" She was already on her feet.

Jerry showed her the fifty and said, "This is for you to dance, but only if you say your real name."

She smiled. "You know my real name."

Jerry tucked the bill deep into the front of her G-string, feeling the graze of stubble against the backs of his fingers. "Do it anyway," he said.

A slow song had just started, some pop-metal ballad. She leaned in close and whispered, "*Girlie.*"

It was what he had called her sometimes, as close as they had come to a pet name. Now, whispered in his ear, it electrified him. Her breath flowed down through his body and settled warm and low.

Annie slid the pedestal in front of him and mounted it. She pulled loose the bow on her teddy. She smiled at him and dropped the teddy onto his lap.

"I think about you sometimes," she said, working her hips smoothly in a figure-eight that hinged around her navel. "I was sorry when you left."

Jerry couldn't think of anything to say, so he just glanced up at her face. He wondered if Betsy could learn that with her hips.

She danced for a while longer, then popped the clasp on her bra and slid it off. "You still going to meetings?" she asked.

"Yeah, sometimes," Jerry said. "How about you?"

"No. Not really. I drink sometimes now. Smoke a joint. But I've stayed away from the junk."

"That's good," said Jerry. "I have, too." She leaned in with her hands against the wall and hung her little pears in front of his face, twitching sideways to shake them. When she pushed away from the wall, she arched her back forward and let a nipple slowly brush his upper lip and the tip of his nose. The touch took on a charged aspect in the noisy club. She faced away from him and bent down. She looked at him over her shoulder and slapped her own behind, leaving red finger marks. She bent lower until her head touched her knees and her vulva was clearly outlined against the sheer, tiny G-string. Jerry's pager went off. He waited until the dance was over to check the number.

As Annie sat back down and fastened her bra a twinge crossed her face, something like shyness, as if her modesty was triggered more by dressing than undressing. Her eyelids fluttered.

"I'd better get back to work. Let's stay in touch. When you come back in, ask for Nina." She stood up.

Jerry felt the warmth from her body on the seat next to him. "Thanks for the dance, Nina."

She kissed his cheek. She whispered, "I'm in the book under Lejeune," and stepped away. "Or just come back here," she said over her shoulder. "I'm here every weekend."

"Okay," Jerry said.

She sauntered away, swaying like a runway model, and leaned over into a group of suits across the room.

On his way to the pay phone, Jerry decided to tell Betsy where he was. She would surely ask, and he was working on personal honesty.

"Are you coming over soon?" she asked.

"Probably not. I'm still with this guy."

"Where are you, a bar? I hear music."

"Yeah," he said, "we're at Sultan's, downtown."

"The strip bar?"

"Yeah, well, this is where he wants to be. He paid my cover. It's better than waiting in the car."

"I'll bet." She paused. "Are you looking at the women?"

"Well. There they are, right in front of me."

"Do you like looking at them?" Her voice took on a wheedling, falsely cheerful lilt that didn't hide her disapproval.

Jerry sighed. "Come on. What am I supposed to do, hate it? I'm not going to close my eyes while I'm in here. It's no big deal. Really."

"Okay, okay," she said. He knew she'd have more to say later. "Do you still want to come over?"

"Sure, when I get done. You want to leave the key under the mat for me?"

"Yeah, I'll do that. Wake me up and kiss me."

"I will."

"Be good."

"I will."

"You know that chick, huh?" Billy asked when Jerry got back to the table.

"Yeah, I used to hang out with her a while back. Before she worked here."

"We come here looking for my old girlfriend and end up finding yours. Ain't that a trip?" Billy smiled and shook his head drunkenly, a little sadly.

Most of the drunks Jerry dealt with in his job served only to reinforce his sobriety with their ugliness and helplessness, but something about Billy, beyond the biker clothes and long hair, reminded Jerry of himself. Something in the way he drank: starting out festive, his goodwill contagious, then just putting one drink in front of the next. Jerry imagined joining Billy in drinking, and instead of the fear and disgust which that thought should have brought, he felt only hard-boiled nostalgia. For the first time in about half a year the slow, muscular body of his addiction began to stir in him – heat uncoiling in his chest. It was a shrewd cousin of panic. His eyes narrowed. He remembered his conversation with Betsy and became suddenly annoyed.

There was a lull in the music. Billy was finishing a drink. He had withdrawn steadily, brooding behind long-ashed cigarettes. He reached forward and stubbed one out in the ashtray. His head snapped up and he said abruptly, "We gotta go."

Jerry said, "Okay, whenever you say."

"I say now. We gotta get back to the rez." He looked as if he had been startled from a nightmare.

In the car on the way down Billy was restless, chain-smoking.

"It's probably nothing," Billy said, "but sometimes I get these feelings. Like something ain't right." He rested his elbow on the lip of the door and flicked his ash out an inch of open window. The sleeve zipper of his motorcycle jacket clicked against the glass and smoke from his mouth rushed for the opening.

"Have these feelings been right in the past?" asked Jerry.

"They're always right. But it might not be anything serious."

"I hope not," Jerry said.

Billy fell silent. Jerry steered the car down the cold highway. He thought about home. Lately he had been sustaining himself through the long workdays, which began and ended in darkness, with thoughts of California. He had his trip figured out. He would see his sister and her family, showing up well dressed and flush with cash, and with charm and gifts he would make up for his past delinquencies. What friends he had left whose lives weren't too deep in the crapper would be impressed with the new Jerry, sober and sporting a beautiful, intelligent girlfriend. Yes, it would be perfect if Betsy went with him. People would be more likely to trust the transformation with her there as evidence.

When they turned into the dirt cul-de-sac where Billy lived, red and blue lights were playing brightly across the trees and snow from the driveway of a small house at the end. A cop car sat there. The flashing lights making no sound made Jerry feel deaf for a second.

"No, Jesus," said Billy. "Pull up there. Pull *up there!*"

Jerry pulled the cab up behind the cop car on the road and Billy jumped out. He ran across the trampled snow on the lawn, nearly falling at every step, his legs bowed out wide like a toddler's. He went in the front door of the tiny, boxlike house. There was no one else outside. Jerry switched on the radio and America was singing, "*After three days . . . in the desert sun . . .*" He had missed the first two days.

Billy came running out of the house, ripped open the car door, and fell into the front seat. "The hospital in Shakopee!" he said.

Jerry turned the car around and headed back for the main road. "Is someone sick?"

"My grandmother. Jesus, get me there." Billy fumbled for a cigarette and lit it.

America was still singing. Jerry reached over and snapped the radio off.

At the Emergency entrance, Billy told him to wait and got out. Four people were smoking outside the entrance, and they greeted Billy and hugged him and spoke to him. Billy ran inside. One of the group, a woman of about forty-five with softly creased, beautiful features, walked over to the cab. Jerry rolled his window down.

"Are you waiting to get paid?" she asked.

"No, not really. He asked me to wait."

"Well, he's better off with us now. I can pay you whatever he owes and you can take off." She took a wallet from her coat pocket.

"I'd feel bad leaving. He told me to wait for him here. He's already given me plenty of money."

She sighed. "I'll go in and talk to him. I think he's going to want to stay." She walked inside. The doorway was empty now, the others finished with their smokes. Jerry waited. Billy and the woman appeared on the other side of the sliding glass door. She was speaking and he was shaking his head and backing away. The door slid open and Billy turned and walked outside. She followed him, screaming his name. As he came toward the cab, she grabbed the sleeve of his jacket and tried to pull him back. He bellowed like a small child and yanked his arm away. He climbed into the passenger seat.

The woman spoke through the window. "Billy. Think of what Grandma'd want. Don't leave her. Stay with us now."

Billy just shook his head, his eyes closed tightly.

She came to Jerry's window and he rolled it down again.

"Take care of him," she said. She had a bill folded in her hand and she pushed it at Jerry. "Don't leave him anywhere. Stay with him and get him home, please."

"Don't take that money," said Billy.

Jerry shook his head at the money and pushed her fist out the window, saying, "Don't worry. I'll get him home."

They went to an all-night diner. Billy told Jerry his grandmother had died in the ambulance.

"That old lady was the one who taught me everything. Her and my big sister. She taught me the old language, she told me stories of her childhood, and I was off looking at titties when she died. She was Grandma Burns. I should have been there."

Jerry didn't know what to say. He settled for "There was nothing you could have done."

"She was always there for me," Billy said. "I could have been there for her."

The diner was a low brick building called Boogie's Kitchen. One wide, friendly waitress worked both the counter and the tables. Bars were still open, so the place wasn't crowded. They sat in a booth near a window and ordered breakfast. Jerry dug into his omelet hungrily, and Billy drank coffee and pushed his fried eggs around the plate, taking a few bites of the sausage links. He talked about his grandmother, his childhood. His mother had run off when he was an infant. His father had enlisted the help of his own mother to raise the two children. She had cared for them when their father was at work, and sometimes he was away for long periods of time on construction crews in far-off states. This had been before the casino. Billy's grandmother had forced them to learn some of their native language, practicing with them after school. "I always got into trouble, and she was the only one who never held it against me. When I came back from my time upstate she never said a word about it, never once."

As if on cue a squad car pulled into the diner's parking lot. Two cops got out and walked in the door. They were sitting down at the counter when one of them looked to the far end where Billy and Jerry sat. He approached their table.

"Oh, great," said Billy, not far enough under his breath for Jerry's comfort. "Fucking pigs."

The cop stopped in front of their booth. He had a thick blond mustache. "Hi, Billy," he said.

Billy looked up at him, then silently back down at his plate.

"I'm sorry about your grandmother. She was a real great lady."

Billy nodded his head and grunted.

"You're not driving, are you?"

Billy sighed angrily, his fork gripped tight and facing menacingly upward.

"No," said Jerry quickly. "I am. That's my cab out there."

The cop nodded. "Good." He paused a moment. That loaded cop pause. "Stay out of trouble tonight, okay, Billy?"

Billy dipped his head lower and shoved his plate into the middle of the table. "Leave me alone," he muttered.

The cop laid a hand on Billy's shoulder before walking away.

Billy paid the check and told Jerry to take him to a bar in Shakopee, just up the road.

"I know it's not my place," said Jerry, "but don't you think it would be good to head home now?"

"I can call another cab if you want me to."

"No, that's all right. My girlfriend's asleep by now anyway."

"Good," said Billy. He peeled another hundred from his roll and gave it to Jerry. "Here," he said, "that other one's run out by now, I guess."

McNeely's had its sign painted in Irish green, the interior small and dark and publike except for the bright booth in the back corner that sold pull-tab lottery tickets and the Black Crowes blasting from the stereo. Billy took the only empty stool at the bar and Jerry stood next to him. The bartender knew Billy by name and served him his drink quickly.

"What'll you have?" the bartender asked Jerry.

"Just a Coke."

"This is my buddy Jerry," Billy said to the bartender. "He's driving me home tonight."

"That's nice of you," said the bartender. He slid Jerry's Coke across the bar. "On the house for designated drivers."

A fat, gray-bearded man built like a small bear swaggered over from a table near the back and slapped Billy on the shoulder. "Billy boy!"

"Don't touch me, Karl," Billy said, looking over his shoulder at the man. "I ain't in the mood to talk to you."

"What are you talking about?" the man asked.

"I just ain't in the mood to talk to somebody who fired me right now." Billy turned away from the man and put his elbows on the bar, spread apart as if expecting trouble.

"Fired you?" The man laughed. "Billy, that's ancient history. I thought we'd forgot about that."

"No, Karl. *You* forgot about that. I pretended to forget, and I ain't in the mood right now. So fuck off."

"Fuck *off*?" The man puffed out his powerful chest.

Jerry took a step between them. "Listen, his grandmother just died, okay? Maybe you could cut him a break." The man was half a foot shorter than Jerry, but solid. His was the kind of fat that hid strength.

"Grandma Burns? She died?" The man stepped back. "Jesus, Billy, come on. I'm sorry about that."

Billy finished his drink. "Fuck off, Karl," he said without looking back.

Karl stood steaming there for a moment, then turned and moved off shaking his head. "Fuck *you*."

Billy ordered another drink, but the bartender had seen the confrontation and cut him off. Billy pleaded with him, but the man stood his ground. Then Karl was back, suddenly there, with his hands on his hips, behind Billy.

"No, Billy," he said. "You don't get to talk to me that way. Your grandmother was a friend of mine, you know she was. You don't get to tell me to fuck off after I hired you when you didn't have no experience. And the only reason I kept you on for as long as I did was out of loyalty to your old man. Just because you got money comin' out your ass now don't give you the right to shit on me. You never did nothin' but cause your family trouble."

Billy spun on his stool, already swinging. His feet hit the floor and he lurched toward Karl, who stepped away from the punch and put his forearm in Billy's neck, slamming him to the floor. Karl hit Billy's face once, just a pop to stun him out of resistance. Jerry put his hand on Karl's shoulder to pull him off, and the big man whirled and stood quicker than Jerry would have thought possible and pinned Jerry against the bar, one hand on his throat, one cocked back in a fist.

"You want some too?" Karl rasped, his eyes wild with booze and adrenaline.

Jerry was ready to back down, but Karl's hand tightened on his throat, cutting off his air, and the older man's teeth were clenched and bared. Jerry had learned never to suppress an impulse in a fight, and he hit the side of Karl's left eye with an elbow-punch. Karl released Jerry's throat and shuffled two steps back like a man doing what he's told. His hand went to his eye, and Jerry put a boot in his balls. Karl knelt, croaking.

Billy was getting to his feet, and Jerry dragged him out the door, one arm around his waist.

In the cab on the way back to the reservation, Billy was quiet for a while, but as they pulled onto the road leading to the houses he let out a low groan, followed by a little yelp of pain, and banged his fist against the door.

"I got to get away from here," Billy said. "Tomorrow. I got to get down to Mankato. I got friends there. I'll give you three hundred bucks to take me there and another three hundred to pick me up when I come back. Unless you want to stay down there with me for a few days. My friends wouldn't mind. They party. They have a great time. They all ride."

"Sure, I could take you down there."

"We'll go in the morning. I can't stay here."

"I'll give you my pager number. You can beep me when you want to go."

"No. You come here at nine in the morning. I'll be ready to go." Billy pointed to a larger house across the street from his. "Drop me off there. That's my dad's house."

Jerry pulled into the driveway and shut off his lights. There were lights on in the house, giving it warmth among the other dark homes. He pulled a pen and a card from the visor over his head and wrote down his name and pager number. "Here," he said. "Call me if you want to change the plan."

"But you'll be here, right? Nine A.M.?"

"Yeah," said Jerry, "I'll be here."

"Thanks." Billy got out. Before shutting the door, he leaned back in, his feet shuffling to keep his balance. "I'll tell you something," he said. He wiped blood from his lip. "You don't ever want to see old Karl again."

"Okay."

Before he got off the reservation, Jerry stopped at a convenience store where they sold tax-free cigarettes. When he stepped out of the store, he slapped the pack against his palm and lit one. He let the cold air deep into himself along with the smoke. His cheeks started to ache. In front of him the car was idling. His nerves were still raw from the fight. It felt good, in a way that he had forgotten about, and he tilted his head back. The cold had expelled every trace of vapor from the atmosphere, and the sky was crazed with stars. He was a warm speck on the frozen prairie. It occurred to him that if he stayed there, he'd freeze solid very quickly. Maybe he had already begun to. He stood and smoked until he began to shiver.

Across the roof of the taxi, in the corner of the lot, he saw a pay phone set low with a long cord so it could be used from inside a car. He climbed in and pulled up to it. He finished his cigarette, put it out, then lowered his window, picked up the receiver, and punched 411. "Minneapolis," he said. "Yes. Lejeune. Anne Lejeune." He wrote the number down on a card with no name and tucked it into his wallet.

Betsy was asleep when Jerry got there. He undressed in the bathroom and slipped into the bedroom carrying his clothes. He stood quietly for a minute, his eyes adjusting to the darkness, until he could see her breathing form under the peach-colored duvet, which looked white in the moonlight from the window. Her cat was curled on the bed next to her, and he picked it up and dropped it on the floor. It stretched and jumped onto a chair in the corner and was sleeping again.

He stole into bed and lay facing the back of her neck. A few locks of hair streaked the smooth skin there, and the rest fell back in a tangle on the pillow. The top of her left ear caught the moon. He was swept up for a second, taken with her. He imagined growing old with her. He imagined being someone else. He stroked her neck, pressed his lips to her shoulder, and she took a deep breath. She moaned, turned over, and mumbled, "Everything okay?"

"Yeah, baby."

Her eyes stayed closed, her breathing even.

"I love you, Jerry."

"Sleep now," he said.

The next morning Jerry got up at eight and dressed to go. He had vague memories of drug-filled dreams. Betsy woke up as he was putting on his jeans. She yawned and stretched. One slender arm reached back and straightened up over the headboard, ending in a sleepy little fist. She was so beautiful, so out of place in his life. Jerry turned away from her and sat on the edge of the bed to put on his boots. She asked him where he was going.

"Work," he said.

"I thought you were going to take the day off with me."

"I was." He was having trouble getting the second boot pulled on. "But this guy said he'd pay me six hundred dollars to take him to Mankato and back. So I'm going to pick him up."

"The same guy from last night?"

"Yeah."

"I don't like him," she said.

"How can you not like him? You don't know him."

"He kept you away from me last night." She reached and hooked her hand into the back of his jeans and yanked as if to hold him back. "He took you to see naked ladies. And he's taking you away from me again today. Come to think of it," she dragged herself over and lay her cheek along his thigh, "I really hate this guy."

"Well, I guess I can understand that," said Jerry. Her cheek was right where Annie's bare thigh had touched him. He slid a hand behind him, unhooked her hand from his belt, and stood up.

"Don't go," she said.

"I can't turn down this kind of money right now," said Jerry. He was suddenly angry at her. She let him finish dressing in silence.

When he had his jacket and wool hat on, he sat back down on the bed and touched her shoulder. She turned onto her back and sat up, holding the sheet over her chest. "Please." The look in her eyes was one he'd never seen before. She was testing him.

"Okay, listen," he said. "This guy's been through a lot. I promised I'd pick him up. I'll just drive down there and tell him I can't do it. Okay?"

"It's all right. You need the money. Go ahead."

"I'm not going. I want to be with you."

"I don't want to hold you back. Don't worry about it."

"Jesus Christ. Come on." He stood up and stepped to the bedroom door, his anger turning over on itself. "I'll be back in an hour or two."

Betsy sighed and nodded, looking at him. Her arms were crossed, and the crooked smile crept across her face. She dropped the sheet to her thighs. "I'll be here."

Insulating cloud cover had moved in, and the morning was less cold than the previous night, the temperature now just above zero. He didn't let the car warm up, and when he eased off down the street the engine sounded raspy as it struggled to circulate the congealed oil. He stopped for gas at a station by the highway entrance. A tanker truck was backed up to the pumps, and the driver waved him off. He pulled up by the door and went in. The counterman was old and shiny-faced, and his black hair looked dyed above his gray eyebrows.

"How long till I can get gas?" Jerry asked.

"Oh, a few minutes yet." The man rubbed one drooping cheek with his fingers thoughtfully, calculating. "Six or seven, maybe."

Jerry bought a pint of steering fluid and listened to the car's running engine suck it up as he poured it in. He pulled out and drove around the block taking the turns tightly, testing the steering. Wind whistled in the imperfect seal of his door. When he came around, the tanker was pulling out.

He had forgotten his gloves at Betsy's, and the pump wouldn't hold itself open, so he alternated hands. It was a big gas tank, and by the time he finished, both hands were completely numb. He went inside and paid for the gas, along with a Styrofoam cup of coffee.

Back in the car, he flipped open the tab on the lid of the coffee and took a sip; warmth spread through his chest. He lit a cigarette. The first drag sent a wave of comfort through his system and he took another quickly to boost it. It felt as only the first cigarette of the day can. He sat for a moment with his two substances. He thought of what the first hit of junk used to feel like when he was strung out, especially when he had thought to save himself a bump for the morning. The best first cigarette was only a feeble imitation of that.

The highway on the way south was not crowded on a Saturday morning, and the farther he got from the city the more empty it became. He began to feel his hands again as the car warmed up inside. He didn't turn on the radio, drinking in instead the hum of the snow tires on dry pavement and the deep growl of the V-8. The light from the overcast sky was diffuse, graying everything like an invisible mist. Suburbs slid past, strip malls, flat, frozen fields. If he stayed on it, this road would take him all the way to Mexico. He wondered how he would make his lease payment to the cab company on Monday, if he was in Mankato with Billy. The taxi rode up onto the bridge, and he tried to feel the exact moment when the gentle arch reached its peak, but then he was beyond it; as he came down the other side, the river passed under him, white and serpentine and hard, and, somewhere below feet of ice, moving.

HEAPED EARTH
David Leavitt

To celebrate her husband's latest movie, a biography of Franz Liszt starring the much-admired John Ray, Jr., Lilia Wardwell wanted to throw a party. The studio had high hopes that the film might win the Oscar that year; *Ben-Hur* had won the year before, and the word was that this time something more intimate might take the prize, so a party was just the thing. The theme, she decided, would be Romanticism. A pianist, done up in Liszt's soutane, would play wonderful music while waiters in nineteenth-century livery circulated with trays of hors d'oeuvres. Also, in addition to the usual Hollywood crowd, she would invite Stravinsky and his wife, Vera.

She called her husband at the studio and said, "Frank, I need a pianist for the party. Any ideas?"

"I'll see what I can do," he answered. As it happened, there was a pianist around the studio, an immigrant called Kusnezov, who, people said, could play any song without the music, just by hearing it hummed. Whenever a piano scene was required, it was Kusnezov's hands that were filmed; in the Liszt movie his hands were substituted for those of John Ray, Jr.

From the associate producer, Wardwell got Kusnezov's number. He expected he would have to do some prodding, as in his experience artist types tended to be sensitive. Instead, however, Kusnezov proved to be extremely cordial, and having first inquired with delicacy as to his fee, agreed instantly to the job – providing, if it was no inconvenience, that he be paid in advance, and in cash. From this Wardwell deduced that he either gambled, drank, or had an ex-wife pressing him for alimony.

At seven o'clock on the evening of the party, Kusnezov, as instructed, arrived at the Wardwells' and knocked at the service entrance. In the kitchen a dozen or so waiters were fighting their way into tight suits from the studio's costume bank, while the cook and her assistants spooned caviar onto toast points, cut sandwiches into the shapes of the card suites, and emptied canned hearts of palm onto silver platters. Having first explained who he was to a man in butler's livery, Kusnezov waited quietly by the refrigerator until Mrs. Wardwell appeared: a woman of heft, with a shelflike bosom and béchamel-colored hair. Her perfume commingled perversely with the cooking smells. "Mr. Kusnezov, so glad to meet you," she said, offering a moisturized hand, and gave him the once-over. His appearance worried her. After all, though he was wearing the requisite soutane, Kusnezov – it could not be denied – was old. When he leaned forward to kiss her hand, his breath smelled of liquor. Also, Liszt (and John Ray, Jr.) had those wonderful, Samson-like locks, whereas Kusnezov was mostly bald, with just a few watery hairs brushed forward over his pate; hardly what she'd envisioned when she'd planned the party.

Still, she was determined to be game, and clasping his hand in hers, took him into the living room, which was harpshaped, sweeping, with ribbed walls. "I'm told the acoustics are sublime," she said, leading him across the polished floor to the piano. Most of the furniture – Scandinavian, of light wood and leather – had been pushed up against the walls. As for the glossy white piano, it stood on a platform before a row of louvered floor-to-ceiling windows, through the glass of which Kusnezov could see a blue swimming pool refracting the sunset, a barbecue pit, and an array of houses in crisp shades of pink and green spilling down the hills toward an ocean you could still make out in those days before smog.

They stepped up onto the platform. "I trust our humble instrument will be to your liking," Mrs. Wardwell said, positioning herself beside the piano like a soprano. "Do sit. It's a Steinway, of course. My husband wanted a cheaper brand, but I said, 'Frank, Steinway is the instrument of the immortals.'"

"And do you play yourself?" Kusnezov asked, adjusting, with a finicky backward motion of the hands, the height of the white leather stool.

"Not seriously, I'm afraid. Still, I do enjoy tinkling out a bit of Chopin now and then . . . Oh, I had the tuner up this morning."

Having first wiped his hands, which were slippery with her moisturizer, onto his handkerchief, Kusnezov sat down and played a scale.

"A lovely tone," he said. "Not too bright."

"Fine. As for the music, as I'm sure my husband explained, it should be romantic, in keeping with the film. Still, this is a party, so we don't want everyone getting down in the dumps, do we?"

"No, Madame."

"So nothing dreary. I would be most grateful."

He bowed his head.

"Oh, haven't you brought any music?"

"There is no need, Madame."

"Of course you're welcome to use any of our scores. My daughter Elise can turn pages."

"There is no need, Madame."

"Fine." She rubbed her hands together. "Well, the guests should be arriving in half an hour or so. Oh, would you like a drink? Burt" – she signaled the bartender – "get Mr. Kusnezov a drink. What will you have?"

"A whiskey and soda. Straight up."

"A whiskey and soda, Burt. And now if you'll excuse me, I must check on things in the kitchen."

He nodded. She left. Burt brought Kusnezov his drink, which he guzzled fast. Smiling, Burt mixed him a second one.

The doorbell rang. The man in butler's livery admitted a group of five into the foyer, all dear friends of Mrs. Wardwell whom she had asked to come early, to "break the ice." Sitting at the piano, Kusnezov played some Chopin waltzes. The next guest to arrive was Lee Remick. And then Mrs. Wardwell strode in, and Mr. Wardwell, who had been drinking alone in his study, and their daughter Elise, who scowled through thick glasses. Everyone except Elise chatted amiably, Mrs. Wardwell allowing her gaze occasionally to rest with approval upon the figure of Kusnezov, who had moved from the waltzes to Liszt's late evocation of the fountains at the Villa d'Este.

After forty minutes, he took a break. Burt mixed him a third whiskey and soda. In the meantime John Ray, Jr., had arrived, an event that had provoked the assembled to burst into a round of applause. Square-jawed, from Texas, the young actor had large hands and thick blond hair, which, to his regret, he had recently been forced to cut in preparation for his next role, as a navy lieutenant. Although his official escort for the evening was a lesbian starlet named Lorna Baskin, he had made a secret arrangement to rendezvous at the party with his lover of the moment, the young professor of musicology at UCLA who had served as musical advisor for the Liszt movie. As instructed, the professor came alone, and late. Kusnezov was by now taking his second break. Most of the guests – Hollywood socialites and actors, though alas no Stravinskys – were out on the patio. In the living room a group of studio executives took advantage of the lull to share Cuban cigars and cut deals. As for Kusnezov, he was leaning against the bar, talking with Burt about the dog races.

The professor asked Burt for a screwdriver. He was a Bostonian of thirty-five, new in Southern California, having taken his position at UCLA only the year before. In the weirdly artificial atmosphere of the party he appeared himself to be in costume, with his bow tie and Eastern tweeds. His face melancholic (for he did not see his lover), he peered out the door at the humming crowd before strolling over to examine the piano. After a few minutes Kusnezov stepped past him and took his place. They nodded at each other.

Kusnezov started to play – a Chopin nocturne in C minor that as it happened was one of the professor's favorites. He sat down to listen. All at once, and quickly, the music carried him away from that ample California living room with its ribbed walls, and into a small house, a winter house, where a coal fire was burning. There was grief in the air, not fresh, but a few years old, its presence as vague as the smell of cooking. No one dared address it. No one dared acknowledge the sprite of memory that danced in the heavy, soot-thickened air. Then the professor smiled, for now he felt sure of something he had long suspected: that Chopin had written this nocturne for a sister who had died in childhood. In Kusnezov's hands, the supposition became a certainty.

Burt was silent. Even the executives fell silent. As for the professor, he was remembering a poem by Oscar Wilde, written also in memory of a sister dead in childhood, a sister buried:

> Tread lightly, she is near
> Under the snow,
> Speak gently, she can hear
> The daisies grow.

From the patio John Ray, Jr., entered the room. He was walking with John Wayne. Their loud conversation dimmed only once they recognized that people were listening to the music, at which point they stopped and stood by the door, both smiling respectfully.

The professor looked at John Ray, Jr. John Ray, Jr., looked over the professor.

> Peace, peace, she cannot hear
> Lyre or sonnet,
> All my life's buried here,
> Heap earth upon it.

The prelude ended. No one applauded. Once again, Kusnezov got up and got a drink, as did John Ray, Jr., John Wayne, and the professor. The lovers did not acknowledge each other.

Only once the two actors had returned to the patio did the professor dare approach Kusnezov. His eyes revealed his knowledge; that he had heard; that he had recognized.

"That was magnificent," he said.

"Yes, it was," Kusnezov answered simply.

"May I ask you a question?" The professor stepped closer. "Who are you?"

"Who was I, you mean. That is the apposite point."

"You mean before the war . . ."

Kusnezov shook his head. "The war is not to blame. I came to live in this country thirty years ago."

"Then what happened?"

"What happened? What happened?" The pianist laughed. And meanwhile Jane Russell had come into the room; Mrs. Wardwell had also come into the room, bringing with her a loud, invasive odor of perfume. She shot Kusnezov a glance, the meaning of which was obvious: *Get back to work, and no more of the depressing stuff.*

"I must go," he said to the professor. And putting down his empty glass, he returned to the piano.

ACCORDION
Aleksandar Hemon

1

The horses are trotting stolidly and the coach is bobbing steadily, and Archduke Franz Ferdinand's eyelids are listlessly sliding down his corneas. The weighty eyelids are about to reach the bottom, but then the horse on the left raises its tail – embarrassingly similar to the tussock on the Archduke's resplendent helmet – and the Archduke can see the horse's anus slowly opening, like a camera aperture.

The coach is passing between two tentacles of an ostensibly exultant throng: they wave little flags and cheer in some monkey language ("Would it be called Bosnian?" wonders the Archduke). Children with filthy faces and putrid, cracked teeth run up and down between the legs of the crowd. The Archduke recognizes the secret police, with their impeccable mustaches, with stern, black hats that look clearly grotesque among bloodred fezzes – much like topsy-turvy flowerpots with short tassels – and women with little curtains over their faces. The secret police stand stiff, throwing skillful side glances, waiting for the opportunity to show off their alertness. The left horse is dropping turds, like dark, deflated tennis balls. The shallow, obscure river behind the back of the Archduke's foreign, cunning denizens is reeking of rotten sauerkraut. In the coach ahead, the Archduke can see only the top of General Potiorek's ceremonial helmet: the elaborate tussock is fluttering annoyingly. He decides to get rid of Potiorek as soon as he assumes the throne.

The Archduke looks at the Archduchess and sees her face in a cramp of disgust. *It would be very unseemly if she starts vomiting in front of all these people*, he thinks. He touches her (cool) hand, carefully trying to convey his manly concern, but she turns to him with the unchanged sickened face and the Archduke quickly recoils.

The coach rolls between two cordons of smirking people waving ridiculous, tiny flags, and vapid, marble-faced secret policemen. The Archduke then sees a man with an accordion stretched over his chest. The man is smiling, sincerely, it appears – he may even be delighted. He doesn't seem to be playing the accordion, just holding it. The Archduke's gaze breaks through the crowd and he can now see the man's strong arms and the accordion belts squeezing the man's strong forearms. He can see the beige-and-black keyboard and he can see that one of the keys is missing; he can see the dark rectangle in place of the missing key. The coach passes the man and the Archduke thinks he can sense the man's gaze on his back. He's tempted to turn around, but that would obviously be unseemly. The Archduke wonders about these strange people, about this man who doesn't seem to possess any hatred toward him and the Empire (not yet, at least) and he begins to wonder, *what happened to that key?* How would "Liebestod" sound with one of the notes never being played? Maybe that man never played that key; maybe he'll never play that note in his entire life. *Strange people*, thinks the Archduke. He decides to tell the Archduchess about the man with the accordion, perhaps it could cheer her up.

"There's a man with an accordion," announces the Archduke into the Archduchess's ear. The Archduchess winces, as though he's delirious.

"What? What are you talking about?"

He leans toward her: "There's a man . . ."

But then he sees a pistol and a straight, tense arm behind it and a young, scrawny man at the end of the arm, with a thin mustache and fiery eyes. He sees the pistol retching and bursts of light at the pistol's mouth. He feels something pushing him against the seat and then it punches him in his belly and all the sounds have disappeared.

Besides the quick-swelling, incomprehensible fear that he can do nothing about and tries to ignore, all he can think of is an evening at

Mayerling: The Archduchess played "Leibestod" on the piano, much too slowly, while he sat in the armchair by the fireplace, feeling the heat on the left side of his back. He wasn't listening to the Archduchess, he was struggling not to doze off, and then he had a rapid thought – which he immediately suppressed – oh my God, how vernacular and ungraceful was the Archduchess's beauty and how unbearably vapid and stupid "Leibestod" really was.

He wants to tell her he's painfully sorry, now, but the Archduchess, her face frozen in repulsion, the Archduchess is already dead.

2

Most of this story is a consequence of irresponsible imagination and shameless speculation. (A case in point: The Archduke died in a car, which took a wrong turn and then virtually parked in front of the assassin, whose pants were soaked with urine.) Parts of it, however, washed against my shores, having floated on a sea of history books, dotted with islands of black-and-white photographs. A considerable part reached me after it passed through tunnels and mazes of the family memories and legends. For the man with the accordion was none other than my great-grandfather, freshly arrived in Bosnia from Ukraine. He was in Sarajevo, for the first and only time in his life, to obtain papers for the promised piece of land – the bait that brought him to Bosnia – from the Austro-Hungarian empire. He was a peasant and had never been in a big city. The fuss and giddiness that he encountered in the city blessed by the Archduke's visit (and then cursed by his death) overwhelmed him, so much so that he spent nearly a fifth of his savings to buy the accordion from a Gypsy at the city market. By the time he got back to his new home, on a hill called Vucijak, the First World War was well on its way. He was recruited within a couple of weeks and went to Galicia to fight for the Empire, where he died of dysentery. The accordion outlived him by some fifty cacophonic years, losing a few more keys along the way. It met its demise with a discordant accordion sight, after my blind uncle Teodor (a hand grenade had exploded in his hands when he was six) threw himself on the bed where the accordion helplessly lay. Uncle Teodor is now stuck in the Serb part of Bosnia. Most of my family is scattered across Canada. This story was written in Chicago (where I live) on the subway, after a long day of arduous work as a parking assistant, A.D. 1996.

OVER BOY
Michael Lowenthal

The cab dropped Keith at Campus, the club halfway between Harvard and MIT where students and their admirers congregated. At nineteen he'd been a regular, but for years now he'd disallowed himself the club, self-conscious of his tenure-track appearance. A shovel-faced bouncer demanded ID from skittish boys, and Keith remembered, from his precocious past, the terror of being carded and denied. Had that been less or more unsettling than his current fear, of not being carded? Mercifully, or perhaps mockingly, the bouncer asked for his license. Keith produced it and the doorman waved him through.

A more scrupulous bouncer would have noted that today was Keith's twenty-ninth birthday. This morning, shaving, Keith had stared glumly into the bathroom mirror. His own reflection had once been a potent masturbation aid – the waifish torso, the glockenspiel abs – but now he had to admit he was no longer his own type. His stomach wasn't fat, but bereft of definition, as uninspiring as a sea without surf. Hair had begun to emigrate from the home shores of his scalp to the new worlds of neck and shoulder blades.

"Come on," said Margaret, a nurse he worked with, when Keith complained at lunch of his failing looks. "You're not even thirty. You're just hitting your prime."

"It's different when you're gay," Keith explained. "It's like Olympic figure skating. The prodigies get younger and younger, and we're forced into early retirement."

Pleased with his witticism, he repeated it at his birthday dinner party. Only two men of the dozen present chuckled.

"We don't all retire," said the host, a balding architect named Mitch. "Some of us turn pro."

Now everybody laughed.

For Keith's friends, the indignities of growing older seemed to be mitigated by the aging of their attractions. They might still appreciate the occasional college freshman in all his gleaming mint-condition glory, but the men they realistically sought and partnered with were graying and sagging just as they were.

Initially Keith had hoped that, just as his childhood yen for grape juice had yielded to cabernet, his sexual tastes, too, might mature. But his hope foundered on a lesson from medical school: the greater venturesomeness of an adult's palate was but a measure of how many taste buds had died. Keith didn't just happen to find youth beautiful. For him, who had been a young beauty, beauty *was* youth, and as he drifted farther from his own ideal, he felt doomed. If he couldn't find himself attractive anymore, how could he trust anyone else who claimed to?

It had been a year and a half since his last boyfriend: Andy, a twenty-year-old concierge at the Park Plaza for whom pleasing others was as instinctual as swallowing. They'd had four months of puppyish fun, but the day Andy found a gray hair on Keith's chest and plucked it with scientific curiosity, like an exotic orchid or heirloom fruit, Keith executed a swift, preemptive dump. Since then, not even a one-night stand (although there had been, in the park last summer, a dispiriting five-minute kneel). He tried the bars, but in his newly unconfident state, every word he spoke was inflected with doubt. He felt like someone who, after years of living abroad, returned home rusty at his own native tongue.

Which is why he should simply have gone to bed. Or accepted Margaret's invitation for a nightcap. But he wanted to take advantage of this last birthday when, if he told people the occasion, and they asked how old he was, he could truthfully say a number starting with twenty. On top of that, it was Groundhog Day – or would become so at midnight – and Keith imagined that by venturing into the dance floor's strobing sun and gauging what effect his presence had, he might predict his emotional weather. How much longer would this winter go on?

* * *

Campus smelled like any club – cigarettes and sour, spilled beer – but layered within that was a more adolescent, locker-room musk of overstraining bodies. Keith checked his coat and readied for the plunge. He avoided the Eighties Room, where the tunes of his teenage years were served up with irony to kids who'd been singing "Old MacDonald" when the tracks were released. Instead he detoured to the lounge, where guys in baseball caps flopped impassively on couches. One sucked a cigarette, then puffed the single sardonic O of a smoke ring. Another blew a bubble of purple chewing gum, then pinched it off and passed it to a friend.

No one seemed to notice him except two thirtysomething men in matching blue tuxedos – what on earth? Standing against the wall with starched and benevolent expressions, they could have been chaperons at the senior prom, and they stared at Keith as if they knew something about him, something perhaps even he didn't know.

Escaping their gaze, he made his way toward the main dance floor, through that odd liminal zone of competing sound systems, like the salt point where a freshwater river gives way to sea, and then past it until he was drenched by repetitive house music. The recessed dance floor was surrounded by a railing at which the non-dancing spectators stood, looking variously predatory and afraid. Keith elbowed his way into a spot and tried to affect an expression halfway in between. There must have been a drink special, because all along the railing, cups filled with some periwinkle liquid glowed in the pulsing light like hokey, outsized shamanic crystals. The comparison seemed apt to Keith, since everyone here, he suspected, including him, relied on a kind of primitive superstition. If I wear my lucky tank top, the boy-gods will smile on me. If I sip my drink before I look, he'll look back.

Beneath the clouds of disco smoke, guys danced with the fervency of a jungle tribe attempting to conjure rain. Keith recognized one kid from the days he used to visit here, pre-Andy. The boy had a wide-eyed, just-slapped appearance and a long Pharaonic goatee. He shook his ass when he danced as though it were a bell and he were trying to wake an entire sleeping village. Keith recalled a previous night of watching the boy, of wanting to deafen himself in that clang, but when he looked closer and saw a reddish snail-shaped birthmark beneath the boy's right ear, he realized it was somebody else. The generations of club kids succeeded themselves as rapidly as lab mice.

He was thinking about budging toward the bar when a skinny shirtless boy pointed at him. The gesture seemed less flirtatious than accusatory. Was he being singled out as too old, an interloper? He pretended he hadn't seen, but again the boy pointed, so Keith touched his chest and mouthed, "Me?" The boy nodded.

Keith felt wooden and ludicrously conspicuous, as though it were he, not the couple in the other room, attired in formal wear, but he sidestepped his way out amidst the throng, using dancers' slippery shoulders for handholds. Just then a billowing thunderhead was released from the smoke machine and he stumbled with a blind man's halting gait.

When the smoke cleared, he was next to the boy, who looked at him with huge baby-seal eyes. His nose was eagerly upward-pointing, his blond hair stringy and dark with sweat. The boy stared fixedly at Keith's necklace – a generic silver strand of chain – then touched it reverently, as if expecting it to emit heat or light. "Cool necklace!" he said.

"Thanks," said Keith. "I like" – he searched for a suitably reciprocal compliment – "your stomach."

But the kid had already rocketed away into another private orbit. Keith stood there, whiplashed with shame and disappointment.

Imagine driving to a distant store to use a coupon, only to find that the coupon has expired; you'd feel suckered to pay full price for the item, but might want to buy something so the trip's not a total waste. Keith began to dance.

Like a pair of rusty scissors, his legs felt blunt and unproductive. His arms were unsynchronized metronomes. He didn't want to be seen searching for the boy, so he closed his eyes, pretending absorption in the music, and after a few awkward unbalanced seconds realized, pleasantly, that he was indeed absorbed, the bass beat like an axis around which his body spun. He relaxed into the motion and the noise.

Then there was a touch on his throat and he opened his eyes to see the boy again, his finger back on Keith's necklace, tracing it, insistent, as though Keith had only imagined his earlier abandonment.

Tentatively, Keith ran his own index finger along the boy's and found his knuckle hairless, smooth as sea glass. His chest was hairless too, but for a sparse patch at his sternum that, like the proverbial fig leaf whose outline it resembled, only drew attention to what it should have hid: his youth.

Nineteen, Keith guessed. A sophomore.

"I'm Keith," he said, offering his hand.

The boy used the hand as leverage and pulled himself close enough to aim his breath in Keith's ear. "Ryan," he said, and kissed Keith on the neck.

It was a small triumph that filled Keith with disproportionate confidence. The local slang was coming back to him.

"Student?" he asked.

Ryan nodded. "Tufts. You?"

Keith was grateful for the open-endedness of the question, as if he, too, might still be a sophomore. "I work in a hospital," he said, using the vague formulation he'd devised as a less off-putting alternative to "gastroenterologist." Most people never pressed for details, perhaps surmising him a lab technician or insurance administrator.

"Cool," said Ryan with the same fixated enthusiasm he'd lavished on Keith's necklace. His gaze was like a needle stitching into Keith's. "Hospitals are so . . . big," he went on. "There's that weird lighting. Hey, do you swim?"

Keith was confused. "In the hospital?"

"Nah, I just thought your neck smelled like chlorine."

In fact, Keith had swum that morning, a half mile at the YMCA pool. "Yeah," he said. "Maybe I should have showered longer."

"I like it. Makes me think of summer, the Good Humor man." Ryan ran his thumbs along the bone of Keith's forehead. "You've got killer eyebrows!"

His burbling stream of consciousness began to drown Keith's self-doubt. Keith made his hand into a cup and mimed sipping. "Want a drink?"

Ryan grinned beatifically. "I'm rolling."

"Rolling Rock?"

"Nah, I'm rolling. I'm on X. Just water for me." He held up a clear plastic bottle in which an orange glow stick fluoresced.

"Gotcha," Keith said. So much for his native speaking.

Keith had never done Ecstasy. A decade back, when he'd started clubbing, his crowd had been mostly drinkers who dabbled with the sporadic line of coke. Then had come the long pleasure-denying hibernation of medical school and residency, and when at last he emerged, and observed the new cult of group-hugging, love-professing ravers, he felt he'd missed a collective conversion.

His doubts, like those of most skeptics, veiled underlying jealousy. Could a pill make him, too, born again? But he feared that without a younger guide, any attempt to enter this new realm would be un-seemly: a geezer at a G-rated cartoon. (He'd hoped at one point that Andy would lead the way, but Andy's youthful high was so naturally powerful that he'd had no need for synthetic help.)

Ryan offered Keith his glowing water, and Keith accepted, half expecting his throat to burn, but the liquid was soothing, analgesic.

"The music!" Ryan said.

"I know," said Keith, not sure if he had just confirmed the Tourettically redundant beat as good or bad. Then he realized that for Ryan right now, everything was good.

Ryan's pupils were huge, like portals into another dimension, and his smile, too, suggested a time traveler's bewildered thrill. He kissed Keith again, this time on the mouth, his breath smelling faintly of banana, then spun to bestow his attentions on someone else. Now Keith understood the kid's turning away not as selfishness, but generosity. Ryan – at least the chemically aided Ryan – was a true philanthropist: a lover of all mankind! And mankind, it was clear, returned the love. Ryan danced with beelike industry, zooming from boy to boy to collect their fawning appreciation. But every few minutes he circled back to Keith.

"Owdy-hay, Eith-kay," Ryan greeted him upon returning from his latest circuit.

"Itto-day, Yan-ray," he said. He appreciated the music of the boy's name in pig Latin: like "ion ray," a high-tech attraction beam.

Ryan turned Keith around and rubbed his cool, clammy fingers on Keith's back, as in the game Keith had played long ago with his mother, when she traced letters on his skin and made him decipher the resulting secret message, except that Ryan seemed to shape only the letter "o," again and again, as though trying to summon a genie from Keith's flesh.

Eventually, Ryan moved up to Keith's scalp, massaging expertly. "God, I love your hair!" he said.

Keith sighed. "What's left of it."

Ryan whipped him around so they were facing, inches apart, his banana breath hot on Keith's lips. "Listen. I'm gay, right? – which means I'm attracted to men. What could be more manly than male-pattern baldness?" He pulled Keith's head down and tongued the path of his receding widow's peak.

Keith noticed people noticing them. The tuxedoed couple had appeared at the railing, blue drinks in hand to match their stiff outfits. He couldn't tell if they looked at him with censoriousness or envy, and he realized, with a bracing free-fall tickle in his groin, that he didn't particularly care.

"Eith-Kay," Ryan asked, "how old are you?"

Keith didn't hesitate. "Twenty-nine. As of this morning."

"Oh my God, are you serious? Why didn't you say something?" Ryan leapt into the air, clapping his hands, then pogo-sticked manically among the crowd. "It's his birthday! It's his birthday!"

Strangers smiled and offered tipsy congratulations, glad for a new reason to celebrate.

"It's so weird," said Ryan, back at Keith's side. "Almost every guy I've ever dated has been either twenty-six or twenty-nine."

"I guess I met you just in time," said Keith.

"Plus, now I can give you a birthday present."

"Come on. That's silly. We just met."

"No, I want to. I do. Will you let me?"

Ryan looked at him with his big dilated eyes – wishing wells into which Keith could aim his fantasies. Keith shrugged. "Well, maybe something small."

"It is small. It's tiny! You're gonna love it."

Ryan dug into his pocket and came up with a mini Ziploc bag, no bigger than a postage stamp. "Happy happy," he said, and handed it to Keith.

The pill inside was the color and size of Tylenol. One side was scored with a line; the other bore the cartoonish outline of a fist, thumb pointing up.

"Thumbs-ups are awesome," Ryan said. "Like Mitsubishis, but not as speedy."

"I don't know," Keith said, returning the bag. "I've never done it."

Ryan gasped. "The first time's totally the best!"

He whirled about Keith like a tetherball in the schoolyard game, spiraling tight, then out, then back. Keith imagined that Ryan's style in bed might be equally schoolboyish, and that he'd find out if he agreed to take the pill.

He checked his watch. Only 11:30. He'd arranged to have no patients until tomorrow afternoon.

He was about to say yes when he saw Ryan pinch open the bag, shake the pill onto his palm, and pop it in his mouth. His hesitation, Keith realized, had caused the boy to renege. Once again his out-modedness – and youth's fickleness – were confirmed.

Then Ryan's mouth was on his, and they were kissing, and Ryan pressed the pill lightly on Keith's tongue.

"You'll see," he said when he pulled away. "Everything changes."

Keith could think of nothing to do but flash the thumbs-up sign. He swallowed.

Ryan said that the X might take thirty or forty minutes to kick in, and that Keith should try just to forget about it and relax. But Keith couldn't. There was so much to keep track of. Drink lots of water, Ryan warned; if you feel nauseous try not to throw up – you might lose the pill; if your jaw grinds, chew gum to keep it loose. Keith felt silly accepting this remedial instruction. He danced on, his feet trippy with nervousness, smiling the tight smile of a gambler who's bet beyond his limit.

"How are you feeling?" Ryan asked after half an hour that seemed like two. And then again, ten minutes later, "Feeling anything?" His blissed-out face was a postcard from a distant paradise: Weather's beautiful, wish you were here.

Ryan's ministrations were entirely well-intentioned, but Keith, who felt nothing other than a late-night stubbornness in his knees, found himself blistering with resentment. He didn't know whether to be angry at Ryan for giving him a dud pill, or at himself for being somehow inadequate, his aging brain perhaps too ossified to assimilate the drug.

He thought of the time, a couple of years after college, he'd gone to City Hall for a Gay Youth Pride dance. The multipierced boy at the door asked his age.

"How flattering," Keith said. "You're doubting that I'm legal?"

"Not quite," said the boy. "No over-twentys allowed." And as Keith had slunk away, too stung to protest, he heard the kid snickering to another teen.

But hadn't Keith himself once been a snickerer? Hadn't he let men sidle up to him on the dance floor and crow over his drum-tight stomach, then ridiculed them as they slaved to bring him drinks? His exclusion now from Ryan's paradise must surely be comeuppance. He deserved this jealousy, this lack of joy.

And then he wasn't feeling that way.

He didn't notice when everything shifted, but at some point it occurred to him that he was no longer wondering if or when the drug would work, no longer questioning himself or his place here, and he thought that perhaps that's what ecstasy truly was: the absence of doubt.

The music's repetitiveness wasn't bothersome any more, but now provided an enveloping, amniotic security. It was the sound a rainbow would make if rainbows made sound. Ryan smiled at him, and Keith saw deep in his mouth the glint of a silver filling, and in that spark a new universe could have been big-banged.

"Have you come up yet?" Ryan asked.

Keith nodded – at least he thought he nodded; his body's movement was hard to distinguish from the overall swirl. "Yeah," he said. "Wow. I think I have."

Up was the perfect word for it, and not the hyper up of cocaine, nothing to do with superiority, with one person higher than another, but a soaring elevation of everything and everyone together. The club was lit as in a dream – inscrutable fogginess punctuated by bursts of clarifying brightness – and in those moments of clarity, Keith saw the dancers around him and recognized their multifarious beauty. Some were beautiful in their bodies, some their faces, some their eyes. Others, like Chinese ideograms, denoted charm or delicacy or sexiness with not-quite-literal but perfectly right approximations.

He saw the couple in the matching tuxes – what a touching, avuncular pair! – and before he quite knew what he was doing had crossed the floor and was introducing himself, kissing each man's cheek. "It's my birthday," he said, "and I want everyone to have a good time. Are you having a good time?"

"Yes," said the one with slightly darker hair, whose name was Gary. "We're celebrating, too. It's our anniversary."

"Really?"

Steve, the blond one, nodded. "We met right here. Ten years ago tonight."

"Oh my God," said Keith, "that's awesome. Come out and dance."

He took each man by the hand and towed them onto the dance floor, their formation like the bow of a human icebreaker, but there was nothing violent in their movement through the crowd; all was gentleness, bonhomie, beneficence. Keith introduced Gary and Steve to Ryan, and Ryan introduced them all to a threesome he had befriended in Keith's brief absence, and the gang writhed as one big multilimbed pod.

Could this be his true vocation, Keith wondered? Not diagnosing intestinal maladies, but facilitating camaraderie among men? He felt born to the task, a retriever pup plunging into its first pond. He complimented Steve's haircut, told Ryan's friend what a wonderful smile he had. He was attentive, doting, generous: the better him he'd always hoped to be.

Next thing he knew his shirt was being tugged out from his jeans. "Come on," Ryan said. "Take it off."

It had been ages since Keith had gone shirtless in a club – six or seven years at least, the point when the grooves of his abdomen had begun, like silt-collecting streambeds, to fill with fleshy sediment. He expected himself to protest, but instead his arms lifted into the air and he let Ryan peel the shirt away.

"That's better," Ryan said, and although Keith hadn't been aware of any problem, he understood at once the necessity of this solution.

With the glee of a child plugging in a new toy, Ryan poked his finger into Keith's exposed navel; Gary and Steve each rubbed a muscle of his shoulders. Keith saw how keeping himself covered would have been presumptuous – who was he to dispute the beauty of creation? Yes, he thought, gazing down at his pooched-out belly, and the soft pewter whorl of hair upon it, even he was beautiful.

He danced, and danced and danced, because it would have taken greater effort not to. That's what the drug did to him. Motion was now his default, as was happiness, and compassion, and the sense that skin was one of God's minor mistakes, that in fact humans were meant to live all within the same membrane, conjoined at the vital organs, Siamese.

Tongues arrived in his mouth, each with a different taste that made his mind change colors. There was Ryan's – salty but fresh, oceanic – which sent blue wavelets through the pleats of his brain. Then, attached to the boy with the church-bell ass, a green tongue: cool, arboreal. Kissing was like breathing now, easy and essential. He felt a rush of sensation and simultaneous deep calm. Was this what a hummingbird experienced, moving at top speed but staying in the same place? He traced the Möbius strip of his emotions: He was happy because everyone here liked him; everyone here liked him because he was happy.

There were fingers – whose? not Ryan's – down Keith's pants and they found something unembarrassedly limp – something miraculous in its tiny limpness! – as different from the usual plump fruit of sexual response as a raisin is from a grape, and likewise concentrated in sweetness, as though its very pliability allowed previously blocked nerve endings to the surface. The fingers tugged and gently tugged, steering Keith down a tunnel of pleasure that he felt could extend indefinitely without reaching the light of orgasm. This trip wasn't about destination, but movement.

Then there was a hand again on his back, circling, circling, calling forth the genie that Keith now realized was his own self, his all-powerful spirit, finally freed from its vessel of doubt. He turned, planning to take Ryan's gifted hand and kiss it, to thank him for showing Keith the way. But the hand, he saw as he spun about and grabbed it, belonged not to Ryan – who was locked in a lambada with some Irish-looking hunk – but to a man Keith hadn't noticed before.

The man's posture was the first thing that struck him: the stalwart uprightness of a lighthouse that has stood, by good design and providence and mindful repair, the battering of countless gales. He had about him, too, something of a lighthouse's anachronistic elegance, his gray hair (the color of weathered Cape Cod shingles) and his roughhewn, unpretentious jaw supporting a fantasy of simpler, better times: They don't make 'em like that any more.

Keith guessed the man at fifty or fifty-five. There were kind crinkles around his mouth and at the corners of his heavy-lidded eyes, which even in the club's light shone an energetic, vernal green. Keith remembered he was holding the man's hand. Instinctively, the way you clutch at an object tossed in your direction, he gripped the hand tighter and brought it to his mouth. He kissed each callused finger in succession.

"Charmed, I'm sure," said the man in a stately baritone that somehow carried over the speakers' soaring anthem.

"More than charmed," said Keith. "My name's Keith."

"Stan," he said. "You didn't mind my being forward?"

"Life's too short. You have to go for what you want."

As the words left him Keith realized that what he wanted was to bury his face in Stan's chest. He didn't question the impulse, didn't think about Stan's being nearly twice his age.

Through his barely damp T-shirt Stan's chest was firm without being overly hard, more forgiving than the skin-and-bones rib cages Keith was used to. His sweat had the pleasantly musty, unhurried scent of the air in a favorite uncle's attic.

"What do you do, Keith?" he asked. "I mean, when you're not kissing strangers' hands in clubs?"

"I work in – " Keith began his standard evasion, but for once, braced by the drug and by Stan's foursquare solidness, he decided to be direct. "I'm a doctor," he said. "Gastroenterologist."

Stan smiled, doubling the lines around his eyes. "I see, a plumber." He sounded neither dismissive nor particularly impressed. "My dad was a plumber. Houses, though, not people."

"Totally right!" Keith said. "Pipes and drains, same basic deal. How 'bout you?"

"Restoration. Tables, chairs, chests – just about anything that can fit through a door, I fix it."

"Wow," said Keith. "That's awesome. That's *amazing*. I mean, saving things that might be thrown away? Salvation?"

The Ecstasy made everything a metaphor. Life was a poem, endlessly enjambing.

"Sorry," said Keith. "Am I gushing? I'm on Ecstasy."

"Aha," said Stan. "I thought you were being a little . . . friendly. Well," he added with mock schoolmarmishness, "kids today. What can you expect?"

"Me? I'm not a kid. I'm twenty-nine. It's my birthday. Or yesterday, before midnight. And I've never done it before. But this guy – he *is* a kid, really really cute, Ryan, he gave it to me, he's the blond one, skinny – "

Keith searched for Ryan, but he and the Irish dreamboat must have decamped to the lounge. This observation wasn't worrisome, it was merely new information, as though someone had repainted the scene's backdrop in a different, equally pleasing shade.

Stan anchored two firm hands on Keith's shoulders. "Listen. Keith.

You said you didn't mind my being forward. It's five minutes to two. I live just down the road."

Stan's voice had an irresistible authority. He beckoned with the promise of comfort, like an old sofa with sags in all the right places. "Do you want to come home?" he asked.

Keith wasn't sure he said "yes," but he was operating in a new language, one without a word for "no." And so they were retrieving their coats from the coat check, and sleeving into them, and approaching the door.

He paused near the exit to scan once more for Ryan. The kid wasn't there, or, if he was, Keith couldn't distinguish him among the crowd of glittering, golden men. He felt the passing shadow of an emotion that he guessed under normal circumstances would be disappointment, but since disappointment did not exist for him just now, nor regret, he only smiled with the memory of Ryan's breath in his ear.

Stan said he lived in a loft in the industrial section of Cambridgeport, fifteen minutes' walk at most. They passed a pair of Indian restaurants, a hardware store, a fire station. The walking didn't bother Keith. It was like dancing but in a different key.

"Warm enough?" Stan asked.

Keith said, "Dandy." He had just been noticing how the cold crystallized his vision into prismatic shards. Each blink clicked the kaleidoscope to a new color scheme. But inside himself he was soupy with warmth.

Stan snugged his hand into Keith's back pocket. "Do you usually go home with older men?"

"I don't usually *leave* home in the first place," Keith said, and they both laughed a disburdening laugh. Keith was enough himself to realize that tricking with Stan broke all his normal rules, but perhaps building your personality was like pumping up your muscles: you had to strain them so when they healed they would be stronger.

A downdraft nipped from an alleyway. It brought a smell Keith couldn't exactly place: fruity and pheromonic and verging on too sweet, with a sultry mulled undertone of clove.

"What *is* that?" he asked.

Stan pointed to the sign on the building they were passing: New England Confectionery Company. Keith then noticed, on the roof, the building's water tower, painted in retro pastel stripes. "Necco wafers?" he said, incredulous.

"Either wafers," said Stan, "or probably Sweethearts – the little candy valentines? This time of year I think they're baking round the clock."

Keith inhaled again. The now-familiar aroma made him nostalgic for his childhood, and, foolishly, for an earlier age, before he was born. It was the smell of gee whiz and backseat drive-in fumblings, the saccharine innocence of romance itself.

In minutes they were at Stan's building, a sprawling brick warehouse that housed a lamp factory and the packing facility for a jigsaw puzzle maker. Styrofoam peanuts were littered about the entry. They rode a clanking elevator to the fourth floor and stepped into the middle of a living room that seemed centered on the elevator itself, the way you might expect to find a room focused on a television. A love seat and couch, upholstered in blood-colored cloth, angled cattycorner around the mechanism. The main source of light was a model of the human skeleton that had been hung from a ceiling beam and fitted with bulbs in the eye sockets.

"I think of the decor as kind of postmodern rummage sale," Stan said.

"It's great," said Keith. "I mean, God, all this space."

But the loft's lack of boundaries was off-kiltering. It stretched unfathomably in every direction, vast and without proper walls. There was a bed in one area, a desk and bookcase in another; under a window Keith saw a sink and stove. It didn't seem like a place where people were meant to live.

He detected the whiff of paint remover and polyurethane, of objects being stripped and reborn. "Is this where you work, too?" he asked.

Stan gestured toward a corner curtained off by drop cloths. "Over there. I'll show you later. In the morning?"

Something about the change from outside to in had made Keith creaky and oversensitive, the way an ice cube cracks when dropped into a drink. He shivered and flapped his ashen hands.

"It's tough to heat," said Stan. "But I've got a few space heaters." He stalked around the room, stooping periodically and flipping switches until a haunted humming filled the air. Keith removed his coat and soaked up the warmth.

Stan came from behind and engulfed him in a hug. "Have I told you how adorable you are?" He kissed Keith on the beginnings of his bald spot. "It's such a nice change to go to Campus and find someone cute but already a grownup. I mean, a doctor! My mother would be thrilled."

Keith hadn't thought of Stan as someone with a mother. "You're a nice change, too," he said. "You're so . . ." but he got stuck, and simply gripped Stan's arms.

Stan moved his hands down and patted Keith's stomach. "I know some guys would say I should just retire gracefully, or spend my time at one of those wrinkle bars. But I don't feel old. Isn't it about how you feel?"

Yes, Keith thought. Hadn't he recently had the very same insight? Or was that just something he had read once in a book? His clarity was receding like a tide.

"If you don't mind," said Stan, "I'm going to hop in the shower, wash the smoke out of my hair. Can I get you something? A beer? Some orange juice?"

"I'm okay," said Keith.

"All right, then. Make yourself at home." And he disappeared into the murk beyond the bed.

Keith mazed his way through the makeshift rooms, acclimatizing to the odd layout. His feet were still floaty, his vision slightly aswirl. The sawdusty air pricked at his skin. He found a stereo and CD cabinet: Lou Reed, Carly Simon, three versions of Handel's *Messiah*. There was jazz, too, and Keith picked a Miles Davis recording, *Kind of Blue*, because the cover was the color of his thoughts.

Returning to the apartment's center, he stared at the hanging skeleton lamp, which seemed an ill-conceived literalization of some cliché he couldn't quite recollect. The lamp swayed in imperceptible currents of air from the space heaters, sending bony shadows skittering on the floor. Keith remembered that it was now almost three hours into Groundhog Day. He searched for his own shadow, but the light was fickle, giving silhouettes and then stealing them away, and in any case he couldn't, in his hazy state, recall which was the hoped-for omen, shadow or none?

He sank into the love seat, which from this proximity was less the shade of blood than of rust. There was an end table between the love seat and the couch, and on it sat a glass bowl filled with candies. They were Necco Sweethearts, those tiny pastel valentines. Stan must keep them handy in honor of his neighbor.

He scooped a handful and read their quaintly old-fashioned memos: BE MINE. I WONDER. IT'S TRUE. Others were more recent messages: E-MAIL ME. GOT LOVE? AS IF. Keith rattled them like dice, then dismissed them back into the bowl. What if people actually conversed in these silly epigrams? Could you conduct an entire romance that way?

He fished for another batch and came up with a reddish heart – cherry? cinnamon? – with its motto inked in purple: OVER BOY. He read it again, confused. "Over boy"? The opposite of "it boy"? Then he studied the candy closer and found a faint impression of the initial "L" the machine had mis-stamped.

The absent letter, like a missing tread on the staircase of his thoughts, sent him tripping into memory: third grade. It was Valentine's Day, and to ensure that everybody received at least one card, each student had been assigned a secret sweetheart. Keith's was Alison Crosby.

In class, he deposited his valentine ("For Alison – true friendship, always") in the milk-crate "mailbox" Miss Kenton had constructed, and wondered whose private passions he would receive. After attendance, Miss Kenton upended the box. One by one she summoned each recipient, reading the names with overenthusiastic titillation, as if, despite her rigged system, getting a valentine should be a big surprise. "Mandy Ryan? Ooh look, someone sent you one! And Daniel Glick – you got one too!"

When Alison's name was announced, Keith watched her read the note, and he filled with a hot hope that he had been her secret sweetheart too. But soon Miss Kenton's pile of cards was gone, and Keith's name still had not been called. He looked enviously at his paper-heart-clutching classmates. He wasn't Alison's sweetheart. He wasn't anyone's.

"Happy Valentine's Day," the teacher said. "Aren't you all just lucky to be so much admired?"

"But I didn't get one," Keith said.

Miss Kenton's face clouded with distress. She shook her mailbox, checking for a final card. "You can be *my* sweetheart," she said, and came over to Keith and hugged him too tightly.

He didn't want to be the teacher's valentine. She smelled powdery. Her arms shook like empty bags.

Keith had fought the sob that was a fist inside his throat. He sat there, squeezed by Miss Kenton's baggy arms and by the shame of being unwanted even when the odds were fixed.

"Good choice," said Stan, snapping his fingers to the jazz.

Keith, startled, as if hiding evidence, popped the OVER BOY heart into his mouth.

Stan was wrapped in a towel, his gray chest hair beaded with water. Wisps of steam rose blurrily from his scalp like muddled thoughts.

"Glad you found the stereo," he said. "I should have shown you. Hope I didn't take too long?"

"No, no, not at all," said Keith, and it was true, he couldn't fault Stan for anything – the man was generous and considerate and squarely handsome – and yet everything, Stan, the music, the apartment, was starting to feel wrong, or not really wrong, but less than perfectly right, and Keith understood that the slow seep back of doubt, and the fact that his brain had allowed such a painful memory, meant the fading of his Ecstasy. Without the drug, he would gradually be returned to himself, and then where in God's name would he be?

On his tongue the candy heart was dissolving to a sludge, its taste not as sweet as the factory fumes, but chalky and bitter, medicinal. Stan approached him, smiling, and embraced him in his damp arms.

Keith felt the knot of Stan's towel pushing into him, and below that, something equally hard, also pushing.

He pulled back for a moment, hoping to overcome his qualms. He tried to look at Stan the way Stan must look at a piece of furniture, beneath the chipping varnish and grimy surface dings to the striking heartwood original. And Keith sensed that he could – he could see Stan's inner grace, or he could learn to. What he wasn't sure he could see again was his own.

Stan kissed him, determinedly, the grizzle of his chin scraping Keith's. Keith kissed back as best as he could. He pressed what was left of the Sweetheart onto Stan's tongue, wishing it were a pill like the one Ryan had given him, and that he could grant that magic to Stan, and to himself.

BEACH TOWN
Amy Hempel

The house next door was rented for the summer to a couple who swore at missed croquet shots. Their music at night was loud, and I liked it; it was not music I knew. Mornings, I picked up the empties they had lobbed across the hedge, Coronas with the limes wedged inside, and pitched them back over. We had not introduced ourselves these three months.

Between our houses a tall privet hedge is backed by white pine for privacy in winter. The day I heard the voice of a woman not the wife, I went out back to a spot more heavily planted but with a break I could just see through. Now it was the man who was talking, or trying to – he started to say things he could not seem to finish. I watched the woman do something memorable to him with her mouth. Then the man pulled her up from where she had been kneeling. He said, "Maybe you're just hungry. Maybe we should get you something to eat."

The woman had a nimble laugh.

The man said, "Paris is where you and I should go."

The woman asked what was wrong with here. She said, "I like a beach town."

I wanted to phone the wife's office in the city and hear what she would sound like if she answered. I had no fellow feeling; all she had ever said to me was couldn't I mow my lawn later in the day. It was noon when she asked. I told her the village bylaws disallow mowing before seven-thirty, and that I had waited until nine. A gardener, hired by my neighbor, cared for their yard. But still I was sure they were neglecting my neighbor's orchids. All summer long I had watched for the renters to leave the house together so that I could let myself in with the key from the shelf in the shed and test the soil and water the orchids.

The woman who did not want to go to Paris said that she had to leave. "But I don't want you to leave," the man said, and she said, "Think of the kiss at the door."

Nobody thinks about the way sound carries across water. Even the water in a swimming pool. A week later, when her husband was away, the wife had friends to lunch by the pool. I didn't have to hide to listen; I was in view if they had cared to look, pulling weeds in the raspberry canes.

The women told the wife it was an opportunity for her. They said fair is fair, and to do those things she might not otherwise have done. "No regrets," they said, "if you are even the type of person who is given to regret, if you even have that type of wistful temperament to begin with."

The woman said, "We are not unintelligent; we just let passion prevail." They said, "Who would deny that we have all had these feelings?"

The women told the wife she would not feel this way forever. "You will feel worse, however, before you feel better, and that is just the way it always is."

The women advised long walks. They told the wife to watch the sun rise and set, to look for solace in the natural world, though they admitted there was no comfort to be found in the world and they would all be fools to expect it.

The weekend the couple next door moved in – their rental began on Memorial Day – I heard them place a bet on the moon. She said waxing, he said waning. Days later, the moon nearly full in the night sky, I listened for the woman to tell her husband she had won, knowing they had not named the terms of the bet, and that the woman next door would collect nothing.

EVIL EYE ALLEN
Ron Carlson

J aney Morrow was a girl who possessed unparalleled beauty, a beauty that stood out like a beacon, the kind of beacon that warns ships of danger, a powerful thing which, though it is intended to serve some greater purpose, inevitably draws attention to itself. I haven't said that very well, but I tried to go that route because even to try to set out her features would be ridiculous. She was beautiful in a transcendent, unconventional way and with such vitality and force that you knew, I did, not to look at her, her chin bones, the dark hair of her eyebrows as they flared, the arch of her mouth, any of it, because to look into or upon or near her bright brooding large-eyed face would seize you with a gravity you couldn't even begin to understand or contend with, and you would be unable to look away, even as the bell rang ending your trigonometry class, and as the eleventh-grade students zipped their backpacks and rose to leave, you would be bound and frozen there to stare at Janey Morrow's perfect, hyperperfect, superperfect face.

There was a relief in all of this, in that even at seventeen I knew she wasn't a girl I was going to have to talk to, ever. I could see her, sense the glow of her aura, but I would never talk to her. It was okay with me. She was in my trigonometry class and I was able to hear Mr. Trachtenberg say her name three or four times every class period, for she was unparalleled also in her understanding of trigonometry.

I was having some trouble in trigonometry even before the real trouble which I will get to by and by, and I needed trigonometry to get into Dickinson College, which was my modest dream. I had heard of a writer there, a woman who actually let her students write stories and then she talked to the students about this work, and that is what I wanted to do. To get into Dickinson I needed to pass trigonometry and I needed thousands of dollars. I started assisting Evil Eye Allen to solve the latter problem, but the power of his Evil Eye did something to the former as well.

My close friend Evil Eye Allen instructed me on more than one occasion, as we reclined on the football bleachers while sloughing pep assemblies, that when I finally arrived at the story of his name to tell it truly yet with some delicacy. "Delicacy is absolutely underrated, Rick," he told me. "Delicacy is a kind of care the real truth requires." We were old friends by then, seventeen, everyone else having given us up as strange, me already known as a guy with notebooks, and Evil Eye, who never recovered from giving himself that name and never wanted to. It made me smile and remember his credo: Posture is message. Part of the reason he was considered too odd for friends was the way he had of posting his body when we sat or walked. He'd look straight up when he spoke to you or answer questions in class with his chin on his chest and his hand on the top of his head. "They'll remember your body," he said to me, "and then what you said. It's pivotal to use the body." He walked sideways or drifted backwards. His hands were always in the air.

I remember his head which bore his own self-administered haircut, a close uneven job that made him look like someone in radical recovery, turning slowly, rolling like a machine part and clicking into place focused right on me there high above the football field. "When you write the story of my name," Evil Eye Allen said to me, his voice now an airy whisper, "write the story truly but with delicacy. You're capable of that; you were there and you know me, and we've got to think of Janey. See what I mean?"

"I guess," I said.

"That would be the wrong answer," he said folding up and realigning himself along the bench. "Leave nothing out. Put everything in the story; put all about Evil Eye and his assistant, but don't change the names. And put in Janey Morrow's election speech." His hand rose into the sky as if lifted by a string. "Word for word."

His name, of course, was not Evil Eye. His real name was Gary, and it would be great to start with something like: He was always a strange kid, but that isn't true. He grew up two houses down from me and we were friends from day one, that is before we went to school, and he was a regular kid, better at chess than I, worse at poker, better at baseball, as good with football, liked by his teachers, my parents, girls. By the time we entered high school, he could have gone with any girl he wanted; he was real and kind and he had something else, an actor's magnetism and what I called poise.

"Poise," he'd say. "Please. Poise is never looking at your hands. I'm a bit beyond that. I'm using my body for something I don't even understand."

And so he got this reputation for being different about then, but it was an enviable different, something we would have imitated if we could have got ahold of it. Sometimes it was his elegant walk, sometimes the way his head seemed to be doing different work than his body, sometimes his mouth opening as he listened or offered you a quick smile. Here I was, a teenager, trying to walk straight, not collapse over my new size 12 feet, and keep my shirt tucked in, and walking with me was this person who embodied grace, a person like I've never seen since, who used every step he took to do two if not three things. "Why do we go up the stairs?" he said to me one day that first year at Orkney High.

"Because we have language arts in 202," I told him, lugging my books up behind him.

"Rick. Oh, Rick. This would be the wrong answer," he said, a phrase I knew by heart. "We are communicating."

"Are we going up to language arts?" I asked.

"If that happens," he said, "so be it. But we are moving upward to say something to the ages." His right hand was clamped on the top of his head and his left under his chin, having given his books to me. "I'm glad you're here to see this." It's what he said later that year when he went a week without closing his mouth and when he went two days, school days, without speaking. That time he told me, "You don't need to talk. It's a luxury. Listen to me right now; I'm enjoying this, but I don't need to do it."

In February of that year, a certain girl came into Evil Eye's sights, a girl everyone else had already seen in that she was the most beautiful girl on dry land anywhere, a girl who was so popular and confident and finished, she seemed already above it all, a girl renowned for her snobbery and style, whom every good soul in our school knew not to greet because there would be no greeting in return. She was self-contained, sealed shut with her abundant talents, and moving on a straight graceful line through high school like a first-class car on the express rail. Her name was Janey Morrow. Evil Eye Allen was astounded at her carriage, her posture, her every manner, and he made it his mission to *cross into her perimeter*. Those are his words, not mine.

He began speaking to her. It was a picture: my tall friend standing on one leg or leaning on his forehead against the wall by her locker as she did everything she could with her shoulder, books, and hands to let him know he should *go away now*. "She has never once looked at me, made eye contact, or spoken in a complete sentence," he told me after the first week. "I don't mean even once, and it has been nine days. Is that magnificent or what?" He brought his hands up in a ball, squeezing his fists together and then springing them open. "She is *there*. She is together. We're not going to see something like this again." Now he took my shirt in both of his gigantic hands and whispered along the side of my face, "I'm going to get to her. Evil Eye Allen is going to *humanize* this angel."

In trigonometry, my teacher Mr. Trachtenberg bathed Miss Morrow, as he called her, in the soft fostering light of his appreciation, and had assumed a stark hostility toward me. I needed a B; it said so in my college application. Trachtenberg had heard that I was Evil Eye Allen's assistant and he was a man who was going to single-handedly use trigonometry to turn around the foolishness that was eroding the decade.

He discovered my alter-ego as a result of our first flyer. We had produced a red and black announcement that offered the services of:

Evil Eye Allen and his able assistant, Igor, for Parties of Every Kind and Magnitude, Including Wedding Receptions, Bar Mitzvahs, Fertility Rites, Séances, Exorcisms, Arbor Day Festivities, Presidents' Day Celebrations, and Any Occasion Where Something Strange and the Presence of Mysterious Objects Would Make a Worthy Contribution and Amplify the Pleasure of Your Friends. "Beware the Power of the Evil Eye" Reasonable Rates.

Mr. Trachtenberg peeled one of these bold goodies off his classroom floor and was not amused to read what appeared to him to be a handbill from the devil. Mr. Trachtenberg's Christianity was famous. His religious zeal protruded from every axiom he scratched on the blackboard. "It is mathematics," he'd say, "which will finally defeat Satan." The previous year a kid named Kenny Albright had quipped, "Well then, Mr. T., which is better against the devil – a crucifix or the quadratic equation?" Mr. Trachtenberg stopped at the board, frozen for ten complete seconds it was said, and then he turned, his black eyebrows already crashing together over his flashing eyes, and he whispered through his gnashing teeth, "Neither is going to save you, Mr. Albright." Kenny Albright, who was a sophomore about to be sixteen, started crying. He transferred into consumer math.

What Evil Eye hadn't told me, his able assistant, was that Mr. Trachtenberg's first name was Igor. And Mr. Trachtenberg made it clear, very clear, that there was room for only one Igor in fourth-period trigonometry. "Is this amusing, Mr. Wesson?" he asked me, waving the flyer before the class. "This, this appeal to the puerile, the ungodly, the evil? Is it?" He wasn't really asking, and he had the class's attention. Everyone was waiting to see if I was going to cry. I needed trig; consumer math wasn't going to get me into college. "I haven't seen the mark of the beast in your work. It's been haphazard and a bit tentative, but not flagitious or depraved. Are you depraved, Mr. Wesson? Or is it *Igor*? Do you think in the hot center of your logical mind, Mr. Igor Wesson, that it would be a good idea for the impotent ant to mock the iron heel of my boot?"

No one moved. Everyone had heard that word, impotent. Everyone was waiting for me to gasp and begin sobbing. And the gasp was right there in my throat waiting to break. I could feel the impeccable presence of Janey Morrow in the desk next to mine. I steadied myself and spoke. "No, sir. It would be a bad idea to mock . . ." I could not go on.

"What, Mr. Wesson?"

"I need this class, Mr. Trachtenberg," I whispered, the edges of a hot tear seared the rim of my eye.

"Well, Igor. We'll see how badly you need it." He turned to the board. And so began the hardest ride in mathematics in the history of Orkney High School. I received that afternoon from the hand of Mr. Trachtenberg the supplemental text I would complete before June, a thick maroon hardback called *Advanced Concepts in Trigonometry*.

Evil Eye and I had several jobs right after our flyer appeared, house parties, a birthday, and after we did the half-hour intermission at the Junior Prom, our calendar filled into the summer. Suddenly, for the first time since my paper route, there was money; we charged forty dollars and then fifty (and there were tips). When Evil Eye would hand me my half, he'd say, "You're going to college."

Our act opened with me coming out in my red vest and white dress shirt buttoned to the collar, setting up our card table and covering it with a black tablecloth. Then I would light the fat black candle in the center and place the Mysterious Objects around it, showing each object to the crowd first. I would hold up a brass doorknob and set it down, a pink plastic shoehorn, a bucket handle, a pair of aviator sunglasses. Sometimes there were other objects.

"What are these for?" I asked him the first time we practiced.

"These are the Mysterious Objects."

"What are the Mysterious Objects for?"

"That's right." He was busy tugging at the sleeves of his cape. It was an old graduation robe he'd found at the thrift shop and then gone at with a pair of pinking shears. "They're Mysterious Objects, which means there is no answer to your earnest question. The Objects have mystery."

"Do you know the mystery? I thought you got these things down at the Salvation Army."

Here he stopped hauling at the heavy garment and turned to me. "Mystery," he said. "Mystery." He wanted the word to be its own explanation. When I just looked at him dumb as the doorknob before us, he went on. "Igor. There are things beyond our knowing." He rolled his head in a big slow circle and brought it back to bear on me: "Do you know what we're doing?"

"No," I said.

Evil Eye crouched down and then rose onto his toes, framing his face in his hands, to announce: "I don't either." He put one hand over his eyes and waved the other in the air. "Do you think the unknown has power?"

"I guess," I said.

"Then," he said, looking at me, his hands now on guard for everything, "this room is full of power, because I don't know what any of this junk means either. We're going to put on a show and try to find some things out!"

I sat down on the couch. "All I have to do is put out the stuff and stand behind you and hand you something if you need it, right?"

"Right. That and look worried. Look worried all the time."

Well, that wasn't hard. I was worried all the time. I was worried about Mr. Igor Trachtenberg and passing trigonometry, and thereby high school; I was worried about getting admitted to college and how I would afford it; I was worried about something else, some unnamed thing, which hovers about me still as a worrying person, and I was particularly worried twice a week about wearing a red vest over my long-sleeved white oxford-cloth dress shirt and placing the Mysterious Objects on a card table in front of thirty people in somebody's living room.

The house parties were the worst for worry, because everyone was so close. At the Junior Prom, for which we received two hundred dollars, there were four hundred people and I couldn't see one of them out there in the dark. I stood at the edge of the spotlight, set out the Mysterious Objects, and looked worried the whole time, but it was easier than standing in front of eighteen people in Eddie Noble's living room or Harriet Middleton's den. But to Evil Eye it was all the same. It didn't matter. He didn't have to set out the Mysterious Objects and then look worried. He had to come out in his hefty gown and wait until the audience, big or small, grew nervous, tittered, and then after a good long dose of silence, he would begin with his routine for the Evil Eye.

"Ladies and gentlemen," he would start. "No one here, not you, not me, not my able assistant, Igor, knows what the next few minutes will bring. Do you understand: no one knows what is about to happen. I'm serious." With that sentence, I'm *serious*, he could make everyone sit up a little; it was obvious he meant it. "I," he'd continue, "am sometimes called the Evil Eye, because of what my look can engender . . ." And then it would all begin. He would cruise, drift, float the perimeter of the stage, whether it was a forty-foot circle, as it was at the Junior Prom, or the width of three folding chairs, as it was at Harriet Middleton's birthday party. From where I stood I always saw the audience sit up and grow still and then imperceptibly at first begin to sway with Evil Eye as he floated, drifted, cruised back and forth before them. When he would stab a foot down and stop and stand straight up like a snake about to strike, I could see the audience sit up, lean back, prepare for the worst. He'd hop backward sometimes and I could see heads bob; and when he spun, everyone flinched; and when he stopped, the shadow of the spell was spilled over us all.

When the room was changed that way, sometimes a boy or sometimes a girl would rise and step forward, standing by the Mysterious Objects, and then the rest would happen in a flurry. Evil Eye would hand them one of the Mysterious Objects, the doorknob, or the sunglasses, and make a request: "What do you feel?" or "Tell us what it's like." And that was really it. Just the picture of the two of them – some stunned boy standing there in a madras shirt with Evil Eye in his monstrous robe – was the climax of the act. Everyone would be leaning forward. And when the boy said, "I'm glad I got my car running," or "This is weird," or "I can be scared and happy at the same time," it would have taken on a layer of danger and importance that made it amazing, and that's what people were really, *amazed*, and they applauded wildly and the subject would sit down and as the evening was retold in the weeks to come, the things the subject said would grow into dire predictions and ponderous epigrams, which only magnified Evil Eye's reputation. After every show, more kids called him Evil Eye, but his name was not carved in stone yet.

Mr. Igor Trachtenberg, the only thing between me and college, continued to try to drum me out of trig. I was doing double assignments anyway, our homework and ongoing chapters in *Advanced Concepts in Trigonometry*, and he would hand back my papers with a little pencil check at the bottom. A check. When I asked him what it meant, he said, "Are you still roving about doing the devil's handiwork?"

"No, sir," I told him, because I'm fairly sure that is the only answer to that question. "I'm doing problems in trigonometry three hours every night. I'm keeping the devil at bay."

Mr. Trachtenberg looked at me, his eyebrows in a dark, threatening arch. "I'll be the judge of that." Then he took my paper and drew a quick circle around the check and put two lines under that and handed my homework back to me. That was all the explanation I was going to get. Check, circle, underlines. It looked like his secret code for F. *It looked like an evil eye.*

Then Janey Morrow's dad called. "I didn't even know she had a dad," Evil Eye told me. "He wants to give Janey a birthday party."

"I hope this isn't anything but a nice birthday party for the most beautiful girl either of us will ever see on earth," I said.

"Meaning?"

"I hope this isn't some special way of incinerating two teenage idiots in a fire of their own design. I hope she's not out to get us."

"I am Evil Eye," he said to me. "It's way too late to get me, and you're a writer, so you're always safe."

Regardless, now charging eighty dollars for house parties, we went out to Janey Morrow's house for her seventeenth birthday party, the party which became the most retold of all of Evil Eye's outings in Orkney, and the one that gave him his name once and for all because something else that happened there was permanent too. If everyone who has told of the night at the little house on Concord Lane had actually been there, it would have been by far our largest crowd, but in fact there were only a dozen people. These were all the kids from school who distinguished themselves by knowing how to dress and knowing the first names of the faculty. I mean, one of the guys wore a sweater vest. These were kids who, when they put their hands in the pockets of their slacks to lean against a cornice for a photograph, felt a fifty-dollar bill. It was this small group that stood around in Mr. Morrow's kitchen about twilight on the day Janey turned seventeen.

It was an odd gathering, as you might imagine; I mean, this was another kind of girl, a girl above and uninvolved with us, and this was her party. She moved quietly among the girls and boys while we all talked to Mr. Morrow in the kitchen, as he set out paper cups and a bowl of punch and a small tray of crackers. He was glad we'd come. He was happy to meet Janey's classmates. He worked at the Texaco refinery. On and on he talked. I realized that he wasn't used to talking, that this was all a kind of spillage brought on by the clear relief on his face, relief that anyone at all had come to Janey's party. This was fun, he said. A party. With the famous Evil Eye! He smiled. He was proud of Janey, her schoolwork, after all she worked so hard and being without a mom and all, and he was glad, well, to meet her classmates. We all nodded at him and finally the girls came and got the tray of crackers and poured everyone a cup of the red punch and it was enough to shake everybody up and have them go into the little living room, and when the girls had sat down in the chairs, and the boys had piled in on the floor, and Mr. Morrow had come into the doorway with his glass of punch, someone turned off all the lights but one, a desk lamp under which Janey Morrow must have been doing her

trigonometry homework for the first eon of her life without knowing
the next was about to begin. When all these things were accomplished,
I came forward, looking worried, and unfolded our little table before
the assemblage, shook out the tablecloth, and set out the Mysterious
Objects.

That night, though the story has a thousand variations, there were
only three. Evil Eye had worn the sunglasses to a football game the
previous Friday and they were lost – another mystery, he told me,
when I asked him where they were – and so I set out the pair of brass
doorknobs, the metal bucket handle, and the pink plastic shoehorn.
I'd learned by now to add a little drama to my part, so after they
were set on the table I went back to my station by the wall and then I
returned to the table and I adjusted the doorknobs, the shoehorn, as
if they needed to be just right for everything to work. Then I stepped
back and gave them a dire look as if I could see Fate itself. Evil Eye
came from behind me, his robe dragging the floor, and handed me
our fat black candle, and I set that in the exact center of the table and
lit a kitchen match and handed it to him and he looked at the yellow
flame as if it were a ragged peephole to the future, that is, with a face
as serious and blank as he could make it, and he ceremoniously lit the
candle, reached back without looking, and handed me the smoking
matchstick.

I then pointed to the desk lamp and said my line: "Could we have
the flow of electric current to that device interrupted?" As always there
was a pause, a "what'd he say?" and finally someone reached up and
turned off the light. The light now collapsed to the point of the pulsing
candle and back along the still profile of Evil Eye Allen. Something was
moving behind his back, flying, flapping toward his face, and it
became his hand as it fell across his eyes. He stood there like that,
like a man in deep concentration or grief. In the new dark he had our
attention again. Evil Eye turned his head toward the gathering. His
hand, as it had so often, stayed right where it had been in space, a
disconnected force, a separate thing suddenly joined by another thing,
a hand in the dark, and then his hands began to float upward and I
could see their movement mirrored by every chin in the room. Heads

lifted. Every eye followed the hands to their apex and held there. I mean, this was fifteen seconds and he had the entire room in the palms of his raised hands. I want to make it clear that from where I stood I could just see the candlelight on the faces turned toward Evil Eye and the occasional sharp glimmer off somebody's glasses and this view was cut into by the dark form of Evil Eye himself, that gown, his raised arms, and so I couldn't see everything he was doing. I knew that he could draw his face into a tight vortex that looked unearthly, bunching his eyebrows down and pulling his mouth up, and then send the parts of his face to the far corners of the field creating a look best described as being *inhabited*. I don't know if he was doing this or not.

But I did see his arms fall and the candle flutter, and then he pulled something from inside his robe and held it up and it was a large red handkerchief. We could all see it. He knelt. He stood. He waved his arm slowly in a big arc, back and forth. Then he stopped. Everyone was watching that handkerchief, and we saw his hand begin to finger it into his palm, slowly gathering it the way a spider eats larger prey, and the look on the faces I could dimly see was a kind of fear. When it was consumed, his fist closed like a rock. It had a kind of pulse, a beat from where I stood, as if the cloth wanted out, and then I saw his hand tremble and falter and it began to open slowly.

I'm trying to be accurate.

The red handkerchief lifted like a little fire and stood on his open palm with a life of its own. For a moment it seemed the only light in the room.

Then the next part, the famous part, began with a scrape, a knee pop somewhere in the middle of the room, and a figure arose, and this was Janey Morrow. Her eyes made two pools of wavering light on her face. This is the part that Evil Eye wanted me to be delicate with, the way the other kids parted to let her drift forward, a look on her face of confidence and ease and utter attention. She came up to Evil Eye and her posture changed in a moment and forever as she straightened up and lifted her face, and I could see her look into his eyes, and what was reflected was something private, and I regret the imprecision of that phrase, but I'm certain of it. The look was something private and I saw her eyes open even wider with it, and then she turned and took the handkerchief from where it stood on his hand. She said, "You're right. This is mine. Thank you."

Her voice was already different, clear and tender.

Evil Eye pointed to the table, the candle, the Mysterious Objects. Janey Morrow went to the table and picked up the doorknobs, hefting them into both hands. She turned back to Evil Eye with an expression of unparalleled joy. I'm a writer and careful of such phrases, but I'm using it now because it is the truth. I'm trying to leave nothing out.

He reached out with two fingers and touched the doorknobs and said in a whisper that everyone heard, "You are now free to do whatever you like."

That was it. I'd never heard him say such a thing before. He had said, "What is it you'd like to say?" and "Tell us the headlines," the responses being various and not without meaning, "My mother has fixed me breakfast all my life," "It takes years for the right rain to fall." Things like that.

But now Evil Eye said, "You are free to do whatever you like," and he stepped back so close to me that the hem of his garment was on my shoes, and Janey Morrow, who was already taller than she'd been a moment before, started to do a little dance, that is, turn and step happily as she turned. Her face shone with what I'll call sureness, and she raised those doorknobs above her head. She was twirling like that, a movement which I'm sure was an expression of happiness, and the twirling was getting a little faster, her skirt in a flare, and we could hear her breath and see her white legs in the unreliable light. This was a person who did not dance in front of people, a girl who had never behaved in such a way. She had never been among us. Now she stopped and her mouth was open breathing and her eyes looked glad and she went to Evil Eye and handed him the doorknobs. "Isn't this why we're here?" she said, turning back to the group. "Isn't this why we're here?" She lifted her black sweater up suddenly over her head and there against her white skin was the red handkerchief like a bikini top and then it billowed and fell. Her breasts lit the room like floating fires. There was a roaring silence. I could see the teeth in Janey

Morrow's gleeful smile. Then her sweater came down on my head and I stumbled against the table.

It was I who bumped the table. It was not Evil Eye or Janey Morrow. Though I'm not sure now it matters. Janey kicks the table in some versions, which is not true, and in some versions she heaves the table over, which is not true, and in some versions the candles catch the curtains and fire chases people from the room, which is not true, and the fire department comes, which they did not, and Janey and her father have to move to Bark City, and Evil Eye, almost consumed in the blaze, is disfigured and still moves among us, a driven ghost, inhabiting our dreams. That last part might be on target.

So now I'll just say it, what happened. I bumped the table and it shivered sharply and collapsed, spilling the remaining Mysterious Objects and our candle onto our front-row spectators. The flickering light in the room rocked, flared, and slid, and in the new dark we all could still see her breasts, bright ghosts in the air. Mr. Morrow turned the lights on, and the scene may as well have been turned inside out, light to shadow, shadow to light, a dozen blinking teenagers scrambling up in the blooming confusion. "Did you see that?" Benjamin Putnam said. "What was that?" But before he'd finished, two things happened that I witnessed at close hand. Evil Eye, stock still and looking surprised for the first time I knew him, locked eyes with Janey Morrow. She had her sweater, that mystery, back on. Their look was as serious as looks get, and I could never read such things, but this one said something like: Something ends here, something begins.

What literally happened next is that Mr. Morrow crossed the room in two steps, pushed me aside, and, lifting Evil Eye to his toes in the raw light, struck him in the face. It was this act that closed the party down. Suddenly there was a lot of scurrying, hauling each other up and out, and we were in the car.

I remember that drive well. Evil Eye was silent, driving the car with one hand over his eye. He turned to me a couple of times as if checking my face for some understanding: Did I see what just happened? Finally, after he'd driven me home, he said to me, "We'll have to get the table next week. Remember, Rick, we've got the Fergusons' tomorrow. Four o'clock. Be there." I wanted to ask him what he'd seen in Janey's eyes. I wanted to ask him what about our candles and the Mysterious Objects. And somewhere inside of me I wanted to ask him if he'd planned the whole thing, if he'd been in control the entire time. There was something about him that day, something different, beyond the wacky act he'd been doing. I wanted to think it was power, but it might have been sadness.

We did the Fergusons', of course, and after that we were in utter demand and we raised our rates again and worked steadily. He'd appeared there with his left eye swollen shut, a purple thing that made your eyes water to look at. To peek at it made your eyes water. Evil Eye indeed, Mr. Ferguson said. Everyone said. I wanted people to call me Igor, regardless of Mr. Trachtenberg's wrath, but no one did. The name appeared in our programs, but everyone just called me Rick. We worked all over the state. Before I left for college we had earned almost nine thousand dollars.

What happened to me that spring is only part mystery to me now. The week of graduation, Mr. Trachtenberg asked for his trig book back, and I thought certainly it was the termination of my hopes for passing, for graduating on time, and I thought I would be six weeks in summer school. He'd given me still no clue as to my ranking, my mark, how I was doing. When I brought it in, he thanked me and set it on his desk beside something I'd seen before: a pair of brass doorknobs. Seeing them gave me a strange feeling that was confirmed on my report card: Trigonometry . . . A. It is now part of my permanent record, as is the look that Janey Morrow gave me when I returned to my seat. Her face had changed, or so I'll say, and I looked right at her and asked, "What did you do?"

She smiled and I could see it there in the second smile I'd ever seen on her face, a face I'd barely seen, a face new in the world and held high. "Mr. Trachtenberg must not believe you're the devil's assistant any longer," she said. Her confidence was overwhelming.

That spring I came to know that she and Evil Eye were going out, though I never saw them together. Things swim under the surface of our lives and there are times when you can sense the rhythms and other times when you can't. Janey sat next to me in trig and I might as well have been sitting by Evil Eye; all the vibrations came through. When he and I went to our shows, her presence was in the car. He had entered her perimeter. When student-body elections came along, Janey ran for student body president. The list was published, and you could hear people in the hallways reading her name and saying, "Why is the snob doing that?" She had been aside from or above everything, and now here she was entering the fray.

Evil Eye and I went to the gym for the election assembly, where each of the kids running for office got to say a little something for two minutes. His eye was better, but he got a reception everywhere he went, signals from boys and girls, odd waves, recognition of Evil Eye. It was almost as if, when we ascended the rows of bleachers, everyone acknowledged him because not to would be to invite harm. Some kids just tugged his shirttail or bumped his leg in passing; everybody touched the Evil Eye.

The assembly was twelve well-scrubbed students acting like little senators or comedians and sometimes both, telling a joke and then saying, "But seriously, we citizens of Orkney High . . ." When they called Janey's name, she stood and came forward on the polished hardwood floor. She was wearing a slim maroon business suit, the skirt a lesson in rectitude, the shoulders of her short jacket flared in a lift that framed her face in a heartbreaking curve. Her speech was one sentence: "I'm asking you to remember that we're all human." Then she bowed her head slightly and pulled a red handkerchief from her bodice and waved it twice. Janey walked back to her seat in the loudest ovation ever created in that fine and ancient edifice. I looked at Evil Eye, his grin, the tears in his terrific eyes.

It was the first and last assembly we'd ever attended. Our custom was to spend assembly time alone in the middle of the football bleachers. Evil Eye would stretch out over three or four seats and set his hand out as if to hold the gymnasium and all of its occupants, and he would say, "Did I tell you about growing up in Orkney, about going to high school in America?"

"You did," I'd always say. "We're still here."

His face would roll to mine and he'd smile as if at a child and say, "My dear Rick, that would be the wrong answer." And then he'd begin what I see now was a kind of rambling beat poem about being *seventeen*, a word he said was a central part of the code of the *unknown*, and then he would invert himself so his head was far below and his magnificent feet were in my face, and he would go on and offer me all the advice I would need if I was going to be a writer.

HER HUSBAND DIDN'T
Yasunari Kawabata

Translated from the Japanese by Michael Emmerich

F i r s t h e r e a r, then her eyebrow, then . . . One by one the various parts of Kiriko's already-married body drifted up before Junji, filling his head. He was thinking his way through the sequence of kisses he would give her that evening.

It takes about an hour to go by train from North Kamakura to Shinbashi on the Yokosuka line. There was enough time for him to imagine a number of different sequences if he liked, and various methods of kissing.

Though Junji and Kiriko both lived in North Kamakura, they met in Tokyo as a rule – Kiriko worried that they would attract attention if they were seen together in their own small town. They took the added precaution of riding in on different trains. Each time they arranged to meet, Junji suggested that he be the one to take the earlier train and wait. Kiriko never even had to ask him to do this. Junji was young, still a student. He seemed to fear that he might discover some flaw in her body.

First the ear . . . Junji started with Kiriko's ear because he still regretted the disappointment he had felt the first time he touched her earlobe – because he was still sorry that it had not excited him. His disappointment had been so acute on that occasion that even the color of his face must have changed.

"Hey." Kiriko had opened her eyes. "What's wrong?"

He had pulled his finger back from her ear the instant he had touched it. No doubt that, too, seemed strange. Junji took Kiriko's ear hurriedly into his mouth. His face was hidden in the hair at the side of her head. The smell of hair engulfed him.

"I wish you wouldn't do that."

Junji caught hold of her head as she tried to pull away.

Kiriko's ear was small and soft but not fleshy, and Junji could fit all of it into his mouth. His disappointment vanished.

But the fact that Junji had felt an urge to touch Kiriko's earlobes at all – there was something in this which filled him with a sense of guilt. Because for Junji, this desire was linked to the abnormal excitement he had felt on a previous occasion, when he had fingered the earlobe of a prostitute.

Junji had scarcely known what he was doing when he had pinched that woman's earlobe – his first earlobe. It wasn't that he had admired its shape, and pinched it for that reason, but then what was it? Why, just when he was feeling such self-hatred, such a powerful aversion to the idea of touching any part of a woman at all – why had his hand moved to her ear? Junji himself couldn't say.

Yet the cold feeling of that earlobe had instantly cleansed him of his filth. The earlobe was just as round and plump as an earlobe ought to be – it was small enough that Junji could squeeze it between the tips of his thumb and forefinger, no bigger than that – yet it filled him with a sense of the beauty of life. The smooth skin, the gentle swelling – the woman's earlobe was like a mysterious jewel. Her purity had remained intact there, inside it. The earlobe held dewlike droplets of the essence of female beauty. A sentimentality like yearning welled up inside Junji. He had never known anything with a texture like this. It was like touching the lovely girl's soul.

"What on earth are you doing?" The woman shook her head cruelly.

Even after he'd left the woman's house, Junji said nothing to his friends about the ear. They would only have laughed at him if he had. And though it would be difficult to bring that sense of excitement to life within him again, ever again, it became Junji's secret – a secret that would probably stay with him for the rest of his life.

Still, when Junji considered that his desire to touch Kiriko's earlobe had originated in his memories of a prostitute's earlobe, he quite naturally suffered pangs of guilt.

Yet for all that, Kiriko's earlobe had betrayed his expectations. It felt thin and flimsy in his fingers. It lacked even the moisture and the silkiness of most earlobes – it seemed crusty and dry. Junji was startled. He was so confused it never even occurred to him that he might never feel the excitement he had felt touching that prostitute's earlobe again – that touching even the loveliest earlobes might not revive that emotion.

Junji's habit of kissing the various parts of Kiriko's body started to form the moment he took her ear in his mouth.

Until then things had been simple. He was still a beginner in the affairs of love, and he had been completely overwhelmed by the surprise he felt on discovering that he could satisfy the middle-aged Kiriko so completely. He came to understand his own masculine charm for the first time through the pleasure Kiriko took in him, and he drifted drunkenly in it.

Junji had believed that Kiriko's body was entirely perfect, so he had to distract himself instantly from what he felt in his fingers – the impoverished flimsiness of her earlobes. He was also conscious of the fact that the ecstatic joy Kiriko had experienced when she was with him at first was growing less ecstatic of late. It was as though the attempt to rekindle her passion had given him an excuse to touch her ear.

Then, during only the third or fourth of their rendezvous, Kiriko said something unexpected.

"Sometimes I used to wonder if I could go to bed with a man without having to worry about any of those difficult ties like marriage or love, you know? I wanted to try sometime – just once. I used to daydream about it."

It sounded to Junji as though that daydream had been realized through him – no other interpretation seemed possible. He felt as though he had been pushed off a cliff.

"You mean – this has all just been a game for you?"

Kiriko firmly denied this. "It's not a game. Men may play games like that, they may fool around and everything – but women aren't like that. At least I'm not like that."

"I don't see how you can say that. What you said just now – you could only have meant you think of this as a game. If it isn't a game . . ."

"I don't know how to explain. There's just something about it – there's this aura of secrecy," she mumbled. "You really don't have the slightest idea how many constraints and burdens a woman my age has to deal with, do you? And in that oppressive pain there's a secret. But I see now that it would have been better if it had ended as it was – as a secret daydream."

"You're sorry that you slept with me?"

Kiriko laughed at this trite, childish line.

"Asking me something like that – if I'm sorry I slept with you! Aren't you just insulting yourself? Even if I criticize myself and even if I feel pain – I still wouldn't want to say that I regret what I did. Regret is the easiest excuse of all. It's just a convenient way to escape . . ."

"So that's all this was? I just happened to end up playing opposite you in these secret daydreams of yours?"

"You didn't find it at all strange that I started seeing you like that? It didn't seem strange that it all happened so easily? I had never had an affair, you know."

". . . . ."

"Think about it – I told you about my late daughter the very first time I met you . . ."

This had happened on a train on the Yokosuka line. Junji had attended a class on Western-style painting that day on an invitation from a friend. They had learned to sketch female nudes. There were four or five young women in the class, but Kiriko was the only one in Japanese dress, and she was older than the other women, so she had attracted Junji's attention. It turned out that they both lived in North Kamakura, and so that evening they went back together on the train. When the conductor came to collect their tickets, Kiriko handed him the money necessary to change Junji's third-class ticket to second-class before Junji could get his money out. It was quicker for her to open the handbag on her lap than it was for Junji to rummage through his pocket, but her movements suggested that she had been planning to pay.

Sometime after they passed Yokohama, Kiriko opened her sketchbook and started to draw something. It seemed to Junji that her face became more and more beautiful as she alternately glanced up at him and looked down at the paper. They were sitting across from one another. Junji leaned forward and looked at the sketchbook – Kiriko was sketching his face. He took the sketchbook from her without saying a word. He looked at it for a moment or two, then took out his own pencil and began adding to the sketch she had started, drawing over it.

"Hey, hey – stop it!" she said, taking the sketchbook back. But Junji felt embarrassed at having his face drawn, so he stole the book back from her and added some more to the sketch. Kiriko leaned forward this time, but she was evidently unable just to sit and watch – she couldn't just leave the drawing to him, it seemed – and she took the sketchbook back again, starting once more to draw. This same cycle of taking and having taken was repeated over and over, and in this manner Junji's face continued to be drawn. The outline of his face grew blurry in certain places, places where the lines Kiriko had drawn and the lines Junji had drawn overlapped excessively. Even a few unnecessary shadows had appeared. But all during the time they drew Junji's face together, a warm affection for Kiriko had been welling up inside of him. It seemed to him that even the drawing expressed this emotion. He had stopped feeling the shyness he had felt at first at having his face sketched – indeed, drawing over the drawing Kiriko had begun filled him with pleasure, as though they were laying the hands of their hearts one on top of the other.

"Well, it's finished." Kiriko stopped drawing and looked back and forth from the sketch to Junji's face, comparing the two. "It does look a bit like you, doesn't it?"

"Here, let me draw a little more."

"Where? Around the eyes?"

"It's my face – if I don't finish it myself . . ."

"You're awfully sure of yourself, aren't you."

"No. But – why did you draw my face?"

"Because we're coming from drawing practice, I would think. But also because when I started drawing I kept being reminded of my late daughter. She was just the right age to marry someone like you. I had her when I was nineteen – she was my only child."

". . . . ."

"Of course, I thought about her even when I looked at that model. Her body wasn't very pretty – I really didn't even want to draw her. But it was fun drawing you."

"You'll have to let me draw your face next time, assuming that we can go home on the same train after the next class." Kiriko did not respond to this.

"If my daughter were alive she would have been able to meet you too." Grief hovered in Kiriko's eyes as she stared at Junji's face. "She had never known love – she died just when the bud of her flower was starting to open. And I think that must have been best for her . . . Maybe that's what happiness is?"

"I didn't think people had any way of knowing whether they're happy or unhappy once they die. Don't you think the people left behind just go ahead and think whatever they like – that they decide for themselves whether the person who died was happy or not?"

"You do have an unpleasantly logical way of thinking, don't you? You know, near the end of winter, when spring was just beginning, my daughter used to wake up in the morning and say – Ah, this is so much fun! – and then she'd stroke her arms. During the course of a single night her skin would turn silky smooth. That's the age she died at."

". . . . ."

Returning home on the day of the next drawing class, Kiriko suggested that they not go straight to Shinbashi station – she invited Junji to go with her to a department store. She bought him a ready-made suit; she seemed to think that they would stand out even more if Junji wore his school uniform.

The things Kiriko said to him didn't sound very affectionate, either – even when they were in the room where they went to be alone. "I'm sorry," she said. "It's just that you're the perfect age to marry my daughter." Still, in her pleasure Junji came to know the pleasure of being a man. It was an awakening that overflowed with strength.

After a time, in a flirtatious voice that disguised her shame, Kiriko said, "I was thinking this before, when we were buying the clothes, but – you're tall, aren't you? Put your legs together for a second." She felt around for Junji's heels with her own, then pressed her face into his chest. "Look, I only come up to here."

She lay still, as though savoring the moment.

Kiriko didn't show up at the next week's class in Western drawing. Junji telephoned her house and asked to speak with her.

"Why didn't you come to class today?"

"The second we met everyone would know – the way you'd act would give us away. There's no way you'd be able to hide it."

They arranged to meet somewhere else for their third date, but Kiriko didn't show up at the appointed time. Junji called again.

By the time he took Kiriko's earlobe in his mouth, Junji had begun to feel both uneasy and irritated himself. Hadn't she just been dragged along by the fact of what they had done together that first time? Wasn't that the only reason she kept coming to meet him? And wasn't it Junji who dragged her along, forcibly? Did she have any choice in the matter? Even Junji could feel that her body was more tightly closed to him than it had been at first. They had drawn Junji's face together, then they had lain with their heels aligned – had that been the last of the pleasure she felt with him? Had Kiriko felt nothing since then but an increasing pain, an ever-growing sense of self-reproach?

Everything seemed to have happened almost as soon as they had met, and so at first Junji had given no thought at all to Kiriko's husband. But after a time he began to be jealous, and with this jealousy he acquired a sense of his own sinfulness.

"How old is your husband?" Junji asked. These were the first words he said which had anything to do with Kiriko's husband.

"Fifty-two. Why, does it matter?"

"I can't imagine you living with someone fifty-two years old."

". . . . ."

"He commutes to Tokyo?"

"Yes, he commutes."

"I might even have met him on the train – maybe in the station. I bet I'll meet him sometime," Junji said.

Kiriko's chest tightened suddenly.

"Why? Do you want to meet him?"

"I don't know the first thing about you – about your mind or about how you live . . . I don't have the slightest bit of influence over you. I want to see your house, you know – secretly."

"What?"

"I mean – I think it's best if I get a look at him."

"No! You can't do that! Look – why don't we just stop seeing one another." Kiriko's voice shook, and she spoke quickly. "Have I really made you so sick?"

"Sick . . . ?"

"Yes. I knew that I'd been hurt, but I really didn't think that you had – at least not so badly. I'm only telling you this because you raised the subject, but my relationship with my husband . . ." She hesitated.

"Your relationship is what?"

"It's not like it used to be. As you said before, my mind and the way I live . . . My husband doesn't seem to have noticed at all, but I've changed. We women are no good."

"What do you mean no good? What do you mean you've changed?"

Kiriko couldn't answer his questions. Junji continued to kiss her body everywhere, in various ways, but Kiriko was still holding back. Her restraint filled Junji with a frantic emptiness. And once this emptiness set in, he had even less of a choice – he had to telephone Kiriko.

She would be coming by the next train on the Yokosuka line. Junji kept imagining her, drawing her inside his head – he kept thinking through the sequence of kisses he would give her, imagining the methods he would use – and he was startled to find that he seemed to have more fun doing this than he did when he was actually with her. He began to wonder if he might not really be sick, just as Kiriko had said. He began to be suspicious of himself.

That night, too, Junji began with her ears. He had yet to find anything wrong with her body in places other than her ears. He was still moving from place to place over Kiriko's body when she muttered, "You don't have to do that, you know."

Suddenly Junji was unable to move. But Kiriko relaxed. She felt as she had that first time, when they lay with their heels together. When Junji realized that Kiriko had spoken as she had because she pitied him, tears suddenly spilled from his eyes, and would not stop. He thought – Is this what it means to break up? And yet Kiriko's cruel words also seemed to suggest that Junji had been doing things that her husband didn't.

COMPASSION
Dorothy Allison

In the last days Mama's mouth cracked and bled. Pearly blisters spread down her chin to her throat. The nurses moved her to a room with a sink by the bed and a stern command to wash up every time you touched her.

"Herpes," Mavis, the floor nurse, told me. "Contagious at this stage."

I held Mama's free hand anyway, stepping away every time the doctor came in to wash with the soap the hospital provided. Mavis let me have a bottle of her own lotion when my fingers began to dry and the skin along my thumbs split.

"Aloe vera and olive oil," she told me. "Use it on your mama, too."

I took the bottle over to rub it into the paper-thin skin on the backs of Mama's hands. She barely seemed to notice, though a couple of her veins had leaked enough to make swollen, blue-black blotches. Mama's eyes tracked past me and even as I rubbed one hand, the fingers of the other reached for the morphine pump. That drip, that precious drip. Mama no longer hissed and gasped with every breath. Now she murmured and whispered, sang a little, even said recognizable names sometimes – my sisters, her sisters, and people long dead. Every once in a while, her voice would startle, the words suddenly clear and outraged. "Goddamn!" loud in the room. Then, "Get me a cigarette, get me a cigarette," as she came awake. Angry and begging at the same time, she cursed, "Goddamn it, just one," before the morphine swept in and took her down again.

That was not our mama. Our mama never begged, never backed up, never whined, moaned, and thrashed in her sheets. My sister Jo and I stared at her. This mama was eating us alive. Every time she started it again, that litany of curses and pleas, I hunkered down further in my seat. Jo rocked in her chair, arms hugging her shoulders and head down. Arlene, the youngest of us, had wrung her hands and wiped her eyes, and finally, deciding she was no use, headed on home. Jo and I had stayed, unspeaking, miserable, and desperate.

On the third night after they gave her the pump, Mama hit some limit the nurses seemed determined to ignore. Her thumb beat time, but the pump lagged behind and the curses returned. The pleas became so heartbroken I expected the paint to start peeling off the walls. The curses became mewling growls. Finally, Jo gave me a sharp look and we stood up as one. She went over to try to force the window open, pounding the window frame till it came loose. I dug around in Mama's purse, found her Marlboros, lit one, and held it to mama's lips. Jo went and stood guard at the door.

Mama coughed, sucked, and smiled gratefully. "Baby," she whispered. "Baby," and fell asleep with ashes on her neck. Jo walked over and took the cigarette I still held. "Stupid damn rules," she said bitterly.

Mavis came in then, sniffed loudly, and shook her head at us. "You know you can't do that."

"Do what?" Jo had disappeared the smoke as if it had never been.

Mavis crossed her arms. Jo shrugged and leaned over to pull the thin blanket further up Mama's bruised shoulders. In her sleep Mama said softly, "Please." Then in a murmur so soft it could have been a blessing, "Goddamn, goddamn."

I reached past Jo and took Mama's free hand in mine. "It's okay. It's okay," I said. Mama's face smoothed. Her mouth went soft, but her fingers in mine clutched tightly.

"That window isn't supposed to be open," Mavis said suddenly. "You get it shut."

Jo and I just looked at her.

Mama's first diagnosis came when I was seventeen. Back then, I couldn't even say the word, "cancer." Mama said it and so did Jo, but I did not. "This thing," I would say. "This damn thing." Twenty-five years later, I still called it that, though there was not much else I hesitated to say. That was my role. I did the talking and carried all the insurance records. Jack blinked. Jo argued. Arlene showed up late, got a sick headache, and left. In the early years it was Jack who argued and that just made things harder. Now he never said much at all. For that I was deeply grateful. It let us seem like all the other families in the hospital corridors – only occasionally louder and a little more careful of each other than anyone at MacArthur Hospital could understand.

"Who do they think we are?" Jo asked me once.

"They don't care who we are." What I did not say is that was right. Mama was the one the medical folk were supposed to watch. The rest of us were incidental, annoying, and, whenever possible, meant to be ignored.

"I like your mama," Mavis told me the first week Mama was on the ward. "But your daddy makes me nervous."

"It's a talent he has," I said.

"Uh huh." Mavis looked a little confused, but I didn't want to explain.

The fact is he never hit her. In the thirty years since they married, Jack never once laid a hand on her. His trick was to threaten. He screamed and cursed and cried into his fists. He would come right up on Mama, close enough to spray spittle on her cheeks. Pounding his hands together, he would shout, "*Motherfuckers, assholes, sonsa-bitches.*" All the while, Mama's face remained expressionless. Her eyes stared right back into his. Only her hands trembled, the yellow-stained fingertips vibrating incessantly.

Gently, I covered the bruises on Mama's arm with my fingers. Jo scowled and turned away.

"They should be here."

"Better they're not."

Jo shoved until the window was again closed. When she turned back to me, her face was the mask Mama wore most of our childhood. She gestured at Mama's bruises. "Look at that. You see what he did."

"He didn't mean to," I said.

"Didn't mean to? Didn't care. Didn't notice. Man's the same he always was."

"He never hit her."

"He never had to hit her. She beat herself up enough. And every time the son of a bitch hit us, he was hitting her. He beat us like we were dogs. He treated her like her ass was gold. And she always talked about leaving him, you know. She never did, did she?"

"What do you want?"

"I want somebody to do something." Jo slammed her fist into the window frame. "I want somebody to finally goddamn do something."

I shook my head, gently stroking Mama's cool clammy skin. There was nothing I could say to Jo. We always wanted somebody to do something and no one ever did, but what had we ever asked anyone to do? I watched Jo rub her neck and thought about the pins that held her elbow and shoulder together. There was my shattered coccyx and broken collarbones, and Arlene's insomnia. At thirty, Arlene had a little girl's shadowed frightened face and the omnipresent stink of whiskey on her skin. I had been eight when Mama married Jack, Jo five, but Arlene had been still a baby, less than a year old and fragile as a sparrow in the air.

"What is it you want to do? Talk? Huh?" Jo rolled her shoulders back and rubbed her upper arms. "Want to talk about what a tower of strength Mama was? Or why she had to be?"

My shrug was automatic, inconsequential.

A flush spread up from Jo's cleavage. It made the skin of her neck look rough and pebbly. Deep lines scored the corners of her eyes and curved back from her mouth. In the last few years, Jo had become scary thin. The skin that always pulled tight on her bones seemed to have grown loose. Now it wrinkled and hung. I looked away, surprised and angry. Neither of us had expected to live long enough to get old.

For all that we fight, Jo is the one I get along with, and I always try to stay with her when I visit. Arlene and I barely speak, though we talk to each other more easily than she and Jo. There have been years I don't think the two of them have spoken half a dozen words. In the ten weeks since Mama's collapse, their conversations have been hurt-filled bursts of whispered recrimination. At first, I stayed with Arlene and that seemed to help, but when Jo and I insisted that Mama had to check into MacArthur, Arlene blew up and told me to go ahead and move over to Jo's place.

"You and Jo – you think you know it all," Arlene said when she was dropping me off at Jo's. "But she's my mama too, and I know something. I know she's not ready to give up and die."

"We're not giving up. We're putting Mama where she can get the best care."

"Two miles from Jo's place and forty from mine." Arlene had shaken her head. "All the way across town from Jack and her stuff. I know what you are doing."

"Arlene . . ."

"Don't. Just don't." She popped the clutch on her VW bug and backed up before I could get the door closed. "Someday you're gonna be sorry. That's the one thing I am sure of, you're gonna be sorry for all you've done." She swung the car sharply to the side, making the door swing shut. If it would have helped, I would have told her I was sorry already.

Jo put me in the room where her daughter, Pammy, stashes all the gear she will not let Jo give away or destroy – shelves of books, racks of dusty music tapes, and mounted posters on the wall over the daybed. I fell asleep under posters of prepubescent boy bands and woke up dry-mouthed and headachy.

Jo laughed when I asked about the bands. "Don't ask me," she said. "Some maudlin shit no one could dance to – whey-faced girls and anorexic boys. All of it sounds alike, whiny voices all scratchy and droning. Girl has no ear, no ear at all."

Pammy had been picking out chords on the old piano Jo took in trade for her wrecked Chevy. She spoke without looking up. "You know what Mama does?" she asked in her peculiar Florida twang. "Mama sits up late smoking dope and listening to Black Sabbath on the headphones. Acts like she's seventeen and nothing's changed in the world at all."

Jo snorted, though I saw the quick grin she suppressed. She kicked her boot heels together, knocking dried mud on the Astroturf carpet. That carpet was her prize. She'd had her boyfriend Jaybird install it throughout the house. "She's eleven now," she said, nodding in Pammy's direction. "What you think? Should I shoot her or just cut my own throat?"

I shook my head, looking back and forth from one of them to the other. They were so alike it startled me, thick brown hair, black eyes, and the exact same way of sneering so that the right side of the mouth drew up and back.

"Hang on," I told Jo. "She gets to be thirty or so, you might like her."

"Ha!" Jo slapped her hands together. "If I live that long."

Pammy banged the piano closed and swept out of the room. My sister and I grinned at each other. Pammy we both believed would redeem us all. The child was fearless.

"We need to talk," I told Arlene when she came to the hospital the day after I moved in with Jo. Arlene was standing just inside the smoking lounge off the side of the cafeteria, waiting for Jack to arrive.

"She's looking better, don't you think?" Arlene popped a Tic-Tac in her mouth.

"No, she ain't." I tried to catch Arlene's hand, but she hugged her elbows in tight and just looked at me. "Arlene, she's not going to get any better. She's going to get worse. If the tumor on her lung doesn't kill her, then the ones in her head will."

Arlene's pale face darkened. When she spoke her words all ran together. "They don't know what that stuff was. That could have been dust in the machine. I read about this case where that was what happened – dust and fingerprints on X rays." She tore at a pack of Salems, ripping one cigarette in half before she could get another out intact.

"God, Arlene."

"Don't start."

"Look, we have to make some decisions." I was thinking if I could speak quietly enough, Arlene would hear what I was saying.

"We have to take care of Mama, not talk about stuff that's going to get in the way of that." Arlene's voice was as loud as mine had been soft. "Mama needs our support, not you going on about death and doom."

Sympathetic magic, Jaybird called it. Arlene believed in the power of positive thinking the way some people believed in saints' medals or a Santeria's sacrificed chicken. Stopping us talking about dying was the thing she believed she was supposed to do.

I dropped into one of the plastic chairs. Arlene's head kept jerking restlessly, but she managed not to look into my face. This is how she always behaved. "Mama's gonna beat this thing," she'd announced when I had first come home, as if saying it firmly enough would make it so. She was the reason Mama had gone to MacArthur in the first place. Jo and I had wanted the hospice that Mama's oncologist had recommended. But Arlene had refused to discuss the hospice or to look at the results of the brain scan. Those little starbursts scattered over Mama's cranium were not something Arlene could acknowledge.

"We could keep Mama at home," she'd told the hospital chaplain. "We could all move back home and take care of her till she's better."

"Lord God!" I had imagined Jo's response to that. "Move back home? Has she gone completely damn crazy?"

The chaplain told Arlene that some people did indeed take care of family at home, and if that was what she wanted, he would help her. I had watched Arlene's face as he spoke, the struggle that moved across her flattened features. "It might not work," she had said. She had looked at me once, then dropped her head. "She might need more care than we could give, all of us working you know." She had dropped her face into her hands.

I signed off on the bills where the insurance didn't apply. For the rental on a wheelchair and a television, I used a credit card. Jo laughed at me when she saw them.

"You are a pure fool," she said. "Send back the wheelchair, but let's keep the TV. It'll give us something to watch when Arlene starts going on about how *good* Mama's doing."

Mama had had three years of pretty good health before this last illness. It was a remission that we almost convinced ourselves was a cure. The only thing she complained about was the ulcer that kept her from ever really putting back on any weight. Then, when she was in seeing the doctor about the ulcer, he had put his hand on her neck and palpated a lump the two of them could feel.

"This is it," Mama had told me on the phone that weekend last spring. "I'm not going back into chemo again."

She had been serious, but Jo and I steamrolled her back into treatment. There were a few bad weeks when we wondered if what we were doing was right, but Mama had come through strong. I convinced myself we had done the right thing. Still, when afterward Mama was so weak and slow to recover, guilt had pushed me to take a leave from my job and go stay at the old tract house near the Frito Lay plant.

"We'll get some real time together," Mama said when I arrived.

"You need rest," I told her. "We'll rest." But that was not what Mama had in mind. The first morning she got me up to drink watery coffee and plan what we would do. There was one stop at the new doctor's office, but after that, she swore, we would have fun.

For three days, Mama dragged me around. We walked through the big malls in the acrid air-conditioning in the mornings and spent the afternoons over at the jai alai fronton watching the athletes with their long lobster-claw devices on their arms thrusting the tiny white balls high up into the air and catching them as easily as if those claws were catcher's mitts. I watched close but could not figure out how the game was meant to be played. Mama just bet on her favorites – boys with tight silk shirts and flashing white smiles.

"They all know who I am," Mama told me. I nodded as if I believed her, but then a beautiful young man came up and paused by Mama's seat to squeeze her wrist.

"Rafael," Mama said immediately. "This is my oldest daughter."

"Cannot be," Rafael said. He never lifted his eyes to me, just leaned in to whisper into Mama's ear. I was watching her neck as his lips hovered at her hairline. I almost missed the bill she pressed into his palm.

"You give him money?" I said after he had wandered back down the steeply pitched stairs.

"Nothing much." Mama looked briefly embarrassed. She wiped her neck and turned her head away from me. "I've known him since he started here. He's the whole support of his family." I looked down at the young men. They were like racehorses tossing their heads about, their thick hair cut short or tied back in clubs at their napes. Once the game started they were suddenly running and leaping, bouncing off the net walls and barely avoiding the fast-moving balls. All around me gray-headed women with solid bodies shrieked and jumped in excitement. They called out vaguely Spanish-sounding names, and crowed when their champions made a score. Now and again one of the young men would wave a hand in acknowledgment.

I turned to watch Mama. Her eyes were on the boys. Her face was bright with pleasure. What did I know? Where else could she spend twenty dollars and look that happy?

When later, Rafael jumped and scored, I nudged Mama's side. "He's the best," I said. She blushed like a girl.

Mama was not supposed to drive, so I steered her old Lincoln town car around Orlando.

"You are terrible," Mama said to me every time we pulled into another parking space. It was an act. She played as if I were dragging her out, but every time I suggested we go back to the house, she pouted.

"I can nap anytime. When you've gone, I'll do nothing but rest. Let me do what I want while I can."

It was part of being sick. She wasn't sleeping, even though she was tired all the time. She'd lie on the couch awake at night with the television playing low. Every time I woke in the night I could hear it, and her, stirring restlessly out in the front room.

It was awkward sleeping in Jack's house. The last time I had lain in that bed, I had been twenty-two and back only for a week before taking a job in Louisville. Every day of that week burned in my memory. Mama had been sick then too, recovering from a hyster-ectomy her doctor swore would end all her troubles. Jo was in her own place over in Kissimmee, an apartment she got as soon as she graduated from high school. Only Arlene's stuff had remained in the stuffy bedroom; she herself was never there. At dawn, I would watch her stumble in to shower and change for school. She spent her nights baby-sitting for one of Mama's friends from the Winn Dixie. A change-of-life baby had turned out to be triplets, and Arlene spent her nights rocking one or the other while the woman curled up in her bed and wept as if she were dying.

"They are in shock over there," Mama had told me. "Don't know whether to shit or go blind."

"Blind," Arlene said. The woman, Arlene told us, was drunk more often than sober. Still, her troubles were the making of Arlene, who not only got paid good money, she no longer had to spend her nights dodging Jack's curses or sudden drunken slaps.

"I'm getting out of here, and I'm never coming back," she told me the first morning of that week. By the end of the week, she had done it, though the apartment was half a mile up the highway, and even smaller than Jo's. I saw it only once, a place devoid of furniture or grace, but built like a fortress.

"Mine," Arlene had said, a world of rage compressed into the word.

Lying on the old narrow Hollywood bed again, I remembered the look on Arlene's face. It was identical to the expression I had seen on Jo when I was packing my boxes to drive to Louisville.

"We'll never see your ass again," Jo had said. Her mouth pulled down in a mock frown, then crooked up into a grin.

"Not in this lifetime."

All these years later I could look back and it was exactly as if I were watching a movie of it, a scene that closed in on Jo's black eyes and the bitter pleasure she took in saying "your ass." I know my mouth had twisted to match hers. We had thought ourselves free, finally away and gone. But none of it had come out the way we had thought it would. I hadn't lasted two years in Louisville, and Arlene had never gotten more than three miles from the Frito Lay plant. Twenty years after we had left so fierce and proud, we were all right back where we had started, yoked to each other and the same old drama.

"Take me shopping," Mama begged me every afternoon, as if no time at all had passed. I had looked at her neck and seen how gray and sweaty the skin had gone and known in that moment that the chemo had not worked out as we hoped.

"Tomorrow," I had promised Mama, and talked her into lying down early. Then gone back to curl up in bed and pretend to read so that I could be left alone. Every night for the two weeks I stayed there I would listen to Jack's hacking through the bedroom wall. Every time he coughed, my back pulled tight. I tried to shut him out, listening past him for Mama lying on the couch in the living room. She talked to herself once she thought we were asleep. It sounded as if she were retelling stories. Little snatches would drift down the hall. "Oh James, God that James . . ." Her voice went soft. I listened to unintelligible whispers till she said, "When Arlene was born . . ." Then she faded out again. In the background, Jack's snoring grated low and steady. I curled my fists under the sheets until I fell asleep.

When she took me shopping, Mama bought me things she said I needed. She made me go to Jordan Marsh to buy Estée Lauder skin potions. "It's time," she said. Her tone implied it was the last possible day I could put off buying moisturizer. I submitted. It was easier to let her tell me what to buy than to argue, and kind of fun to let her boss around the salesladies. I even found myself telling an insistent young woman that, no, we would not try the Clinique, we were there for Estée Lauder. Afterward, we went upstairs to do what we both enjoyed the most – rummage through the sale bins.

"I need new underwear," Mama said. "Briefs. Let's find me some briefs. No bikinis, can't wear those anymore. They irritate my scar." She gestured to her belly, not specifying if she meant the old zipper from her navel to pubis, or the more recent horizontal patches to either side. I sorted the more garish patterns out of the way, turning up a few baby-blue briefs in size seven.

"Five now," Mama muttered. "Find me some fives, and none of those all-cotton ones. I want the nylon. Nylon hugs me right, and I hate the way cotton looks after a while. Dirty, you know?"

Sevens and eights and sixes. I kept digging.

"Excuse me." The two women at Mama's sleeve looked familiar.

"Mam," the first one said, pushing into the bin. "Excuse me." She reached around Mama's elbow to snag a pair of blue-green briefs. "Excuse me," she said again.

The accent was even more familiar than her flat grayish features and tight blond cap of hair. Her drawl was more pronounced than Mama's, more honeyed than the usual Orlando matrons. It was a Carolina accent, and a Carolina polite hesitation, too. The other woman reached for a pair of yellow cotton panties, size seven. Mama moved aside.

"So I told him what he was going to have to do," the first woman said to her friend, continuing what was obviously an ongoing conversation. "No standing between me and the Lord, I told him. We've all got a role in God's plan. You know?"

Her friend nodded. Mama looked to the side, her eyes drifting over the woman's figure, the pale white hands sorting underwear, the dull gold jewelry and the loose shirtwaist dress. That old glint appeared in Mama's eyes and a little electrical shock went up my neck. I moved around the corner of the bin to get between them, but Mama had already turned to the woman.

"I know what you mean." Mama's tone was pleasant, her face open and friendly. The woman turned to her, a momentary look of confusion on her face.

"You do?"

"Oh yes, there is no fighting what is meant. When God puts his hand on you, well . . ." Mama shrugged as if there were no need to say more.

The woman hesitated, and then nodded, "Yes. God has a plan for us all."

"Yes." Mama nodded. "Yes." She reached over and put both hands on the woman's clasped palms. "Bless you." Mama beamed. This time the woman did frown. She didn't know whether Mama was making fun of her, but she knew something was wrong. Her friend looked nervous.

"Just let me ask you something." Mama pulled the woman's hands toward her own midriff, drawing the woman slightly off balance and making her reach across the pile of underpants.

"Have you had cancer yet?" The words were spoken in the softest matron's drawl but they cut the air like a razor.

"Oh!" the woman said.

Mama smiled. Her smile relaxed, full of enjoyment. "It ain't good news. But it is definite. You know something after, how everything can change in an instant."

The woman's eyes were fixed and dilated. "Oh! God is a rock," she whispered.

"Yes." Mama's smile was too wide. "And Demerol." She paused while the woman's mouth worked as if she were going to protest, but could not. "And sleep," Mama added that as it had just occurred to her. She nodded again. "Yes. God is Demerol and sleep and not vomiting when that's all you've done for days. Oh, yes. God is more than I think you have yet imagined. It's not like we get to choose what comes, after all."

"Mama," I said. "Please, Mama."

Mama leaned over so that her face was close to the woman's chin and spoke in a tightly parsed whisper. "God is your daughter holding your hand when you can't stand the smell of your own body. God is your husband not yelling, your insurance check coming when they said it would." She leaned so close to the woman's face, it looked as if she were about to kiss her, still holding on to both the woman's hands. "God is any minute pain is not eating you up alive, any breath that doesn't come out in a wheeze."

The woman's eyes were wide, still unblinking; the determined mouth clamped shut.

"I know God." Mama assumed her old soft drawl. "I know God

and the devil and everything in between. Oh yes. Yes." The last word was fierce, not angry but final.

When she let go, I watched the woman fall back against her friend. The two of them turned to walk fast and straight away from us, leaving their selections on the table. I felt almost sorry for them. Then Mama sighed and settled back. With an easy motion, she snatched up a set of blue nylon briefs, size five. She turned her face to me with a wide happy smile.

"God! I do *love* shopping."

"Wasn't she from Louisville, that woman had the sports car? The one with those boots I liked so much?" Jo and I were folding sheets. We had cleared about a month of laundry off the bed, shifting sheets and towels up onto shelves, and stacking the T-shirts, socks, and underwear in baskets. Jo's rules for house-keeping were simple; she did the least she could. All underpants, T-shirts, and socks in her house were white. Nothing was sorted by anything but size – when it was sorted at all. If I wanted to sleep, I had to get it all off the bed.

"No," I said. "Met her after I moved to Brooklyn."

"Sure had a lot of attitude. And Lord God! Those boots. What happened to her, anyway?"

"Got a job in Chicago working for a news show."

"Oh, so not the one, huh?" Jo made a rude gesture with her right hand. "You talked like she had your heart in her hands."

"For a while." I shook out a sheet and began to refold it more neatly. "But when I moved in with her, things changed. Turned out she had Jack's temper and Arlene's talent for seeing what she wanted to see."

"That's a shock." There was a sardonic drawl in Jo's tone. "Didn't think there was another like Arlene in the world."

"There's a world of Arlenes," I said. "World of Jacks, too, and a lifetime of scary women just waiting for me to drag them here so you can talk them out of their boots."

"Well, those were damn fine boots."

Jaybird came in then, dragging his feet across the door-sill to knock loose the sand. Jo waved him over. "You remember the red boots I bought in Atlanta that time?"

"They hurt your feet." Jay took a quick nibble on Jo's ear-lobe and gave me a welcome grin.

"Just about crippled me. But you sure liked the way they looked when I crossed my legs at the bar that weekend."

"You look good any way, woman," Jay said. "You come in covered in dog shit and grass seed, I'll still want to suck on your neck. You sit back in shiny red high-heeled boots and I'll do just about anything you want."

"You will, huh?" She snagged one of his belt loops and tugged it possessively.

"You know I will."

"Uh huh."

They kissed like I was not in the room, so I pretended I was not, folding sheets while the kiss turned to giggles and then pinches and another kiss. Jo and Jaybird have been together almost nine years. I liked Jay more than any other guy Jo ever brought around. He was older than the type she used to chase. Jo wouldn't say, but Mama swore Pammy's daddy was a kid barely out of junior high. "Your sister likes them young," she complained. "Too young."

Jay was a vet. He had an ugly scar under his chin and a gruff voice. Mostly, he didn't talk. He worked at the garage, making do with hand gestures and a stern open face. Only with Jo did he let himself relax. He didn't drink except for twice a year – each time he asked Jo to marry him, and every time she said no. Then Jay went and got seriously drunk. Jo didn't let anyone say a word against him, but she also refused to admit he was little Beth's daddy, though they were as alike as two puppies from the same litter.

"To hell with boots," Jo joked at me over Jay's shoulder. "Old Jaybird's all I really need." She gave him another kiss and a fast tug on his dark blond hair. He wiggled against her happily. I hugged the worn cotton sheet in my arms. I'd hate it if Jo ran Jay off, but maybe she wouldn't. Sometimes Jo was as tender with Jay as if she intended to keep him around forever.

Arlene lived at Castle Estates, an apartment complex off Highway 50 on the way out to the airport. It looked to me like Kentucky Ridge where she was two years ago, and Dunbarton Gardens five years before that. Squat identical two-story structures, dotted with upstairs decks and imitation wood beams set in fields of parking spaces and low unrecognizable blue-green hedges. Castle Estates was known for its big corner turrets and ersatz iron gate decorated with mock silver horseheads. It gleamed like malachite in the Florida sunshine.

When I visited last spring, I went over for a day and joked that if I wanted to take a walk, I'd have to leave a trail of bread-crumbs to find my way back. Arlene didn't think it was funny.

"What are you talking about? No one walks anywhere in central Florida. You want to drown in your own sweat?"

In Arlene's apartments, the air conditioner was always set on high and all the windows sealed. The few times I stayed with her, I'd huddle in her spare room, tucked under her old *Bewitched* sleeping bag, my fingers clutching the fabric under Elizabeth Montgomery's pink-and-cream chin. Out in the front room the television droned nondenominational rock and roll on the VH-1 music channel. Beneath the backbeat, I heard the steady thunk of the mechanical ratchets on the stair-stepper. Since she turned thirty, Arlene spends her insomniac nights climbing endlessly to music she hated when it was first released.

The night before we moved Mama into MacArthur, the thunking refrain went on too long. I made myself lie still as long as I could, but eventually I sneaked out to check on Arlene. The lights were dimmed way down and the television set provided most of the illumination. The stair-stepper was set up close to the TV, and my mouth went dry when I saw my little sister. She was braced between the side rails, arms extended rigidly and head hanging down between her arms. I watched her legs as they trembled and lifted steadily, up and up and up. A shiver went through me. I tried to think of something to say, some way to get her off those steps.

Arlene's head lifted, and I saw her face. Cheeks flushed red; eyes squeezed shut. Her open mouth gasped at the cold filtered air. She was crying, but inaudibly, her features rigid with strain and tightened to a grotesque mask. She looked like some animal in a trap, tearing herself and going on – up and up and up. I watched her mouth working, curses visible on the dry cracked lips. With a low grunt, she picked up her speed and dropped her head again. I stepped back into the darkened doorway. I did not want to have to speak, did not want to have to excuse seeing her like that. It was bad enough to have seen. But I have never understood my little sister more than I did in that moment – never before realized how much alike we really were.

Jack has been sober for more than a decade, something Jo and I found increasingly hard to believe. Mama boasted of how proud she was of him. Her Jack didn't go to AA or do any of those programs people talk about. Her Jack did it on his own.

"Those AA people – they ask forgiveness," Jo said once.

"They make amends." She cackled at the idea, and I smiled. Jack asking forgiveness was about as hard to imagine as him staying sober. For years we teased each other, "You think it will last?" Then in unison, we would go, "Naaa!"

Neither of us can figure out how it has lasted, but Jack has stayed sober, never drinking. Of course, he also never made amends.

"For what?" he said. For what?

"I did the best I could with all those girls," Jack told the doctor, the night Arlene was carried into the emergency room raving and kicking. It was the third and last time she mixed vodka and sleeping pills, and only a year or so after Jack first got sober, the same year I was working up in Atlanta and could fly down on short notice. Jo called me from the emergency room and said, "Get here fast, looks like she ain't gonna make it this time."

Jo was wrong about that, though as it turned out we were both grateful she got me to come. Arlene came close to putting out the eye of the orderly who tried to help the nurses strap her down. She did break his nose, and chipped two teeth that belonged to the rent-a-cop who came over to play hero. The nurses fared better, getting away with only a few scratches and one moderately unpleasant bite mark.

"I'll kill you," Arlene kept screaming. "I'll fucking kill you all!" Then after a while, "You're killing me. You're killing me!"

It was Jo who had found Arlene. Baby sister had barely been breathing, her face and hair sour with vomit. Jo called the ambulance, and then poured cold water all over Arlene's head and shoulders until she became conscious enough to scream. For a day and a half, Jo told me, Arlene was finally who she should have been from the beginning. She cursed with outrage and flailed with wild conviction. "You should have seen it," Jo told me.

By the time I got there, Arlene was going in and out – one minute sobbing and weak and the next minute rearing up to shout. The conviction was just about gone. When she was quiet for a little while, I looked in at her, but I couldn't bring myself to speak. Every breath Arlene drew seemed to suck oxygen out of the room. Then Jack came in the door and it was as if she caught fire at the sight of him. For the first and only time in her life she called him a son of a bitch to his face.

"You, you," she screamed. "You are killing me! Get out. Get out. I'll rip your dick off if you don't get the hell out of here."

"She's gone completely crazy," Jack told everyone, but it sounded like sanity to me.

The psychiatric nurse kept pushing for sedation, but Jo and I fought them on that. Let her scream it out, we insisted. By some miracle they listened to us, and left her alone. We stayed in the hall outside the room, listening to Arlene as she slowly wound herself down.

"I did the best I could," Jack kept saying to the doctor. "You can see what it was like. I just never knew what to do."

Jo and I kept our distance. Neither of us said a word.

By the third morning, Arlene was gray-faced and repentant. When we went in to check on her, her eyes would not rise to meet ours.

"I'm all right," she said in a thick hoarse whisper. "And I won't ever let that happen again."

"Damn pity," Jo told me later. "That was just about the only time

I've ever really liked her. Crazy out of her mind, she made sense. Sane, I don't understand her at all."

"What do you think happens after death?" Mama asked me. She and I were sitting alone waiting for the doctor to come back. They were giving her IV fluids and oral medicines to help her with the nausea, but she was sick to her stomach all the time and trying hard not to show it. "Come on, tell me," she said.

I looked at Mama's temples where the skin had begun to sink in. A fine gray shadow was slowly widening and deepening. Her closed eyes were like marbles under a sheet. I rubbed my neck. I was too tired to lie to her.

"You close your eyes," I said. "Then you open them, start over."

"God!" Mama shuddered. "I hope not."

Jo was a breeder, Ridgebacks and Rottweilers. A third of every litter had to be put down. Jo always had it done at the vet's office, while she held them in her arms and sobbed. She kept their birth dates and names in lists under the glass top of her coffee table, christening them all for rock-and-rollers, even the ones she had to kill.

"Axl is getting kind of old," she told me on the phone before I came last spring. "But you should see Bon Jovi the Third. We're gonna get a dynasty out of her."

After her daughter Beth was born, Jo had her own tubes tied. Still she hated to fix her bitches, and found homes for every dog born on her place. "Only humans should be stopped from breeding," she told me once. "Dogs know when to eat their runts. Humans don't know shit."

Four years ago Jo was arrested for breaking into a greyhound puppy farm up near Apopka. Mama was healthy back then, but didn't have a dime to spare. Jaybird called me to help them find a lawyer and get Jo out on bail. It was expensive. Jo had blown up the incinerator at the farm. The police insisted she had used stolen dynamite, but Jo refused to talk about that. What she wanted to talk about was what she had heard, that hundreds of dogs had been burned in that cinder-block firepit.

"Alive. Alive," she told the judge. "Three different people told me. Those monsters get drunk, stoke up the fire, and throw in all the puppies they can't sell. Alive, the sonsabitches! Don't even care if anyone hears them scream." From the back of the courtroom, I could hear the hysteria in her voice.

"Imagine it. Little puppies, starved in cages and then caught up and tossed in the fire." Jo shook her head. Gray streaks shone against the black. The judge grimaced. I wondered if she was getting to him.

"And then" – she glared across the courtroom – "they sell the ash and bone for fertilizer." Beside me Jaybird wiggled uncomfortably.

Jo got a suspended sentence, but only after her lawyer proved the puppy farmers had a history of citations from Animal Protection. Jo had to pay the cost of the incinerator, which was made easier when people started writing her and sending checks. The newspaper had made her a Joan of Arc of dogs. It got so bad the farm closed up the dog business and shifted over to pigs.

"I don't give a rat's ass about pigs," Jo promised the man when she wrote him his check.

"Well, I can appreciate that." He grinned at us. "Almost nobody does."

"How'd you get that dynamite?" I asked Jo when we were driving away in Jay's truck. It was the one thing she had dodged throughout the trial.

"Didn't use no dynamite." She nudged Jaybird's shoulder. "Old Bird here gave me a grenade he'd brought back from the army. Didn't think it would work. I just promised I'd get rid of it for him. But it was a fuck-up." She frowned. "It just blew the back wall out of that incinerator. They got all that money off me under false pretenses."

Every time Jack came to the hospital, he brought food, greasy bags of hamburgers and fries from the Checker Inn, melted milk shakes from the diner on the highway, and half-eaten boxes of chocolate. Mama ate nothing, just watched him. The bones of her face stood out like the girders of a bridge.

Jo and I went down to the coffee shop. Arlene, who had come in with Jack, stayed up with them. "He wants her to get up and come home," she reported to us when she came down an hour later.

Jo laughed and blew smoke over Arlene's head in a long thin stream. "Right," she barked, and offered Arlene one of her Marlboros.

"I can't smoke that shit," Arlene said. She pulled out her alligator case and lit a Salem with a little silver lighter. When Jo said nothing, Arlene relaxed a little and opened the bag of potato chips we had saved for her. "He's lost the checkbook again," she said in my direction. "Says he wants to know where we put her box of Barr Dollars so he can buy gas for the Buick."

"He's gonna lose everything as soon as she's gone." Jo pushed her short boots off with her toes and put her feet up on another seat. "He's sending the bills back marked 'deceased.' The mortgage payment, for God's sake." She shook her head and took a potato chip from Arlene's bag.

"He'll be living on the street in no time." Her voice was awful with anticipation.

Arlene turned to me. "Where are the Barr Dollars?"

I shook my head. Last I knew, Mama had stashed in her wallet exactly five one-dollar bills signed by Joseph W. Barr – crisp dollar bills she was sure would be worth money someday, though I had no idea why she thought so.

"Girls."

Jack stood in the doorway. He looked uncomfortable with the three of us sitting together. "She's looking better," he said diffidently.

Arlene nodded. Jo let blue smoke trail slowly out of her nose. I said nothing. I could feel my cheeks go stiff. I looked at the way Jack's hairline was receding, the gray bush of his military haircut thinning out and slowly exposing the bony structure of his head.

"Well." Jack's left hand gripped the doorframe. He let go and flexed his fingers in the air. When the hand came down again, it gripped so hard the fingertips went white. My eyes were drawn there, unable to look away from the knuckles standing out knobby and hard. Beside me Jo tore her empty potato chip bag in half, spilling crumbs on the linoleum tabletop. Arlene shifted in her chair. I heard the elevator gears grind out in the hall.

"I was gonna go home," Jack said. He let go of the doorjamb.

"Good night, Daddy," Arlene called after him. He waved a hand and walked away.

Jo twisted around in her chair. "You are such a suck-ass," she said.

Arlene's cheeks flushed. "You don't have to be mean."

"I can't even say his name. You call him Daddy." Jo shook her head. "Daddy."

"He's the only father I've ever known." Arlene's face was becoming a brighter and brighter pink. She fumbled with her cigarette case, then shoved it into her bag. "And I don't see any reason to make this thing any worse."

"Worse?" Jo twisted further in her chair. She leaned over and put her hand on Arlene's forearm. "Tell me the truth," she said. "Didn't you ever just want to kill the son of a bitch?"

Arlene jerked her arm free, but Jo caught the belt of her dress. "He ain't got shit. He ain't gonna give you no money, and he can't hurt you no more. You don't have to suck up to him. You could tell him to go to hell."

Arlene slapped Jo's hand away and grabbed her bag. "Don't you tell me what to do." She looked over at me as if daring me to say something. "Don't you tell me nothing."

Jo dropped back in her seat and lifted her hands in mock surrender. "Me, you can say no to. Him, you run after like some little broken-hearted puppy."

"Don't, don't . . ." For a moment it was as if Arlene were going to say something. The look on her face reminded me of the night she had screamed and kicked. Do it, I wanted to say. Do it. But whatever Arlene wanted to say, she swallowed.

"Just don't!" She was out the door in a rush.

I took a drink of cold coffee and watched Jo. Her eyes were red-veined and her hair hung limp. She shook her head. "I hate her, I swear I do," she said.

I looked away. "None of us have ever much liked each other," I said.

Jo lit another cigarette and rubbed under her eyes. "You ain't that bad." She pulled out a Kleenex, dampened it with a little of my black coffee, and wiped carefully under each eye. "Not now anyway. You were mean as a snake when you were little."

"That was you."

Jo's hand stopped. An angry glare came into her eyes, but instead of shouting, she laughed. I hesitated and she pushed her hair back and laughed some more.

"Well," she said, "I suppose it was. Yeah." She nodded, the laughter softening to a smile. "You just stayed gone all the time."

"Saved my life." I laced my fingers together on the table, remembering all those interminable black nights, Jo pinching me awake and the two of us hauling Arlene into the backyard to hide behind the garage. Bleak days, shame omnipresent as fear, and by the time I was twelve, I stayed gone every minute I could.

"You were the smart one." Jo looked toward the door. I watched how her eyes focused on the jamb where his hand had rested.

"You were smart, I was fast, and Arlene learned to suck ass so hard she swallowed her own soul."

I kept quiet. There was nothing to say to that.

"I dreamed you killed him." Mama's voice was rough, shaped around the tube in her nose.

"How?" I kept my voice impartial, relaxed. This was not what I wanted to talk about, but it was easier when Mama talked. I hated the hours when she just lay there staring up at the ceiling with awful anticipation on her face.

"All kinds of ways." Mama waved the hand that wasn't strapped down for the IV. She looked over at me slyly.

"You know I used to dream about it all the time. Dreamed it for years. Mostly it was you, but sometimes Jo would do it. Every once in a while it would be Arlene."

She paused, closed her eyes, and breathed for a while.

"I'd wake up just terrified, but sometimes almost glad. Relieved to have it over and done, I think. Bad times I would get up and walk around awhile, remind myself what was real, what wasn't. Listen to him snore awhile, then go make sure you girls were all right."

She looked at me with dulled eyes. I couldn't think what to say.

"Don't do it," she whispered.

I wanted to laugh, but didn't. I watched Mama's shadowy face. Her expression stunned me. Her mouth was drawn up in a big painful smile, not at all sincere.

"Did you want to kill him?"

I turned away from the black window, expecting Jo. But it was Arlene, her eyes huge with smeared mascara.

"Sure," I told her. "Still do."

She nodded and wiped her nose with the back of her hand.

"But you won't."

"Probably not."

We stood still. I waited.

"I didn't think like that." She spoke slowly. "Like you and Jo. You two were always fighting. I felt like I had to be the peacemaker. And I . . ." She paused, bringing her hands up in the air as if she were lifting something.

"I just didn't want to be a hateful person. I wanted it to be all right. I wanted us all to love each other." She dropped her hands. "Now you just hate me. You and Jo, you hate me worse than him."

"No." I spoke in a whisper. "Never. It's hard sometimes to believe, I know. But I love you. Always have. Even when you made me so mad."

She looked at me. When she spoke, her voice was tiny. "I used to dream about it," she whispered. "Not killing him, but him dying. Him being dead."

I smiled at her. "Easier that way," I said.

Arlene nodded. "Yeah," she said. "Yeah."

That evening Mavis stopped me in the hall. She had a stack of papers in one hand and an expression that bordered on outrage.

"This ain't been signed," she said. Her hand shook the papers. I looked at them as she stepped in close to me. She pulled one off the bottom.

"This is from Mrs. Crawford, that woman was in the room next to your mama. Look at this. Look at it close."

The printing was dark and bold. **"Do not resuscitate." "No extraordinary measures to be taken."**

I looked up at Mavis, and she shook her head at me. "Don't tell me you don't know what I mean. You been on this road a long time. You know what's coming, and your mother needs you to take care of it."

She pressed a sheaf of forms into my hand. "You go in there and take another good long look at your mother, and then you get these papers done right."

Later that evening I was holding a damp washrag to my eyes over the little sink in the entry to Mama's room. I could hear Mama whispering to Jo on the other side of the curtain around the bed.

"What do you think happens after death?" Mama asked. Her voice was hoarse.

I brought the rag down to cover my mouth.

"Oh hell, Mama," Jo said. "I don't know."

"No, tell me."

There was a long pause. Then Jo gave a harsh sigh and said it again. "Oh hell." Her chair slid forward on the linoleum floor. "You know what I really think?" Her voice was a careful whisper. "I'll tell you the truth, Mama. But don't you laugh. I think you come back as a dog."

I heard Mama's indrawn breath.

"I said don't laugh. I'm telling you what I really believe."

I lifted my head. Jo sounded so sincere. I could almost feel Mama leaning toward her.

"What I think is, if you were good to the people in your life, well then, you come back as a big dog. And . . ." Jo paused and tapped a finger on the bedframe. "If you were some evil son of a bitch, then you gonna come back some nasty little Pekingese."

Jo laughed then, a quick bark of a laugh. Mama joined in weakly.

Then they were giggling together. "A Pekingese," Mama said. "Oh yes."

I put my forehead against the mirror over the sink and listened. It was good to hear. When they settled down, I started to step past the curtain. But then Mama spoke and I paused. Her voice was soft, but firm.

"I just want to go to sleep," she said. "Just sleep. I never want to wake up again."

The next morning, Mama could not move her legs. She could barely breathe. There was a pain in her side, she said. Sweat shone on her forehead when she tried to talk. The blisters on her mouth had spread to her chin.

"I'm afraid." She gripped my hand so tightly I could feel the bones of my fingers rubbing together.

"I know," I told her. "But I'm here. I won't go anywhere. I'll stay right here."

Jo came in the afternoon. The doctor had already come and gone, leaving Mama's left arm bound to a plastic frame and that tiny machine pumping more morphine. Mama seemed to be floating, only coming to the surface now and then. Every time her eyes opened, she jerked as if she had just realized she was still alive.

"What did he say?" Jo demanded. I could barely look at her.

"It was a stroke." I cleared my throat. I spoke carefully, softly. "A little one in the night. He thinks there will be more, lots more. One of them might kill her, but it might not. She might go on a long time. They don't know."

I watched Jo's right hand search her jacket pockets until she found the pack of cigarettes. She put one in her mouth, but didn't light it. She just looked at me while I looked back at her.

"We have to make some decisions," I said. Jo nodded.

"I don't want them to . . ." She lifted her hands and shook them. Her eyes were glittering in the fluorescent lighting. "To hurt her."

"Yeah." I nodded gratefully. I could never have fought Jo if she had disagreed with me. "I told them we didn't want to do anything."

"Anything?" Jo's eyes beamed into mine like searchlights. I nodded again. I pulled out the forms Mavis had given me.

"We'll have to get Jack to sign these."

Jo took the papers and looked through them. "Isn't that the way it always is?" Her voice was sour and strained. The cigarette was still clenched between her teeth. "Isn't that just the way it always is?"

"Mama's pissed herself," Arlene told me when I came back from dinner. I was surprised to see her. Her hair was pushed behind her ears and her face scrubbed clean. She was sponging Mama's hips and thighs. Mama's face was red. Her eyes were closed. Arlene's expression was unreadable. I picked up the towel by Mama's feet and wiped behind Arlene's sponge. Jo came in, dragging an extra chair. Arlene did not look up, she just shifted Mama's left leg and carefully sponged the furry mat of Mama's mound.

"Jo talked to me." Arlene's voice was low. Without mascara she seemed young again, her cheeks pearly in the frosty light that outlined the bed. Behind me, Jo positioned the chair and sat down heavily. There was a pause while the two of them looked at each other. Then Mama opened her eyes, and we all turned to her. The white of her left eye was bloody and the pupil an enormous black hole.

"Baby?" Mama whispered. I reached for her free hand. "Baby?" she kept whispering. "Baby?" Her voice was thin and raspy. Her thumb was working the pump, but it seemed to have lost its ability to help. Her good eye was wide and terrified. Arlene made a sound in her throat. Jo stood up. None of us said a thing. The door opened behind me. Jack's face was pale and too close. His left hand clutched a big greasy bag.

"Honey?" Jack said. "Honey?"

I looked away, my throat closing up. Jo's hands clamped down on the foot of the bed. Arlene's hands curled into fists at her waist. I looked at her. She looked at me and then over to Jo.

"Honey?" Jack said again. His voice sounded high and cracked, like a young boy too scared to believe what he was seeing. Arlene's pupils were almost as big as Mama's. I saw her tongue pressing her teeth, her lips pulled thin with strain. She saw me looking at her, shook her head, and stepped back from the bed.

"Daddy," she said softly. "Daddy, we have to talk."

Arlene took Jack's arm and led him to the door. He let her take him out of the room.

I looked over at Jo. Her hands were wringing the bar at the foot of the bed like a wet towel. She continued to do it as the door swung closed behind Arlene and Jack. She continued even as Mama's mouth opened and closed and opened again.

Mama was whimpering. "Ba . . . ba . . . ba . . . ba . . . ba . . . ba."

I took Mama's hand and held it tight, then stood there watching Jo doing the only thing she could do, blistering the skin off her palms.

When Arlene came back, her face was gray, but her mouth had smoothed out.

"He signed it," she said.

She stepped around me and took her place on the other side of the bed. Jo dropped her head forward. I let my breath out slowly. Mama's hand in mine was loose. Her mouth had gone slack, though it seemed to quiver now and then, and when it did I felt the movement in her fingers.

Across from me Arlene put her right hand on Mama's shoulder. She didn't flinch when Mama's bloody left eye rolled to the side. The good eye stared straight up, wide with profound terror. Arlene began a soft humming then, as if she were starting some lullaby. Mama's terrified eye blinked and then blinked again. In the depths of that pupil I seemed to see little starbursts, tiny desperate explosions of light.

Arlene's hum never paused. She ran her hand down and took Mama's fingers into her own. Slowly, some of the terror in Mama's face eased. The straining muscles of her neck softened. Arlene's hum dropped to a lower register. It resounded off the top of her hollow throat like an oboe or a French horn shaped entirely of flesh. No, I thought. Arlene is what she has always wanted to be, the one we dare not hate. I wanted Arlene's song to go on forever. I wanted to be part of it. I leaned forward and opened my mouth, but the sound that came out of me was ugly and fell back into my throat. Arlene never even looked over at me. She kept her eyes on Mama's bloody pupil.

I knew then. Arlene would go on as long as it took, making that sound in her throat like some bird creature, the one that comes to sing hope when there is no hope left. Strength was in Arlene's song, peace its meter, love the bass note. Mama's eye swung in lazy accompaniment to that song – from me to Jo, and around again to Arlene. Her hands gripped ours, while her mouth hung open. From the base of the bed, Jo reached up and laid her hands on Mama's legs. Mama looked down once, then the good eye turned back to our bird and clung there. My eyes followed hers. I watched the thrush that beat in Arlene's breast. I heard its stubborn tuneless song.

Mama's whole attention remained fixed on that song until the pupil of the right eye finally filled up with blood and blacked out. Even then, we held on. We held Mama's stilled shape between us. We held her until she set us free.

RED DRESS
Kevin Canty

I wanted to be a mixologist. I don't know where I got the
desire, or even the word, which still has a kind of magic for me:
mixologist. In the syllables of those letters are my parents' parties,
nights of smoke and laughter and lipstick. I borrowed the Mr. Boston
bartender's guide from the liquor cabinet and read it in my bed,
imagining myself pouring, shaking, stirring, holding the sugar cube in
a slotted spoon and drizzling the red liquor through. I learned the
difference between lemon zest and lemon peel, I memorized the steps
for a perfect Ramos Gin Fizz, I knew how to pour a Manhattan, a
Stinger, a Grasshopper, a White Russian.

My sister was gone to college by then, and our only television was
downstairs. On party nights, I could neither sleep nor read; I lay on my
bed with the light on and listened to the undifferentiated oceanic
hubbub from downstairs, louder as the night went on, the whole house
gradually filling with cigarette smoke. Occasionally a guest, a man
trying to find the upstairs bathroom, would come through the door of
my room and find me on the bed, awake – which seemed to come not
only as a surprise but as an embarrassment to him, as if he had caught
me at some shameful act. He would shut the light off on the way out.

Other nights I would sit in the dark at the top of the stairs and listen.
I would try to imagine myself among the guests, try to imagine what
they were talking about. I could hear my mother's high-pitched, brittle
laughter, imagine her mixing and drifting from guest to guest in her
red party dress. I didn't want to be one of them; I just wanted to know
what made them so loud and excited, what they were hoping for.

I promoted myself to doorman at some point. My job was to answer
the bell, great the guests, take their coats and point them toward the

bar. It's always winter, the way I remember it. I think now that it might have been just one year, one winter giving way to spring and summer, but I remember it as always, world without end. This job as doorman was unsatisfying. I was closer to the action but I was visible. I was always being called by the doorbell just as the conversation was becoming interesting, just as they were starting to forget that I was among them; or coming back after the punch line, the joke I was too young to hear, the women still giggling. They couldn't help themselves. Or else, as I drifted or sidled to the edge of the group, I would be noticed, I would be called attention to with a greeting or a wave of a cigarette, and the talk would instantly turn toward the innocuous – the lives of pets, movies that had been seen, *West Side Story* or *Doctor Zhivago*. My parents' life and the lives of their friends seemed even more jumbled and fragmentary than they had before.

My mother, for instance. In everyday life, she was vague, sometimes absent-minded, wandering the house while my father was at work like she was half asleep. In my dreams, I see her standing in an almost dowdy, unrevealing floral dress, an *I Love Lucy* dress, standing just inside the doorway of her bedroom, pausing, with one hand on the dresser, and trying to remember – you could see it in her face – what she had wanted from there. Was it laundry? Jewelry? Was she going out or staying in? I still don't know what she was thinking about, or dreaming about.

When she put on her red dress and her lipstick and descended into a party, though, she became an altogether different person – energetic, intense, almost uncomfortably alive. She was everywhere at once, laughing at jokes, holding her white cigarettes to be lit, carrying trays of olives and crackers and little squares of cheese on toothpicks. When someone spoke, especially if they were talking lightly or playfully, she was lit with concentration, her mouth moving into a half-smile or a half-frown as each new sentence came spilling out. Her attention was as urgent and narrow as a flashlight beam. Yours was the one face in the world, the one joke, the only scandalous story or amusing anecdote. She lit her subjects, one by one, and then moved on, and on. Never to me. The one place her attention never lit was on my face;

and if, sometime after eleven, she happened to notice that I was still awake – watching her, as ever, from my station by the door – all the old puzzlement would return to her face, and she would stare at me, wondering who I was and how I had gotten there, for a long moment before ordering me off to bed.

She would tuck me into the sheets in her red party dress and she would kiss me goodnight and then leave, down the hall in a rustle of fabric. I would lie on my bed with the door open, drifting in and out of sleep, awakening to singing, to arguments and fights, sleeping again to dream of flowers and smoke, the laughter penetrating the thin screen of my sleep. Once I came to the top of the stairs, awake or nearly awake, in time to watch two men carry another out into the snow, a trickle of blood at the corner of his mouth. Once I heard somebody singing "Mairzy Doats," which I recognized from an old cartoon. Always the sound of my mother's laughter.

In the morning, before my parents woke up, which was never before ten-thirty or eleven, the house was mine: the ashtray-smell of dead cigarettes, lipsticky glasses, the toothpicks with their frilly cellophane tops scattered at random on the tablecloth. Only the flowers, the flowers which my mother and I had picked out so carefully the day before, had managed to stay fresh. I would wander barefoot through the wreckage, sniffing the half-finished drinks, the bourbon-smell of my father in each of them, and having little conversations. I was winning. I was charming. I left laughter behind me wherever I went.

Sometime in spring, I was promoted to bartender. Not without an argument, though – my mother roused herself into one of her fits of motherhood, which were always a little hypothetical. She was acting as if she were my mother, as if I were her son.

"I don't think he needs to stay up that late," she said.

This was the eve of another party – I can't understand how they could have had so many parties; it must have been two or three or four years altogether, not just one. My father, with my help, was setting up the drinks table, watching me carefully prepare the bowl of lime wedges, arrange the ice and shakers and Angostura bitters.

"He likes it," my father said. "Besides, he's always up till the wee small hours anyway."

"I always send him to bed."

"Doesn't mean he goes to sleep," my father said, turning his attention on me. "What do you do up there, anyway, Champ? You aren't sleeping, are you?"

I didn't know how to respond to this. I didn't know what this was code for, or what the secret response might be.

"I never could stand to be left out myself," he said.

"Could I talk to you for a moment?" my mother asked.

They disappeared into the kitchen, leaving me to bustle, straighten and cut, laying out ashtrays, putting the glasses in an accurate row: wine glasses, cocktail glasses, highballs. If I could make myself indispensable, they would have to let me stay. The pleasure that I found in this kind of work – tidying, straightening, fussing – was intense, illicit. I straightened the flowers in their vases until they looked attractive from every angle. I placed ashtrays, coasters, bowls of pretzels and mixed nuts while my parents were arguing in the kitchen. My father would win, eventually, as he did. He would wear her down like water. I took uneasy pleasure in knowing that he would prevail, knowing that I was fooling him. He thought I was pretending to be the little man.

Her face, when they came out of the kitchen, had a mixed, unsettled, lost look that made me feel lost with her. She was right and it didn't matter.

"You're on, Champ," said my father. "Let's see if we can find you a necktie."

"Just until ten-thirty, though," my mother said.

"Ten-thirty or eleven," said my father. "We'll see how it's going."

She looked at him helplessly. He shouldn't have contradicted her in front of me, but she could do nothing about it. And then she looked at me and it was strange; it felt like she could really see me, like the fog had cleared away momentarily and she recognized something.

"You be careful," she said to me.

"What does that mean?" my father asked her. "He's in his own living room, for Christ's sake. What could go wrong?"

She didn't answer for a moment; abstract, musing, she stared into my eyes, wondering what she saw there. I didn't know myself. I knew it was guilty, I knew it was something to hide, but I didn't know what it's name was.

"He could cut himself," she said, turning away from my face, back to my father. "That's all I meant."

"He's not going to cut himself," said my father; though I did, in fact, slice my finger wide open with a paring knife while cutting up a second batch of limes, at almost midnight.

Sixty or seventy men and women milled and perched and chatted in the first floor of the old house that night, a few of the men – hardy souls in wool sport jackets – out on the patio smoking cigarettes, a group around the stereo listening, I remember distinctly, listening to Olatunji and His Drums of Passion. The night had gone quickly, up until then. It amused them all to treat me as a genuine bartender, to make jokes about stiff ones and wet ones that I didn't quite understand – though I laughed eagerly – and to stuff dollar bills and loose silver into the jar that my father had insisted I put on the table in front of me. I had the glassware and the bottles and the mixers and the utensils all neatly aligned, near at hand. I wore a dish towel around my waist, as a sort of apron, to tidy up any spills; and I thought that I had fulfilled my duties as well as any grown-up bartender could, that I had been crisp and professional and nearly invisible, and I was proud of myself.

All of this changed in the course of one second. I was cutting a lime and something – a shout, a burst of laughter – distracted my attention. When I looked down again, I saw that I had cut myself, and cut myself badly – that moment before the blood begins to flow, before anything starts to hurt, when the cut flap of skin turns white. I was immediately filled with shame. Quickly, before any of them could see me, I wrapped the cut finger in three or four thicknesses of cocktail napkin and slipped away from my post, through the kitchen and up the back stairs to the third, hard-to-find bathroom in the old part of the house.

I sat on the edge of the toilet and gingerly unwrapped the napkins. Blood seeped eagerly from the cut. In the bright, palegreen florescent light, the hand looked disembodied, already dead. I thought that if I lifted up the flap of skin I might see all the way to the bone; but I was already a little dizzy, a little queasy, and I didn't. What if I died there? What if I bled to death while the party raged downstairs?

But I wasn't going to die. I was going to get caught. I had over-stepped myself, had pretended to be what I was not: competent, reliable, safe. In fact I was just a child, pretending.

I cut the light so that nobody would find me, and waited for the bleeding to subside. Clear moonlight came through the window, through the leafless trees outside. Stupid boy, I thought, stupid stupid boy. Soon I would have to face them, and they would all know. The bleeding continued, slower and slower. I soaked the blood up with toilet paper. It hurt, by then, considerably, and I had to bend and unbend my finger several times to convince myself that I had not severed something vital.

After a few minutes, the blood slowed to a manageable trickle. In the moonlight – my eyes had adjusted perfectly well – I found gauze and adhesive tape in the medicine cabinet over the sink. Clumsy, singlehanded, I wrapped the wound in bandages, finishing off with a pair of flesh-colored Band-Aids, in the hope I would not be discovered; in the hope that I could return to my post behind the bar. I hid the bloody paper under a magazine, artfully placed over the top of the trash basket, slipped the lock and went out into the hallway.

There in the moonlight was my mother with a man: Kendellan, my father's college friend. They weren't touching, but something about their bodies alerted me, awkward, like frozen bodies in a game of freeze-tag. Something had been started, interrupted. They must have been kissing – that blank unseeing look on her face that only slowly cleared, the flush on her neck – but I didn't know that then. I was an unwelcome surprise. Apart from that, nothing was clear.

"Ray," she said. "What are you doing up here?"

I held my injured hand behind my back, as casually as I could.

"Nothing," I said; and then, when I realized this didn't make any sense, I said, "The other bathrooms were all full."

"It's late, sweetie," she said, stepping away from Kendellan, who wouldn't give me his face. She bent toward me and I smelled her perfume. "It's late. Off we go. Let's go."

She took my hand – the innocent hand – and led me down the back hallway to my bedroom. The ebb and surge of conversation spilled up the stairs but it was not for me, not that night. She led me to my door and kissed me briefly, dryly on the top of my head, as she had for most of my life, an assertion of normalcy, a statement that everything was, after all, in the right place, where it had been before. She was wearing the red dress, same as always.

Then she turned, and closed the door, and went back to wherever she was going, leaving me, again, alone in my room. And maybe she was right – maybe I was overtired, maybe it was not right for me to be out so late – because when I caught sight of myself in the mirror, my crisp white shirt and real bow tie that my father had tied for me, it struck me as awful, and wrong, and unfair, and I didn't even have a name for it. I curled into a ball on my bed and cried, until I fell asleep in my clothes.

The finger became infected in the following days. I concealed it from my mother as long as I could, as the swelling grew and the pain drummed along with every beat of my heart; I didn't know exactly where I stood with her, I didn't want any new event between us until the old one had subsided. Kendellan and my mother, my mother and Kendellan, like something out of a dream – and in fact I did see the moment replayed in dreams, with photographic literalness; and I nearly managed to convince myself that it had never happened. If anything had happened at all.

By mid-week, though, I had to do something. I couldn't sleep, and strange colors were appearing around the swollen cut. Awake, asleep, I felt like I was half-body and half-finger, every part of me focused on this one throbbing spot.

I confessed; I was examined, taken to the doctor, pronounced purulent. The cut was drained and cleaned and freshly bandaged, I was put on antibiotics and ordered to stay home for the rest of the week. I may have been seriously ill – I felt a kind of pleasant haze or fog in the edges of my vision, and the doctor and my mother were worried. It was in their faces. The gifted child does not miss this kind of thing.

Home, then, and a short week of television-watching, soup and crackers, the sound of the washing machine and the hot breath of the dryer. I was special, once again. This should have been perfect; home alone, my mother and I, the chance to see the daily life she led, the life that was hidden while I was at school. I don't think I was sick any more than the next child, but I did enjoy being sick more than most of them. But this week was different; in the afterimage of that party – the dream of Mr. Kendellan, the interrupted moment – I felt like I was always on the verge of a question, I had to hold it back, a box I knew I didn't want to open. And my mother, when she saw me at all, seemed always about to launch into some new explanation. We were not easy with each other.

So I slept, and I read, and I slept some more, and I waited for the weekend, and after the weekend I would be back at school.

On Friday, though, I woke from my nap midway through the afternoon and my mother was gone – shopping, I thought, drycleaning, general errands. Nothing was planned for the weekend, no flowers or special foods, no trips to the liquor store and hundred-dollar bills. My sister was coming home that evening. All the pieces of my world were in place. I went to my parents' bedroom, overlooking the street, and I looked out on the place where her car had been, the outline of her car in dry pavement on the rain-darkened street. It was three or three-thirty, overcast and dark. The light in the room was dim and gray, softshadowed, a delicate touch on skin.

I went to my mother's closet and I opened the folding doors and I touched the red dress. I was alone in the house. There was nobody to stop me, nobody to see. The barriers between my dream life and my waking one had been let down. My own clothes felt like a mistaken costume; quickly I took them off and threw them under the bed, where I wouldn't have to look at them. Now I was alone with the mass of dresses, the colors spilling out into the dim light, the disorderly crowd of shoes on the floor. Dresses and dresses but there was only one for me. I was almost exactly my mother's size. My skin was soft as hers was, softer. I could feel the softness of my own skin. I slipped the dress on, the red dress. I looked at the lipsticks, the bottles of perfume; I looked at my shoulders in the mirror. A strange face stared back at me, a girl's face, mine.

A car door slammed shut outside.

I ran to the window – stupid stupid boy – and that was where she saw me, maybe nothing more than a flash of red but she saw me. In a moment she would be in the house and upstairs and what would happen after that? I couldn't imagine. I took my clothes and ran to my room, closing the door behind me as the front door opened and closed downstairs but it was no use – there was no time. She was bound to find me. She had already found me. I sat at the edge of my bed and waited.

She didn't come.

A minute passed, another minute. As quietly as I could, I slipped out of the dress, into my boy's clothes, watched over by models and dinosaurs. I opened my door as gently as I could and put the dress back in the closet. When the door was closed, everything was where it had started. I went back to my room and waited, but she wasn't coming up. After ten or fifteen minutes, I went downstairs. She was waiting in the kitchen.

"How are you feeling, sweetie?" she asked, putting the cereal box in the pantry, the milk in the refrigerator door. She didn't even look.

"I'm fine," I told her.

"I'm glad to hear it," she said; and that was all. She looked at me once, and I knew that she had seen me, if ever I had doubted it. But we never spoke about it – never spoke about that afternoon, or Kendellan, never spoke openly to each other again. She was still my mother, I was still her son. But everything after that was in code, ambiguous, the silences full of unasked questions, the words empty of answers. And now I am grown, and my mother is dead, and my father is dead. And this is all the childhood I will ever have.

BALL

Tara Ison

My sweet little dog Tess is what they call "apricot." She has tiny blue eyes, almond shaped and set close together like Barbra Streisand's, and the prettiest little dog vagina. I spent twenty minutes examining and marveling at it once with my best friend Dayna, before she had a boyfriend and we spent a lot of our time together appreciating Tess; Dayna is a biologist, which gave the experience a legitimizingly clinical spirit. It's a tidy, quarter-inch slit in a pinky-tip protuberance of skin, delicate and irrelevant and veiled with fine, apricot hair. Tess rolled over and spread out happily, trustingly for us; she lives almost pathetically for love, for attention, like a quivering heroine from some fifties romance novel. She also lives for food and naps, but mostly for Ball. Tennis balls, squishy rubber ones with bells inside, any spherical object to love will do. I've learned hard rubber balls are the best – the last time she had a flimsy plastic one she worked it down to bits, chewed it with such passion there was almost nothing left.

She came with a ball. I'd been living alone in my big new house with a fireplace for six days, came home on a Thursday evening to the still-lingering smell of paint and spackle and fresh-sliced carpet fibers and realized I can have a dog, here. Apartment living hadn't allowed for that, but now I had my own house, with a fireplace and a small fiberglass Jacuzzi in a small chlorine-scented backyard, all to myself. I was only twenty-five, and very proud of having my own house. I walked around and around, and my heels clacked resoundingly on the hardwood floors. Dayna had mentioned maybe coming over, but we'd hung out together the last five nights out of six, she was in a needy, boyfriendless phase, and her presence was becoming a cloying and oppressive force. She hated sleeping alone – she's always scared of an earthquake, a fire combusting out of nowhere, a serial-killer-rapist-burglar breaking in – but I wanted my big new house all to myself, and a dog, and a fire in the fireplace. I went right back out and bought a newspaper and called the first ad for a cockapoo: *eleven mos, shots, fxd, hsbrkn, plyful*. A cockapoo, to me, meant the large dark eyes of a baby harp seal and a silky spaniel coat, a body thick-limbed but compact and floppy. The true, Platonic image of a cockapoo. I drove to an apartment complex in Northridge. The dog was hideous, at first sight, more blurred, crossbred terrier and poodle than anything else, with skinny crooked legs that needed to be broken and reset, and those creepy blue eyes. A brown nose, faded like over-creamed coffee. And she was covered with fleas, little dark, leaping specks visible through her beige fur. I made polite chat with the owner, a heavy, sixtyish black woman named Gloria – *That isn't beige, dear, they call that color "apricot" on a poodle* – who couldn't be bothered with the dog anymore, and then told her that yes, I *knew* the ad said she'd be eleven months, but I really did want a puppy. The dog dropped a soiled, shreddy, lime-colored tennis ball in front of me and looked up, her tiny eyes squinting with hope and expectation: *You want to play with my ball? Here, look, here's a ball! You want to play? Please, please!* When I ignored her she pounced on the ball with her skinny front legs, her paws shoving it toward me – *Ball! Ball! Ball!* – until I gave in and threw it for her. But when I got up to leave, I suddenly realized that if I didn't take her, it meant I would have to keep interviewing dogs. This seemed like an exhausting prospect: continuing to call deceptive ads, inquire about worms, meet imperfect dogs, choose. Also, it meant that I would be going home that night to my big house alone. I told Gloria I would take the dog, thinking, literally, that if it didn't work out I would just get rid of it somehow. I wrote Gloria a check for seventy-five dollars – the cost of getting the dog fixed at five months, and the shots – and she gave me the dog's leash, a quarter of a bag of Puppy Chow, and the dog. At the last moment, Gloria put the soiled tennis ball in the Puppy Chow bag, like a parting gift. *The dog's gotta have that ball*, she said, *or any kind of ball, you'll see.* I stopped at the drugstore on the way home with the dog, to buy flea shampoo and dog treats, and I dumped the dirty, lime-hairy ball in a Dumpster. Through the window of the car the dog watched me do this, anxious, her squinty little eyes made wide and round by alarm.

At home she suffered submissively, mournfully, through the kitchen-sink flea bath and a towel-drying in front of a fire in the fireplace, then curled up tight as a snail shell at the foot of my bed, looking orphaned and weepy. She wouldn't touch the doggy rag tug thing I'd bought, nor the faux-bone treats, nor the plastic squeaky toy shaped like a garish hamburger with the works. I went to bed wondering how to unload an ugly and sentient animal. Several hours later I heard a light thud sound, then a *thump-roll, thump-roll,* and I looked across my room to see the little dog trotting happily toward the bed with a large green apple in her mouth. She jumped up on the bed with it, dropped it, peered up squintily with hope and expectation, and shoved it toward me with her crooked apricot paws. I knew I'd bought apples during the week, but how she'd found one I had no idea – some desperate, biologically driven search for Ball. I threw the apple across the room for her for a while, and each time she brought it back to me, thrilled, suffused with intimate joy at our connection. She finally tired, snail-curled on the empty pillow next to me, and went to sleep. When I awoke in the morning her brown nose was breathing in my face and her almond-shaped blue eyes blinked at me with drowsy adoration, and I was abruptly slapped swollen with love. I went out first thing and bought her a real ball, periwinkle blue, hard rubber, just the right size and with a solid, stable bounce.

Now it isn't just my echoing footsteps in the house, it's her happy, scratchy nail scrambles, the thud and roll of a ball that I hear.

I loved her so much it was numbing, and sometimes, to jab a feeling at myself, I fantasized about her dying. Getting hit by a car, drinking from a contaminated puddle of water when we went on walks (how my accountant Jill's dog died), or succumbing to an attack of bloat (some disease my friend Lesley's dog almost died of, when the intestines bunch up out of nowhere). Or I would whet the fantasy by imagining that I had to sacrifice her for some reason. Put her out of some misery. I'd have her dying of encroaching cancers, where I forced myself to give her a mercifully quick and lethal shot of morphine because keeping her alive and in pain would only fill my own selfish needs. This usually made me cry, and once, picturing that and crying, I called Dayna and made her promise me if Tess ever did get sick she'd get drugs and a syringe from the lab, and we'd take care of it so Tess would never suffer. Or I'd think about an epic disaster, a nuclear bomb or a nine-point earthquake that somehow destroyed all the food and left me with nothing but Tess, and would I be willing to starve to death instead of eat her. How bad something would have to get to force me to do such a thing. I wondered what Tess would taste like. I imagined her flesh was tender and sweet. Her paw pads were the color of cracked, grayish charcoal, and smelled of burnt popcorn. When she yawned I poked my nose into the gap of her jaw and inhaled. I ran my hands over the wiry pubiclike hairs at the base of her spine, the fine, clumped curls at her throat. She let her head fall all the way back when I did this, so trusting, her throat stretched to a soft, defenseless, apricot sweep. I just wanted to crawl inside of her sometimes, or have her crawl inside of me, keep her safe there forever.

In hindsight, Gloria's ad was accurate; Tess was indeed *fxd* – you could still feel the barbed wire of subcutaneous stitches in her belly, another thing Dayna and I always marveled at, or used to, before Dayna met her boyfriend, back when hanging out meant admiring and playing Ball with Tess for hours at a time – and *hsbrkn*, and I was spared all the yipping, newspaper-thwacking, stick-her-nose-in-it hassles of a puppy. The idea of disciplining her horrified me, and I was glad I didn't have to. Her one unfortunate habit was her way of hurtling herself at people to greet them when they came in the door, invariably impacting at ovary- or testicle-crushing height. Dayna encouraged this, finding the hurtling a consistent and unconditional show of love; she'd catch Tess in mid-leap, grab her at each side's delicate, curving haunch, and swoop her around the living room or the backyard like a clumsy, older puppy-sister. Tess's exuberance, her insistence on playing Ball, worked as sort of a litmus test for other people – how much grace they mustered up told me a lot about who they were. But most people adored her. Some friends perfected a knee-dip-and-swivel, so that Tess landed smack against a fleshy mid-thigh. Eric showed a congenial grace about it the first time he came over to my house, but after that it became his means to set the evening's tone; if he was feeling generous he petted her, threw the ball for her, and we had a stressless, fun, prurient kind of time together, but if he wasn't in the mood or thought I was paying too much attention to her, he got nasty. Sometimes there was a faintly sinister quality to it, especially when she wanted to play Ball and he didn't. Sometimes it became an enraging, bitter thing. He'd hide the ball, laughing as she searched the house in a growing panic. Or he'd pretend to throw it but then hide it behind his back, and smirk at her bewilderment. If she shoved the ball at him once too often – and she could be relentless, needy, *You want to play with my ball? Here, look, here's a ball! You want to play? Please, please!* – his annoyance built to the point where I got very nervous and protective, almost scared he was going to explode and hurt her. I'd try to distract him with food or sex. Sometimes I think he hated her, but then he'd be so sweet and loving I'd figure it would all be okay. He liked coming to my place because of the fireplace and the Jacuzzi, but it still usually felt safer to me if I just went alone to his.

I met Eric two years ago, when Dayna had a big party to celebrate getting a promotion at her lab, something that involved a bonus and increased time with rabbits. She told me she'd invited a couple of young guys who'd moved in across the street; one of them had a girlfriend but the other was exactly my type, and also the type who probably wouldn't go for her, anyway. Dayna is very beautiful, she just has a way of thrusting herself at men, emotionally stripping for them on a first date. She assumes men prefer me because I'm smaller – she's six feet tall, stunning, but six feet tall – while I think it's just because she tries too hard, opens up too massively. She drowns you with all of herself, with a flood of vulnerability, trust, need, and I know that the success of sex depends on contrivance, in holding yourself back. It's the tease, not the strip. You offer up your soul for a taste, it's like an invitation to feed on it. Once I went out with a guy she'd dated for a while – to her despair, only a sexless, buddy sort of dating – who told me he'd been attracted to her honesty, but was a lot more attracted to my sexuality, which made me feel bad for her but also sort of smug. I only went out with him once, and didn't sleep with him – he wasn't really my type, just almost, a little too short – but when I mentioned it a few years later to Dayna she thought it was a hateful, disgusting thing for me to do, go out with someone she'd liked, that I hadn't been a good friend. She kept insisting she would never do a thing like that. This was bullshit – of course she would, she'd do anything for a guy, ditch any friend, I could think of examples, she's so painfully desperate for intimacy and marriage and babies – but I let it go. She needed to think herself more moral than I was, as if it balanced things out. I never told her his comment to me, but it's the sort of thing she'd be likely to come to all on her own and kick herself for.

Eric turned out to be twenty-three, six years younger than Dayna and me, and striking, a wonderfully alpine six-feet-four, which was certainly tall enough for Dayna, but I saw what she meant by my type – tall and bold men always make me feel sexual, nymphetish – and also what she meant by he probably wouldn't go for her, anyway. He didn't want a drowning torrent of intimacy; he wanted to get laid. We sat on the floor of Dayna's apartment for an hour at the party's wane, drinking beer and making suggestive, clever comments to each other while he played Ball with Tess. He petted her and scratched her tummy, not realizing that being sweet to my sweet little dog was a litmus test of sexual acceptability, a wildly effective and endearing form of foreplay. She adored him, draped herself trustingly across his lap, her little almond eyes slanted closed in bliss. But that wasn't why I wanted him, badly, really; it was the adamant and unabashed sex look of him, his way of dirty, lustful regard. His look said *Sex*, said *Fuck, suck me, I'm hard*, said *It's specifically, singularly, because of you*. His hands stroking Tess's tummy – I wanted them on me, working me, shoving my thighs apart, pressing me facedown by my shoulders or the back of my neck into a pillow, raising my hips high from behind, guiding my head. I suddenly remembered Malcolm, the guy of Dayna's I'd once gone out with, regarding me like that. Almost . . . three years ago? Four? Right, four years, it was just before I'd bought my own house, found Tess. I suddenly realized I hadn't been fully looked at that way in a while, maybe since. It used to happen all the time, but not so often anymore. Eric looked at me that way, and I wanted to get his cock inside me, fast, to grip at and hold onto that look. I wanted to leave with him that second, but I knew Dayna would be upset. So I waited another half-hour to suggest he show me his new place across the street, and in answer he circled me hard around the waist, leaned over, and kissed me – more gently than I'd expected, but still his arm was firm, ruling – and then we left. I took Tess with me, and her latest in the series of hard rubber periwinkle blue balls; Dayna had wanted us to sleep over, but hey, she was the one who tossed me this guy in the first place.

I hate fucking men who get moony or coy about it, who act as if there's an element of accident that you're here, doing this, as if you both tripped and wound up landing naked in bed. Eric was brusque and unsheepish, as fearless of sex as a porn star. He had the hard, tapered male torso I like, skin so fluid and seamless your hand slides, slides. My own skin is starting to dry, slightly – I shouldn't go in the Jacuzzi too often – I've noticed fine, thin wrinkles when I twist the loosening flesh of my upper arms, I've grown a little self-conscious of my babyish pout of belly. But the sex was an endlessly wet, vehement, pounded smooth kind of sex that wiped out doubt.

During the first surge of it, on Eric's living room sofa – a velour playpen-style couch still smelling faintly of frat house joints and beer – Tess had stretched out drowsily at the far end, behind Eric's hunching, jarring back, out of his view. We reeled to his bed afterward, while he was still solid and driven and I could still jolt at a slightest touch of his tongue, to start all over. She picked up her ball and padded after us, climbed upon a bolster we'd thrown on the floor, and went back to sleep. I'd had Tess for a little over four years by then, but had never fucked anyone with her in the room before; I typically went to the guy's house and left afterward, because, after all, Tess would be home, waiting for me, needing to go out. I liked my bed all to ourselves. After the second time, I got up, awkwardly – my legs felt permanently locked apart at the hips, hinged wide – and fumbled for clothing, but Eric grabbed an ankle and pulled me back onto the quilted bedspread. Mock-wrestle, mock-struggle, and Tess jumped up on the bed with us to play, her mouth full of periwinkle ball. He had me pinned on my side, was fumbling with himself, aiming, when Tess dropped and shoved her ball at him – *Get out of here, dog, go on*, he said – wedging it under his thigh – *You want to play with my ball? Here, look, here's a ball! You want to play? Please, please!* – and kept shoving, desperate for his attention, his affirming and engaged throw of the ball. I tried squirming upward, trying to glide, grasp him inside me, distract him, but one more ball-shove from Tess – *Would you get her the fuck out of here?* he snapped at me – and he jerked out a leg, catching her just at her midsection's arching curve, and hurled her off the bed. She yelped, I saw in the streetlamp's light through the window an apricot blur, and heard her smack the wall, heard her flurry slide to the ground.

I was up and to her in a second – *Hey, I'm sorry, I didn't mean to do that, okay?* – and she was fine, just bewildered. She poked her damp pink tongue in my ear and hiccuped like a little human baby, and I cradled her, rubbing her tummy. She was fine, but I wanted to cry. Eric kept apologizing, coaxing me back, and when I looked at him in disgust, finally said I was overreacting, just being neurotic, I shouldn't indulge her so much, I was probably going to wind up some weird old lady living alone with forty-seven poodles. I carried her out of the bedroom, slamming the door behind us. Then I didn't know what to do. It was almost three, I knew Dayna was asleep, and I didn't want to go wake her up, explain what had happened. She'd be furious; worse, she'd be smug. And Tess's ball was still in the bedroom with Eric; I wasn't leaving without it, I wasn't going to leave her without a ball.

I carried her into Eric's roommate's bedroom – he was staying at his girlfriend's, Eric had told me – and crawled with her into the unmade bed, into unwashed sheets with that odor of careless, straight young bachelor guys. She dozed on the greasy pillow next to me, in her spine-defying, shell-curled way, her nose in my face. I tried to go to sleep. My jaw ached; I scratched away some flakes of dried semen on my cheek, craved a drink of water, but didn't want to get up. My insides felt still stretched open, rooted out. My hips kept twitching in the rhythm I'd found sent him over. I'd already gotten to know the thick vein in bas-relief on the left side of his cock, and the exact, utmost length within me his fingers could go, and I wanted all of that back. For some reason I thought of Malcolm, the guy of Dayna's – though he wasn't really ever that, she'd just hoped for it – and his hungry, wanting look. His slight nervousness, the jiggling knee, the fumbling with a spoon, had lost it for me; it meant he wasn't fully consumed or absorbed by lust, there was room left for consciousness, thoughtfulness, diffusion. Eric's lust was heated and direct and unrefracted as rays of light through a magnifying glass, focused to burn you down to death. I wanted that back. I heard Tess yawn, and I craned to face her, needing the comforting, starfish scent of her breath.

I waited until she was asleep, then got up, closed the roommate's door behind me, and crept back into Eric's room. He'd thrown half the bedspread over himself and lay sleeping, sprawled out and mammoth and lustrous. I molded myself small up against the length of him, and felt a flutter of pulse down his arm; I crawled on top of him and slid myself around until he grew big and hard and I could grip at that vivid, affirming burn one more time.

In the morning we glanced disdainfully at each other, and rolled quickly out of opposite sides of the bed. I retrieved Tess's ball, and hurried to free her from the other room; she kissed me wildly, whimpering, as though she'd feared something had happened to me or that I'd left her forever. He watched me nuzzle her for a moment – *I guess that's the deal breaker, huh?* he said – then shrugged and went back into his room. Dayna looked at me like a resigned, just slightly reproachful good loser when I came in, then shrieked a greeting to Tess, whipped her up to a leaping, hurtling frenzy, and swooped around the room with her. We spent the rest of the morning cleaning up the party's dismal mess and playing Ball. Eric called me at home the next day, and I invited him over for the following Saturday night; he came bearing a single iris for me, and a bag of pricey lamb-and-rice treats for Tess. He let her climb onto his lap, and she spread herself out happily for him, unguarded, unselfconscious, arching her head and exposing her throat to his fondling, stroking hand. He threw the ball for her that night, again and again. But after that I usually insisted on going to his place and leaving Tess with Dayna, where it was safe.

I was careful to never fall asleep at his place again, even after a year. I didn't want to get slack, or too accessible, and actually sleeping together was hardly the point. The only time, after that first grotesque night and morning, was just an accident, a slip. Tess was across the street with Dayna, and the plan, as always, was the requisite dinner with Eric while we watched a movie or a rerun of *The Simpsons*, then sex, and then I leave. I just wanted pizza or Chinese delivered, something quick, because the dinner was not the point either, just a feature he liked to insist on, but I got to his apartment and smelled onions cooking, mushrooms, the acrid snap of garlic. He was making dinner. His roommate was out, and he was making an evening, trying to, out of a Lyle Lovett CD and a head of romaine lettuce and a jar of Ragu sauce spiffed up with fresh onions and mushrooms – *Hey come on, I really like to cook, my mom told me to add all these veggies*, he said, nodding – and a gleaming bottle of red zinfandel. A boiling pot of spaghetti fogged the kitchen with starch; the table was set with melamine plates and paper towel napkins folded in big squares. Fine, okay. I started on the wine, had half the bottle down by the end of salad, and listened to him talk about some old college girlfriend, some Shannon or Nicole, who he'd been with for a couple of years and really cared about but just was never ready to commit to and how he'd heard the other day she was getting married and he really did hope she was happy but it still really hurt, you know, and it was probably time he started really thinking about what he was going to do with his life, about what he wanted in life, and what did I think about all that. And what I was thinking was that it was getting late and we'd never had sex yet on his kitchen table and can we get going? And that Tess was waiting for me over at Dayna's and I've finished my spaghetti and can we get going? I tipped the last of the wine into my mouth, got up, slid off my underwear from under my skirt, and he shut up. I sat on his lap, straddling him, pushed his hand down in the crotch of space between us, used my hand against the buttons on his jeans, and his breathing quickened. I traced the rim of his ear with my tongue, worked myself against his fingers, everything I knew would do it, and it did, his cock jutting out from his split-open fly and the table edge gouging my spine when he lunged forward at me. I leaned back with my elbows on the table, skirt raised and legs open, for him to get me up and onto it, but instead he picked me up – *Uh-uh, not here*, he mumbled – clutching and carrying me like a sack of fragile groceries, kissing me before we even got to his room. He fell with me on the bed, fell onto me with a great, weighted crush, but when I squirmed to get up on my hands and knees for him he gently pushed me flat again, face down, nudging my legs apart – *Good, I like that*, I said, *do that* – and then twisted my shoulders around so that while he thrust into me from behind, lying on me, he had my face against his, or his face in my neck, still kissing me. That kind of twist was a strain, everything went taut and seized up until it hurt so I couldn't stand it anymore; I finally had to pull back away from him, turn away. I pressed my face down into the pillow but he wouldn't let me do that, wanted my arm around his shoulders or his neck, holding on, wanted me facing him, and twisted me back. It took a long time. He kept slowing down and every time I was about to come he wouldn't let me, he'd just stop, still looking at me, and when we both finally came in the middle of a kiss that was like breathing straight into each other's lungs we stayed like that, still, all twisted up around each other. When my spine and the rest of me finally relaxed, went aimless, all of my muscles eased into place and I strayed off to sleep. Eric still on top of me, holding me. A branch hitting the window lurched me awake well after midnight, and my first aware thought was a glad one, *Thank God that woke me up so I can get out of here.*

I pulled away from Eric and called Dayna – yeah, Tess was okay, she was right there on the pillow next to her. I told Dayna I was coming over, I'd be there soon. Proof I was a good friend, always there for her, this guy doesn't mean anything to me, see, and she wasn't just a baby-sitter. Eric tugged on the phone in my hand, *No, come on, don't leave, she's fine*, but I shook my head at him until he let go. He was angry, I could see in the light from the streetlamp through the window, and that pleased me. I could imagine him thinking there was something wrong with me that I'd leave him to go running off to my dog. He rolled over to the other side of the bed, a big, spoiled baby, *Fine, go*, his back to me; I got up and straightened out my clothes and left without saying good-bye. He needed to learn, I thought, that he can't have everything he wants. That he was only there to fuck, I'd never be lulled, and in the end, if he ever pushed me, I would always choose my sweet little dog.

When I went to Sausalito, Tess stayed with my mother. An artist friend asked me to house-sit for six weeks while he went to Eastern Europe to study iconography; I decided leaving town would wave a giant Fuck You flag at Eric, a banner of my insusceptibility. I decided it was time for a more sporadic arrangement, that it would keep everything fervent and honed. I told my artist friend I'd love to get out of town for a while. The only problem: no dogs. He was wildly allergic. I insisted to him that poodles don't shed, and that Tess was mostly poodle, I thought, but he wasn't about to come home to dander and tracked-in spores. He was apologetic, but that was the deal. I decided it was worth it, that Eric needed to be reminded what this was, and I reminded myself that contrivance works. It does, I'm telling you. Dayna was hurt and upset, as if I were abandoning her. She was also upset she couldn't take Tess – her hours at the lab made it impossible. So I packed up Tess's food and water dishes, her special high-quality food the vet had recommended, her leash, her blue rubber ball, and drove her over to my mom's. I started crying when I hugged her goodbye – *Don't worry, honey, she's my grandchild, isn't she? I'll take very, very good care of her* – and she burrowed her face in the crook of my neck. I was a terrible mother to do this to her, and for what, for him? I pushed my nose into her charcoal-colored paw pads to breathe in the salty, furry, puppy-sweat smell, then forced myself to leave. I cried for a few hours afterward, choked with guilt, still seeing her forlorn, confused face as I drove off without her.

Not waking up to Tess was awful. I walked through Sausalito two or three times a day – gift shop, gallery, gift shop, gallery, driftwood seagulls everywhere – and when I found people with dogs, I would befriend them. Guys with dogs thought I was coming on to them, but I just wanted the dogs. One Sunday I met a retired policeman from Oakland, walking a docile, regal Borzoi. This was an odd dog for a policeman to have, a guy with a movie cop's burly swagger and black kangaroo-leather shoes. Long before Tess, I'd thought of having a Borzoi one day; they're hugely magnificent art deco dogs with dear, shy temperaments, but they're also congenitally stupid. This one was skittish, too, and pulled nervously from my greeting – the guy told me she'd been part of a case he'd investigated, that she'd been abused and abandoned by some volatile, coked-up perp, and afterward he'd adopted her. Cynthia. He said abused dogs broke his heart, even more than abused kids, because dogs are even more vulnerable and trusting, their lives are in our hands and they know it. And they are like kids, they even love the people who abuse them, you know? There's that innate instinct to adapt, adjust. He'd like to see animal abuse laws toughened up. Cynthia was his baby now, *Yeah, my precious little girl, Daddy's always gonna take good, fine care of you, uh huh.* She bumped her long muzzle into his stomach, leaned against him so fully and hard he almost lost his balance. She trusted me to pet her for a while, then, and I ran my fingers through her long, sheening white coat, wishing for Tess. The guy looked like he maybe wanted to keep talking, or go for coffee, but I just wanted to pet Cynthia. Yeah, I told him, because animals had purer souls than human beings – everybody has their own agenda and wants something from you, even friends, even lovers, even your mother, and you can't let your guard down, ever, that's when they get you, hurt you – and so animals were more honest, more deserving of love and care. I told him I had a little apricot cockapoo I just loved to death, who was every-thing pure and innocent and sweet in the world, who I'd do anything for, and the idea of actually getting married and having actual children was revolting to me, because you couldn't fully ever trust a human being, a friend, a parent, a lover, they love you, they hurt you, you can't even trust yourself, whereas a dog like Tess would be there for you, always. I told him I shouldn't even be away from her here in

Sausalito, I should hurry home, because I was just wasting six weeks of her life – she wasn't a puppy anymore, she was a grown-up dog, and I'd sacrificed six precious weeks of her life away from her, just to be here alone, a big, gaping crater of a person with nothing to hold inside. I told him I felt I could never get close enough to her, keep her safe enough from harm, because I wasn't really worthy of her, and because the world and everyone in it was so profoundly fucked. I asked him if he wanted to go get coffee or a drink or something, but he tugged a little on Cynthia's leash, and said it was nice meeting me, but they had to get going.

My mother always apologized on the phone that she couldn't possibly give Tess the kind of attention I gave her – she just couldn't play Ball all the time, it was too much. It was like having a child in the house again, Like when you were little, honey, she'd say, always wanting attention, so needy, a person could go nuts from it, from the constant demand, a person can't help losing her patience. A person can't help losing it, now and then. Sometimes something just snaps, she would say, her voice a remembered echo, a long-lost refrain. And you can't give in to giving them love all the time, the real world's not like that and they have to learn. If you do, it just spoils a child, they learn how to be manipulative, and Tess, well, she is a little spoiled, honey, she could use some discipline. And she was acting maybe a little depressed. I assured my mother that Tess loved being at her house and I knew she was taking very good care of her, doing the best she could, but part of me felt a little nervous and protective. I drove home a week early; I sort of expected to find Tess ragged and thin and hungry, like the orphans at the beginning of *Oliver*, and my mother clutching a hairbrush, a spatula, a coiled fistful of telephone cord. But Tess was fine, hurtling herself at me in joy, whimpering when I clutched her, quivering with unrestrained love. On the way home in the car she lay down with a happy exhalation and put her head in my lap.

Her ball, however, was on its last gasp. Somehow the hard rubber ball I'd left her when I went to Sausalito had gotten lost, and my mother had bought her a flimsy yellow plastic one with fake, porcupiney spikes. I'd been so clear with my mother about this, very specific about what Tess needed in a ball, but of course she hadn't listened, my mother. I should never have trusted her. The plastic had split under Tess's vehement play, and only an inch or so of its circumference seam held the ball together – it wasn't even really a ball anymore, there wasn't much left, it was an asymmetrical yellow plastic flap. But for some reason, Tess was madly in love with it. When we got home and I gave it to her she ran around and around with it, the chewed yellow plastic flapping from either side of her mouth.

I checked my answering-machine messages, something I'd airily refrained from doing the entire time I was away. One, from Dayna, of course, welcoming me home. I hadn't called Eric to tell him I was leaving, but Dayna had mentioned to him where I was. I assumed he'd learn I was back, or when I was coming back, in the same way. I'd assumed he'd call, want us to get together. Maybe he'd call later. *Call me, call me, call me*, I chanted to the phone. I dialed his number. His roommate's voice answered, and I hung up. Tess perked her ears, and hopefully dropped the plastic flap in front of me, expecting it to roll like a ball. When it wouldn't, she just made do, picked it up again, dropped it closer so I could reach, and shoved it my way. But my spine was petrified from the long drive home, and I decided to go in the Jacuzzi; that way, when Eric called, I wouldn't be just sitting there, waiting for him.

The hot water sent up pungent steam; I'd poured in way too much chlorine before leaving for Sausalito, and it was now like boiling myself in disinfectant. It felt good; I let the jets pound on my back. Tess trotted up, dropped the yellow ball-flap at the Jacuzzi's lip – *No, honey, not now*, I said – and then shoved it into the bubbling water; it swirled around then flapped closed, trapping in the water's weight, and sank slowly to the bottom. I ignored it, but Tess went wild, whining desperately to have it back. I had to dive under to retrieve it, the heat and the chlorine searing my eyes, then tossed it back to her with a firm admonition – *That's it, Tess, no more Ball, not now* – but she did it again, then again, in that relentless, needy *Ball! Ball! Ball!* way, just when I needed something, to relax – *Stop it, just stop it!* I snapped – then again, just to get me, I knew it, until finally I came up with it, burning, just in time to hear a phone ring's trill. Or, I thought, listening for it. The jets were loud and I wasn't sure I heard a ring, but then I was sure I did, but then Tess barked at me, crying for the ball I still held, and so then I wasn't sure. But then there was nothing. She began to whine and whine – *All right, you want it, you want the fucking ball?* – and I threw it as far as I could over the backyard fence, probably into a neighbor's yard or garage space. *Go get it, go!* She whimpered pitifully, and I hated her, suddenly, wanted to punish her for all the obsessive, manipulative Ball bullshit, her pathetic, obvious need for love that I'd always given in to and had made me such an idiot, had cost me so much. I shoved her hard away from the edge of the Jacuzzi, ready to snap her spine, ready to make it all stop. She just looked at me, bewildered and wounded, and meekly rolled over on her back on the Jacuzzi-splashed concrete, her crooked little paws raised in supplication.

The only message on the machine was the old one from Dayna. I hurriedly got dressed, got Tess back in the car – she crept into the backseat this time, burrowed herself down behind my seat like she'd done a horrible, inexcusable thing – and drove over to Dayna's. Eric's car was parked in front of his place, but if he saw me, hey, I was just there to see Dayna, my friend Dayna. But she had someone over, a guy, some short, rabbity fellow biologist from the lab, who smiled and poured me a glass of wine but kept gazing at her with a moony, indulgent expression. She didn't even marvel at Tess, just let her jump up once or twice, then told her nicely to get down. I waited an hour to ask her if she'd seen or talked to Eric recently, and she mentioned something about their going to the grocery store together a few times, a jog in the park. He'd taken a weekend trip to La Jolla with some buddies, but that was a few weeks ago; he'd told her the trip was great, they'd all gotten laid. And she'd seen him a few times since with some really cute girl, coming or going from his building. She looked at me, smugly, I thought, maybe sort of challengingly. As if I'd tell her anything. As if I'd tell her I pictured him fucking some moist-skinned twenty-two-year-old, spreading her legs and eating her on the velour playpen couch or the kitchen table, telling her *Fuck me*, his look saying *Suck me, I'm hard, and it's specifically, singularly, because of you,* and how it made me want to drive nails into both of them, all of them. It was pretty late, and obvious Dayna and her biologist wanted to be alone, so I picked up Tess and we left. I was glad Dayna had found someone, but it seemed just a little sad to me, pathetic, that she'd grabbed at the first guy not smashed flat by the plunging, falling safe of her need.

Outside Tess started pulling on her leash. As if to get away from me. I apologized, I bent over and tried to rub her tummy, *It was my fault,* I told her, *I was the one who took away your ball, I'm sorry, I just lost it for a minute,* but she wouldn't even look at me. Even if she did, I suddenly knew I'd see hate in her little blue eyes, betrayal, distrust, disgust, and that made me want to bawl, crumple up, just die. Pound her into loving me again. She seemed to want to cross the street, or I thought she did, so I let out the leash a few feet and let her go. She trotted directly across to where the streetlight was in front of Eric's apartment house, the one that always shone through the tree branches into his bedroom window. She sniffed around the grass, squatted and peed, but then still tugged me, really, she did, across the patch of landscaping, toward the dark window at the side of the building. And I looked through the window, knowing what I was going to see, the heat and the wet, the feral rocking, a thing to draw blood, flaming and lethal as love. But all I could see, I thought, was a still, dull gleam of torso, and then a curve, maybe, of breast, a rumple of long dark hair, a girl sleeping curled up inside his arms, the quilted bedspread half thrown over both of them, all of it, both of them, still. I looked over at Tess; she gazed at me with innocence, the light from the streetlamp making a nimbus of her fine apricot fur.

She would have been seven on her next birthday, and that's starting to get old, sort of, for a dog. She would have gotten arthritis, or canine diabetes, and I couldn't do that to her. I wouldn't be able to bear seeing her in any pain, or seeing her hurt, and I bet Dayna would be just too busy with her drooly boyfriend when the time came to help. I got a fire going in the fireplace, and I brought her onto my lap and held her for a while. I felt the tiny staple-stitches inside her belly where she'd been *fxd*, and admired her trim, unused vulva that always kept her sort of a puppy, and inhaled her furry, spongy, tartar smell. I rubbed her tummy until she relaxed and went limp and trusting the way she used to, with me, her little almond-shaped eyes closing in warm, sleepy peace, and I knew she loved me again and she knew how much I loved her. She let her head drop back, and the soft, clumped curls along her throat weren't any problem at all, because I'd been very, very careful to sharpen the blade.

I'd bought a new ball to put in with her, but afterward I realized the rubber wouldn't burn, it would just melt to a smoky, periwinkle blue lump in the fireplace. And the aroma of her was so good, like rich, roasting, crackling kernels of popcorn. So I just buried the ball in the backyard. Sometimes now I awake alone in the middle of the night, thinking I hear its thump, roll, or feel her shove it under my thigh: *You want to play with my ball? Here, look, here's a ball! You want to play? Please, please!* Please, please, love me love me love me. Sometimes I hear her nail scrambles on the floor.

I just wish I'd tasted her before she burnt all away. I'm sure she would have tasted so sweet. Like apricots.

BLOOMS
Peter Rock

I took a job no one else wanted, and I learned many things I would never have believed. Here's an easy one, to start with: fungus can bloom inside books. Different kinds of molds, mostly, in dark, damp libraries where the air isn't too good. Fungi cannot make their own food; they take what they can from other organic matter. They start on the fabric and cardboard of the books' covers, then feed on the pulp wood in the pages, the vegetable dyes in the ink – kind of like how moss grows on tree trunks, swings from branches.

Samples are taken, and sent to a laboratory, to check if the bloom is virulent. Usually, it's not – it's only Penicillin or Aspergillus – and then they send in a team to clean it up. This is no job for librarians. They hire other people, whoever they can get. It's not exactly skilled labor.

An injury had forced me from my previous occupation. I'd been working down the shore, on the boardwalk. I wore a suit with three inches of padding, a hockey mask painted with a fanged smile. I leapt around behind fake trees, in front of a canvas backdrop, and people shot paintball guns at me. Ten shots for three dollars – I had targets on my suit, my helmet, a bull's eye on my crotch that everyone found hilarious. I wore two cups, with padding between them. Tough-talking boys couldn't touch me, cursing with their cracked voices, slapping their temporary tattoos; it was their girlfriends – bikini tops, slack expressions, baby fat under their arms – who had the deadly aim. At the end of the day, in the shower, I counted the round bruises on my skin.

One day I was recounting a story to a friend of mine, holding the mask in my hand. He had one of the guns, twirling it around his finger like Jesse James. When it went off, it caught me in the face – sideswiped me, actually, not even as hard as a punch. Dark red paint splattered across my temple, into my ear. I was left with this detached retina, where my vision's crooked and everyone I talk to thinks I'm trying to say something else; it's still shadowy on that side, but some days I believe it's clearing. Some days I'm not so sure.

My boss said he couldn't be held accountable for a time I wasn't working. Playing grab-ass – those were his words. And, of course, with my vision wrecked, my depth perception completely gone, I did not make a very challenging target. I was sore all over. We gave away half the stuffed animals in one afternoon.

Fortunately, none of this impaired me for the new job – the blooms did not move so fast. I answered an ad and was hired over the phone, told where to be the next morning.

They said I'd work on a team; what that meant was one other guy, Marco. He was forty, at least, from South Philly, where he still lived. Older than me, and heavier, with gray flecks in his hair, which was thick on the sides but you could see through it on top, his scalp shining. He had a heavy way of walking, almost sliding his feet. His hands would hang down at his sides, opening and closing with each step. My first impression was that he would never surprise me. Nothing he would do, nothing he would say.

We didn't shake hands when we first met, he just started to show me how things worked. Hair pushed out the collar of his T-shirt, both front and back. He'd done this kind of work before, and he told me there were worse jobs.

I've had them, I said.

He told me he was only working long enough to make enough money to get out of town, and I nodded and said that sounded wise.

I have to get out, he said. The reasons are personal.

We went through a side door, on a kind of loading dock, down a flight of stairs. The books we were dealing with were on two floors – a basement, and then another basement beneath that. There was not one window. Marco had already isolated the area with clear plastic sheeting, hung up the warning signs.

He helped me into my suit, that first day. They were white, made of

Tyvek, with a long zipper up the front, and zippers on the sides of the legs. We wore latex gloves, and baggy paper booties we had to replace every time we went outside. The hoods on our heads had clear plastic face panels; we wore battery packs on our belts, a fan with a tube that blew filtered air in front of our faces. It took one morning of breathing my own breath in that hood before I quit smoking. That's one positive thing that came of that job.

The blooms, they were a green fuzzy mold, streaked with black. Fibrous, like nothing you'd want in your lungs. They rested atop books, forced the covers open where they weren't tight in the shelves and squeezing each other. We started out with the vacuums, fitted with HEPA filters that trapped spores. Marco would work one aisle and I'd do the next. The shelves were tall, but sometimes I'd pull out a book and see him there, on the other side, his face close but his expression hidden. We kept moving, slowly and methodically, as if we were underwater.

The days went fluid, each like the one before it, progress marked only by the bookshelves left behind. Sections of maps, then encyclopedias. Novels, even poetry. It was strange to spend so much time so close to a person without being able to talk with them. We went our separate ways at lunch, and the rest of the time we were inside the suits and ventilators. It was all white noise, down there – the fans, the rustle of Tyvek, the sound of pages being flipped under our gloved thumbs.

At least a week passed before we first had lunch together. He asked me to join him. We walked half a block, bought sandwiches from a truck, then headed toward a little park. When the children in the playground saw us coming, they started screaming Astronauts! We always got a kick out of that.

The wooden bench we sat on had been chewed by pit bulls – the owners train them to do it, to strengthen their jaws. Next to the jungle gym, the plastic swings were so gnawed they looked melted. When we bit into our sandwiches, shredded lettuce fell onto the ground, tangled with cigarette butts.

Marco stood and tried to touch his toes. He stretched his arms and grunted. All that work in the damp library tightened his joints.

I wonder, he asked, if you wouldn't mind rubbing my knee a little.

I'd give it a try, I told him.

Not everyone would, he said.

If it helps, I said.

I kind of kneeled down and tried to get a decent hold, through the slippery Tyvek, using both hands. Marco picked up his sandwich, closed his eyes. He obviously shaved, but there were always these long whiskers along his throat, ones he missed. I rubbed his knee. The sun stayed where it was, straight overhead, stuck there.

You're probably wondering what I'm going to do for you, Marco said.

I told him not really. My knees felt fine.

I live in a rowhouse, Marco said. So I share walls with my neighbors. Thin walls.

A couple lived there, and he'd hear their arguments – threats, recriminations, then the usual coming to terms. Marco would turn up his radio, or go out walking around his neighborhood.

Italians, he said, almost spitting.

I thought you were Italian, I said.

I am, he said.

There was an Indian spice shop near that park, so it always smelled a little foreign. The air was thick. Marco picked his teeth with his fingernail as he spoke.

Pay attention, he said. This won't turn out any way you expect.

I told him I had no expectations.

Sometimes on the mornings after the arguments, Marco would run into the man from next door. You're lucky, the man would say, you were safe – a wall between you and her. Pray for me, these nights! He and Marco would laugh together.

What happened to him? I asked, guessing ahead.

I just stopped hearing him through the wall, Marco said. Stopped seeing him in the front yard. He was gone.

And that was your opening, I said. Don't tell me – she's incredibly beautiful.

Yes, Marco said. But that's not the point.

We took our time in the basements of the library, though we weren't being paid by the hour. It wasn't that I got a lot of thinking done, exactly; it was almost a different plane of some sort, listening to my own breathing, a kind of meditation. Sometimes I even thought of the people who would follow, who would be able to read the books because I'd saved them.

Sometimes people came down the stairs, descended by mistake, and I'd catch glimpses, twice-distorted by my face shield and the clear plastic barriers. The people seemed to have no feet, to move fluidly, as if they were growing their way smoothly upward again, beyond my sight.

Sometimes, on my break, I'd climb those stairs; I'd hold the door slightly open, my ventilator around my neck and the cool air on my sweaty face. I spied into the library, and it was quiet up there, just like it was supposed to be. A green and yellow parakeet hung onto its perch, inside a bamboo cage. I heard the sound of pages turning. If I held the door open a little further, I could see the desk where the librarian sat. She was about my age, with dark black skin, gold eyeglasses; her hair was braided close to her head, in curving lines, the loose ends like ropes whipping her shoulders. Her fingers were thin, her smile wide as she answered someone's question. Whenever I turned away from her and began to descend into the basement, it was as if my body grew heavier with every step. I wanted her to know there were real people underneath her, that I was beneath her every day. I wanted to tell her I'd wiped mold from musical scores and hummed the melody, that I'd read a Russian story about grown men swimming in the rain, another where people could see into the future and still couldn't change it.

If I could tell the librarian one story, it would be this one. And I would tell her only a little at a time, the way Marco told me, until she had to know what would happen next, until she couldn't stand it.

He never used the woman's real name, since he said I was his friend and he was afraid I'd try to track her down, once I'd heard it all, that I'd only get myself in trouble. Louisa – that's the name he chose for her.

Their houses shared a porch, so all Louisa had to do was reach over the railing to ring Marco's doorbell. She wanted to ask him a favor. Groceries. She had the list in her hand, and he took it when she held it out.

It's my eyes, Louisa said. I can't see a thing. She told him that the doctors had found nothing wrong, physically, but that didn't help her.

Marco looked at her eyes, and she didn't seem to see him. Her eyebrows had always been tweezed into a narrow arch; now they were returning, thickening. She stood there, barefoot on the concrete porch, the toenails of her left foot painted red. All the words on the list in Marco's hand tilted, and some stretched off the edge of the paper, cut short. Others were written right on top of each other; he struggled to untangle them.

When he returned from the store, he offered to put the things away for her, and she said she could do it. Stay, she told him. You can talk to me while I do.

She held the door open and then led him, moving deftly around the furniture, hitting the lightswitch exactly and just for him. Later, he tried it in his own house, his eyes closed. He bruised his shins and tore his fingernails; he cursed and stumbled and wondered if she heard him, if she guessed what he was doing.

In the kitchen, she reached and found the knobs on the cupboards; inside, they were carefully organized, all the cans lined up.

I've got it all figured out, she said. I miss being able to read, but that's about it. I was halfway through a book when it happened.

Marco asked if it happened all at once, and she told him she had one day where everything went dim – that gave her a chance to prepare – and then the next day that was it.

Is it just pitch black? he said. Or is it like nothing at all? Marco wasn't sure what he meant, exactly. He couldn't stop watching her hands.

Somewhere in-between, she said.

He stayed until all the groceries were put away, and then said he'd be happy to help her again.

I remember what you look like, Louisa said, but do you mind? She reached out, and slowly her soft fingertips moved down his face.

Yes, I said, when he told me that. I knew this was going somewhere.

You know nothing, Marco said.

I learned not to say things like that, eventually; it only made him stop talking – it was as if I'd sullied the way it had been. If I asked, he'd say to wait, to be patient. He could only tell it a little at a time; otherwise, it made him too sad.

The conversation at lunch would turn to other things. We'd walk to the park, stripping off our latex gloves, the sweat between our fingers going cool, the zippers of our suits pulled down and their white arms dragging behind us. The weather turned hot and dark, overcast. Trains came and went, slowly, sat on the tracks behind the playground. We watched the dogs, betting on which owners would pick up after theirs and which would pretend oblivion. Down there they had dogs of all shapes, with their tails lopped off, their ears pinned up. Marco knew the names of all the breeds and what they were for. He'd have his arm across the back of the bench, fingers drumming next to my shoulder. I didn't mind. Once we saw a guy crash his bicycle into a parked car as he tried to look behind him, to check the ass on a girl he'd passed. Marco got a good laugh out of that – a little shift like that would bring him around again.

All right, he'd say, turning toward me. Where did I leave off?

The next time Louisa rang his doorbell, she was holding a book in her hand. She asked what he was doing; when he said nothing, she asked if he wouldn't mind reading to her.

She had already read the first three chapters. It was a novel where all the characters were rabbits, but it was for adults. Thick. Later, he borrowed it, to catch up on the beginning.

Louisa wanted him to read to her in the bedroom, so she could lie down and imagine it all. She set a chair next to the bed, then took off her shoes and stretched out.

This isn't right, she said, after a few pages.

The way I'm reading? Marco said.

She said it was strange, because she couldn't see him. She said that his voice was kind of disembodied, and that distracted her from following what was going on in the story.

Is it all right if I reach out and touch you? she said. While you read?

They tried it for another few pages, but she still couldn't get a sense of him.

What is it? he said.

Your clothes, Louisa said. It might be better if I didn't have to feel you through them. Is this turning too weird? You don't know what it's like, like this; I start to need different things to feel anything, to understand.

At first it seemed it would be enough to take off his shirt, to strip down to his underwear. Part of it was to test her, maybe, to see if she was having him on somehow, and part of it was that it excited him.

Did she know you were all the way naked? I said, afraid to interrupt.

I believe so, he said.

He had never been involved in anything like that, he told me, never felt that way. He'd been married before, even, and this was different – he felt it in his heart, he said, knowing how ridiculous that sounded. And he never even touched Louisa, not once, yet sometimes, as the weeks passed, he'd wake up in the middle of the night because he'd been laughing in his sleep. He'd just lie there, smiling in the darkness.

Are you happy? Louisa asked him, a little later, that first night.

I guess so, he said.

She told him it seemed like an uneven trade.

Well, he said. I can see. I can read. I can see you.

Are the lights on? she said. Can you see well enough?

Yes, he said, except you're wearing clothes. As soon as he said that, he was sorry, and he wanted to take it back. He wanted to say it was a joke, but it was too late for that. Louisa had already begun to answer.

One piece at a time, she took off her clothing, folded it, and stacked it at the foot of the bed. She lay back, her hand on his leg again. He knew he was not allowed to touch her, just as she could not see him.

Now, read, she said.

And that's how it always was, after that. There was nothing showy about it, as if she was alone, unlacing her shoes, unbuttoning her shirt as he began to read. He turned the lamp up high and moved it closer to her; her shadow twisted low across the opposite wall, attached to his by her hand, checking that he was there. He flexed his bare toes on the cool floorboards.

Louisa's skin was dark and smooth, solid, hiding her bones. She wasn't skinny. Her thighs were heavy, a scar above one knee. Stretching and turning over, she'd laugh and hold a smile, showing her teeth, listening. She had a faded tattoo of a rose on her right hip, and a smaller, clearer one over her right nipple. Perfume rose from her skin as Marco read; sometimes he'd look up into the full-length mirror on the wall, and see her thin waist angling out to her rounded hips, and himself, the book in one hand and a glass of water in the other.

He drank between chapters, rested his voice. He counted the few hairs that circled her nipples, watched how her breasts slid across each other when she turned, enough space between them to hide a flattened hand. The hair under her arms matched that between her legs, where the edges, unshaven, were growing back. Her eyes stared and stared, shining.

Are you happy? she asked him.

He told me that she wore no jewelry at all, that there was nothing on her. Nothing. She and Marco hardly spoke, except for his reading, or deciding on the time they'd next meet. He never asked about her husband, and Louisa never brought it up. He felt there were many silent understandings between them.

Of course it took him weeks to tell me all this, and even in pieces the information was not easy for me to process. It was difficult to shake. Sometimes, even now, I set a glass of water beside me and I hold a book in one hand. I read aloud, my voice echoing off the tight walls of the room I rent, not letting my eyes wander from the page, and I imagine my other hand belongs to Louisa, and that she is listening to me, and that she can't see a thing.

Marco's story was farfetched, but I had never known him to lie. Still, I'd sometimes watch him at work, pausing with a book open in front of him, and I'd wonder if he was coming up with stories to tell me, or searching for something for her, or if he was just staring into the words without reading them, trying to think.

We both slowed as the weeks went on; he slacked off worse than I did, but I didn't mind. Mostly, we spent our time reading. We were using the rubber sponges, then, so there was no longer the vacuums' roar. The reflection of the face shields made it difficult to read; sometimes we let the hoods slump over our backs and wore only the ventilator masks with the HEPA filters, our eyes clear and uncovered. In the books where the fungus had really taken hold, it bled down into the pages in red and purple stains, blurring letters, eating words that we could not recover.

Louisa and Marco did not always meet at the same time. Once she'd called him at three in the morning, saying she couldn't sleep, saying she could hear his footsteps and wouldn't he like to come read? They finished the first novel, then went through another, and another. She liked books about animals, others where women took charge.

One of their understandings was that she had to come for him, and not the other way around; after all, he was doing her a favor. It was on a night when he waited – listening for the doorbell, the phone, her knock on the wall – that he heard the man's voice. Next door, and it was not the voice of Louisa's husband.

Marco was jealous, partly, but he also feared something was wrong. He took a can of corn from his own cupboard, so he could use it as an excuse, say he forgot to give it to her.

He tried the doorknob before the bell, and the door swung open. He stepped inside, the can of corn in his fist, ready to hit someone with it. In the dim living room he moved around the furniture as easily as she had that first day. He'd come to know her house that well.

In the hallway, closer to the bedroom, he listened; something about the man's voice seemed strange, the rhythm too regular and Louisa never interrupting. He stepped to the doorway and looked inside.

She was stretched out on the bed, wearing a long flannel nightgown, her face turned to the ceiling. On the bedside table, a tape recorder was playing, and the man's voice looped out from it, a hiss behind his words.

Marco took another step, into the room, and waited there, silently. He could tell she sensed him, that she knew he was in the room, and the fact that she said nothing made it all worse. As the taped voice looped around, Marco turned and walked back down the hall. He locked the front door and gently pulled it closed.

The next day, she told him the news. Her vision was returning; it was clearer each day. And the reading couldn't be the same if she could see the shape of him, his slumped shadow and the words coming out. Closing her eyes wouldn't work, when she knew she could open them. Awkward – that's the word she used. Soon she'd be able to read, once again, on her own.

When he told me that, I couldn't stop thinking about it. He'd been right – something in me wanted to find her, to hold her down until she saw some sense.

Marco never read to her again. He did find a place, though, where they made those tapes; he went there and volunteered, read a whole book into a microphone. He hoped Louisa might hear his voice, and remember, and have second thoughts. The sadness I felt, hearing this, was like I'd breathed in the spores and they'd thickened in my throat, blooming darkly through my organs, cold, one at a time like the way a blackout spills over sections of a city.

There was a time I believed and hoped that job could continue indefinitely, that I might persuade Marco to stay on, but those blooms are seasonal, mostly. Nothing stands still.

We were finishing up, just wiping down the shelves with the Clorox solution, when he told me the end of the story. In fact, Marco left before the job was finished, without any warning, and I handled the last few days – tearing down the plastic barriers, taking down the signs – by myself. He left that way, I believe, so he wouldn't have to say goodbye.

It wasn't as if he thought things between him and Louisa could have continued – he knew the balance had changed, that they couldn't return – but he expected it all had to go somewhere, that it couldn't just trail off into nothing.

She refused to speak about it. She was cool, not quite unfriendly. She turned down the simplest favors. She said that had been a different time, that they had been different people who needed different things.

He felt that they were the same, inside the changes. He needed her, and he couldn't stand the way she looked at him, every day, watching him with those same eyes as he came home from work with his hood and ventilator bouncing along his back, the arms of the Tyvek suit tied off around his waist. Her gaze rested cold on him, settling so he felt it even after he was inside his house. He sat alone, shivering; it was very, very quiet on the other side of the wall.

If I ever see Marco again, I'll tell him that I know what happened, even if she was ungrateful, even if she never understood.

He healed her.

THE INTERVIEW
Helen Schulman

How the hell do they interview a child who cannot speak? It was the start of twinset season, and Mirra, that shameless imposter, was carefully donning the creamy sleeveless cashmere mock-turtle and cardigan that she had stuffed away so victoriously when she'd twice hit the bell with her two older daughters, so many years before. Fat envelopes of acceptance. Fat tuition bills. Mirra peered at herself in her bedroom mirror. She looked ropy and European; she looked like her body was younger than her skin. Her brown hair was blown back into a glossy ponytail. She added lipstick and earrings to further the artifice. Of course both her girls had aced their way into appropriate girls' schools – brainy Lilia at the challenging, no-nonsense Brearley and popular fun-loving Charlotte at the fizzier, partying Spence – they'd proven superior from the get-go; they had her husband, Dr. Dan's, genes after all, and he was a brilliant neurosurgeon, always flying off to here or there to operate on some famous actor or world leader or the sultan of Brunei – it seemed Dan was always operating on the sultan of Brunei. Mirra sighed. In the mirror her face was older and her hips thinner than she felt inside. She buttoned up the top three buttons of her cardigan. Both her girls had been talking since the age they could walk. Not little Adam.

Adam was her afterthought, her oops!, her late-in-life baby, the product of Dan's and her infrequent and increasingly irritating erotic couplings – that little hiccupy sound he made in the back of his throat! the staccato predictability of his thrusts! Adam, with his golden curls and creamy blue eyes, with his snotty nose and sturdy little body, his sporadic outbursts, the dark storm of his temper tantrums, the whirl of his legs, the power of his baby punches, his thighs as cut and defined as that skater Eric Heiden's, he was the child of Mirra's heart, but he was not a talker. Adam could push both of his big sisters in a shopping cart through the crowded aisles of Food Emporium. Adam could, in the midst of one of his terrible-three-plus explosions, require both herself and Miss Lucille, the most recent in a string of reluctant baby-sitters, to quiet his flailing arms and fold him into a taxi to bring him safely home. Adam could shout and laugh and cry with the best of them. But aside from the words *Momma* and *mine*, the kid was mute. This hadn't exactly worried Mirra much before she had to face a brand-new round of nursery school interviews; in fact, before this newest twinset season, her son's lack of language had sort of comforted her.

Mirra liked the fact that she and Adam communicated silently. Physically. Through slippery kisses and big bear hugs. Those girls were such chatterboxes. Often Mirra found herself standing behind one of them as the kid in question prattled on and on about the portraits of Joseph Roulin – Joseph Roulin? "Van Gogh's postman, Mom!" – or some dopey new boy band, Mirra mouthing the words *Shut the fuck up*. Adam was her confidant. When they were home alone she did not even have to whisper. Adam would be building a tower of blocks and Mirra would say: "Daddy's so fat, all those rolls around his belly, I can barely find his penis," and "One day I'm going to pack our bags and you and I are going to leave all of them," stuff like that, stuff that she would never, ever dare say to someone who was capable of repeating it. Mirra liked the fact that after she finished with whatever tirade seemed to spew independently out of her mouth, Adam would stare at her goggle-eyed, press his goobery cheek to hers, and then ignore her. She liked the fact that he still took a bottle and a pacifier, she liked that he could stuff both simultaneously between his lips and that when he did the house was completely noiseless except for the sound of their breathing. She liked when they breathed in sync, effortlessly, yogically, when they were one.

Night after night, after the girls had gone to bed when Dan was working late – operating on someone's brain, for Godssake! the hubris! the Dan-ness! – Adam would fall asleep in her arms, his sweaty little curls pressed against her thin chest. Mirra liked more than anything that he was still a baby. She could kiss him anywhere on his body that she wanted – his tummy, his chest, his tush – whenever she wanted. The luxury of it all!

In the kitchen, Miss Lucille was feeding Adam a banana. How cute he looked, cramming the soft white fruit into his rounded cheeks. He was all gussied up too; blue cords and a big-boy button-down shirt. Miss Lucille had brushed his hair so that it lay slick and wet across his forehead, but still his little curls were springing into action.

"Miss Lucille," Mirra said, "could you pick up Charlotte and take her to ballet? Today is the day of Adam's school interview, so he's coming with me." Miss Lucille nodded her bored, sullen nod, but Mirra could sense her rolling her inner eyes.

Miss Lucille's calling had been the raising of children. Mirra, on the other hand, was a former divorce attorney, a fine one, although she never planned on going back to work, never; she'd gotten her husband! Dan had been her favorite client. So for the past eleven years, Mirra had raised children, three of them, but it had hardly been her calling, and she wasn't terribly good at it. She didn't bake, she'd given up on art projects long ago. She was unevenly skilled at discussing matters of the heart. Plus, she gave in to just about everything. First Barbies and Barbie Dream Closets, snacks and treats, television and computer games, now music videos, Britney Spears, Kate Spade bags. She didn't have the strength to fight. Miss Lucille had a hard, unflappable countenance, which was why Mirra had hired her.

But at the moment, Adam was a lamb. Mirra had learned the hard way that as long as she asked Adam for permission first, with a little luck, she could mostly get him to do what she wanted. "Sweetie," she said, "can we put on our jackie now?" He allowed his chubby little arms to be pulled through the sleeves of his dressy blue jacket; he gurgled and smiled as Mirra buttoned him up. It was a Tuesday. Tuesday mornings he always accompanied Mirra on her various errands, on her secret missions. Tuesday mornings for Adam were Mommytime. He walked out of the apartment without a fuss, Miss Lucille closing the door behind them with a thunk. Mirra would never ask, but she hoped with Adam out of her hair, Miss Lucille would make some inroads into the mountain of clean laundry lying on the living room sofa.

Out in the crisp fall air, Mirra asked Adam to hail her a taxi. This he was good at. Why, if the interviewer could see him now, his determined little expression, his hand shooting up into the air so masterfully, they would recognize his superiority, take note of the fact that this particular child had management capabilities, he could lead. Mirra should have put this specific skill down on his application. After all, the various admission forms had had a space for "your child's special interests and talents." What were Adam's? Applied physics? Avant-garde theater? He was terrific at knocking a tower of blocks down – so Mirra had marveled in her essay about his large motor capabilities – and proficient at scribbling across Lilia's precious paintings with indelible Magic Marker, so she'd waxed on and on about his love of art. When the theme song for Sesame Street began to warble throughout the house at the end of the day when Mirra was already deep in the bottle and ready to tear her hair out – she'd buy cases of Beaujolais Nouveau, the cheap stuff, and drink it past its prime – little Adam would come running to the TV like a homing pigeon. So she'd emphasized his passion for music, its ability to both delight and calm him. But Mirra had forgotten to mention his expertise at hailing a cab. Spatial relationships, physical prowess, confidence confidence confidence.

Now, her brilliant, commanding, potent son deftly waved a taxi down. They climbed in without a fuss, although during this ride, like all the others, she had her heart in her throat, because he refused to sit in her lap. He refused to sit period, Mirra couldn't slip the seat belt around him the way she'd always done with his sisters, instead the backseat was alive with activity, Adam rolling around, standing up, pushing buttons, the window, good God, the locks, forcing the little Plexiglas change sleeve back and forth so that the scratchy sound would drive anyone in earshot nuts. Mirra apologized over and over again to the driver, saying "Adam, please sit, Adam, please – baby danger," just so the cabbie wouldn't think she was a disaster as a mother, when really all she wanted to do was look out the window and space out, daydreaming a tragic accident in which both mother and son could escape from this messy, clamorous world, together, and find a united solace in the heaven of another. By the time the cab pulled up in front of the apartment building of her lover, both Mirra and Adam were in a sweat, she could feel her underarms staining that damned sweater set, and Adam had a little pearly string of moist beads gracing his upper lip and brow. She wiped it away with her lips. Mirra tipped the cabbie a couple of dollars and hightailed it out of there, afraid as always to turn into Lot's wife, to look back.

Jacob, Mirra's lover, was Charlotte's English teacher. Mirra had met him first at a parent-teacher conference and then, after some strategic volunteering, she had virtually thrown herself at him at a series of book fair meetings. Mirra had always been willing. In high school, in college – thank God she'd grown up in the seventies when lunatic sexual behavior was expected; why, back then you were practically forced to sleep around – she'd been able to have her cake and eat it whenever she wanted without any damage to her reputation. In truth, her desirous nature had been one of the things that helped her rope in her husband – Dan's first wife had been a more of a once-a-monther. Now, since Dan's interest had waned to the point of being a surprise, her fulsome and needy sexuality had become a liability. As a lonely middle-aged mother of three, Mirra had seen this transgression – throwing herself at the younger, vulnerable Jacob – as an act of self-preservation. She flirted and flirted until the poor guy had had no choice but to ask her out. She would never forget it, Jacob's shambling shy and bookish manner, the way he wouldn't meet her eye when he said, "Mrs. Eichler?" Mrs. Eichler! "I could use your advice, uh, around, uh, book ordering; perhaps we could have a cup of coffee?" He was as young and smart and nerdy and sweet as Dan had been in his prime.

A cup of coffee indeed. Right then, Mirra had known that some time in the immediate future he'd be left standing and she'd be on her knees, and she'd wondered to herself if when he came, a gorgeous and enlightening string of poetry would ejaculate from his mouth. But first a proper courtship had to ensue. There was no cut to the chase with matters this delicate, Mirra knew this much. She was in her forties, she'd had enough experience to now know not to rush things, when all she ever wanted to do was rush things. She wanted to rush Jacob right into her bed, his face between her thighs, her hands in his hair, the bedroom air moist and fertile as a rain forest, her favorite TV show on in the background. But with age comes wisdom, restraint, this she told Adam as she stirred his oatmeal one morning, after the girls had gone to school and Dan had strutted off to the office and she was plotting about Jacob and doing the breakfast dishes and fixing Adam a healthy snack all at the same time – multitasking. Wisdom, restraint. Growing old.

So Mirra had agreed to join Jacob's committee of two. They'd meet in a neighborhood coffee shop, Adam persistently emptying all the sugar sachets, the salt and pepper shakers, the little individually packaged jams and honeys, the ketchup and mustard packets, into some weird cosmic soup on the table, while Mirra and Jacob put their heads together over the book orders. How many Eric Carle? How many Dr. Seuss? Jacob's hair was black and curly, with a pattern of silver threads bejeweling his well-stocked head. He reminded Mirra of a rabbi, his gentle searching manner, his tender avuncular humor, the wisdom of his anecdotes, that little yarmulke of a bald spot. Still, he was cute. And bespectacled in a cool, Armani way – silver frames perched lightly on his nose – and even through that thick glass his eyes were an iridescent, mesmerizing blue. With the wafting odor of fry fat perfuming their hair, the coffee that looked and tasted like melted brown crayon water, the soggy BLTs wilting on the chipped china plates that squatted on chintzy paper place mats, Mirra and Jacob would press their knees together under the table, in the corner booth – Adam under the table with his toy cars to document this – until the day they graduated to Jacob's apartment.

Every Tuesday morning, while Jacob with his Ph.D. from Princeton, his M.A. from Yale, his B.A. from Columbia (all Ivy, Mirra noted with pride) was home doing "course prep" – Charlotte's school was famous for "course prep," for instructor sabbaticals and all-expense-paid trips to Europe for further study – while Jacob the academic was preparing to teach the privileged and the gifted, and his artist wife, Shoshanna – the heiress to a fortune amassed from the manufacturing of labels for designer underwear – worked at her studio out in Long Island City, Adam and Mirra paid him their weekly visit. They'd fuck in the maid's room, the little portable TV turned on to some dumb cowboy game show, the "hee-haws" drowning out the escalating arpeggios of their moans, with the door open while Adam busied himself, pulling the pots and pans out of all the lower kitchen cabinets. From the announcements of the crashing metal, Mirra could assure herself that Adam was safe.

Today's visit was not a sex visit. Too bad. Sex would be great on a day like today, interview day, a day when she was anxious. But sex had to be put on hold for a while. At least with Jacob. He met them eagerly at the door. He put his hand out for a high-five, but Adam would have none of it. Like a little homing pigeon, Adam headed straight for the pots and pans in the kitchen.

"I am so very glad you've come," said Jacob to Mirra, and he looked glad, he looked desperate, he looked sweaty and shaky and, well, unattractive. He looked a little like a grad student. He had recently been caught embezzling book fair funds by one of the more dastardly administrators at the school, a cold-hearted spinster graduate of the very same institution. He'd been trying to collect enough money to escape, so that he could get out from under the economic thumb of the wife who neither respected nor coveted him. Mirra understood his situation. So although Mirra had been privy to his ridiculous plan, she hadn't bothered to stop him. If he hung his own rope, she'd have a graceful exit strategy. And actually, she'd been a little flattered, because Jacob had made noises about her and Adam accompanying him. Fat chance, she'd told Adam.

Jacob took her hand. His palm was sweaty. "Yuck," said Mirra. Of course Jacob was miserable, he faced certain termination, perhaps an indictment, or worst of all, a nose-holding acquiescence to the wretched and desperate administrator's sexual advances, but did he have to wear his misery so obviously? Here's where an icy narcissistic self-confidence like Dan's took on a certain luster. Far preferable to this wilting lettuce leaf of a man. She shook herself loose and followed her son into the kitchen.

"Would you like a cup of tea?" asked Jacob, following her. "We are in possession of a particularly interesting leaf, termed, appropriately enough, gunmetal. Perhaps I could use it to off myself. Shoshanna brought it back from her sabbatical in India."

"Lemon Zinger," said Mirra. She sat down at the undersize round table; the light spilled in inexplicably through the air shaft and warmed a little square of the butcher block where she rested her arms and waited for him to serve her. Another reason she'd liked Jacob, besides that he was smart and actually liked to go down on her, was that he served her. At this point in her life no one ever served her, unless you counted the knowing, smirking waitress in the coffee shop. At this point in her life Mirra served everyone around her – Mommy, juice please, Sweetie, drop off the dry-cleaning? – everyone except him. Too bad Jacob was such a loser. As an academic, as a husband, as a thief. But as criminals went, wasn't he the best kind? Taking from the rich to give to the poor, stealing from her and her overprivileged children? Mirra felt dizzy with confusion, as if she were tumbling down a long tunnel, internal compass, as always, failing her.

"You look so beautiful in that light," said Jacob. "You look like a Sargent, in that sweater you look moneyed and elegant like a Sargent. You look lit from within like a Vermeer."

What was this, a tour through the Metropolitan Museum of Art? Still Mirra was flattered. She knew she was not beautiful, but it was kind of him to think so, kinder still to lie to her about it, because a lie took so much more effort than the truth.

"Today is Adam's interview," said Mirra by way of explanation. Jacob nodded an "of course" nod. He remembered. This fact made her like him again. Her concerns were his concerns. He was practiced in the art of empathy. As if he could sense this, her subtle shift, Jacob sank to his knees by her side and placed his head in her lap.

How pink and shiny was his bald spot. Mirra petted his hair anyway around the exposed, pathetic skin.

Mirra petted away with one hand, and with the other she dug deep into her pocket.

She and Adam had gone to the bank that very morning, before Miss Lucille had arrived and after dropping the girls off at their bus stops. She and Adam had written a check out of her brother Michael's account made out to cash. Mirra managed his finances, Michael's. Mirra the attorney had power of attorney. Michael had been run over by a car or a truck or something down in Florida, three years prior. Mirra hadn't known what hit him, and neither, she suspected, had her brother, because the alcohol level in his blood was three times the legal limit. He was found by the side of the road, in the A.M., about a hundred yards beyond a local bar where he'd been seen drinking the night before by various ruffians of dubious reliability. Since her parents were both dead, and her other two siblings, a sister and a brother, lived in London and Alaska respectively, Michael was her charge. She set him up in a nursing home on upper Fifth Avenue. He could neither speak nor eat, he was fed through a tube in his belly. No one knew if he could hear or perceive or register. He was a gnarled and twisted-up piece of rotting human driftwood, riddled with bedsores that burrowed from his skin down to the bone. And he hadn't been exactly great shakes when he was still animated. As a child he'd been a cruel, vicious bully. As an adolescent a delinquent and an addict. As an adult he'd been a lowlife, two-bit gambler; human scum. Still, he was Mirra's charge. She'd reluctantly supervised his medical treatment, visited him with Adam once a week, handled his finances and his inheritance. But this was the first time that she'd stolen from him. She and Adam had withdrawn five thousand dollars, enough to cover the embezzlement, to get Jacob off her back. Hush money. Jacob could see it as a loan, or whatever. He could pay back what he owed and then some. He could take off. Do with it what he desired. He could steal from Michael if he wanted. As long as he effectively disappeared. It had all gotten a little too complicated.

Three weeks ago, Jacob had been down on the floor then too, rubbing her feet with some peppermint foot lotion that he'd swiped off Shoshanna's shelf, when he'd said, "I love you, Mirra." Mirra had felt dizzy with regret when he'd said it. His love was not the love she wanted. And when Mirra looked up and away from Jacob's beseeching gaze, she could have sworn she saw Adam roll his eyes and make a cutting motion with a finger at his throat, validating her response.

Now Adam stopped his building and his crashing, his big blue eyes locked on his mother. He gave her a subtle nod. Together they had planned this moment.

"Jacob," said Mirra.

He looked up. He was still on his knees but he looked up at her.

She reached into her pocket, pulled out the check, handed him the dough.

It took Jacob a moment to make sense of the thing. Then he began to smile.

"So you, you and Adam, you will come?" asked Jacob, half as a question, half as a statement. He said it with hopeful hope.

Adam shot her a look.

"No," said Mirra. "It's for you." She winked over her head at her son.

"Without you, I don't want it," said Jacob.

"Sure you do," said Mirra. "Without it you could go to jail."

For a moment the room was silent.

"I'll pay you back," said Jacob, looking at the floor. There was some spaghetti sauce splashed on the tiling.

"Of course you will," said Mirra. Let him believe whatever he wanted.

Outside, in the soft warm early-autumn sunshine, Mirra looked at her watch. There was still enough time to take Adam and visit her brother. As the years had passed, her visits had become shorter and shorter. Michael had grown so thin, his muscles had atrophied so that not only his hands and feet but his arms and legs had clawed. Adam was a welcome menace around the breathing and feeding tubes, the IV and the catheter – chasing after him in Michael's room had kept her busy; and she'd won points with the nursing home staff by bringing her little boy with her. "What a devoted sister," the health-care attendants said when they made their weekly visits. The health-care attendants did not know what Mirra whispered in her brother's ears: "You got what you deserved." Only Adam knew. Only Adam knew how much she reviled the sibling who had forced her head between his legs, who had beaten her roundly and often as a child. She hated those visits, but she liked them too. She liked that Michael was in a position where he could no longer harm her. Now, leaving Jacob's, they were in Michael's neighborhood. There was enough time to run over there, make nice to the nurses, earn her medal of honor, and then whisper into her brother's ear the fact that she was now stealing money from him. There would have been some new form of grim satisfaction in the visit. But then again, she and Adam could go get a cookie and a coffee before walking over to the school.

Mirra strolled down Madison Avenue with her little boy's hand in hers. They stopped in at one of those Parisian fancy food shops. Mirra bought a cupcake for Adam and one for herself, they'd earned this little repast, and a cappuccino to fortify her. He ate quietly and diligently as they watched the traffic go by outside the store's ceiling-to-floor plate glass. So many mothers with their children. So many well-dressed mothers with their well-dressed children. Mothers with ponytails like hers, mothers with manicures like hers, with good shoes and good bags, mothers with custodianship of designer cashmere twinsets. If Mirra scratched their surfaces, would they all be in possession of secret lives as knotty and ugly as hers? Or would she just end up with a fingernail-full of eighty-dollar face cream?

When the Muffy mommies glanced into the food shop's window, when they saw Mirra and her little Adam, gorgeous and calm and eating a cupcake, did they believe she was one of them?

Mirra brought her cappuccino to her lips, but somehow a tiny bit of milky coffee dribbled out her mouth, landing on the creamy perfection of her already pit-stained mockturtle. Shit. She dabbed at the blot with a napkin that she dipped into Adam's plastic cup of water. Too bad some of the sprinkles from his cupcake had already fallen in. Her sweater was now marred with a small rainbow-colored blemish. The more she worked it, the more the rainbow began to spread, the colors continuing to bleed. It was too much. In the frame of the plate glass window Mirra began to weep.

With all those people watching, Mirra wept, silently and wetly, mascara running down her cheeks. Adam was the only one who tried to comfort her. He placed his little chocolaty cheek on her good wool slacks. It was a sartorial disaster. And in the lexicon of independent schools, dishevelment was a dealbreaker. But without entry into the proper preschool, one could not hope for a first-tier ongoing school. Without a first-tier ongoing school, what would be his prospects for college? More than anything, she wanted this child to have a good life.

After a quick trip to the ladies' room in the Hotel Wales across the street, Adam's face was scrubbed, Mirra's face was scrubbed, and the cardigan of her sweater set was buttoned closed into one smooth long schoolmarmy line, conservative and smart, appropriate once again for the task at hand. As she studied herself in the mirror, Mirra's racing heart went back to normal. She could do this, she told herself. She could pull it off. A swift glance at the lobby clock informed her that they were ten minutes away from liftoff. She picked up Adam in an effort to run him across the street to the school. Dan would be outside the building, wondering where they were. He'd be tapping his foot in annoyance. He never waited for anyone. People waited for him. Dan was a surgeon. At times like this, Mirra was sure, he would happily rearrange her brain if he could retain his license.

But picking up Adam was Mirra's great mistake, her fatal one, in a day that had been so thoughtfully and still – how did this happen? – so recklessly calibrated. She'd picked Adam up without asking his permission first. She'd lost her head. Forgotten protocol. She'd neglected to say, "Sweet boy, can Momma go uppie?" As soon as she lifted his little body into the air she realized her error in judgment, for his calm, peachy-skinned, clean and shining face instantly turned purple, his little legs began to bicycle, his arms began to windmill, his body to torque and arch. And then, after a moment of delay, as with a sonic boom, came the ear-shattering screams. "Please, baby, please," said Mirra, as she struggled to get him out of the lobby, "Please, honey, not now." Time was running out.

When she reached the sidewalk, Adam was going fullthrottle; she could barely hold on to him. He hit her in the face, the neck, his feet kicking at her stomach, her legs, her knees; after a particularly good wallop, she almost dropped him and his strong little body sagged close to the ground. Fortunately Dan was waiting on the opposite corner, looking judgmentally at his watch. Dan was short and vaguely fit and wearing the blue suit she'd laid out for him. His cheeks were tan, he'd just returned from some surgical conference in Palm Beach. Somehow, through aging and accomplishments he'd become a formidable, cold-hearted, portly man. Why didn't he care enough now to glance across the traffic, see Mirra's predicament and rescue her? She tried to scream for help but Adam's cries far out-distanced her own. It must have been this familiar sound, the bloodcurdling shrieks, that forced Dan to look up and notice them. When the light changed, he slowly crossed the street, in clock time, disgust plastered across his fat face.

"What now?" said Dan, as way of greeting. "We're late enough as it is."

"This wasn't exactly my idea," Mirra hissed at him. A mother from Charlotte's school was getting out of a taxi. Mirra didn't want her to see them. She turned her back, which set Adam's wails to a higher frequency.

"Adam, you must quiet down," said Dan, with a distanced fatherly authority. But Adam didn't listen to him. And when Dan reached out to take Adam from Mirra's arms, Adam punched him in the nose. A little trickle of bright red blood debuted out of Dan's left nostril. He reached for his linen handkerchief, the one she had ironed and so carefully folded and placed in his breast pocket that morning, and used it to staunch the flow.

"God damn it, Adam," Dan said.

"Don't you swear at him," said Mirra.

"Oh, hey, Mirra!" called Charlotte's friend's mother from down the block. Shit, thought Mirra. She turned to smile at her through her teeth.

"Everything all right there?" said the mother. She was dressed head to toe in Prada. She looked serene and calm, like she'd just come home from a massage.

"You know, terrible twos," said Mirra, as Adam tried to stuff his fist down her throat.

"I thought he was three," said the mother.

There was a pregnant pause, while Mirra glared at her, and then the woman said: "Well, we'll see you at the school auction," and gave a little ladylike wave goodbye as she headed downtown, hand already in her pocketbook to search for her cell phone, probably readying to call some other mother to gossip about Mirra's misfortunes.

"The little bastard, he could have broken my nose," Dan said, gazing at his handkerchief like he'd never seen blood before. "Who was that woman?"

"Don't call him that. He's upset," said Mirra. He looks, she thought, just like how I feel. "She's one of Charlotte's friend's mothers."

"I know he's upset," said Dan. "But this behavior is unacceptable. Maybe we should just call and cancel," said Dan.

"We can't cancel now," said Mirra. "We'll never get another interview. I can't believe you, Dan, I . . ."

Husband and wife stared angrily at each other. Drastic times call for drastic measures, Dan reached into Mirra's purse with disdain, as she held their egg beater of a son away from him, and pulled out their secret weapon.

The interviewer was a woman named Mrs. Wallace. Her husband and her two boys had attended the school as children; she'd volunteered for years, she said, before getting a job in the admissions office. She wore flesh-colored stockings, Pappagallo flats and something vaguely reminiscent of a Chanel suit, tweedy and buttoned and boxy. Dr. Eichler and his wife, Mirra, sat on the brown leather couch, with their son, Adam, on her lap. The walls were covered with pictures and several of the bookshelves were lined with little porcelain figures all in the shape of pigs. Mrs. Wallace collected pigs, she told them with a little laugh. Then she eschewed the swivel chair behind her desk for a damask-covered rocker she pulled out to get a better look at them. After the usual pleasantries, Mrs. Wallace leaned forward and tried to make nice with little Adam. "How old are you, Adam?"

No answer.

"So I hear you have two charming older sisters?"

Nary a sound. How could there be? Adam couldn't talk. And he had both a pacifier and a bottle in his mouth. His parents' secret weapon. It was the only way Mirra and Dan could think to calm him down. He was all plugged up.

"He doesn't usually take a bottle or a pacifier anymore," Mirra stammered. "I, I, I guess he's just a little anxious."

"Of course," said Mrs. Wallace, "we are keenly aware of how trying new situations can be for little boys."

"Thank you for understanding," Dan said.

The adults all smiled wanly at each other.

Mrs. Wallace leaned in close to Adam again.

"You know, Adam," said Mrs. Wallace, "if you come to this school you're going to have to leave your pacifier and bottle at home."

Adam smiled at her, his adorable little smile, and the pacifier slipped out. Mirra's heart began beating wildly. Mrs. Wallace smiled a Cheshire cat grin. Emboldened, she reached out and grabbed the bottle out of his mouth.

Adam reached out to pull the bottle back in again. Mrs. Wallace gently tugged. It came out with a little pop.

"Shut yer piehole," said Adam.

He put the bottle snugly back in again.

In the first second of shocked silence that followed, Mirra's heart swelled with pride. The woman was a bitch. Her little boy had put her in her place. He had shown strength, resolve, confidence confidence

confidence. It was only when the reality of the full horror of the moment began to dawn on her that she recognized Adam for the traitor that he was.

He could talk.

The fat letter of acceptance arrived at the Eichlers' apartment in the spring. But Mirra no longer lived there to open it.

HABITS OF HAPPINESS OR STILL LIFE WITH BOOT
Julie Benesh

One, in effect, *creates* happiness . . .
—Alan Epstein, Ph.D.,
How to Be Happier Day by Day

[Stretch and Breathe]

Dear Angel, she reads, would you mind terribly if I went without you blah-blah-blah . . . The words swim on the screen. Okay, how would a habitually *happy* person respond? How the hell would *she* know, Angel wonders, logging off without reply after her semi-long-distance boyfriend, Paolo, e-mails her that he has changed his mind and would rather she not accompany him to the exotic Santa Fe retreat center where he is delivering a paper on something that, he points out helpfully, she wouldn't understand anyway. He does explain, nicely enough, he has all this catching up to do with important people in his field, all these conversations that will sail right over her head at this conference in the romantic red desert where his old girlfriend the Teri Hatcher look-alike will be, the Teri Hatcher look-alike with the 753-word faculty bio on the Yale University Department of Art History Web site. The Teri Hatcher look-alike and who knows how many other art groupies with whom he involved himself before he fell in love with Angel.

[Complete Each Task You Begin]

Something constructive and matter-of-fact, Angel decides, is what she must do to get her mind off herself and take this most recent disappointment in stride. Chores and errands. Lots of chores and errands, bunches of them, dozens of them, to pull her out of her own head and into the world. She strides to the closet and energetically digs out the cat litter box, bags up the kitty litter, and bundles up her boot (black leather, multicolored embroidered trim along the center seam) with the broken heel. She throws on her red coat and sweeps on some red lipstick, ready to face the world and smile at the nice old man at the shoe repair shop with the sign in the window that says, *time wounds all heels.* She stops at the trash chute in the hall to toss the litter and hears a wump-wump-wump. She realizes that, in her determination to be constructive, she has just consigned her cute, wounded boot down the chute and into the trash bin in the basement.

[Acknowledge People Who Serve You]

Now what? Take a nap, she answers, start smoking, then – no, a happy person would persevere. She goes downstairs to locate the super, Desmond, ready to salvage her boot – and her day! – silently congratulating herself for giving him the Christmas bribe money last month. He pulls on gloves and wades around in the big blue bin before concluding that her lovely inadvertently trashed boot has been compacted already. He glances obliquely at her gray sweatpants and from his semi-toothless gold-sprinkled smile emanates, Are you still exercisin', Miss Johnson? 'Cause he remembers how nice she looked when she took off that extra weight . . . She manages a tight smile and says, oh yes, she finds that exercise gives her strength, stamina, and energy and reduces stress. He looks at her solemnly. "Stress," he intones. "Well, after all, you *alone.*"

[Join a Support Group]

Angel arranges to meet Supportive Friend Gloria at the Greek diner down the street. SFG embraces her briskly, her Laurel Burch tabby cat earrings glinting in the pale afternoon light. She has some questions and comments about Angel's crisis du jour: "Is it just that you see Paolo so seldom as it is? Or more that you really wanted to go and share in his professional triumph and meet his colleagues from around the world? Compounded by the fact that he told you in what you might consider an insensitive way? Or that he asked you then rescinded the invitation, which may indicate he is cooling off? Because it's surely not, well, you know . . . it's not like he *invites* attention from women. You are really lucky Paolo picked you, you must know that. He said himself that you were the first girlfriend he ever had that he was never tempted to cheat on. That says something. Especially since, just between us, you're a little . . . hey, *we're* a little . . . I count myself in this category, too . . . well . . . *difficult*, high-maintenance, you know, moody and all. Don't get me wrong, you *deserve* to have someone like Paolo. But now that you have him you should be happy . . . You should feel really good about yourself – hey, what's *wrong?*"

[Bargain with Someone]

When Angel's boyfriend Paolo calls her up the day after hurting her feelings by e-mailing her a disinvitation to an important professional event, the first thing he does is ask is she pissed. *Pissed?* It's a trick question. If she says yes, she's a shrew. If she says no, then he did nothing out of line and thus she deserves no comfort. So she feigns nonchalance, but he asks if she got his e-mail. Oh, that. Well, he persists, about her not going with him . . . She says it's his decision, of course, and she's not mad at him, exactly. Good! He chatters on about other things. Finally she screws up her courage and tells him she did, she does, have some feelings about it. Well, he responds, he can feel a fight brewing, so they'd better stop talking about it now. Angel consults her Artist's Way calendar. It's ten weeks until this trip – a pretty lengthy gag order. Gotta go, she says, brightly, see you this weekend, sweetie. Later she gets another e-mail from him. He has made his reservations and wants to stay at her house before and after to break up his trip to O'Hare. He's very polite about it, says he knows this is a thankless request. She writes back that they are a team, they help each other out, as one prospers, so does the other. She finds it's possible to feel both smug and dissatisfied simultaneously.

[Seek Professional Help]

Angel's Jungian analyst, Father Dante Travanti, a former Catholic priest, has the following distinctions: 1) being the exact same age (b. 10/ 28/22), to the day, as Angel's father, 2) having an artificial hip, and 3) having experienced firsthand two psychotic breaks of his very own. He gets befuddled sometimes, but they have been through a lot together in his cluttered office with the royal blue, scarlet, and gold magic carpet and the white ceramic Buddha planter and the burbling feng shui fountain; Angel has advanced in her career, bought a condominium, and fallen in love with Paolo. But sometimes she covets those days before she had so much to worry about losing. Father Travanti is still her last stand, the place where if she has to go there, he has to take her in. They spend a lot of time, even in her sessions, talking about professional concerns – Angel is a social worker who does art therapy with hospitalized children; they hang out collegially at conferences; and Angel has referred many of her friends to Father Travanti. If anyone can help her, it's him. If he can't . . . well, she doesn't want to think about that. Imagine Angel's delight when she hears his voice on her voicemail returning her call saying, "Angel! Where art thou? I'd misplaced your number and I wanted urgently to contact you. God must have sent you. I've been meaning to tell you – I raised my rates two years ago, but I just kept forgetting to tell you or it wasn't the right time, and so now I thought it would be best to call you up when you weren't having any other issues going on, you're seeing that wonderful man and things are going well, you got that big promotion at work and that raise you told me about. I really think it's only fair to ask you for some back pay. I know this is highly unusual, but I so need the money and under the circumstances . . . I'm feeling a little taken advantage of, and I'm sure you don't want that . . ."

[Keep a Journal]

When he's not talking mental-health shop with her, one of the things Angel's Jungian analyst Father Travanti tells her is that she should write a novel. Shaping her emotions into salable prose fit for public consumption would be good for her mental hygiene. And since she's a painter, she can even do the cover art for the book when it gets published (if she starts painting again). There are two problems with taking a writing workshop: a) it costs money that she then cannot use for therapy, let alone Travanti's back pay resulting from his own casual billing practices but for which she nonetheless feels guilty, and b) she can only write in the second person, and everyone always complains about it. But she thinks in the second person and when she tries to transcribe her moody, intimate second-person prose into third or even first, it's not the same, it sounds flat and boring, and there's always a stray pronoun or verb disagreement or two left over. Still, she keeps her journal, no one can criticize her there, as long as she's alive and keeps it hidden.

[Have a Slumber Party]

From *A Journal in the Second Person*, by Angel Johnson:

At night when you can't sleep, count your boyfriend's exes instead of sheep. Imagine your guy's entire romantic past, woman by woman. Elspeth the architect posing languidly in front of her latest billion-dollar mixed-use project, Dr. Cassandra with her blue-green blood-spattered scrubs complementing her tawny complexion, delivering a baby; songstress/composer Pam(accent on the *el*)a swaying in her gauzy garb, accepting a Grammy; the art groupie quintuplets, etc., etc. Try to focus equally on the fatal attractions and flaws of each. What brought them together, what tore them asunder? (Alternate between deep empathy for them because they must still want him and fearing them because they may represent your Paolo-less, empty future.)

[Do Something out of Character]

Angel and Paolo are sitting in the Starbucks on Rush on a Saturday afternoon when Paolo's former girlfriend composer-songstress Pam (accent on the *el*)a appears. Angel is prone to spontaneous visitations from Paolo's old girlfriends not extant in consensual reality, and assumes at first this is another such incident. Angel has never seen Pamela in person before but recognizes her from her CD cover photo and music video. She is frustratingly beautiful, like a Botticelli, or Cirque du Soleil, you don't know where to look first or how not to miss anything important. Angel wonders idly if success and expensive stylists have made her that way, or whether she has always had some inevitable star quality. Suddenly Pamela looks their way and shouts, "Paolo," strutting over to them, holding out her hand, then reaching toward Paolo for a hug. They tell each other how great they look while Angel looks on as if from a distance. When Paolo says this is my friend, Angel, Angel makes eye contact, smiles warmly and says, "It's so wonderful to meet you in person. I love your CD – and the video, too." (She thinks, but does not say: I have your lamp in my bedroom; Paolo, practical and unsentimental guy that he is, gave it to me. Perhaps if you get famous enough I can sell it for a large amount of money on eBay.) After Pamela excuses herself to proffer a few autographs, Paolo tells Angel how much he loves her when she's not being her usual difficult, touchy, oversensitive, and jealous self – just kidding, sweetie!

[Strive for Perspective]

Paolo is perennially and vocally surprised, almost betrayed, when Angel fails, as she frequently does, to demonstrate what he is convinced is her monolithic and pathological jealousy. In Angel's mind he confuses the exception with the rule, or what an artist would describe as the figure (her small bright touchiness) with the ground (her subdued backdrop of mature understanding and perspective). Angel knows people who know people who page their boyfriends hourly to ask them if there are any women around who are prettier than them, women who won't leave Victoria's Secret catalogs lying around, women who snoop. Angel lives a hundred miles from Paolo and never checks up, is benevolent and approving of his female friends, and has accompanied him to sex museums on three continents where they later watched adult pay-per-view videos back at the hotel. What

Paolo sees as "jealous" Angel sees as a legitimate political, psychological, and spiritual code of honor. To wit: 1) Angel resents the pressure put on women by the media to conform to society's consumerist expectations (the fact that she largely succumbs makes her resent it all the more); 2) Angel believes that utter unconcern over potential rivals usually indicates a lack of investment and that while jealous paranoia is often implicated in a relationship's demise, it is usually well justified, grounded in fact, and merely used by the clever villain (and endorsed by a brutal war-mongering culture) to blame the innocent victim; and, most importantly, 3) Angel's concerns are not so much about wandering attentions as about the inevitability of endings and the inherent disloyalty of existential separateness and ultimate mortality. She is Margaret in the Hopkins poem, grieving over fallen leaves, mourning for herself and her own relationships and everyone else's, past, present, and future.

[Visualize the Future]

Angel hates hospitals, fears illness, obsesses about deaths actual and metaphorical, and is more or less a blocked painter and perhaps an artist manqué, but she is excellent as an art therapist for sick children. This is what her Jungian analyst calls a "compensatory attitude" – by confronting one's fears head-on, one conquers them in the way that truly counts, by integrating them. Angel has boundless empathy for the children she works with, empathy that seems superfluous at times, given the grace of many of them, grace that humbles her frequently, shames her occasionally, and comforts her invariably, like when Bethany sketches a dazzling pastel of a butterfly in Easter hues of sky blue, lavender, sea-foam green, and chick yellow. It's a self-portrait, Bethany's pet name is Butterfly. The next sketch shows her family: Mom, Grandmom, and little sister in a garden with pink peonies and yellow roses, but no Bethany and no butterfly. "I'm there," she explains. "You just can't see me."

[Look at All Sides of an Issue]

Is Angel's lover Paolo a bad romantic risk?

Yes. He's clearly beyond the land of double-digit conquests, and if he's faithful for Angel in the long run it'll be a first. He's an extrovert who enjoys the stimulation of new people, though he quickly tires of them. He and Angel live far apart and don't see each other that much. Paolo admits to being superficially sexually attracted to his better-looking undergraduate students and insists that all male professors are, and any who say they are not are lying. He admits to being driven to distraction by the mere sight of a woman's legs. Once on the Boulevard St. Germain in Paris he practically licked a poster of Emmanuelle Béart, and got mad at poor Angel when she shot him a wounded glance. At his age (forty), he's unlikely to change.

No. He's deeply in love with Angel, who, he claims, brings out in him a soft and tender side he never knew he had. As sensitive as Angel is, she has never noticed him so much as look at another woman in her presence, not counting the Emmanuelle Béart poster incident; that's what made it so shocking. He says the minute he reads his students' exams any sexual interest he has in them vaporizes. Paolo doesn't hide things from Angel, the way he thinks her past lovers have, and the way he has from women in his own past.

Maybe. This is one of those things that are known only in retrospect, and surprises abound.

[Look at All Sides of an Issue (II)]

Is Angel projecting her own deeply denied, promiscuously lustful desires onto the innocent Paolo?

Yes. Angel has a deep need to be wanted, and was actually a notorious tease during her single dating days. She envies Paolo his experience and wants it for herself, though she's apparently afraid to go get it honestly. One wonders if she is a latent lesbian or repressed omnisexual, or something, the way she obsesses about Paolo's sexual history.

No. Angel has proven herself capable of (serial, at least) monogamy, with a demonstrated ability to focus her attention on a particular special someone with no regrets. She adores Paolo, thinks he is the most interesting and attractive guy around, feels like they complement one another very well.

Maybe. Angel glamorizes the image of Paolo as a bad boy, glamorizing herself by association, simultaneously allowing herself to be "the good one."

[Take a Nap in the Afternoon]

After a cathartic, if exhausting, journal-writing session, Angel has a dream in which, urged on by her Supportive Friend Gloria, she uncharacteristically peruses Paolo's desk: papers, bills, checks, junk mail, a Pamela CD, then a glossy, glistening, lurid-looking leather-bound photography book. Eureka – a pornographic photo album! Angel's limbs quiver as she leans in and she sees it is Jan Sovak's butterfly illustrations, which morph into photos of butterflies, which morph into mounted butterfly corpses, which come to life, fly around the room, and disappear into an unfamiliar stained-glass skylight. Father Travanti appears, robed as the pope, nodding his blessing, holding out a chalice in his withered, ringed hand, which Angel takes in exchange for a chunky-heeled boot. Angel's building super, wielding push broom, eases Father Travanti and Gloria out the door in front of him and Angel is alone, her journal at her feet.

[Pay Attention to Synchronicities]

Angel realizes that if she were to never again see Father Travanti, he will nonetheless always be with her. The defining moment in their pre-dispute therapeutic relationship? Angel crying over Peter Pan-ish *puer* Abe, the last man she was involved with before she met Paolo. Her story: Coffee dates with poor recently jilted Abe met at a Jung Institute workshop ultimately end up naked and horizontal. Then, a month later, Abe calls her from O'Hare to say hey, he just got married and is moving to Japan, and thanks for being such a pal. On this basis Angel proclaims to Travanti that everything in life is either trivial or else it breaks your heart. Father Travanti shakes his head at her outburst, lifts his grizzled chin, and proclaims, "But it's not either-or! It's both-and!" Angel stares at him. Both-and! Both-and! Is that supposed to be consoling? And then she laughs imagining the Frost poem about the crow shaking the snow from the hemlock tree on the depressive's head, cheering him up, possibly averting his suicide, and Travanti laughs, too, whether he knows why or not, and it is a good inter-vention, whether it was really all intended that way or not, whether that matters or not. So when the phone rings mid-ponder and it's Travanti inviting Angel to a lecture he is doing on Intuitive and Outsider Art at the Museum of Contemporary Art, reminding her she is an artist, as well as a therapist, and her young patients are intuitive outsiders, she figures she ought to go.

[Connect with Someone Once Important to You]

Art critic Paolo and art therapist Angel are at the Museum of Contemporary Art, where Father Travanti is about to lecture. "You want me to talk to him?" Paolo asks. "Ask him if his *malpractice* premiums are up-to-date?" No, Angel does not. Paolo thinks the following are fraudulent: Intuitive and Outsider Art, Jungian analysis, analysts who request back pay. He goes to look at the normal exhibit, the sparrows' corpses dressed in baby clothes, simultaneous videos of performance artists energetically conjugating verbs, chairs made of beef jerky. At least those artists had M.F.A.s. (Angel doesn't have an M.F.A., just a B.F.A. and an M.A. in art therapy.) Angel sits down near the exit in the lecture hall, receiving Father Travanti's nebulous nod. He rambles as usual; Angel has often heard people complain about his lacking linearity, which never fails to mobilize her loyalty. But today she feels prickly, as if she is getting hives. Gradually she notices an off-white cashmere scarf, fringed, trailing around her neck, arranged by recognizable hands caressing her collarbone and creating an involuntary, familiar frisson. Abe, her old whatever, muttering

Angelinuschka, my Slavic princess, who you sleepin' with these days, who's the lucky guy? Angel, flushing and confused, covers his hand with hers, reaches around to pat Abe's curls, and, in turning, looks up to see Paolo at the door of the auditorium, arms folded, eyes like charcoal. About-face.

[Trade Roles with Someone]

Angel is practically running, with rising panic, dodging people and sculptures. Paolo is moving briskly but, she calculates that he calculates, slowly enough for her to catch him, with effort, his hands in his pockets to preclude their characteristic clasp with hers. (When they started going out he told her he had not held hands with a woman on a public thoroughfare for more than a decade, but that hers are so beautiful, and soft, and so even with his . . .) She runs up behind him and laces her arm through his. His arm is stiff but he doesn't pull away, at least. "You know why I'm pissed?" he asks, without preamble. "I want to be sure you understand. If you don't understand that's bad. If you understand, that's bad. Either way, why would you do that? What were you *doing*? The worst part was, I saw you in that red coat and felt this wave of love for you – yes! I said to myself – I'm with her! The *painter* in the red coat. Who then allows herself to be manhandled by some foppish goofball . . ." Angel tries to explain she was merely responding to the unexpected greeting of an old friend. Paolo wants her to understand that it's not as if he is jealous or possessive, he just doesn't like to see her taken advantage of in any way or see that someone feels free to take liberties, physical ones, in public, he can only imagine what their private moments were like, speculating how they must have robbed poor Angel of her essential dignity, thus explaining the burdensome insecurity with which *he* must so often contend. Angel feels a hot surge of righteous anger immediately followed by a cool geyser of relief, which shoots from the soles of her feet and out the top of her head. "I'm sorry, Paolo, but I can't follow all your subtle, refined distinctions." She squeezes his arm. "It all just sounds like *jealous* to me." He looks down and smiles, recognizing himself as the source of these words of dismissive wisdom, pokes her with an elbow to concede her the point, leans in for a small, contained embrace, takes her hand. "But Paolo, we still need to talk about something."

[Have a Lively Conversation]

– But, wallowing in emotions never makes anything better. We're not kids anymore. I'm tired of the Sturm und Drang. I thought you were different. Why do all the women I meet start out sane and independent and end up crazy and obsessive? It should all be about respect and sharing experiences . . .

– You mean outer experiences, Paolo, but we should be able to respectfully share inner ones, too.

– Inner experiences not independently confirmed by outer ones are known as delusions. If you don't like it, just fix it, why don't you?

– It's not about fixing. All I want is to express myself. That's all I need. And I don't feel right talking to someone else about you. Why can't I talk to you?

– Okay, what?

– I feel sometimes like you're slumming around with me, like I'm not accomplished enough, or flashy enough, or . . . enough. I'm like some wholesome habit you're using discreetly to temporarily cleanse your jaded palate . . .

– Where are you *getting* that? I'm with you, aren't I? And who cares about flash? *You*, apparently. With your red coat and matching lipstick, your shiny hair, and your fancy footwear . . . You help people in ways I can't even begin to understand.

– But you disinivited me to that conference . . .

– What? You're upset about *that*? I told you I didn't want any distractions.

– But why did you invite me in the first place?

– I suppose I thought I needed you there to prove that everything is different now. Like some kind of image thing. But then I realized I *don't* need you there, precisely *because* everything *is* different now.

There's nothing to prove, or so I thought. I wasn't thinking about second-guessing you. Don't you have a better way to express yourself?

[Immerse Yourself in Color]

On this they can agree. Paolo is like a small, dark Chardin still life: knife, apple, skinned rabbit, perfectly proportioned, defined, structured, and grounded, whereas Angel is like a colorful Chagall with bridal couples flying over the Eiffel Tower juxtaposed with Bible scenes and dream sequences flowing and floating. Paolo's a host carrier of chaotic emotions, experiencing minimal symptoms himself (he has two emotions – happy and angry – Angel claims he doesn't paint with a full palette) yet propagating them extravagantly in others. What they have together is like a mosaic laid with tweezers, a constellation of habits, vibrant as viscera, bright as blood, hard and fragile as bone, easily scattered as ash; significant and insubstantial as a mandala traced in sand, a pattern discernible only from outer space. They both like Picasso and Pollock and Yves Klein. A certain shade of blue can move them both to tears. (People think ~~you~~ they look cute together.)

WE ARE NOT FRIENDS
Fred Leebron

When they're not sailing their boat or hiking in places where nobody recognizes them, the two take their friends with them to Tuscan villas, where everybody cooks, drinks good wine, and stays up late talking and waiting for something unexpected to happen.

"We fly them in if they don't have money," she says of her mates. "One of the hard things about dealing with wealth is that you don't want to lose your friends. And a lot of that is saying, 'We happen to be very fortunate and very lucky – so let's all enjoy it.'"

—From a profile of Nicole Kidman, in *Vogue* magazine, June 1999

There is something about the way the phone rings that lets you know it's Them – a kind of glitter in the chime, a certain *je ne sais quoi* to the cadence, which seems to skip a beat as if it can't quite believe that They are calling. You pick up, heart throbbing, getting ready to move your mouth, a sly frisson of sweat striking your palms.

"They asked me to call," Their assistant says. "They want you at the house next Thursday. And then you'll all go somewhere. A plane will be involved. You'll want to bring a passport. Until Monday, let's say. Can I pen you in?"

Of course, you say. Because, really, you know no other response. And you want to. And you like Them.

All week you attend to dropping everything – meetings at work, the children at your mother's, the cats at the kennel, your own self-involvement into the basement of your brain. You feel a wonderful tingle at the top of your head – someone likes you and it is Them. You shop for clothes, scout the itinerary that will get you to the house on time, and concentrate on biting your lip when anyone asks you if you have any special plans. One of your attributes is discretion, another is your wry or winning or self-deprecating humor, a third the fact that your personality doesn't change when you drink. Beyond that, you're not sure. It's certainly not your looks or your bitterness or your propensity toward self-pity – which They simply will not tolerate. Maybe it's just you. You're a special friend, a member of the inner circle, a trusted one. You have watched Their back and They have watched you watch it. Together you've skinny-dipped, drunk too much expensive single-malt, fallen down stairs and off trampolines. You know things about Them that you've made yourself forget, so fearful are you of being quoted by anyone who hounds you for tidbits.

At Their house – an ascetic zen bowl sink in the bathroom, ten-thousand-dollar rococo couches opposing each other on the hard-wood floor, flames roaring in the marble fireplace even though it is spring outside – you sit dazed with the other friends, some of whom you don't know at all and others whom you know too well. "I'll tell you," a loud brunette whispers, "the most surprising thing in my life is that I am Their friend." You nod politely – you've been on many such junkets with her, you know her for the starfucker she is and you believe you are not – and yet your face saddens and you cast around inside yourself for some kind of truth – what does this summoning really feel like, this performance of friendship?

They saunter down the steps, smiles dazzling, eyes secreted behind sunglasses, the room growing brilliant in the light that great success can shed. "We set?" He says, in that muscular grunge way. "Shall we?" She offers, with that sweet slope of her voice. A tinted Mercedes van instantly pulls up. The assistant shoos you in, calling, "Disposable cameras are in your favor bags. I've made sure dinner is vegan." And you drive off, people clicking off cell phones, everyone grinning as if in on a great secret, terrifics and excitings strewn about the interior like petals in the aisle at Their wedding. You're not even sure where you're going.

At the airport in the descending darkness waits a camp of paparazzi. Within the plush hush of the van you listen to His instructions: all friends off first, meet in the celebrity lounge. You open the door to the frantic glare.

"Who's that?"

"Is it Them?"

"Don't shoot, don't shoot! It's no one."

Needlessly grinning, you hurry inside. From behind the heavy glass you can't help turning and watching. Eventually, He descends, stands smirking for an instant as flashes pop and spray, agreeably removes his sunglasses momentarily, mouths some ironic remark you cannot hear, and shoulders his way through. Finally, it is Her. Dressed in white. Bright red lipstick. Sunglasses off. Smiling with élan. Then they let Her go.

In the lounge you're all panting hard from the near-celebrity exertion. The flight is called. Wait, you're told. You sip a seltzer. The clock turns. "That time at Moomba," one friend says. "What a bitch," someone sneers. "Then Kenny did that thing to her." Uproarious laughter when She laughs, solemn nods when He is pensive. There is industry chitchat which you cannot follow, names tossed out like so much parade candy. Five minutes before departure, you all rise. Those of you who have sunglasses put them on. At the wordless direction of the oldest friend, a multimega exec in a double-breasted suit with an electronic device in each pocket, you form a phalanx of escorts around Them and stride through the dark airport onto the dark plane.

"Should I know you," an older stewardess nervously giggles to Them, taking the new dress on its hanger that She has somehow managed to purchase as She charmingly entertained in the airport. "I know I should know you. I'm sure my son would know you."

You sit back in your seats, marveling at how hard it must be to be Them, to be commented to and on at every available turn, to surrender any iota of private embarrassment or pain or joy, to have all elements of life cut up into smaller and smaller pieces to be chewed and emitted by the bulemic media, to pose and play in full nudity in scenes that can be viewed and reviewed until everyone everywhere knows just where the coiffed curl of pubic hair gives way to scraggly fur. To be so exposed. You shudder honestly and sip your cocktail as the plane lifts and lifts.

In Italy there are ten times as many paparazzi and their hands beat at the metal flanks of the Volvo bus as you sail by and away and the shutters stop, the road empties, and you are up past olive trees and lines of vineyards into the tender hills. The eight or ten of you who have made it this far beam radiantly and when a relative newcomer offers cigarettes you dismissively decline as you wisely await further instructions on protocol. Up front, by the driver, the Two who've brought you hold hands across the aisle. In the distance a white compound with red tile roofs rises, destined peaks of emotion and indulgence fronted by the tiny heads of many ingratiating servants and the bursting frills of bougainvillea and hyacinth.

Of course, you understand, this will all come to an end. Someday you will arrive late for a command appearance, flustered by a rough business lunch and the fact that you will have performed too much beforehand, and one of Them will tease you and you will tease Them too much in return, perhaps you will even talk back, perhaps you will even be rude. The assistant will snap her carnivorous jaws at you, He will look away in disappointment, She will wait you out in silence until you recognize that you must leave. You will stumble at the door, unwilling to apologize, unable to sense anything but the exhilaration of yourself unmasked as a person. Their look has lit you in a thousand different ways, at gala benefits and in cozy restaurants, on Page Six of the *Post* and in a dozen weekly magazines, on the beach and in lift lines, but now the gold has gone out of it. Is it something you have done to Them, or They have done to you, or you have done to yourself, or – incredibly – They have done to Themselves? What has this friendship meant if, in the instant you watch it slip from your hands, you feel both relieved and regretful, nostalgic and enraged, redeemed and vilified, negligible and tangible? Who knows, but in this long moment of first and last betrayal – Their impatience, your indiscretion; your transgression, Their dismissal – shines the only time that They will ever remember that you were there.

MY MOTHER'S GARDEN
Katherine Shonk

S pring had come to my hometown. When I got off the bus at the entrance to the contamination zone, Oles was standing at the guard station in a lightweight uniform instead of his padded military jacket, his gun swung loosely over his back. The thaw seemed to have improved his usually sullen mood; he nodded his appreciation of the flowered fabric I'd brought for his wife, and let me pass through the gate without even looking at my documents.

I strayed from the silent, wide street that led into the abandoned town, turning instead into the forest. I prefer to take the long route to my mother's house in the village, averting my eyes from the town's yawning high-rise apartment buildings, the rusting yellow Ferris wheel, and in the far distance, the plant itself. Here the trees grew dense and undisturbed, and the familiar scent of spring filled the air. The fresh, heady smell hadn't yet reached our new home – funny that after twelve years I still think of it as "new" – less than fifty kilometers away on the barren, flat steppe.

I emerged from the woods into the broad field where I used to play as a child. During my last visit, just a month ago, it had been a smooth blanket of snow, but now feathery grass reached my knees. Across the field, the village looked almost as it did just before the evacuation, the little pastel houses rising in two neat rows, shaded by budding trees. White clouds meandered across a sky the color of periwinkles. A breeze blew up from the river, rustling the grass and swaying the sign that leaned in the middle of the field, its red warning chipped and peeling.

"Yuuuulia!" Mama cried, brandishing her ax in greeting. She and her friend Ganna, their aprons filled with pine branches, met me in the field. They smiled, wide and gap-toothed, squinting in the cool sun-light, their soft fat faces framed with kerchiefs. They were waiting for me to touch them, a kiss or a pat, but I hesitated, and the moment passed.

"Ganna, take some of these logs I've brought Mama," I said. But they had begun to divvy up their branches, each scolding the other for not taking her fair share.

Inside the house, I stacked the logs I'd brought by the stove. "I've got a perfectly good forest in my backyard, and you bring me fire-wood," Mama complained.

She made me a cup of tea and examined my loot, grunting her approval at the sausage links, the bag of sugar, the box of tea. "Enough for a dress," I said, unfolding a length of flowered fabric. The white material shone like a beam of light in the rundown house, where the teacups were stained brown, the wallpaper roses buried beneath a layer of grit.

Mama showed me a bucketful of green onions she'd grown in her garden. "Delicious," she said, chomping on one. "Here, you try."

"Mama, you know I won't eat that," I said.

"Summer is coming," she said. "Ganna's Oksana is bringing her little girls here in a few weeks."

"They should be arrested for bringing children here." Each time I visit, my mother hints that she'd like me to bring my thirteen-year-old daughter, Halynka, to see her. She doesn't seem to understand that it is something I will never do.

"Look at this beautiful onion." She sliced the tip off a stalk and held it beneath my nose. It smelled sweet. Juice coated the tender white rings like syrup on a cut pine. "They come up earlier than before, and they taste better, too."

"How many times do I have to tell you, Mama? Just because it looks healthy doesn't mean it is." With the possible exception of God, my mother only believes what she sees.

"I had a visitor the other day," she said in a singsong voice that told me she was planning to win the argument with a sneak attack. "I heard something rustling outside, and I thought it was a deer or a rabbit. I looked out the window and nearly jumped out of my skin. There was a man poking around my garden with one of those counters, wearing white clothes and a mask. He looked like a cosmonaut."

"We should all dress like that around here."

"'What are you doing in my garden?' I shouted. He came to the door and started speaking to me in Russian."

"Who was he?"

"He told me that he was an American and he didn't speak Ukrainian."

"An American? What did he want?"

"Some of my onions. He told me he was a scientist and he wanted to do a test on them."

"Did you give him some?"

"I did, but only to teach him a lesson in hospitality. This American, he was trespassing on my property, wearing a mask, like the very air he's stealing isn't good enough for him."

"Maybe he'll come back and put some fear into you."

"There's nothing to be afraid of here." Her fingers fluttered over the fabric daisies and carnations. On the bus, I had pictured myself draping the material around her waist, taking measurements, then cutting and stitching. Mama's fingers were so stiff and callused that I doubted she could thread a needle anymore. But now I was ready to leave.

She filled one of my plastic bags with onions. "Here. These'll make Mykola strong."

"Thank you, Mama." There was no sense in refusing.

"Soon the grandchildren will be here," she said.

"You just told me that, Mama."

"Healthy, playful kids, they are. Not a one of them sick."

"For now, maybe."

"They'll eat our berries. Drink water from the well."

"Halynka's not coming here, Mama." I gave her a swift kiss, my lips glancing her cheek, my hand grazing her sweater. It never ceases to shame me, this fear I have of touching my mother, of carrying the poison in her skin and clothes to my daughter. And I could tell by her rigid posture, her refusal to yield to my touch, that Mother was ashamed of me too, and that she had been ashamed outside when I stood stiffly in front of her and Ganna. "Mama, would you do something for me?"

"Eh?"

"If the American comes back, see if he can stop by here next Saturday, say at two o'clock."

"I know what I'll say if he tells me he didn't like my onions: 'Go back home and eat American onions, then!' We'll see what he has to say to that."

"Just ask him, all right, Mama? I'll come back again next week."

"Don't trouble yourself. I do just fine on my own."

I walked out the front way, down the dirt road, past the tottering, deserted houses of former neighbors. I was born in this village and lived here until I was twenty-three, when I moved into my husband's apartment in the nearby town. The windows of the cottages are still framed with hand-carved woodwork, but the paint is bleached and flaking, and many of the panes are broken. I usually avert my eyes as I walk past, out of respect for those who left their homes so quickly, in such disarray. But this time as I passed the Teslenkos', I turned, just for a second. An old loom was set up in the front room, strung with gray yarn, or perhaps just cobwebs, and something pink hung out of an opened bureau drawer. Their daughter, my daughter's best friend, died six months ago. I tossed the bag of onions down the side of the road and watched it disappear into the weeds.

At home, my husband was standing in the scruffy yard of our sinking apartment building in his track suit and house slippers, talking to the old women seated on the bench. He was gesturing wildly, knees bent and feet apart in an anchoring stance, as if he expected the world to take off at any moment. Mykola was once considered a handsome man – certain people were surprised he chose someone as plain as me to marry – but the neighbors do not notice his wavy hair and solid build anymore. I am grateful that we settled here with our own people after the accident, rather than among strangers in Kiev. Mykola can wobble about the yard, shouting nonsense, and no one will talk about him behind his back. Here, people make allowances.

"The pistons need to be kept clean," he was saying. "It's the most important thing. The most important!" The women were nodding; like me, they have learned to pretend they understand his discourses on automobile repair. Mykola was one of the first men to participate in the cleanup at the reactor, and shortly afterward he began to suffer from dizzy spells. He was fired from his job as a mechanic five years ago, after he lost control of a car and crashed into a tree. That day marked the beginning of his confused thoughts and odd behavior.

"Be careful, I'm dirty," I said, backing away when Mykola reeled toward me.

"How's Mama?" one of the women asked about their old friend.

"As stubborn as ever," I sighed.

"We should all be as stubborn as her," said Evhenia Vlodimirovna. "She's living in her own home, happy as can be."

"She wants me to bring Halynka to visit her."

"Why shouldn't you?"

"Sure, why not?" echoed Maria Sergeyevna. "Not for long, of course."

Mykola picked up a candy wrapper and disappeared inside the building. I heard him shuffle up the stairs, then the whine of the garbage chute.

"I'm not taking her there," I said. "It's bad enough that I go."

"Listen to me, Yulia." Evhenia wagged her finger at me. "You know why they don't want us to move back?"

"Why?" I asked.

"It would cost too much to start up the town again after all these years. They'd have to redo the electricity and telephone lines and such. That's the only reason why. I saw it on television."

"An American scientist came by my mother's house," I said. "He's going to do a test on her onions."

"See?" Evhenia said. "He'll tell you there's nothing to worry about, and you can let your mother have a nice visit from her granddaughter before she dies."

"We'll see," I said.

Upstairs, I undressed in the bathroom, dumping everything in the bathtub, even my muddy boots. Then I turned on the shower, hot, and scrubbed my skin until it was red and raw. I lathered my hair with shampoo, stomped my clothes underfoot, and rinsed the boots, inside and out, until finally I felt clean again. Then I fetched Halynka from the Teslenkos' place, where she was watching television with Danylo, their son. Halynka left the apartment without saying goodbye, as if she were just going off to the bathroom.

"Grandmama says hello," I told her on the stairs, but she had nothing to say to that. She hasn't seen her grandmother since Mama disappeared two years ago, leaving only a note that read: "I've gone home. Come and visit me." Halynka cried for days after that. Her grandmother practically raised her; I've worked as a bookkeeper for the grocery store since we moved here twelve years ago. Halynka didn't understand when I explained that she couldn't visit her grandmother because the village would make her sick. After a while, Halynka simply stopped asking about her. I suspect she feels abandoned by her grandmother, though she has never said this to me directly.

Halynka does not like to reveal herself to me. I began to notice this fact a year ago, when the Teslenkos' daughter was diagnosed with thyroid cancer. During the next six months, Halynka often slept on the floor next to Viktoria's bed, and even traveled with the family to the hospital in Kiev. Lilia, Viktoria's mother, told me that Halynka would rub her friend's back for hours to help ease the terrible pain. In the months since Viktoria's death, Halynka has spent most of her time outside of school with the Teslenkos, returning home only to sleep and eat. She has developed an attachment to Lilia that I envy, and a closeness to sixteen-year-old Danylo that worries me.

We cooked supper in silence, cutlets and fried potatoes. When the food was almost done, Halynka went to the balcony to call in her father, but he wasn't outside.

I found Mykola in the bedroom, lying in the dark. "Please," he whispered.

One of his migraines had descended, so I placed a damp towel on his forehead and shut the door. I would sleep on the couch, so as not to disturb him with my snoring. I knew that the next evening I would find the apartment in perfect order, the dishes put away, my clothes ironed, the rugs vacuumed. He has grown increasingly tidy since the car crash, taking over responsibilities I assumed in the early years of our marriage. But I try not to compare our present life to the past. We are two different people now; it is the only explanation that makes sense.

Coming home from work a few days later, I found Lilia Teslenko waiting for me in the yard. She was trim in her housedress, her short, dark hair neatly curled, and she smiled at me as I approached, her hand shading her eyes. Ignoring Mykola, who was talking with his lady friends, she asked me up for tea. She had sent Danylo and Halynka off on an errand, she told me, so that we could have a nice, quiet chat.

I sat at the kitchen table, dreading whatever it was she had to say.

"I haven't taken the opportunity, Yulia, to express how grateful I am that my Viktoria had such a wonderful friend as Halynka," she said as we sipped our tea.

"Viktoria was a precious gift to Halynka," I said. "She misses her terribly."

"Yes, I know." Lilia looked into her cup. "She often talks to me, and to Danylo, about her feelings, her grief. It has been difficult for all of us."

I was silent, steeling myself.

"Yulia, I'm worried about Halynka." She met my eyes. "I feel she depends on me and Danylo too much. It's as if she expects us to be her family. As if she hopes to take over Viktoria's place in our hearts."

"I'm sure she would never expect that," I said. But in truth, I wasn't sure of this at all.

"Perhaps I'm overstating it. But I am worried about her, and I just don't have the energy . . ." Her hands were laced tightly on the table. "To be frank, I don't want another daughter. And Danylo doesn't want a sister, or a girlfriend – do you understand what I'm saying?"

I stood up. "I understand. I'm sorry Halynka has been such a burden."

"Oh, not a burden. Please, don't think that. But . . . I think she needs to spend more time with her family – with you, at least."

I felt a surge of protectiveness for my husband. Why were his eccentricities more shameful than Viktoria's illness, when they both flowed from the same source?

"I'll make sure she doesn't bother you anymore," I said. "You've had a difficult enough time. I should have intervened earlier."

Halynka came home an hour later and went straight to her room. Finding her lying on the bed, I sat down and squeezed her shoulder. The narrow angel wings of her back rose up in defense, and I moved my hand away.

"I had a talk with Lilia Teslenko today," I said.

"I know," she said. Her voice was small and weary.

"I told Lilia that I wanted you to visit them less often. Your father and I hardly see you."

"I want to go stay with Grandmama for the summer," she said.

"Darling, you know I won't let you go there."

"There are some little kids who spend the whole summer with their grandparents," she said.

"Their parents are making a mistake. Those children will get sick, like Viktoria."

"I don't care if I get sick."

"Halynka, don't say that." I longed to cradle her thin body in my arms, but I thought of my own need to protect myself from my mother – an urge perhaps less warranted than my daughter's need to wall herself off from me – and I restrained myself.

"Papa wouldn't care if I went to Grandmama's," she said. "He doesn't even notice me."

"Halynka, that's not true." But in a way it was. As he slowly lost his mind, Mykola had become more and more perplexed by Halynka, avoiding her until they were like neighbors in a communal apartment. "We would both miss you very much."

"I've never even seen the place where I was born," she said. Her voice was high and slow; she was drifting off to sleep.

"It was just like any other Soviet town. There was nothing special about it." This was true, except, of course, that it had been our home. But I didn't want her to get any romantic notions about the town. I wanted her to look ahead to the future, to go to college, to move away, to Kiev or even to Europe. I wanted her to forget that she had been born in a place so elusive and unnatural that its entire population had disappeared overnight.

"Drink, drink," I heard my mother say as I approached her house the next Saturday.

A man was sitting at the kitchen table, his body covered in brilliant white, from his jumpsuit to a cloth mask that revealed only his eyes – brown, crinkled at the edges – to a stiff white cap. Mama was wafting a cup of tea under his nose. Between them lay several onion stalks, a notebook and pen, and a tape recorder, its spools turning.

"Please turn that off," I said.

"I was hoping to interview you and your mother," the man said. His Russian was more pure than my own. "My name is George. George Hayes. I'm an environmental toxicologist." He rose, and I saw that he was wearing rubber gloves.

"This is Yulia, my daughter," Mama said.

I had no intention of talking to a stranger about my life, and I felt protective of my mother's privacy as well. "Please," I said. "We don't want to be recorded."

He turned off the machine and we both sat down.

"Go on, tell her," Mama said. "Tell her what you told me about my onions."

"I ran a Geiger counter over them, and there's no question they're highly contaminated. She shouldn't be eating anything from that garden. She shouldn't drink the well water or burn wood from the forest. She shouldn't be living here at all."

"I've told her all of this a thousand times," I said.

"Tell her the rest," Mama said.

"I did some tests on these onions," the American said. "Despite the radiation, or maybe even because of it, they're quite robust. You can tell just by the size and color, but the cell structure and nutritional value are both strong as well."

"It's like I told you, they're even better than before," Mama said.

"What difference does it make, if they're going to make her sick?" I said.

"Well, yes, exactly. There's no doubt they're inedible," he said.

"He says it's healthy," Mama said.

"Not healthy, exactly . . . let me explain. I've been testing mice in the area, and I've found that they're actually becoming bigger and stronger with each generation." He spoke quickly, with increasing fervor. "All over the zone I'm finding these amazing examples of nature's ability to preserve itself, and even to advance genetically. But the acceleration we see in these onions – and that I've noticed in my mice – is abnormal. It may lead to mutations as the years go by."

"I'll give you some tomatoes when they're ready, and potatoes in the fall," Mama said. "Real beauties. I'll make you some soup."

I scraped back my chair. "May I speak to you outside?"

"Of course," the scientist said.

We stood by the garden fence. "I want you to stay away from my mother," I said.

"Stay away?"

"You're confusing her, and I'm the one who has to cope with her."

"I'm sure I can make her understand – "

"She's trying to talk me into bringing my thirteen-year-old daughter here for a visit."

"Oh, you shouldn't do that."

"Of course not. But she points to her onions, her berries, her clear water, and she tells me there can't possibly be anything wrong with them, because they look healthy and they taste good."

"But doesn't she know . . ."

"She ran away from our new home seven times in the first ten years after we moved, until she finally convinced the guard to let her back in. She's determined to die here. No, she doesn't understand. She doesn't believe that something she can't see can hurt her."

He shook his head. "I guess it would be hard to argue with that point of view."

"Her friends' grandchildren visit them every summer. The parents let their kids drink the dirty water and breathe the dirty air, and she thinks I'm unreasonable for not letting my daughter join them." I frowned at him. "The wind goes right through that mask of yours. I can see it."

He looked away. "It's better than nothing. Would you like me to bring you some gear?"

I shook my head. "I don't worry about myself."

"For your daughter's sake, you should."

I turned back toward the house.

"I won't confuse your mother anymore, I promise," he called after me. "In fact I'll try to talk some sense into her."

"Good luck," I said over my shoulder. "I've been trying to do that for the past twelve years."

I thought I would wait another month before returning to the village. My visits seemed only to agitate my mother and myself, and I knew there was nothing I brought that she truly needed or even wanted. Her little community of elderly squaters – these are about ten of them – gathers on Sundays at the village prayer house, and there is a delivery of bread twice a week. Sometimes the old men share the fish they catch in the polluted river with Mama and the other women. A doctor comes by to check on their health and distribute their pensions, and some teenage boys bring them provisions for a fee. It is a pleasant life for my mother, and perhaps a more peaceful end than might have been predicted for a child who was born in the aftermath of the famine and grew up during the German occupation.

There was another reason I stayed away: The children would be arriving soon. I did not want to see the wistful expression on my mother's face as she fed them bread with jam made from contaminated cranberries. I did not want to see them playing in the sun, their little bodies soaking up the poison that was resting in my own daughter's body, waiting to attack.

In the next two weeks, I felt hopeful that life was getting back to normal. Halynka began to come home straight from school and study with her bedroom door ajar, music playing softly. She told me shyly one day that she was going to be presented with an award for her high marks. I watched her walk across the school stage, fresh and pretty in her pale blue dress, a matching ribbon trailing in her shiny brown hair. There was a moment of silence for the three students who had died in the past year, Viktoria and two others. Lilia Teslenko approached us afterward, her eyes brimming with tears, Danylo at her side. I'm ashamed to say that I felt a certain satisfaction when Halynka pulled away from the woman's embrace.

On the first day of summer vacation, Halynka was gone when I returned from work. When she still hadn't come home by the time supper was ready, I called down to Mykola and the old women from the balcony. "I saw her walk off this morning, and I haven't seen her since," Evhenia Vlodimirovna yelled. Mykola only gazed at me blankly. I went to the Teslenkos', and Lilia woke Danylo from a nap, but he said he hadn't seen Halynka all day.

Mykola was agitated during supper, giving me a long lecture on carburetors and crankshafts. While I cleaned up the kitchen, he pulled the chairs away from the table and ran his homemade vacuum over the rug again and again. I looked up from the dishes and was startled to see a man standing in the hallway, dressed in tan pants and a blue pullover shirt. As I moved toward Mykola to snap off the machine, I realized it was the American scientist, stripped of his protective clothing.

"I'm sorry – I knocked but there was no answer," he said. He was balding, and his face was round, childlike, though he was at least forty.

"Pleased to make your acquaintance," Mykola said when I introduced them. Sometimes strangers provoke him to emerge momentarily from his little world.

"I was just at the entrance of the zone," the American said. "Your daughter's there."

"What?" I cried. "Where is she now?"

"Oles is holding her there. She said she wanted to see her grandmother, but he wouldn't let her in. Did you tell her that she could go there?"

"No, no, of course not."

"Have you come from Moscow?" Mykola asked. "Have you come for the cleanup?"

"The cleanup?"

"George is American, Mykola," I said. "He's a scientist."

"Your daughter wouldn't let me drive her home. Can I take you there?"

"I would be so grateful if you would," I said, grabbing my purse. "Mykola, I'll be home soon with Halynka."

The American drove an old Lada that stalled frequently as we drove along the wide dark road toward the town. George told me that he was a professor back in Boston, but had studied in Moscow when he was young, and returned there often to work with Russian scientists. He had been living here in Ukraine for a couple of months, renting an apartment in New Martinovichi and going into the zone every day to collect samples for his experiments.

"Your family back in America must miss you," I said.

"Well, I'm divorced, and I don't have any children. But I suppose my parents miss me."

"I'm sure they're proud of the work you do."

"They don't understand what I do." He smiled at me. "Just like your mother. I've been talking to her, by the way. I've been trying to convince her that it would be dangerous for your daughter to visit her."

"I appreciate that, but I think you're wasting your time. She's a stubborn old woman. Unfortunately, as you've found out, my daughter takes after her."

The border crossing was a circle of light surrounded on all sides by darkness, the tall abandoned buildings of the town rising like black monoliths in the distance. Halynka was sitting inside the little guard station with Oles, drinking tea.

"Halynka," I said. "Your father and I were worried sick about you."

"I was going to visit Grandmama." I noticed a duffel bag by her chair, packed full.

"I told her she couldn't go anywhere without her parents' permission," Oles said.

"Thank you, Oles. Halynka knew she was forbidden to come here." I tugged her roughly by the arm. "Hurry up. We've taken enough of Mr. Hayes's time already."

We rode back in silence, save for the rattling of the car and its tendency to putter to a stop every few kilometers. Halynka sat in the back seat and stared out the window. For a moment I imagined that we were an American family on vacation, driving through Colorado or California, looking for a hotel where we could spend the night. It was a silly fantasy, and not one that I wished would come true. Americans had their own problems, after all. George had had a wife, and had somehow failed to keep her. My husband and I loved each other, in our peculiar way, and our precious daughter was healthy and safe.

Back at home, I thanked George for his help and followed Halynka up to her bedroom.

"Young lady, I want you to explain why you ran away," I said.

"I wanted to see Grandmama." She was pulling clothes out of her bag, not looking at me.

"You know, your grandmother could have stayed here, but she didn't. She decided to leave us."

Halynka looked at me with tears in her eyes. "Does she know about Vika?"

"Yes, darling, I told her. But she doesn't understand what made Viktoria sick."

"Maybe she's right. Maybe it wasn't the town. Maybe Vika got sick for no reason."

"It's possible, sweetheart, but you know what the doctors said."

"I was going to talk to Grandmama about her."

"You could write a letter and I could bring it to her. Would you like that?"

"I don't want to write her a letter. I want to talk to her."

"I wish I could let you, darling. Would you like to talk to me instead?" She shook her head.

I left her room and went out on the balcony. Down below, Mykola was bent over the American's car, his hands darting like a pianist's under the hood. George shone a flashlight and handed tools to Mykola. The old women watched from their bench. The windows of the other buildings in the settlement were lit up, gold and flickering blue boxes. Children were playing ball off on the horizon, barely visible against the black sky and black earth, their cries punctuating the still air. Other men gathered at the car, shaking George's hand, and Mykola began to narrate his gestures for the benefit of the crowd. A man lit a cigarette for George. Slender plumes of smoke drifted in the dim light, disappearing into the blackness.

Two little blond girls in summer dresses were playing in the sunlit field when I emerged from the pine forest the following Saturday. One dropped, disappearing into the tall grass, and then the other stumbled about with her eyes closed until she tripped over her friend. When I approached, they stared at me, still as statues, waiting until I had crossed the field before continuing their game.

My mother met me at the door. She had made a dress from the fabric I'd brought; the carnations and daisies widened across her broad belly. "What do you have?" she asked, grabbing my bags.

"Aren't you even going to say hello?" I asked.

She pushed past me. "Tara, Olya, come here!" The little girls ran up to her from the field. "Girls, take these things to Grandmama, and tell her this is what you're to eat. All right?" The girls looked into the bags at the flour and salt, the sticks of wood, and nodded solemnly. "Go on home, now."

"What was that all about?" I asked.

"Ganna doesn't feed them right," Mama said, settling heavily into her chair.

"Oh?"

"That American's been coming around, talking to us, taking pictures."

"Has he?" I wondered if he had told Mama about Halynka's attempt to visit her, and decided he was probably more discreet than that.

"Here, I want you to see this." She picked up a photograph from the table. Her face was in the center of the picture, unsmiling, determined. "He gave this to me yesterday." The photo was printed on thick paper in tones of green, and the image was strewn with faint white dots. "See the snow?" she said. "The American said it's radiation. He said he has a special camera that can see it."

I stared in fascination at the photograph. It did look as if snow were falling inside the house, swirling around my mother, speckling her face.

"Yulia, do you think the American is an honest man?" Mama asked as she fiddled with a handkerchief.

I put the photograph aside. "Yes, Mama. I do think he's an honest man."

She stood up. "I don't want you to come here anymore."

"Why not, Mama?"

"I should never have told you to visit." Her voice quavered, and she brushed her eyes with the back of her hand.

"Mama." I reached for her, but she pushed me away.

"The American and I showed the picture to Ganna, but she just laughed. Stupid old fool. That's what we all are – stupid old fools."

"The girls will be all right," I said. "They'll go home soon."

Mama cupped her face in her hands. "Halynka was outside the entire day after the accident."

"Shh, shh, Mama." I held her shoulders, trying to draw her near, but she shrugged me away. "Halynka's all right," I said.

"She's healthy."

"She used to have such a terrible cough, it would keep her awake at night."

"She hasn't had it for a long time."

"Her little friend died, the blond girl. They were the same age." She crumpled against me, sobbing.

I held her tight, wanting to both shake her and kiss her. After twelve long years she finally understood. She had only needed to see it with her own eyes.

I took the picture home. "Come with me," I said to Mykola, and he followed me up to the apartment. Halynka watched in surprise as I turned off the television and placed the photograph on the coffee table. "You wanted to see your grandmother," I said. "I brought you a picture of her. Don't touch it – it's dirty. But I want you to look at it, closely." Then I went into the bathroom to cleanse myself.

When I came out in my robe, Mykola and Halynka were facing each other on the couch. "They gave us two counters to keep track of the levels, one in your boot, the other in your pocket," Mykola said, slapping his chest. He jumped to his feet. "Into the uniform. Heavy aprons, lined with lead. Gloves. A big mask." He pantomimed pulling on the uniform. "Then up to the roof of the reactor. Five minutes at a time, that's all we had." He pushed an imaginary shovel against the carpet. "Quick, quick, push through the rubble, look for the rods. Watch your step. Helicopters loud overhead." He whirled around, staring at the ground. "Here's some." He made a scooping motion. "Collect as much as you can. Dark rods. Find the trash bin. Careful – it'll burn through your boots. Hard to see. Time's running out, hurry up." He dashed around the living room, staring intently at the ground. "Ah, here's one. And here's some more. They're calling now, time's up." He tossed the shovel aside. "They grab the counters, no chance to read them." He collapsed into a chair, panting. "Time for a smoke."

I stood at the edge of the room, watching as Halynka helped Mykola light a cigarette. "Good job, Papa," she said softly, and retreated to the couch.

Mykola wiped sweat from his forehead as he puffed smoke into the room. "Just enough time for a smoke. Then up to the roof. Up to the roof again."

When I came home from work on Monday, Halynka was lying on the couch reading, and there was a stack of library books on the floor beside her. For a moment I was hopeful that she would spend the summer absorbed in literature, but when I flipped through some of the books, I saw that she was reading about the accident. The writing was dense and technical, illustrated with complicated graphs. When I asked if she found the books interesting, she only shrugged.

The next evening after supper we took the bus to New Martinovichi. The American answered his door wearing his casual clothes. "Yulia," he said. "And Halynka. Hello. Please come in."

"I'm sorry to stop by unannounced," I said. "I got your address from Oles."

"I'm glad you're here. Would you like some tea?" The apartment was terribly messy. Papers were strewn about the tables and floor, and there were half-filled cups of coffee everywhere.

"I'll get the tea," I said. "Halynka has some questions she'd like to ask you."

"Of course." He cleared a space on the kitchen table and they sat down.

I moved about the apartment gathering the dirty dishes and washed them slowly. I heard my daughter's shy voice gaining confidence as she asked the American about safety procedures at the reactor and the odds of a meltdown happening again. George answered her questions directly and thoroughly, using simple terms. I could tell he was being careful not to frighten her, yet expressing concern about the damage caused by the accident and the possibility that some day it could happen again, here or in another part of the world.

I served them tea and sat quietly at the other end of the table.

"Were you alive when it happened, Halynka?" George asked when she had run out of questions.

Halynka looked at me. "I had just had my first birthday. Right, Mama?"

"Yes. We had a party the day after the accident. Before we knew anything was wrong."

"No one had any idea, did they?" George asked.

I shook my head. "They waited two days to evacuate us." I felt my throat tightening.

"Were you scared?" Halynka asked.

"Not scared . . . it's hard to describe." They both looked at me, waiting. "We should be going," I said, standing up.

George insisted on driving us home. The car ran smoothly, and he praised my husband's repair job. In front of our building, Mykola ran up and opened Halynka's door, then mine. He greeted the American and trotted off. "Wait, Papa," Halynka called after him.

"Thank you for talking to her," I said to George.

"I can only tell her the facts. She'll have to find out the rest from you."

His tape recorder was lying on the seat between us. "Could I borrow this?" I asked.

"Sure. I won't need it anymore." He showed me how to use the machine, testing it on his own voice. Before I got out of the car, George told me that he was returning to America in a few days, but that he hoped to see me next summer. As I climbed the stairs behind my husband and daughter, I imagined George walking into his empty, quiet apartment in Boston. Entering my own home, I smiled, for it occurred to me that he too was probably feeling sorry for me as he drove away.

"Halynka?" my mother shouted. "This is Grandmama."

"You don't need to talk so loud, Mama," I whispered. We were sitting at her kitchen table and I was holding the tape recorder up to her mouth.

"Halynka, this is Grandmama talking to you on the machine," she shouted. "Your Mama said you'll be able to hear me. I want to say hello to you. I hope you're doing well. Everything's fine here. My tomatoes are growing. The flowers are blooming." She paused and looked out the window, breathing loudly through her nose. "I heard about Viktoria. I'm so sorry, my dear." She looked at me.

"You can stop if you like."

She turned back to the machine and cleared her throat. "I told your mama that she wasn't allowed to visit me anymore, but she came anyway. She said you can talk back to me on the machine if you want. I would like that very much. I miss you terribly, my darling."

When we had finished, I walked down the road in front of the house. Reaching the main street, I turned toward the town rather than heading back toward the border. I held the tape recorder to my mouth and began to speak.

"Halynka, I'm walking into your hometown. Since I won't let you come here, I thought I would describe it for you. I myself haven't been here since we left. I was afraid to come here, to see our old home looking so empty and desolate.

"The reactor is off in the distance, towering over the town. There are two great smokestacks, striped, and huge buildings shaped like a mountain. From here it all looks normal. This was a young city, built for workers in the plant. So many of us were just starting our families, and there were lots of children here. I'm passing some apartment buildings now. It almost seems as if they're not empty at all. There are curtains on the windows and I can see furniture inside.

"Here's a store where I used to shop. I brought you with me, of course." I looked through the window. "There are still a few cans of food on the shelves – I recognize the old paper labels. I remember the day you first walked into the store by yourself, holding my finger. The women behind the counters clapped, and I was so proud.

"I'm turning onto the street where we used to live." I heard some birds chirping, but that was all. "I can see the Ferris wheel between some buildings. It was brought in especially for May Day. Your papa and I had planned to take you to the carnival. But of course we all left just a few days before.

"Here it is, our building." My voice caught, and I lowered the recorder from my mouth. I stared up at the window, waiting until my breathing was even. "It's just six stories high, and we were on the top floor. It looks like the pink curtains I sewed have faded. We left the apartment neat as a pin. Your father used to tease me about the way I tidied up before we went anywhere. I swept and did the dishes that day, even though we only had a few hours to get ready."

I peered through a scratched plastic window. "The entryway is dark and dingy, paper and garbage everywhere. We stood there waiting for the buses – by that time we knew better than to stand outside. It was hot and crowded, and you cried."

I had planned to go upstairs, look for the spare key under the doormat, enter our home and describe it for Halynka. But now that I was here I was frightened. The apartment might have been looted; at the very least it would be dusty and terribly quiet. I turned back to the road, knowing that I had come as close as I could.

"The accident happened in the middle of the night, as George told you. In the morning there was a steady dark line of smoke coming out of the reactor. Your papa told me he had heard an explosion. I had slept through it. We turned on the radio, but nothing was said about it on the news.

"Of course we didn't have time to think about the reactor. It was an important day: your first birthday party. I put on my nicest dress, and your papa wore a suit and tie. I had sewn you a yellow dress edged with lace.

"We walked over to the park around noon. I'm heading there now. It was a warm spring day and everyone was outside. Women were shopping at the market, and children were playing. There was no sign that anything was wrong. Here, here is the park. Back then the grass was worn away, but now it's overgrown with weeds.

"Your Uncle Ivanko butchered a pig the week before, and my friends and I prepared sausages, dumplings and meat pies. Your grandmama made pancakes, and Lilia Teslenko baked a four-layer frosted torte. We had gone to little Viktoria's birthday celebration just a month before at their home in the village. Lilia was a great beauty, and when we were growing up, I used to be jealous of her. But after we both had baby girls, we became friendly. You and Viktoria took to each other immediately. Even when you were just a few months old, you seemed to have your own private language, cooing and laughing together.

"All of our friends were at the party. Most of them worked at the reactor, like your papa. There was talk of the explosion, and we watched the dark smoke rising into the sky. Someone said that foamy water had been gushing onto their street, and that children were playing in it. But no one was really worried. You have to understand, we never imagined that anything bad would happen to us, and we were sure we would be notified if there were any reason to be concerned. But I still feel guilty for taking you outside that day. Sometimes I wonder if I would have been more sensible if I hadn't been distracted by the party. Maybe we would have all stayed inside with our windows closed. Sometimes I wonder if Lilia blames me for this.

"In the late afternoon we woke you up for the ceremony – your first haircut. Your papa stood you on a chair at the head of the table, and everyone gathered around. Your grandmother took up the scissors and snipped off a lock from your forehead. She did the same at the back of your head, and then on each side, so that she had cut from north, south, east and west, the four directions of the world. Then she passed the scissors to your Uncle Ivanko, and it was his turn. Then Lilia and Yuri Teslenko cut your hair.

"You were always a good baby, rarely fussing, but on that day you were especially quiet and still, as if you realized something important was happening – almost, I thought later, as if you knew that everything was about to change. To me, your haircut was a reminder that you would grow up and leave me, just as I had left my own mother. I got a little teary, and your papa hugged me, and everyone laughed, understanding why I was sad."

I began to walk back toward the border. I was ready to see the look on Halynka's face when she heard her grandmother's voice. And, I confess, I was eager for my daughter to hear my own story for the first time.

"The evacuation began the next day. They told us that we would be able to come home in three days. The envelope with your locks of hair was the only memento I packed when we left. I suppose part of me realized that we might never return, though I don't remember thinking this at the time. I threw the envelope away later, crying as I did. I threw away everything we had brought with us from the town. Of course you didn't understand when I tried to explain that I had thrown out your favorite doll because it was dirty. How cruel I seemed to you. Do you understand now, Halynka? I didn't feel I had a choice. I had to get rid of everything from the past."

I turned off the recorder. The bus was pulling up to the gates, and Oles waved and shouted at me to hurry. I began to jog, laughing at the spectacle I was making, a middle-aged woman running to catch a bus, as if in my rush to leave the town I had forgotten myself, just for a moment, and thought that I was still a young girl.

ON HIS DEATHBED, HOLDING YOUR HAND, THE ACCLAIMED NEW YOUNG OFF-BROADWAY PLAYWRIGHT'S FATHER BEGS A BOON

David Foster Wallace

THE FATHER: Listen: I did despise him. Do.

[PAUSE *for episode of ophthalmorrhagia; technician's swab/flush of dextrocular orbit; change of bandage*]

THE FATHER: Why does no one tell you? Why do all regard it as a blessed event? There seems to be almost a conspiracy to keep you in the dark. Why does no one take you aside and tell you what is coming? Why not tell you the truth? That your life is to be forfeit? That you are expected now to give up everything and not only to receive no thanks but to expect none? Not one. To suspend the essential give-and-take you'd spent years learning was life and now want nothing? I tell you, worse than nothing: that you will have no more life that is *yours*? That all you wished for yourself you are now expected to wish for him instead? Whence this expectation? Does it sound reasonable to expect? Of a human being? To have nothing and wish nothing for *you*? That your entire human nature should somehow change, alter, as if magically, at the moment it emerges from her after causing her such pain and deforming her body so profoundly that ne – that she will herself somehow alter herself this way automatically, as if by magic, the instant he emerges, as if by some glandular bewitchment, but that you, who have not carried him or been joined by tubes, will remain, inside, as you have always been, yet be expected to change as well, drop everything, freely? Why does no one speak of it, this madness? That your failure to cast yourself away and change everything and be delirious with joy at – that this will be judged. Not just as a quote unquote parent but as a man. Your human worth. The prim smug look of those who would judge parents, judge them for not magically changing, not instantly ceding everything you'd wished for heretofore and – *securus judicat orbis terrarum*, Father. But Father are we really to believe it is so obvious and natural that no one feels even any *need* to tell you? Instinctive as blinking? Never think to warn you? It did not seem obvious to me, I can assure you. Have you ever actually seen an afterbirth? watch drop-jawed and unblinking as it emerged and hit the floor, and what they do with it? No one told me I assure you. That one's own wife might judge you deficient simply for remaining the man she married. Was I the only one not told? Why such silence when –

[PAUSE for episode of dyspnea]

THE FATHER: I despised him from the first. I do not exaggerate. From the first moment they finally saw fit to let me in and I looked down and saw him already attached to her, already sucking away. Sucking at her, draining her, and her upturned face – she who had made her views on the sucking of body parts very plain, I can – her face, she had changed, become an abstraction, The Mother, her natal face enraptured, radiant, as if nothing invasive or grotesque were taking place. She had screamed on the table, *screamed*, and now where was that girl? I had never seen her look so – the current term is "out of it," no? Has anyone considered this phrase? what it really implies? In that instant I knew I despised him. There is no other word. Despicable. The whole affair from then on. The truth: I found it neither natural nor fulfilling nor beautiful nor fair. Think of me what you will. It is the truth. It was all disgusting. Ceaseless. The sensory assault. You cannot know. The incontinence. The vomit. The sheer smell. The noise. The theft of sleep. The selfishness, the appalling selfishness of the newborn, you have no idea. No one prepared us for any of it, for the sheer unpleasantness of it. The insane expense of pastel plastic things. The cloacal reek of the nursery. The endless laundry. The odors and constant noise. The disruption of all possible schedule. The slobber and terror and piercing shrieks. Like a needle those shrieks. Perhaps if someone had prepared, forewarned us. The endless reconfiguration of all schedules around him. Around his desires. He ruled from that crib, ruled from the first. Ruled her, reduced and remade her. Even as an infant the power he wielded! I learned the bottomless greed of him. Of my son. Of arrogance past imagining. The regal greed and thoughtless disorder and mindless cruelty – the literal *thoughtlessness* of him. Has anyone considered this phrase's real import? Of the *thoughtlessness* with which he treated the world? The way he threw things aside and clutched at things, the way he broke things and just walked away. As a toddler. Terrible Twos indeed. I watched other children; I studied other children his age – something in him was different, missing. Psychotic, sociopathic. The grotesque lack of care for what we gave him. Believe me. You were of course forbidden to say 'I paid for that! Treat that with care! Show some minim of respect for something outside yourself!' No never that. Never that. You'd be a monster. What sort of parent asks for a moment's thought to whence things came? Never. Not a thought. I spent years drop-jawed with amazement, too appalled even to know what – noplace to speak of it. No one else even appeared to see it. Him. An essential disorder of character. An absence of whatever we mean by "human." A psychosis no one dares diagnose. No one says it – that you are to live for and serve a psychotic. No one mentions the abuse of power. No one mentions that there will be psychotic tantrums during which you will wish – even just his face, I did, I detested his face. He had a small soft moist face, not human. A circle of cheese with features like hasty pinches in some ghastly dough. Am – was I the only one? That an infant's face is not in any way recognizable, not a human face – it's true – then why do all clasp their hands and call it beauty? Why not simply admit to an ugliness that may well be outgrown? Why such – but the way from the beginning his eye – my son's right eye – it protruded, subtly yes, slightly more than the left, and blinked in a palsied and over-rapid way, like the sputter of a defective circuit. That fluttery blinking. The subtle but once noticed never thenceforth ignorable bulge of that same eye. Its subtle but aggressive forward thrust. All was to be his, that eye betrayed the – a triumph in it, a glazed exultation. Pediatric term was "exophthalmic," supposedly harmless, correctable over time. I never told her what I knew: not correctable, not an accidental sign. That was the eye to look at, into it, if you wished to see what no one else wished to see or acknowledge. The mask's only gap. Hear this. I loathed my child. I loathed the eye, the mouth, the lip, the pinched snout, the wet hanging lip. His very skin was an affliction. "Impetigo" the term, chronic. The pediatricians could find no reason. The insurance a nightmare. I spent half my days on the phone with these people. Wearing a mask of concern to match hers. Never a word. A sickly child, weak and cheese-white, chronically congested. The suppurating sores of his chronic impetigo, the crust. The ruptured infections. "Suppuration": the term means ooze. My son oozed, exuded, flaked, suppurated, dribbled from every quadrant. To whom does one speak of this? That he taught me to despise the body, what it is to have a body – to be disgusted, repulsed. Often I had to look away, duck outside, dart around corners. The absent thoughtless picking and scratching and probing and toying, bottomless narcissistic fascination with his own body. As if his extremities were the world's four corners. A slave to himself. An engine of mindless will. A reign of terror, trust me. The insane tantrums when his will was thwarted. When some gratification was denied or delayed. It was Kafkan – you were punished for protecting him from himself. "No, no, child, my son, I cannot allow you to thrust your hand into the vaporizer's hot water, the blades of the window fan, do not drink that household solvent" – a tantrum. The insanity of it. You could not explain or reason. You could only walk away appalled. Will yourself not simply to let him the next time, not to smile and let him, "Have at that solvent, my son," learn the hard way. The whining and wheedling and tugging and towering rages. Not really psychotic, I came to see. Crazy like a fox. An agenda behind every outburst. "Too much excitement, overtired, cranky, feverish, needs a lie-down, just frustrated, just a long day" –

the litany of her excuses for him. His endless emotional manipulation of her. The ceaselessness of it and her inhuman reaction: even when she recognized what he was up to she excused him, she was charmed by the nakedness of his insecurity, his what she called "need" for her, what she called my son's "need for reassurance." Need for reassurance? What reassurance? He never doubted. He knew it all belonged to him. He never doubted. As if it were due him. As if he deserved it. Insanity. Solipsism. He wanted it all. All I had, had had, never would. It never ended. Blind, reasonless appetite. I will say it: evil. There. I can imagine your face. But he was evil. And I alone seemed to know it. He afflicted me in a thousand ways and I could say nothing. My face fairly ached at day's end from the control I was forced to exert over – even the slight note of complaint you could hear in his breathing. The bruised circles of restless appetite beneath his eyes. Exhalation a whimper. The two different eyes, the one terrible eye. The redness and flaccidity of his mouth and the way the lip was always wet no matter how much one wiped it for him. An inherently moist child, always clammy, the scent of him vaguely fungal. The vacancy of his face when he became absorbed in some pleasure. The utter shame-lessness of his greed. The sense of utter entitlement. How long it took us to teach him even a perfunctory thank you. And he never meant it, and she did not mind. She would – never minded. She was his servant. Slave mentality. This was not the girl I asked to marry me. She was his slave and believed she knew only joy. He played with her as a cat does a toy mouse and she felt joy. Madness? Where was my wife? What was this creature she stroked as he sucked at her? Most of his childhood – memory of it – most renders down to seeing myself standing there some yards away, watching them in appalled amazement. Behind my dutiful smile. Too weak ever to speak out, to ask it. This was my life. This is the truth I've hidden. You are good to listen. More important than you know. To speak it. *Te ju* – judge me as you wish. No, do. I am dying – no, I know – bedridden, near blind, gutted, catarrh, dying, alone and in pain. Look at these bloody tubes. All these tubes. A life of such silence. And this is my confession. Good of you. Not what you – it is not your forgiveness I – just to hear the truth. About him. That I despised him. There is no other word. Often I was forced to avert my eyes from him, look away. Hide. I discovered why fathers hold the evening paper as they do.

[PAUSE for FATHER's attempted pantomime of holding object spread before face]

THE FATHER: I am recalling now just one in un – something, a tantrum over something or other after dinner one evening. I did not want him eating in our living room. Not unreasonable I think. The dining room was for eating; I had explained to him the etymology and sense of "*dining* room." The living room, where I reserved for myself but half an hour with the newspaper after dinner – and there he was, suddenly right there before me, on the new carpet, eating his candy in the living room. Was I unreasonable? He had received the candy as his reward for eating the healthy dinner I had worked to buy for him and she had worked to prepare for him – feel it? the judgment, disgust? that one is never to say such a thing, to mention that one paid, that one's limited resources had been devoted to – that would be selfish, no? a bad parent, no? niggardly? *selfish?* And yet I had, had paid for the little colored chocolate candies, candies which here he stood upending the little bag to be able to get all of the candy into that mouth at once, never one by one, always all the sweets all at once, as much as fast as possible regardless of spillage, hence my gritted smile and carefully gentle reminder of the etymology of "*dining* room" and far less a command than – mindful of her reaction, always – *request* that, please, no candy in the – and with his mouth crammed with candy and chewing at it even as the tantrum began, puling and stamping his feet and shrieking now at the top of his lungs in the living room even as his mouth was filled with chocolate, that open red mouth filled with mashed candy which mixed with his spittle and as he howled overran his lip as he howled and stamped up and down and running down his chin and shirt, and peering timidly over the top of the paper held like a shield as I sat willing myself to remain in the chair and say nothing and watching now his mother down on one knee trying to wipe the chocolate drool off his chin as he screamed at her and batted the napkin away. Who could look on this and not be appalled? Who could – when was it determined that this sort of thing is acceptable, that such a creature must be not only tolerated no but *soothed*, actually *placated*, as she was on her knees doing, tenderly, in gross contradiction to the unacceptability of what was going on. What sort of madness is this? That I can hear the soft little singsong tones she used to try to soothe him – for *what?* – as she patiently brings the napkin back again and again as he bats it away and screams that he hates her. I do not exaggerate; he said this: hates her. *Hates* her? *Her?* Down on one knee, pretending she hears nothing, that it's nothing, cranky, long day, that – what bewitchment lay behind this patience? What human being could remain on her knees wiping drool caused by *his, his* violation of a simple and reasonable prohibition against just this very sort of disgusting mess in the room in which we sought only to *live?* What chasm of insanity lay between us? What was this creature? Why did we go on like this? How might I be in any way culpable for lifting the evening paper to try to obscure this scene? It was either look away or kill him where he stood. How does doing what must be done to control my – how is this equal to my being remote or ungiving unquote or heaven forfend "cruel"? Cruel to *that?* Why is "cruel" applied only to those who pay for the little chocolates he spews onto the shirtfront you paid for to dribble onto the carpet you paid for and grinds under the shoes you paid for as he stamps up and down in mindless fury at your mild request that he take reasonable steps to avert precisely the sort of mess he is causing? Am I the only one to whom this makes no sense? who is revolted, appalled? Why is even to speak of such revulsion not allowed? Who made this rule? Why was it I who must be seen and not heard? Whence this inversion of my own upbringing? What unthinkable discipline would my own father have –

[PAUSE for episode of dyspnea, blennorrhagia]

THE FATHER: Did. Sometimes I did, no, literally could not bear the sight of him. Impetigo is a skin disorder. His scalp's sores suppurated and formed a crust. The crust then turned yellow. A childhood skin disease. Condition of children. When he coughed it rained yellow crust. His bad eye wept constantly, a viscous stuff that has no name. His eyelashes at the breakfast his mother made would be clotted with a pale crust which someone would have to clean off with a swab while he writhed in complaint at being cleaned of repellent crust. About him hung a scent of spoilage, mildew. And she would nuzzle just to smell him. Nose running without cease or reason and caused small red raised sores on his nostrils and upper lip which then yielded more crust. Chronic ear infections meant not only a spike in the incidence of tantrums but an actual smell, a discharge whose odor I will spare you describing. Antibiotics. He was a veritable petri dish of infection and discharge and eruption and runoff, white as a root, blotched, moist, like something in a cellar. And yet all who saw him clasped their hands together and exclaimed. Beautiful child. Angel. Soulful. Delicate. Break such hearts. The word "beautiful" was used. I would simply stand there – what could I say? My carefully pleased expression. But could they have seen that inhuman little puke-white face during an infection, an attack, a tantrum, the piggy malevolence of it, the truculent entitlement, the rapacity. The ugliness. "Barked about most lazar-like with vile" – the ugly truth. Mucus, pus, vomit, feces, diarrhea, urine, wax, sputum, varicolored crusts. These were his dowry to – the gifts he bore us. Thrashing in sleep or fever, clutching at the very air as if to pull it to him. And always there bedside she was, his, in thrall, bewitched, wiping and swabbing and stroking and tending, never a word of acknowledgment of the sheer horror of what he produced and expected her to wipe away. The endless thankless expectation. Never acknowledged. The girl I married would have reacted very, very differently to this creature, believe me. Treating her breasts as if they were his. Property. Her nipples the color of a skinned knee. Grasping, clutching. Making greedy sounds. Manhandling her. Snorting, wheezing. Absorbed wholly in his own sensations. Reflectionless. At home in his body as only one whose body is not *his* job can be at home. Filled with himself, right to the edges like a swollen pond. He was his body. I often could not look. Even the speed of his growth that first year – statistically unusual, the doctors remarked it – a rate that was weedy, aggressive, a willed imposition of self on space. That right eye's sputtering forward thrust. Sometimes she would grimace at the weight of him, holding him, lifting, until she caught the brief grimace and wiped it away – I was sure I saw it – replaced at once with that expression of narcotic patience, abstract thrall, I several yards off, extrorse, trying not –

[*PAUSE for episode of dyspnea; technician's application of tracheobronchial suction catheter*]

THE FATHER: Never learned to breathe is why. Awful of me to say, yes? And of course yes ironic, given – and she'd have died on the spot to hear me say it. But it is the truth. Some chronic asthma and a tendency to bronchitis, yes, but that is not what I – I mean nasal. Nothing structurally wrong with his nose. Paid several times to have it examined, probed, they all concurred, nose normal, most of the occlusion from simple disuse. Chronic disuse. The truth: he never bothered to learn. Through it. Why bother? Breathed through his mouth, which is of course easier in the short term, requires less effort, maximizes intake, get it all in at once. And does, my son, breathes to this very day through his slack and much-loved adult mouth, which consequently is always partly open, this mouth, slack and wet, and white bits of rancid froth collect at the corners and are of course too much trouble ever to check in a lavatory mirror and attend to discreetly in private and spare others the sight of the pellets of paste at the corners of his mouth, forcing everyone to say nothing and pretend they do not see. The equivalent of long, unclean, or long nails on men, which I tirelessly tried to explain were in his own best interest to keep trimmed and clean. When I picture him it is always with his mouth partly open and lower lip wet and hanging and projecting outward far further than a lower lip ought, one eye dull with greed and the other's palsied bulge. This sounds ugly? It was ugly. Blame the messenger. Do. Silence me. Say the word. Verily, Father, but whose ugliness? Are we certain? For is she – that he was a sickly child as a child who – always in bed with asthma or ears, constant bronchitis and upper flu, slight chronic asthma yes true but bed for days at a time when some sun and fresh air could not poss – ring for, hurts – he had a little silver bell by the rocket's snout he'd ring, to summon her. Not a normal regular child's bed but a catalogue bed, battleship gray they called Authentic Silvery Finish plus Postage and Handling with aerodynamic booster fins and snout, assembly required and the instructions practically Cyrillic and yes and whom do you suppose was expec – the little silver tinkle of the bell and she'd fly, fly to him, bending uncomfortably over the booster fins of the bed, cold iron fins, minist – it rang and rang.

[PAUSE for episode of ophthalmorrhagia; technician's swab/flush of dextrocular orbit; change of facial bandage]

THE FATHER: Bells of course employed throughout history to summon servants, domestics, an observation I kept to myself when she got him the bell. The official version was that the bell was to be used if he could not breathe, in lieu of calling out. It was to be an emergency bell. But he abused it. Whenever he was ill he continually rang the bell. Sometimes just to force her to come sit next to the bed. Her presence was demanded and off she went. Even in sleep, if the bell rang, however softly, slyly, sounding more like a wish than a ring, she would hear it and be out of bed and off down the hall without even putting on her robe. The hall was often cold. House poorly insulated and ferociously dear to heat. I, when I awoke, would take her her robe, slippers; she never thought of them. To see her arise still asleep at that maddening tinkle was to see mind control at its most elemental. This was his genius: to *need*. The sleep he robbed her of, at will, daily, for years. Watching her face and body fall. Her body never had the chance to recover. Sometimes she looked like an old woman. Ghastly circles under her eyes. Legs swollen. He took years from her. And she'd have sworn she gave them freely. Sworn it. I'm not speaking now of *my* sleep, *my* life. He never thought of her except in reference to himself. This is the truth. I know him. If you had seen him at the funeral. As a child he – she'd hear the bell and without even coming fully awake pad off to the lavatory and turn on every faucet and fill the place with steam and sit for hours holding him on the commode in the steam while he slept – that he made her trade her own rest for his, night after – and that not only was all the hot water for all of us for the entire next morning exhausted but the constant steam then would infiltrate upstairs and everything was constantly sodden with his steam and in warm weathers came a rank odor of mold which she would have been appalled had I openly credited to him as its real source, his rocket and tinkle, all wood everywhere warping, wallpaper peeling off in sheets. The gifts he bestowed. That Christmas film – their joke was that he was giving angels wings each time. It was not that he was not sometimes truly ill, it would not be true to accuse him of – but he *used* it. The bell was only one of the more obvious – and she believed it was all her idea. To orbit him. To alter, cede herself. Vanish as a person. To become an abstraction: The Mother, Down On One Knee. This was life after he came – she orbits him, I chart her movements. That she could call him a blessing, the sun in her sky. She was no more the girl I'd married. And she never knew how I missed that girl, mourned her, how my heart went out to what she'd become. I was weak not to tell her the truth. Despised him. Couldn't. This was the insidious part, the part I truly despised, that he ruled *me*, as well, despite my seeing through him. I could not help it. After he came some chasm lay between us. My voice could not carry across it. How often on so many late nights I would lean weakly in the doorway of the lavatory wiping steam from my spectacles with the belt of the robe and was so desperate to say it, to utter it: "What about *us*? Where had our lives gone? Why did this choking sucking thankless thing mean more than we? Who had decided that this should be so?" Beg her to come out of it, snap out. In despair, weak, not utter – she would not have heard me. That is why not. Afraid that what she would hear would – hear only a bad father, deficient man, uncaring, *selfish*, and then the last of the freely chosen bonds between us would be severed. That she would choose. Weak. Oh I was doomed and knew it. My self-respect was a plaything in those clammy little hands as well. The *genius* of his weakness. Nietzsche had no *idea*. Ballocks all reason for – and this, this was my thank-you – free tickets? A black joke. *Free* he calls them? And airfare to come and applaud and shape my face's grin to pretend with the rest of – *this* is my thank-you? Oh the endless sense of entitlement. Endless. That you understand eternal doom in all the late-night sickly hours forced in a one-buttock hunch on the booster's bolted fin of the ridiculous rocket-shaped bed he cajoled her – more plaything than bed, impossible instructions on my knees with the wrong tool as he stood in my light – ironized fin no broader than a ham but I'm damned if I'll kneel by that ill-assembled bed. My job to maintain the vaporizer and administer wet cloths and monitor the breathing and fever as he lay holding the bell while again she was off unrested out in the cold to the all-night druggist to hunch there on the booster-stage fin awash in the odor of mentholate gel and yawning and checking my watch and looking down at him resting with wet mouth agape and watching the chest make its diffident minimal effort of rising and falling while he through the flutter of that right lid staring without expression or making one acknowledgment of – rising then up out of an almost oneiric reverie to realize that I had been wishing it to cease, that chest, to still its sluggish movement under the Gemini comforter he demanded to have upon him at – dreaming of it falling still, stilled, the bell to cease its patrician tinkle, the last rattle of that weak and omnipotent chest, and yes I would then strike my own breast, crosswise thus –

[FATHER's weak pantomime of striking own chest]

– in punishment of my wish, ashamed, such was my own thrall to him. He merely staring up slackly at my self-abuse, with that red wet lip hanging wetly, rancid froth, lazar-like crust, chin's spittle, chest's unguent's menthol reek, a creamy little gout of snot protruding, that blank eye sputtering like a bad bulb – put it out! put it out!

[PAUSE for technician's removal, cleaning, reinsertion of O_2 feed into FATHER's nostril]

THE FATHER: That cramped on that fin and dabbing tender at his forehead and wiping away some of the chin's sputum and sitting gazing at it on the handkerchief, trying to – and – yes at the pillow, looking at the pillow, gazing at the pillow and thought of it, how quickly it – how few movements required not just to wish but to will it, to impose my own will as he so blithely always did, lying there pretending to be too feverish to see my – but it was, it was pathetic, not even – I was thinking of my weight on the pillow as a man in arrears thinks of sudden fortune, sweepstakes, inheritance. Wishful thinking. I believed then that I was struggling with my will, but it was mere fantasy. Not will. Aquinas's velleity. I lacked whatever it seems to take to be able to – or perhaps I failed to lack what must be lacking, yes? I could not have. Wishing it but not – both decency *and* weakness perhaps. *Te judice*, Father, yes? I know I was weak. But listen: I did wish it. That is no confession but just the truth. I did wish it. I did despise him. I did miss her and mourn. I did resent – I failed to see why his weakness should permit him to win. It was insane, made no sense – on the basis of what merit or capacity should *he* win? And she never knew. This was the worst, his *lèse-majesté*, unforgivable: the chasm he opened between her and I. My unending pretense. My fear that she'd think me a monster, deficient. I pretended to love him as she did. This I confess. I subjected her to a – the last twenty-nine years of our life together were a lie. My lie. She never knew. I could pretend with the best of them. No adulterer was more careful a dissembler than I. I would help her off with her wrap and take the small sack from the druggist's and whisper my earnest little report on the state of his breathing and temperature throughout her absence, she listening but looking past me, at him, not noting how perfectly my expression's concern matched her own. I modeled my face on hers; she taught me to pretend. It never even occurred to her. Can you understand what this did to me? That she never for a moment doubted I felt the same, that I ceded myself as – that I too was under the sucking thing's spell?

[PAUSE for episode of severe dyspnea; R.N.'s application of tracheo-bronchial suction catheter]

THE FATHER: That she never thenceforth knew me? That my wife had ceased to know me? That I let her go and pretended to join her? Might I hope that anyone could imagine the –

[PAUSE *for episode of ocular bobbing; technician's flush/evacuation of ophthalmorrhagic residue; change of ocular bandage*]

THE FATHER: That we would make love and afterward lie curled together in our special position preparing to sleep and she'd not be still, whispering on and on about him, every conceivable ephemera about him, worries and wishes, a mother's prattle – and took my silence for agreement. The chasm's essence was that she believed there was no chasm. Our bed's width grew day by day and she never – not once occurred to her. That I saw through and loathed him. That I not merely failed to share her bewitchment but was appalled by it. It was my fault, not hers. I tell you this: he was the only secret I had from her. She was the very sun in my sky. The loneliness of the secret was an agony past – oh I loved her so. My feelings for her never wavered. I loved her from the first. We were meant to be together. Joined, united. I knew it the moment – saw her there on the arm of that Bowdoin twit in his fur collar. Holding her pennant as one would a parasol. That I cathected her on the spot. I had a bit of an accent then; she twitted me for it. She would impersonate me when I was cross – only your life's one love could do this – the anger would vanish. The way she affected me. She followed American football and had a son who could not play and then later when he mysteriously ceased being sickly and grew sleek and vigorous would not play. She went instead to watch him swim. The nauseous diminutives, Wuggums, Tigerbear. He swam in public school. The stink of cheap bleach in the venues, barely breathe. Did she miss even one event? When did she stop following it, the football on the misaligned Zenith we would watch together – hold it still, the – making love and lying curled like twins in the womb, saying everything. I could tell her anything. When did that all go then. Just when did he take it from us. Why can't I remember. I remember the day we met as if it were yesterday but I'm bollixed if I can remember yesterday. Pathetic, disgusting. They do not care but if they knew what it – felt to hurt to bloody breathe. Enwebbed in tubes. Bastards, bleeding out every – yes I saw her and she me, the demurely held pennant I was new over and could not parse – our eyes met, all the clichés came instantly true – I knew she was the one to have all of me. A spotlight followed her across the lawn. I simply knew. Father, this was the acme of my life. Watching – that "she was the girl for all of me / my unworthy life for thee" [melody unfamiliar, discordant]. To stand before Church and man and pledge it. To unwrap one another like gifts from God. Conversation's lifetime. If you could have seen her on our wedding – no of course not, that look as she – for me alone. To love at such depth. No better feeling in all creation. She would cock her head just so when amused. So much used to amuse her. We laughed at everything. We were our secret. She chose me. One another. I told her things I had not told my own brother. We belonged to one another. I felt chosen. Who chose *him*, pray? Who gave informed consent to everything hitherto's loss? I despised him for forcing me to hide the fact the fact that I despised him. The common run is one thing, with their judgments, the demand to see you dandle and coo and toss the ball. But her? That I must wear this mask for her? Sounds monstrous but it's true: his fault. I simply couldn't. Tell her. That I – that he was in truth loathsome. That I so bitterly regretted letting her conceive. That she did not truly see him. To trust me, that she was under a spell, lost to herself. That she must come back. That I missed her so. None. And not for my sake, believe – she could not have borne it. It would have destroyed her. She'd have been destroyed, and on his account. He did this. Twisted everything his own way. Bewitched her. Fear that she'd – "Poor dear defenseless Wuggums your father has a monstrous uncaring inhuman side to him I never saw but we see it now don't we but we don't need him do we no now let me make it up to you until I drop from bloody trying." Missing something. "Don't need him do we now there there." Orbited him. Thought first and last. She had ceased to be the girl I'd – she was now The Mother, playing a part, a fairy story, emptying everything out to – No, not true that it would have destroyed her, there was nothing left in her which would even have understood it, could so much as have *heard* the – she'd have cocked just so and looked at me without any comprehension whatever. It would have amounted to telling her the sun did not rise each day. He had made himself her world. *His* was the real lie. *She* believed his lie. She believed it: the sun rose and fell only –

[PAUSE for episode of dyspnea, visual evidence of erythruria; R.N.'s location and clearing of pyuric obstruction in urinary catheter; genital disinfection; technician's reattachment of urinary catheter and gauge]

THE FATHER: The crux. The rub. Omit all else. This is why. The great black enormous lie that I for some reason I alone seemed able to see through – through, as if in a nightmare.

[PAUSE for episode of severe dyspnea; R.N.'s application of tracheobronchial suction catheter, pulmonary wedge pressure; technician (1)'s application of forcipital swabs; location and attempted removal of mucoidal obstruction in FATHER's trachea; technician (2)'s administration of nebulized adrenaline; pertussive expulsion of mucoidal mass; technician (2)'s removal of mass in authorized Medical Waste Receptacle; technician (1)'s reinsertion of O_2 feed into FATHER's nostril]

THE FATHER: Thrall. Listen. My son is evil. I know too well how this might sound, Father. *Te judice.* I am well beyond your judgment as you see. The word is *evil*. I do not exaggerate. He sucked something from her. Some discriminatory function. She lost her sense of humor, that was a clear sign I clung to. He cast some uncanny haze. Maddening to see through it and be unable – and not just her, Father, either. Everyone. Subtle at first but by oh shall we say middle school it was manifest: the wider world's bewitchment. No one seemed able to see him. Began then in blank shock at her side to endure the surreal enraptured soliloquies of instructors and headmasters, coaches and committees and deacons and even clergy which sent her into maternal raptures as I stood chewing my tongue in disbelief. It was as if they had all become his mother. She and they would enter into this complicity of bliss about my son as I beside her nodding with the careful, dutifully pleased expression I'd fashioned through years of practice, out of it as they went on. Then when we'd off to home and I would contrive some excuse and go sit alone in the den with my head in my hands. He seemed able to do it at will. Everyone around us. The great lie. He's taken in the bloody world. I do not exaggerate. You were not there to listen, drop-jawed: oh so brilliant, so sensitive, such discernment, precocity without vaunt, such a joy to know, so full of promise, such limitless gifts. On and on. Such an unqualified *asset*, such a *joy* to have on our roll, our team, our list, our staff, our dramaturgid panel, our minds. Such *limitless gifts* unquote. You cannot imagine the sensation of hearing that: "*gifts*." As if freely given, as if not – had I even once had the backbone to seize one of them by the knot of his cravat and pull him to me and howl the truth in his face. Those glazed smiles. Thrall. If only I myself could have been taken in. My son. Oh and I did, prayed for it, pondered and sought, examined and studied him and prayed and sought without cease, praying to be taken in and be-witched and allow their scales to cover mine as well. I examined him from every angle. I sought diligently for what they all believed they saw, *natus ad glo* – headmaster pulling us aside at that function to take us aside and breathe gin that this was the single finest and most promising student he'd seen in his tenure at middle school, behind him a tweedy defile of instructors bearing down and leaning in to – such a joy, every so often the job newly worthwhile with one such as – limitless gifts. The sustained wince I'd molded into what appeared a grin while she with her hands clasped before her thanking them, thank – understand, I'd *read* with the boy. At length. I'd probed him. I'd sat trying to teach him sums. As he picked at his impetigo and stared vacantly at the page. I had circumspectly watched as he labored to read things and afterward searched him out thoroughly. I'd engaged him, examined, subtly and thoroughly and without prejudice. Please believe me. There was not one spark of brilliance in my son. I swear it. This was a child whose intellectual acme was a reasonable competence at sums acquired through endless grinding efforts at grasping the most

elementary operations. Whose printed S's remained reversed until age
eight despite – who pronounced "epitome" as dactylic. A youth whose
social persona was a blank affability and in whom a ready wit or
appreciation for the nuances of accomplished English prose was
wholly absent. No sin in that of course, a mediocre boy, ordinary
– mediocrity is no sin. Nay but whence all this high estimate? What
gifts? I went over his themes, every one, without fail, before they were
passed in. I made it a policy to give my time. To this study of him.
Willed myself to withhold prejudice. I lurked in doorways and
watched. Even at university this was a boy for whom Sophocles'
Oresteia was weeks of slack-jawed labor. I crept into doorways,
alcoves, stacks. Observed him when no one's about. The *Oresteia*
is not a difficult or inaccessible work. I searched without cease, in
secret, for what they all seemed to see. And a *translation*. Weeks of
grinding effort and not even Sophocles' Greek, some pablumesque
adaptation, standing there unseen and appalled. Yet managed – he
fooled them all. All of them, one great audience. Pulitzer indeed. Oh
and all too well I know how this sounds; *te jude*, Father. But know the
truth: I knew him, inside and out, and this was his one only true gift:
this: a capacity for somehow *seeming* brilliant, *seeming* exceptional,
precocious, gifted, *promising*. Yes to be *promising*, they all of them
said it eventually, "limitless *promise*," for this was his gift, and do you
see the dark art here, the genius for manipulating his audience? His gift
was for somehow arousing admiration and raising everyone's estimate
of him and everyone's expectations of him and so forcing you to pray
for him to triumph and live up to and justify those expectations in
order to spare not just her but everyone who had been duped into
believing in his limitless promise the crushing disappointment of seeing
the truth of his essential mediocrity. Do you see the perverse genius of
this? The exquisite torment? Of forcing me to pray for his triumph? To
desire the maintenance of his lie? And not for his sake but others'?
Hers? This is brilliance of a certain very particular and perverse and
despicable sort, yes? The Attics called one's particular gift or genius his
techno. Was it *techno*? Odd for "gift." Do you decline it in the dative?
That he draws all into his web this way, *limitless gifts,* expectations of

brilliant success. They come thus not only to believe the lie but to depend upon it. Whole rows of them in evening dress rising, applauding the lie. My dutifully proud – wear a mask and your face grows to fit it. Avoid all mirrors as though – and no, worst, the black irony: now his wife and girls are bewitched this way now as well, you see. As his mother – the art he perfected upon her. I see it in their faces, the heartbreaking way they look at him, holding him whole in their eyes. Their perfect trusting innocent children's eyes, adoring. And he then in receipt, casually, passively, never – as if he actually *deserved* this sort of – as if it were the most natural thing in the world. Oh how I have longed to shout the truth and expose and break this spell he's cast over all who – this spell he's not even *aware* of, not even conscious of what he's about, what he so effortlessly casts over his – as if this sort of love were *due* him, itself of nature, inevitable as the sunrise, never a thought, never a moment's doubt that he deserves it all and more. The very thought of it chokes me. How many years he took from us. Our gift. Genitive, ablative, nominative – the accidence of "gift." He wept at her deathbed. Wept. Can you imagine? That he had the right to weep at her loss. That *he* had that right. I stood in abject shock beside him. His arrogance. And she in that bed suffering so. Her last conscious word – to him. *His* weeping. This was the closest I ever came. *Pervigilium.* To speaking it. The truth. Weeping, that soft slack face red and eyes squeezed tight like a child whose sweets are all gone, gobbled up, like some obscene pink – mouth open and lip wet and a snot-string hanging untended and his wife – *his* wife – lovely arm around, to comfort him, comforting *him, his* loss – imagine. That now even my loss, my shameless tears, the loss of the only – that even my grief must be usurped, without one thought, not once acknowledged, as if it were his right to weep. To weep for her. Who told him he had that right? Why was I alone undeluded? What had – what sins in my sad small life merited this curse, to see the truth and be impotent to speak it? What was I guilty of that this should visit upon me? Why did no one ever ask? What acuity were they absent and I cursed with, to ask why was he born? oh why was he born? The truth would have killed her. To realize her own life had been given for – ceded to a lie. It would have killed her where she stood. I tried. Came close once or twice, once at his wed – not in me to do it. I searched within and it was not there. That certain sliver of steel one requires to do what must be done come what may. And she did die happy, believing the lie.

[PAUSE for technician's change of ileostomy pouch and skin barrier; examination of stoma; partial sponge bath]

THE FATHER: Oh but *he* knew. He knew. That behind my face I despised him. My son alone knew. He alone saw me. From those I loved I hid it – at what cost, what life and love sacrificed for the need to spare them all, hide the truth – but he alone saw through. I could not hide it from him whom I despised. That fluttered thrusting eye would fall upon me and read my hatred of the living lie I'd wrought and borne. That ghastly extrusive right eye divined the secret repulsion its own repulsiveness caused in me. Father, you see this irony. She herself was blind to me, lost. He alone saw that I alone saw him for what he was. Ours was a black intimacy forged around that secret knowledge, for I knew that he knew I knew, and he that I knew he knew I knew. The profundity of our shared knowledge and complicity in that knowledge flew between us – "*I know you*"; "*Yes and I you*" – a terrible voltage charged the air when – if we two were alone, out of her sight, which was rare; she rarely left us alone together. Sometimes – rarely – once – it was at his first girl's birth, as my wife was leaning over the bed embracing his and I behind her facing him and he made as if to hold the infant out to me, his eyes on me, holding my eyes whole with his and the truth arcing back and forth between us over the lolling head of that beautiful child as he held it out as if his to give, and I could not then refrain from letting escape the briefest flicker of acknowledgment of the truth with the twist of my mouth's right side, a dark little half-smile, "*I know what you are*," which he met with that baggy half-smile of his own, what doubtless all in the room perceived as filial thanks for my smile and the blessing it appeared to imply and – do you now see why I loathed him? the ultimate insult? that he alone knew my heart, knew the truth, which from those I loved I died inside from hiding? A terrible charge, my hatred of him and his blithe delight at my secret pain oscillating between us and deforming the very air of any shared space commencing around shall we say just after his Confirmation, adolescence, when he stopped coughing and grew sleek. Though it's become ever worse as he's aged and consolidated his powers and more and more of the world has fallen under the – taken in.

[PAUSE]

THE FATHER: Rare that she left us alone in a room together, though. His mother. A reluctance. I'm convinced she did not know why. Some instinctive unease, intuition. She believed he and I loved one another in the strained stilted way of fathers and sons and that this was why we had so little to say to one another. She believed the love was unspoken and so intense that it made us awkward. Used gently to chide me in bed about what she called my "awkwardness" with the boy. She rarely left a room, believed she had somehow to mediate between us, complete the strained circuit. Even when I taught him – taught him sums she contrived ways to sit at the table, to – she felt she had to protect us both. It broke – oh – broke my – oh oh bloody Christ please ring it the –

[PAUSE for technician's removal of ileostomy pouch and skin barrier; FATHER's evacuation of digestive gases; catheter suction of edemic particulates; moderate dyspnea; R.N. remarks re fatigue and recommends truncation of visit; FATHER's outburst at R.N., technician, Charge Nurse]

THE FATHER: That she died without knowing my heart. Without the entirety of union we had promised one another before God and Church and her parents and my mother and brother standing with me. Out of love. It was, Father. Our marriage a lie and she did not know, never knew I was so alone. That I slunk through our life in silence and alone. My decision, to spare her. Out of love. God how I loved her. Such silence. I was weak. Bloody awful, pathetic, tragic that weakn – for the truth might have brought her to me; I might somehow have shown him to her. His true gift, what he was really about. Slight chance, granted. Long odds. Never able. I was too weak to risk causing her pain, a pain which would have been on his behalf. She orbited him, I her. My hatred of him made me weak. I came to know myself: I am weak. Deficient. Disgusted now by my own deficiency. Pathetic specimen. No backbone. Nor has he a backbone either, none, but requires none, a new species, needn't stand: others support him. Ingenious weakness. World owes him love. His gift that the world somehow believes it as well. Why? Why does *he* pay no price for his weakness? Under what possible scheme is this just? Who gave him my life? By what fiat? Because and he will, he will come to me today, here, later. Pay his respects, press my hand, play his solicitous part. Fresh flowers, girls' construction-paper cards. Genius of him. Has not missed a day I've been here. Lying here. Only he and I know why. Bring them here to see me. Loving son the staff all say, lovely family, how lucky, so very much to be grateful. Blessings. Brings his girls, holds them up for me to see whole. Above the rails. Stem to stern. Ship to shore. He calls them his apples. He may be in transit this very – even as we speak. Fit diminutive. Apples. He devours people. Drains. Thank you for hearing this. Devoured my life and left me to my. I am loathsome, lying here. Good of you to listen. Charitable. Sister, I require a favor. I wish to try to – to find the strength. I am dying, I know it. One can feel it coming you know, know it's on its way. Oddly familiar the feeling. An old old friend come to pay his – I require a favor from you. I'll not say an indulgence. A boon. Listen. Soon he will come, and with him he will bring the delightful girl who married him and adores him and cocks her head when he delights her and adores him and weeps shamelessly at the sight of me here lying here in these webs of tubes, and the two girls he makes such a faultless show of loving – *Apple of my eye* – and who adore him. Adore him. You see the lie lives on. If I am weak it will outlive me. We shall see whether I have the backbone to cause the girl pain, who believes she does love him. To be judged a bad man. When I do. Bitter spiteful old man. I am weak enough to hope in part it's taken for delirium. This is how weak a man I am. That her loving me and choosing and marrying me and having her child by me might well have been her mistake. I am dying, he impending, I have one more chance – the truth, to speak it aloud, to expose him, sunder the thrall, shift the scales, warn the innocents he's taken in. To sacrifice their opinion of me to the truth, out of love for those blameless children. If you saw the way he looked at them, his little apples, with that eye, the smug triumph, the weak lid peeled back to expose the – never doubting he deserves this joy. Taking joy as his due no matter the. They will be here soon, standing here. Holding my hand as you are. What time is it? What time do you have? He is in transit even now, I feel it. He will look down again at me today on this bed, between these rails, entubed, incontinent, foul, wracked, struggling even to breathe, and his face's intrinsic vacancy will again disguise to all eyes but mine the exultation in his eyes, both those eyes, seeing me like this. And he will not even know he exults, he is that blind to himself, he himself believes the lie. This is the real affront. This is his *coup de theatre*. That he too is taken in, that he too believes he loves me, believes he loves. For him, too, I would do it. Say it. Break the spell he's cast over even himself. That is true evil, not even to *know* one is evil, no? Save his soul you could say. Perhaps. Had I the spine. Velleity. Could find the steel. Shall set one free, no? Is that not promised Father? For say unto you verily. Yes? Forgive me, for I. Sister, I wish to make my peace. To close the circuit. To deliver it into the room's air: that I know what he is. That he disgusts me and desp – repels me and that I despise him and that his birth was a blot, unbearable. Perhaps yes even yes to raise both arms as I – the black joke my now suffocating here as he must know he should have so long ago in that rocket I paid for without.

[PAUSE]

THE FATHER: God, Aeschylus. The *Oresteia*: Aeschylus. His doorway, picking at himself in translation. Aeschylus, not Sophocles. Pathetic.

[PAUSE]

THE FATHER: Nails on men are repellent. Keep them short and keep them clean. That is my motto.

[PAUSE for episode of ophthalmorrhagia; technician's swab/flush of dextrocular orbit; change of facial bandage]

THE FATHER: Now and now I have made it. My confession. To you merciful Sisters of Mercy. Not, not that I despised him. For if you knew him. If you saw what I saw you'd have smothered him with the pillow long ago believe me. My confession is that damnable weakness and misguided love send me to heaven without having spoken the truth. The forbidden truth. No one even says aloud that you are not to say it. *Te judice.* If only I could. Oh how I despise the loss of my strength! If you knew this hurt – how it – but do not weep. Weep not. Do not weep. Not for me. I do not deserve – why are you crying? Don't you dare pity me. What I need from – pity is not what I need from you. Not why. Far from – do stop it, don't want to see it. *Stop.*

YOU [cruelly]: But Father it's me. Your own son. All of us, standing here, loving you so.

THE FATHER: Father good and because I do I do do need something from you. Father, listen. It must not win. This evil. You are – you've heard the truth now. Good of you. Do this: hate him for me after I die. I beg you. Dying request. Pastoral service. Mercy. As you love truth, as God the – for I confess: I will say nothing. I know myself and it is too late. Not in me. Mere fantasy to think. For even now he is in transit, bearing gifts. His apples to hold out to me whole. Wishful thinking, to raise myself up Lazarus-like with vile and loathsome truth for all to – where is my bell? That they will gather about the bed and his weak eye will fall upon me in the midst of his wife's uxorious prattle. He will have a child in his arms. His eye will meet mine and his wet red wet labial lip curl invisibly in secret acknowledgment between he and I and I will try and try and fail to raise my arms and break the spell with my last breath, to depose – expose him, rebuke the evil he long ago used her to make me help him erect. Father *judicat orbis*. Never have I ever begged before. Down on one knee now for – do not forsake me. I beg you. Despise him for me. On my account. Promise you'll carry it. It must outlive all this. Of myself I am weak bear my burden save your servant *te judice* for thine is – not –

[PAUSE for severe dyspnea; sterilization and partial anesthesis of dextral orbit; Code for attending M.D.]

THE FATHER: Not consign me. Be my bell. Unworthy life for all thee. Beg. Not die in this appalling silence. This charged and pregnant vacuum all around. This wet and open sucking hole beneath that eye. That terrible eye impending. Such silence.

CONTRIBUTORS

Dorothy Allison is the author of *Bastard out of Carolina, Cavedweller*, and a memoir, *Two or Three Things I Know*. She is also the author of *The Women Who Hate Me*, a collection of poetry; and *Skin: Talking About Sex, Class, and Literature*, a collection of essays. Her collection of short stories, *Trash*, was reissued in 2002. Born in Greenville, South Carolina, she currently lives with her partner and her son in Nothern California.

Tom Barbash's short fiction has received the Nelson Algren Award from the *Chicago Tribune*. He was a recipient of the James Michener Award from the Iowa Writers' Workshop for his novel, *The Last Good Chance*, which was published by Picador in 2002. He lives in San Francisco with his wife.

Julie Benesh grew up in Iowa, attended Washington University in St. Louis, and now lives in Chicago. She is working on a story collection, *Loves of Her Lives*, and a novel, *Attempting Romance*.

Kevin Canty is the author of the short-story collection *Stranger in This World* and the novel *Into the Great Wide Open*. He won the Transatlantic Review Award for the opening chapters of *Nine Below Zero*. His work has been published in *Esquire*, the *New Yorker*, *Details*, *Story*, the *New York Times Magazine*, and *Vogue*. Currently living in Montana with his wife, the photographer Lucy Capehart, and two children, he teaches fiction at the University of Montana.

Ron Carlson is the author of six books of fiction, including the collections *The Hotel Eden* and *At the Jim Bridger* and the novel *The Speed of Light*. He has been awarded a National Endowment for the Arts Fellowship in Fiction, a Pushcart Prize, and the *Ploughshares* Cohen Prize. He is a professor of English at Arizona State University and lives with his wife Elaine and their two sons in Scottsdale, Arizona.

Lydia Davis is the author of seven books of fiction, including *Almost No Memory, Break It Down, The End of the Story,* and, most recently, *Samuel Johnson Is Indignant.* Her stories have been published in the *New Yorker, Antaeus, City Lights Review, Conjunctions, Grand Street, Harper's* and the *Paris Review,* among others. She is a noted translator of works by Maurice Blanchot, Michel Butor, Pierre Jean Jouve, Michel Foucault, Jean-Paul Sartre, Michel Leiris, and other French writers. She was awarded the French-American Foundation's 1992 Translation Prize, and has received fellowships from the National Endowment for the Arts and the Ingram Merrill Foundation, as well as a Whiting Writers' Award for Fiction. She lives in upstate New York and teaches at Bard College.

Stuart Dybek is the author of two collections of stories, *The Coast of Chicago* and *Childhood and Other Neighborhoods,* and a collection of poems, *Brass Knuckles.* His fiction, poetry, and nonfiction have been published in numerous magazines, including the *New Yorker, Atlantic Monthly, Harper's,* the *Paris Review, Antaeus, Poetry, Tri-Quarterly, Ploughshares,* and the *New York Times.* Awards include the 1995 PEN/Bernard Malamud Prize "for distinctive achievement in the short story form"; an Academy Institute Award in Fiction from the American Academy of Arts and Letters in 1994; a Guggenheim Fellowship, two fellowships from the National Endowment for the Arts, a residency at the Rockefeller Foundation's Bellagio Center, and a Whiting Writers' Award. He has received four O. Henry prizes, including first prize for his story "Hot Ice." He lives in Kalamazoo, Michigan.

Michael Emmerich has translated numerous works from both pre-modern and modern Japanese, including Yasunari Kawabata's *First Snow on Fuji*, Banana Yoshimoto's *Asleep* and *Goodbye Tsugumi*, and Mari Akasak's *Vibrator*, published by Faber & Faber in 2003.

Mary Gaitskill grew up outside of Detroit. She is the author of two collections of short stories, *Bad Behavior* and *Because They Wanted To*; a novel, *Two Girls, Fat and Thin*; and numerous articles and stories. She lives in Rhinebeck, New York.

David Gates is the author of the novels *Jernigan* and *Preston Falls* and the short-story collection *The Wonders of the Invisible World*. He has been a Guggenheim Fellow, twice a finalist for the National Book Critics' Circle Award and once for the Pulitzer Prize. His stories have been published in *Esquire, GQ, Grand Street, Ploughshares, TriQuarterly, Best American Short Stories*, and *O. Henry Prize Stories*. His nonfiction has appeared in many magazines, including the *New Yorker*, the *New York Times Book Review, Bookforum, Esquire, GQ, Rolling Stone, Smithsonian, Spin*, and the *Journal of Country Music*. He is a senior writer at *Newsweek*, where he writes about books and music, and he teaches in the M.F.A. Writing Program at the New School for Social Research.

Aleksandar Hemon was born in Sarajevo in 1964. He moved to Chicago in 1992 with only a basic command of English. He began writing in English in 1995. He has been published in *Granta*, the *New Yorker, Best American Short Stories 1999*, and *Best American Short Stories 2000*. He is the author of the short-story collection *The Question of Bruno* and the novel *Nowhere Man*. He lives in Chicago with his wife, Lisa Stodder, a Chicago native.

Amy Hempel is the author of the story collections *Tumble Home, Reasons to Live*, and *At the Gates of the Animal Kingdom*. She has edited, with Jim Shepard, *Unleashed: Poems by Writers' Dogs*.

Tara Ison's novel, *A Child out of Alcatraz,* was a finalist for the 1997 *Los Angeles Times* Book Award for "Best First Fiction." She is the acting chair of the M.F.A. Program in Creative Writing at Antioch University and lives in Los Angeles.

Yasunari Kawabata was born in 1899 and died in 1972. He is best known for his novels *Thousand Cranes, The Sound of the Mountain,* and *Snow Country.* His influences range from French writing to Japanese linked verse, from the resonance of traditional culture to the radical modernism that was the artistic weather of his time. He was the first Japanese writer to be awarded the Nobel Prize for Literature, in 1968, and was a mentor to Yukio Mishima.

James Kelman's novels include *A Chancer; A Disaffection;* the Booker Prize–winning *How late it was, how late;* and *Translated Accounts.* His story collections include *Greyhound for Breakfast, Busted Scotch,* and *The Good Times.* He lives in Glasgow, Scotland.

Dylan Landis has just finished a novel, *Floorwork,* and is writing a collection of interlocked stories. She has won the Ray Bradbury Fellowship and numerous fiction competitions. In a previous life she wrote six books on interior design. She lives in Los Angeles.

David Leavitt is the author of several novels and story collections, including *Family Dancing, The Lost Language of Cranes, A Place I've Never Been, Arkansas, The Page Turner,* and *Martin Bauman.*

Fred G. Leebron's novels are *Out West, Six Figures,* and *In the Middle of All This.* His work has received Michener, Fulbright, Stegner, and Pushcart prizes. He lives in Gettysburg with his wife and two children.

Jonathan Lethem has written six novels, including *Motherless Brooklyn* and *The Fortress of Solitude.* He lives in New York.

Michael F. Lowenthal is the author of the novels *The Same Embrace* and *Avoidance*, as well as the editor of numerous nonfiction books. His short stories have appeared in the *Kenyon Review, Witness, Other Voices, Crescent Review,* and in more than a dozen anthologies. A recipient of fellowships from the Bread Loaf Writers' Conference, the Massachusetts Cultural Council, and the New Hampshire State Council on the Arts, he has also written for the *New York Times Magazine,* the *New York Times Book Review,* and the *Washington Post Book World.* He teaches writing at Boston College and is currently completing his second collection of stories.

Max Ludington's stories have appeared in *Tin House, Nerve, Meridian,* and other publications. His first novel, *Tiger in a Trance,* will be published in August 2003. He lives in New York.

Chris Offutt is the author of the story collections *Kentucky Straight* and *Out of the Woods,* the novel *The Good Brother,* and the memoir *The Same River Twice.* His nonfiction book *No Heroes* was published in 2002 by Simon & Schuster.

Emily Ishem Raboteau is an M.F.A. student in the creative writing department at New York University, where she holds a *New York Times* Fellowship and a Jacob Javits Fellowship. Her writing has appeared in *Transition, African Voices,* and the *Chicago Tribune.*

Nancy Reisman's short-story collection *House Fires* won the Iowa Short Fiction Award. Her work has appeared in *Five Points, Michigan Quarterly Review, New England Review,* the *Kenyon Review, Glimmer Train,* and other journals, as well as in *The Iowa Award: The Best Stories 1991–2000.* "Illumination" was selected for *Best American Short Stories 2001.* Reisman grew up in western New York and now teaches fiction at the University of Michigan.

Peter Rock was born in Salt Lake City, Utah. He is the author of the novels *This Is the Place, Carnival Wolves,* and *The Ambidextrist.* Many projects are under way and will become visible.

David Schickler is the author of the story collection *Kissing in Manhattan*, published by the Dial Press. His stories have appeared in *Tin House*, the *New Yorker*, and *Zoetrope: All-Story*, among others. He lives in New York with his wife and is at work on a novel.

Helen Schulman is the author of the short-story collection *Not a Free Show* and the novels *Out of Time*, *The Revisionist*, and most recently *P.S.* She is co-editor, with Jill Bialosky, of the essay anthology *Wanting a Child*. Her nonfiction and fiction have appeared in such publications as *Time*, *Vanity Fair*, *GQ*, *Vogue*, the *New York Times Book Review*, the *New York Times Style Section*, *Bookforum*, the *Voice Literary Supplement*, the *Paris Review*, and *Ploughshares*, among others. She has been a Sundance Fellow, a recipient of the New York Foundation for the Arts Award, and a Pushcart Prize winner.

Jim Shepard is the author of, most recently, the novel *Nosferatu* and the story collection *Batting Against Castro*. His new novel will be published by Knopf in September 2003. He teaches at Williams College and lives in Williamstown, Massachusetts, where he and his wife and two sons enjoy tormenting their 110-pound Labrador retriever.

Katherine Shonk's short-story collection, *The Red Passport*, will be published by Farrar, Straus & Giroux in fall 2003. Her stories have appeared in a number of literary journals. "My Mother's Garden" was selected for *Best American Short Stories 2001*. A graduate of the University of Illinois and the University of Texas, she lives in Evanston, Illinois.

David Foster Wallace is the author of the short-story collections *Girl with Curious Hair* and *Brief Interviews with Hideous Men*, the essay collection *A Supposedly Fun Thing I'll Never Do Again*, and the novels *Infinite Jest* and *The Broom of the System*. A recipient of a MacArthur Foundation award, his writing has appeared in the *Paris Review* and *Harper's*, among other publications.

Liza Zeidner is the author of four novels, most recently *Layover,* and two books of poems. Her stories, articles, and essays have appeared in the *New York Times, GQ, Atlantic Monthly,* and elsewhere. She directs the Graduate Program in English at Rutgers University in Camden, New Jersey.

A NOTE ON THE TYPE

The text of this book is set in Linotype Sabon, named after the type founder, Jacques Sabon. It was designed by Jan Tschichold and jointly developed by Linotype, Monotype, and Stempel, in response to a need for a typeface to be available in identical form for mechanical hot metal composition and hand composition using foundry type.

Tschichold based his design for Sabon roman on a fount engraved by Garamond, and Sabon italic on a fount by Granjon. It was first used in 1966 and has proved an enduring modern classic.